THE DEATH OF EDITH TODD

Anne L Walsh

ANNE L. WALSH

◆ FriesenPress

One Printers Way
Altona, MB R0G 0B0
Canada

www.friesenpress.com

Copyright © 2023 by Anne L. Walsh
First Edition — 2023

All rights reserved.

Author photograph by Michelle Fleming 2022

This book is a work of fiction. Names, characters, places, and incidents are either products of the author's imagination or are used fictitiously. Any resemblance to actual events, locales or persons, living or dead, is entirely coincidental.

No part of this publication may be reproduced in any form, or by any means, electronic or mechanical, including photocopying, recording, or any information browsing, storage, or retrieval system, without permission in writing from FriesenPress.

ISBN
978-1-03-915921-1 (Hardcover)
978-1-03-915920-4 (Paperback)
978-1-03-915922-8 (eBook)

1. *Fiction, Mystery & Detective, Amateur Sleuth*
2. *Fiction, Mystery & Detective, Cozy*
3. *Fiction, Mystery & Detective, Crime*

Distributed to the trade by The Ingram Book Company

❧ ❧ ❧

ONE

Thursday, November 4, 1999

Beth Langille saw the cluster of bright flashing lights long before she slowed to make a left turn from Nanaimo Street. She guessed it was the destination of the shrieking ambulance that had raced past her along East Twelfth Avenue. The glimpse of someone being eased onto a stretcher caused her to stiffen and quickly bring her eyes back to the road. Streetlights, headlights of oncoming cars, and flashes from a police cruiser strobe made colourful kaleidoscope-like patterns on the wet road. Beth braked with care and focused on her driving as she turned onto her street.

Though she normally worked alternate Fridays since retiring from her position as an infection control nurse at Highcrest Hospital—her replacement in the infection control program had negotiated alternate three-day weekends—Beth had been called in to help with routine hospital surveillance as well as some contact tracing when an unexpected tuberculosis case was diagnosed on day eight of a patient's stay in a four-bed room. The man was promptly moved to a single room and placed on airborne precautions as work began to identify all discharged or transferred patients who had shared the room, staff assigned to the room and visitors. Vancouver Public Health had been notified for community follow-up.

The longer-than-usual day resulted in Beth's decision to take a short detour to her nearest Safeway. The aroma of barbecued chicken tempted her all the way home. *Won't be long*, she thought as she anticipated the meal, which would soon be ready with leftover vegetables from the night before. In the back lane, she waited for the familiar grating sounds of her garage door to stop while she glanced at a few of the neighbouring homes. Sofia Martinelli's kitchen windows were ablaze, while the house next door was dark. That was no surprise. Edith Todd would be visiting her husband at Vancouver General Hospital.

Edith, long-time resident and Block Watch captain, had called Beth the evening before to update her about Ken's progress and talk over some Block Watch concerns.

"I feel like I work in infection control these days, keeping an eye on staff handwashing," she'd said.

"Good for you," Beth had replied, "we appreciate all the help we can get. How's Ken doing?"

"Better now, but he has to finish the intravenous antibiotic. Not too long till he'll be home. Listen, I want you to come over for dinner one evening soon to thank you for fielding my many calls." She'd continued over Beth's protests, "We haven't had a proper visit recently. And I have a very serious matter to run by you; I need your opinion. It's 'for your ears only' as they say—James Bond, right?"

"You might be thinking of 'for your eyes only.' Mission Impossible maybe?" Beth had said with a chuckle.

They'd moved on to discuss the recent Block Watch potluck party held at Beth's to celebrate Edith's planned year-end retirement from her role as captain.

"I'm almost eighty now and some people think I'm past it

with my grey hair and wrinkly face," she'd said.

"Edith, many women half your age aren't as active as you," Beth had replied. "Anyway, I think ten years watching over us all is a nice round number."

"And it's been exactly ten years since Block Watch officially began in Vancouver," Edith had said. "I'm proud I've have been in from the start. Of course, I'll still be involved, just in a less obvious way."

Eventually, it was settled that Beth would come for dinner Friday.

In the East Vancouver neighbourhood Beth called home, there were a variety of newcomers and old timers—a description that took twenty years to achieve in Edith's eyes. That left Beth three years before she qualified. On both sides of the laneway, the cultures of China, Italy, Portugal, and the Philippines were represented along with the United Kingdom. Beth felt she was a good fit with her roots in England and Scotland.

It hadn't taken long after moving to the area for Beth to learn that Edith had a natural tendency to keep tabs on what was happening with her neighbours. Fortunately, her thirst for gathering information was complemented by a kind heart buried under her forthright exterior. Edith's frequent curiosity may have been a source of irritation for some, but on the whole, she was appreciated for being caring, discreet, and demonstrably dedicated to following the golden rule. It took a while for newer residents to appreciate this—still, there were some who remained skeptical. Beth may have remained more of a neighbourly acquaintance had it not been for a chance encounter with Edith at Forest Lawn Cemetery twelve years previous. On that day, a firm bond had developed based in the discovery of a loss in common.

A meowing tabby cat rushed to meet Beth as she pushed open her back door to a laundry area. Monty wanted his dinner pronto, if you please. Beth draped her Gore-Tex jacket over the dryer and brushed some damp strands of greying blonde hair away from her face. The short walk from her garage had been enough to leave her dripping.

"Hang on, let me get my shoes off."

Over the years, talking to her cats had become a natural habit. *What pet owner doesn't do that?* she thought. She had noticed her inclination to speak aloud to herself as well. Since it usually involved sorting something out—like the various pros and cons when faced with a dilemma—she found it helped keep her generally centred and calm, as she wasn't left dwelling on the problem for days. She tended to talk some things through with some family and a few good friends who were easy to talk with, but she took care not to overdo it. It had been many years since she'd had Alex to discuss feelings and problems with. They'd been a devoted couple, destined, she'd thought, to raise a family and live comfortably into old age together. Beth shook her head to set aside the thought that their deep love and mutual respect had not been enough to overcome the ordeal that became their undoing.

"Okay, Monty, what'll it be tonight?" She opened a lower cupboard and picked out a new tin of Cat's Meow tuna. Upon hearing the can opener, the cat wove around her legs, mewing loudly.

Preparations for her own meal were delayed by the ringing telephone. Sofia, across the back lane, was calling to ask if Edith was with Beth.

"No. I imagine she's still with Ken. I know she's been staying later to encourage him to eat his evening meal. I think it's delivered quite early, but she wouldn't get away till well after five. The traffic's pretty heavy. Felt almost like a Friday. What's up?"

"She's supposed to be here for dinner by now. I thought she might have dropped in to discuss Ken with you. I guess she must have missed her bus connection."

"What do you mean? Is something wrong with their car?"

"No, it's just she decided to take the bus given the forecast. Don't you remember? Last winter after a close call, she started to feel nervous about driving in the rain after dark."

"Right. Now I do." Beth drew out the next words slowly, "Oh… dear."

"What?" said Sofia. "What?"

"Well, there was an incident of some sort near the corner store. Since I was driving, I didn't see much. Anyway, someone was put in an ambulance." Beth heard a gasp. "Don't panic, Sofia. It was about ten minutes ago. I'll run down to the shop right now. Bill likely knows something. I'll call you as soon as I'm back."

Clutching her jacket hood against the wind and rain, Beth neared the Good Luck Corner Grocery. There was a police officer talking to a man on the sidewalk under a large umbrella while another was speaking with Bill Yeung in the store. When Beth entered, both Bill and the officer turned to look. Bill's face was stone-like. He stared at her and gave his head a little side-to-side shake. Beth blurted out her name and said she lived up the lane and was worried that a neighbour who had not arrived home on time might have had an accident. There was a moment's silence. The officer faced her and spoke politely. He couldn't discuss the person hurt until the next of kin had been notified. He was sorry, but he needed her to leave while he spoke with Mr. Yeung in private.

❦

For Edith Todd, the day began much like any other day since her husband had been admitted to the hospital for heart bypass surgery—a creamy bowl of oatmeal porridge and vanilla yogurt with some sliced banana followed by a leisurely cup of tea while she scanned *The Sun* newspaper. She missed Ken, but the radio kept her from feeling alone. A leg wound infection had delayed his discharge, and though his appetite had waned along with his mood, a slice or two of her homemade pumpkin tea bread was bound to perk him up.

Midafternoon, umbrella raised against the pelting rain, she strode purposefully along the back lane on her way to visit her husband. Her alert gaze roamed over each backyard she passed. Once, Edith paused just long enough to cast an appraising look over one yard. She shook her head slightly. Against the side of a garage were tottering towers of green and black plastic plant pots, an untidy stack of ragged lengths of wood, and several rusty garden tools amongst other unidentifiable "good finds." Maggie had been a sucker for garage sales for years. There was a time when her sister Pearl kept her in check, but not recently. *Both of them are getting on,* Edith thought, then chided herself since she was older. *Maybe I'll have a tactful word with them.* She could remind Pearl that Dennis Greene, a young former neighbour, was indispensable in helping clean up the basement when Ken had the renovations done. It was worth a try.

Later, having left Ken in the capable hands of his evening nurse, she headed for home. In the gathering gloom brought on earlier by the recent return to standard time, Edith, her mind abuzz with neighbourhood business, abandoned her usual care as she hurried to catch a bus home. She was scarcely aware of the swaying tree tops or the now-blowing rain. Two menacing notes sent to her in the past few weeks claimed brief attention until she almost slipped on the sodden rusty-brown and gold autumn leaves that carpeted the sidewalk.

Stepping aboard a Broadway bus, Edith was most gratified to be offered a seat by a man young enough to reassure her that proper manners were not a thing of the past. She'd stopped dying her hair some years ago and found the transition to grey had a few benefits. She murmured her thanks, bestowed a grateful smile on her benefactor, folded her dripping umbrella into the side pocket of her flowery plasticized carry bag, and relaxed into the seat. She took a moment to veer off into thinking about how pleased she was with Ken's improvement. The antibiotic was working, and he was in better spirits now that he could see his hospital stay coming to an end.

Her thoughts returned to the letters, the most recent of which had been left at Halloween. A frown momentarily creased her face. Scare tactics wouldn't work on her. While she would admit she'd taken a few risks as Block Watch captain, she'd never felt unsafe. Edith had certain ideas about how to be an effective captain since she saw herself as the on-site defender of the neighbourhood. She enjoyed conducting random afternoon patrols in the guise of walking Sofia and Gino Martinelli's placid beagle Rusty. Constable Argento, the Block Watch liaison, had cautioned her against putting herself in harm's way. She reassured him she understood and was being careful.

Before she'd stepped away from the volunteer position she'd held for ten years, Edith had wanted to discover tangible information about the current rash of car and garage break-ins in her immediate area. She thought it was likely related to a certain newcomer. It was too bad that if she was right, as so often she was, someone she'd known from babyhood might also be implicated, so it would be best to have it out in the open soon and be done with the bad influence.

As the bus stuttered east along Broadway, Edith's mind moved on to the locket, which laid nestled between her still ample, albeit saggy, breasts. It was safe there. The chain had been broken, so she'd found an old one of her own to use. A grave problem like this brought home how much she missed her neighbour Evie Whitman, who had died in late January and who had been an excellent confidante. What was meant to be a routine cholecystectomy for gallstones had uncovered a more sinister cause for Evie's symptoms. She and her husband Alan had lived next door for forty years, good friends to her and Ken.

Edith had been avoiding troubling thoughts about the meaning of the appearance of Emma's locket. It presented a dilemma that was causing more strain than the worry about Ken's leg wound and the serious infection that had spread to his blood. At least her uncertainty about Ken had been lessened thanks to Beth. With her long years in infection control, she had been able to calm Edith's fears with some simplified explanations. It hadn't been a big leap to realize Beth would be the perfect person to help with her quandary over the locket. In fact, even if Evie had still been there, it might be better to share with someone who hadn't been around in that long-ago September when Emma had disappeared. Beth was sure to help her decide the right course of action.

With the late arrival of the connecting bus at Nanaimo, Edith decided against making a quick detour to see a parishioner from her church whom she often helped. Old Harry Anders lived in a senior's residence on the south side of Trout Lake not far from her home. With a small smile, Edith remembered he was exactly her age. She hadn't visited him for over a week. It was about time she found out more about his no-account nephew Frank—there was something shady going on there. Harry, a widower, was a gentle soul whose advancing blindness made him more dependent and therefore, she believed, more vulnerable to the questionable attentions of his nephew. It was too bad Harry's level-headed niece had moved to the States. Edith decided she would call to ask if he needed a drive to the late morning mass on Sunday. She could quiz Harry on the way.

Thus it was, Edith disembarked from the number seven bus into the perfectly awful, typical wet and windy west coast November day, content with the prospect of tying up a few loose ends, entirely unaware that she herself had been designated a loose end.

※

Sofia picked up on the first ring.

"The police were talking to Bill at the store," said Beth, rushing on to try to reassure Sofia. "There's no way of knowing who it was. We're just going to have to wait. Edith will turn up—it's not even six thirty yet. The buses could be running late with this weather. It'll be okay, Sofia, don't cry."

"I'll try," Sofia said with a sob. "What can I say, blame it on my Italian genes. But really, Edith has been in my life almost as long as Gino. I'm worried. What'll we do?"

"Wait a little longer; give her another fifteen or twenty minutes maybe. If she doesn't come by then, call me, and I'll check with Ken's ward. Hopefully, there hasn't been any further complications with him."

Beth called the hospital, and as she hung up, the phone rang.

"Is she still with Ken?" asked Sofia hopefully.

"No. I wonder if she's simply forgotten. Remember, she's had a lot to deal with lately, and she is, after all, getting up there, though she wouldn't thank me for saying that. Edith's likely with her daughter. Why don't you call Susan? You know her well."

Close to eleven, Sofia called to say there was no answer at Susan's, though she'd tried a couple times then left a message. "I've got a really bad feeling about this," she said, her voice quivering.

"Yes, I have to agree. Me too. Let's get some rest. It's late, Sofia, time we both got to bed. You're bound to get a call in the morning."

Beth whispered a few quiet thanks for the blessings in her life as she snuggled into her flannel sheets. She hoped Edith's absence was some sort of simple mix-up. She was aware of Monty's soft footfall on the bed when he came to curl up in his usual place on the flowered duvet. With his comforting weight warm against her back, Beth settled slowly into a restless sleep.

TWO

Thursday, November 4

At precisely 5:59 p.m., less than two blocks from home and a mere four days from her eightieth birthday, Edith Todd was knocked to the pavement with a force that propelled her toward heaven. She looked down in bewilderment from somewhere near the orange glow of the streetlamp to see her usually tidy, plump self sprawled in a most un-Edith-like fashion, head askew against the unyielding curb. Her blue raincoat was splashed with grime and her skirt had whipped above her knees in the gale. One boot was half off and her handbag gaped open. Her sensible black umbrella had been flung nearby where it lay like a huge bat, wings akimbo. It was far too much to comprehend. Edith hovered at the edge of the dark haze that pulled at her, telling herself to hold on.

❦

The sharp sound of peeling tires, an odd shriek, and accompanying thump had attracted the immediate attention of Bill Yeung, owner of the Good Luck Corner Grocery. He had stared at the grim scene though the front window, mouth agape. A blur of disappearing red taillights was all he could make out in the darkened street as he grabbed the phone to call 911. He was relieved to see two pedestrians hurry to the woman lying on the street. One hovered over the body with a large golf umbrella, which threatened to blow away, and the other—an anorak-hooded figure—waved what looked like a white plastic bag to divert oncoming traffic. A car came to a halt with its flashers on. *Another good Samaritan,* Bill thought while he willed the ambulance to arrive as soon as possible.

❧

Friday, November 5

Morning rain drummed on the roof like impatient fingers, nudging Beth awake to the unsettling memory of Edith's unknown whereabouts. Monty, who had gone roaming earlier, jumped up on the bed and walked over her chest to lick her cheek. He began a loud purr.

"I know, I know, you want your breakfast. Let me wash my face first. Why don't you go turn up the heat?"

Beth sighed; it was a small joke she repeated often in the winter. Today, it wasn't very funny. She flung the covers back and grabbed her flowered fleece robe, hugging it to her as she headed for the thermostat in the hall.

After a bowl of porridge with chopped apple and nuts, Beth sat, a steaming mug of mocha coffee at her elbow, losing herself in a crossword book. She knew she would find out soon enough what was happening with Edith. No point phoning Sofia. She was glad it wasn't one of the Fridays she worked. Beth was content with the part-time arrangement for now. It was pleasant to keep some connection to the profession she'd loved and to various staff who seemed like family after thirty-plus years.

Sofia called about nine thirty. She sobbed, barely able to speak at first, while Beth tensed, wondering how bad the news would be.

"It was Edith you saw, Beth. Susan says her mom was hit by a car and the driver took off. Edith's in intensive care at Vancouver General. She had surgery through the night. No way to tell the outcome, but right now, the doctor says she's stable. Ken's in a state. Sue said she'll keep in touch."

Some time later, a calmer Sofia phoned with an update. "Sue's taken time off work to be there with Ken. Her brother is on his way."

"Is Edith conscious? Has she said anything?"

"I don't think so. Sorry, I barely slept a wink. I hardly remember what she said," Sofia ended, tearful once more. "She's been there all night and she'd really appreciate if you or I could come down to relieve her from her dad and see her mom. Sue gave our names to the ICU head nurse. But I'm not sure I can do it, Beth. I'm sorry, I don't think I can bear to see Edith that way."

"I understand. It's all right. I'll have an early lunch so I can give Susan a break to eat. I'll let you know what's what as soon as I can."

❧

An unopened summer issue of *Maclean's* lay on Beth's lap as she registered that the plain round wall clock had advanced to 11:56. Only five minutes since she had last looked. She was alone, surrounded by the moss green walls of the intensive care unit waiting room. A shrill ring startled her. Picking up the receiver of the beige telephone that sat by the magazines strewn on the wooden coffee table, she identified herself as asked. The voice at the other end told her she could come in. Beth walked along the terrazzo-floored corridor and turned through the main ICU doors. There were signs everywhere. 'Two visitors maximum allowed per patient unless otherwise ordered.' 'Cell phone use is strictly forbidden.' 'Staff and visitors must clean their hands upon entering and when leaving.' The latter clearly pointed to a wall-mounted dispenser of hand sanitizer. Beth knew the drill by heart. Pressing one squirt of the liquid into one hand, she rubbed both hands together and all over as if she were washing them. The alcohol-based fluid dried quickly. Through large north-facing windows, she could see some of downtown Vancouver with a misty suggestion of mountains beyond. As she passed beds on either side, she lowered her eyes and felt the familiar embarrassment of being whole and full of life while others lay broken. Despite a long career in health care, or perhaps because of it, this was a feeling she had never quite shaken.

"I'm here to see Edith Todd please," she said, offering her name to the unit clerk who cast a sympathetic look her way.

The bedside nurse verified her relationship a second time and remarked that Susan Todd had mentioned Beth's health care background and had told staff to consider her family.

"You likely know that Mrs. Todd—Edith—suffered a severe head injury," she said. "She's about twelve hours post-surgery. She's been unresponsive except to deep stimulus so far. Did the unit clerk mention that if you'd like to see Mr. Todd and his daughter, they may be in family room two?"

Beth shivered. It was like stepping into a cold shower. She understood the practice of providing immediate family with a place to have privacy did not augur well.

The still body was attached to a maze of tubes and wires. Beth looked down on the ashen face of her friend with bandaging around her head and recoiled from the fragility she saw. She pushed away the emotions that threatened to engulf her. *Edith, how the hell did this happen? This isn't right—you're the extra careful one.*

She reached out to hold Edith's one free hand, encouraged by its warmth. She searched for what to say. "Edith, it's me, Beth. Sofia and Gino send their best. You mustn't worry about the Block Watch newsletters; Jenny will look after them. I'll ring her later." She paused, wondering what else to say. She decided on a few words about the weather and went on to cover whatever neighbourhood news came to mind.

Beth jumped slightly when she felt Edith's fingers move. Her eyelids quivered but remained closed.

"Edith, can you hear me? It's Beth." She raised her voice to the nurse who sat charting just outside the open door, "Edith might be coming to."

Then Edith's mouth began to move, and slowly from her throat came a slew of indistinct sounds. "Aw ih, uh, ih… way ten, ih wheh ten, uh, aw me, way ten, wheh ten." Edith repeated it again. At the same time, she squeezed Beth's hand with growing urgency.

"It's okay, it's okay, Edith. You're asking about Ken?" Beth spoke over a third repetition. "Ken's okay. He's close by. You're at VGH."

A call to the family room brought Ken and Susan, each pale-faced and hopeful as they approached Edith's bedside. Beth had slipped on her jacket, ready to go. She touched Susan's arm in sympathy and gave Ken a gentle half-hug. "Edith's asking for you. I'll pop back to see you later, Ken."

Once Beth was home and had made calls to Sofia and Jenny Lee, the Block Watch co-captain who lived next door, she found herself replaying Edith's voice in her mind. The more she thought about it, it didn't really sound like asking after Ken. If not Ken, then it could be something about the accident. Wouldn't that be just like Edith to struggle out of a coma and provide information to catch the runaway driver. A small smile was wiped away by her concentration on Edith's garbled communication. Beth settled at the kitchen counter with paper and pen. She shut her eyes and focused on the sounds she could remember. *Aw ih. Way ten. Wheh ten. Aw nee. Aw mee.* She would try what she did with some crossword clues that stumped her when she had some of the letters. She worked through the consonants first. When she got to *s*, Beth felt she'd cracked one of the words.

Saw. So likely—saw me? Meaning Edith knew the driver saw her? That would be logical just before impact. Beth gave up on the other sounds. Maybe Edith had been able to say more to Ken and Susan.

THREE

Saturday, November 6

When the phone rang, Beth was chewing the last of her tuna sandwich and wishing the rain would stop. *Likely Sofia,* she thought. But it was Susan Todd's splintered voice with news that her mother had passed away around ten that morning.

"I just talked to Sofia and Dad's close friend Alan. I wanted to let you know in person too. Mom just couldn't hold on," Susan said, blurting it in a rush of weary words. "There was more bleeding and swelling in her brain overnight. They didn't think she'd survive more surgery. Dad knew what she wanted if something like this happened, so we let her go. We're thankful we could be there with her when she slipped away."

"I admit, I was dreading news like this," said Beth. "I'm so sorry. I'm really going to miss your mom," she managed, keeping tears at bay and feeling inarticulate, as she often did in such situations. "Your poor dad. How is he? Both of you will be worn out. What about your brother?"

"Dad's okay, not taking it in I think, especially not being at home where it might feel more real. Says it's like a bad dream. I'm grateful he still needs to be in hospital and has caring staff around. Gives me a chance to arrange some more time off and prepare to have him at home with me for a while. Glen's upset but okay, has to get back to Victoria for the time being."

"What can I do to help? Please tell me."

"Dad wants other neighbours to know as soon as possible. I mentioned it to Sofia. Asked if you and she could call everyone you think appropriate. And maybe one or both of you could drop in on Dad tomorrow?"

Beth composed herself, and after a soothing cup of tea, she made a few calls. She first checked on Sofia, who answered with a tentative hello, and upon hearing Beth's voice, broke into coarse sobs.

"I hardly know what to do with myself. Gino's gone with Leon and the grandkids to the aquarium to give me some time to myself, but I can't seem to settle at anything. I have lots to do. I was planning to make cannelloni for dinner. But all I can think of is Edith in that crosswalk with a car coming at her. I wish she would come walking up the lane like she did before. It felt like a miracle. Did Edith ever tell you?"

"Yes, she told me one time. She said there was a Mrs. Dodd who passed and had lived on the same avenue but over near Victoria. Your church office had misheard the name and sent a priest and nun to the Todd address to say prayers. But no one was home, and they came to ask you if you knew anything."

Sofia sniffled. "I was a basket case wondering what to do, thinking Edith was alone in the house, dead … and then I saw her."

"Yes, Edith said she was very touched by how you rushed halfway down the lane and hugged her. You can take comfort—Edith knew very well how much you cared about her."

With Sofia calmed, Beth first made a call to Jenny, who offered to call half the Block Watch team members. Then Beth flipped through her book to find Dennis's number, got an answering machine, and left a message for him to call her as soon as possible.

✤

Dennis Greene replaced the receiver of the kitchen phone in slow motion and stared at blurred wallpaper. His lanky frame slumped into the nearest chair as he pushed a cold empty mug aside. He couldn't imagine Edith's neighbourhood without her. They'd had frequent contact in the past couple months, during which Edith's plans for changes to the Todd's backyard were discussed. Only Thursday morning, Edith had phoned to say she hadn't forgotten his bill, that she'd been very busy what with hospital visits and such and would he like to pick up his cheque Monday? That conversation was their last. It would be tactless to ask about money at such a time. Hopefully Edith's daughter would find the invoice in the coming week, and he might see the money sooner rather than later since his business waned over the colder months when there was less to do outside. Still, he did have a side income from odd jobs. Five years on construction crews stood him in good stead.

Dennis's business, which he had dubbed Greene Yards and More, was his pathway to a dream. He and two friends had rented a house on the east side of Beth for several years before he moved into a small house near Commercial Street with his girlfriend. Since his aim was to establish himself as reliable and capable as quickly as possible in order to save money for his private dream, he'd started out simply, offering reasonably priced help to people he knew in parts of East Vancouver. His old neighbourhood had been the perfect place to launch his modest business. Many knew him as a good guy willing to lend a hand and were more than happy to hire a 'known entity.' Little did they know, they were contributing to Dennis's vision of being a director of one of the two large botanical gardens in Vancouver.

Dennis was grateful for the garden planning time he'd spent with Edith recently, as well as the social time they'd had the evening of the neighbourhood Block Watch get-together. He thought back to the work he'd completed. It had been just over a week ago, he recalled—the day before the potluck. On that dull grey day, the gardener and general handyman had been doing what he liked best—carrying out the initial part of a plan to rearrange and replant some of the Todd's garden beds. Showers had been predicted, but he'd planned to get the job done before lunch and hopefully remain dry.

🌺

He was digging out the thick bed of Hypericum alongside Edith and Ken's garage between a sidewalk and the outer west-facing wall. Edith had agreed it would be a perfect place for a display of assorted spring flowers and would then be home to some of their favourite annuals. It could be enjoyed from both the kitchen and dining room windows as well as from the back lane where many neighbours lingered to chat. They'd decided on a scattering of narcissi, snowdrops, and crocuses with clusters of tulips. On the south coast of British Columbia where winter freezes were often short-lived, spring bulbs could be planted until late fall. All the more satisfying to be doing this work with the promise of bright colour in just a few months' time. With that thought, he grabbed the spade and garden fork from the back of his 'rusty but trusty,' as he called it, 1972 red Dodge pickup. He credited his mechanically adept brother with its reliability.

Bending his sturdy six-foot body to the job, his unruly red hair protected by a ball cap, Dennis plunged the fork over and over into the soil to loosen the tenacious roots of the St. John's wort. He knew it had enjoyed complete reign here since around 1960 when the garage was first built. Edith had said she was tired of it in that location, and so it was to be moved. From midsummer into early fall, the easy-care evergreen bore pretty, long-lasting, cup-shaped, yellow flowers with an array of filament-fine red stamens. The sky had gradually lightened as he worked and a burst of sun illuminated the side of the garage like a large spotlight just as he was pulling out some roots that had extended under the garage. A tiny star gleamed from the tangled darkness. Dennis reached for the star and found himself holding a grimy, hinged gold locket, which might have gone unnoticed except for a scratch that had caught the momentary sun. He guessed the damage was his fault. He brushed away some encrusted dirt to read the initials EJT. He smiled anticipating the pleasure Edith would undoubtedly feel when she saw his find. He was interested to know what was inside. Maybe a photo of her and Ken?

He slipped the locket into his vest pocket, zipped it shut, and resumed his work. He relocated some of the plants to a spot by the back fence to help camouflage a composting area and turned to preparing the spring bed. By half past twelve, with the first bulbs nestled in their allotted spots and the soil tamped down, Dennis stood back to admire the stretch of dark ground. He'd be back to do more before long. He turned his attention to bagging what could be composted and put his tools away, wondering as he did why Edith wasn't yet back from Safeway. On Wednesday mornings, she helped fill delivery orders and was usually home by noon. Sitting in the passenger seat of his truck, Dennis ate his cheese sandwich, washing it down with now-lukewarm milky tea. For the hundredth time, he made a mental to note to get a new thermos. It was disappointing Edith wasn't home so he could give her his find right away. Not trusting his memory, he decided to leave it for her and rooted out a wrinkled envelope from the glove compartment. He jotted a note on the outside: *Look what I found! See you soon, Dennis.* He walked around the house and slipped it through the front door mail slot.

Retracing his steps to the backyard, he saw Nina Mahoney across the lane, her chestnut hair gathered into a sleek ponytail at the nape of her neck. She was standing outside her back gate by the garbage can. He didn't know Nina well but had done yard work and other jobs arranged with her husband over the past few years.

"Dennis," Nina said, more a statement than a greeting. "Lucky the rain held off for you this morning. That looks like a big job."

"Yeah," he said, searching for what else to say. He'd never felt completely at ease in her presence. She was always smartly dressed like she'd just walked out of a Holt Renfrew store window. Though he considered himself a poor judge of age, he figured she was in her late fifties and wondered if she coloured her hair. Today, she was more casual in black jeans with boots, but a fitted rain jacket and silky scarf added class.

"I've got to get on to my next job," Dennis said to limit the interruption. "Does Michael want me to help clean out his eaves again this year or is young Mike going to do it? Edith mentioned he's still living at home."

"What?" She raised her finely tweezed brows and brought her gaze back from the far distance. "What did you say?"

"Just about the eaves—should I call Michael or is Mike doing it?"

"Yes, call my husband, or you can ask him tomorrow night. Mike Junior's busy with more important things. I gather you'll be at Beth's?" A small frown played across Nina's brow.

"Wouldn't miss it. See you soon." Dennis ended the exchange by turning away from her. He sensed that Nina was one of the few who didn't feel he was still part of the neighbourhood since he'd moved to rent further afield.

❧

Many neighbours had gathered to celebrate the tenth anniversary of Block Watch in Vancouver and to honour Edith's tireless efforts as captain on Friday evening, October 24. Not that Edith had ever required a title to watch over the neighbourhood—it was simply in her nature to care about what was going on around her. With Ken Todd in hospital recovering from heart bypass surgery, Beth and Sofia felt the occasion would provide a lift for Edith and could serve as a surprise early birthday party.

"Come over here, Edith." Beth guided her to a comfortable armchair in the living room.

"I'll set up a TV table for you. We're not standing on ceremony tonight. There's enough room between here and the dining room—we'll bring in some extra chairs. You can hold court here."

"Who all's coming?" Edith asked.

"Oh, the Mahoneys, Nina and Michael that is, I doubt we'll see Mike. And there'll be Alan and his niece, and Jenny of course. Sofia is here and Gino will come soon. There's Dennis now, I hear him in the back porch. With all the work he does around the neighbourhood, he's still a fixture. Pearl said sorry, she wasn't sure she could make it when she dropped off some sausage rolls—she seems to feel tied to Maggie more these days, I think. There're at least three or four others. It'll be a full house. Oh, and Constable Argento will drop in for dessert as long as no emergencies pop up."

Beth turned away toward a noise in the back porch and called out, "Dennis, come on in."

"Hiya, thanks for including me, Beth. I brought garlic bread and a bottle of wine, that's okay, is it? Do you need me to pick up anything else? What can I do?" Dennis asked.

THREE | 23

"We'll have more than enough. Wait'll you see—there's usually food to feed an army. You can keep Edith company and put a little more wood on the fire if you think it's needed. I got it started—you're in charge now."

Dennis settled on the end of the chocolate leather couch nearest Edith. He was in familiar territory here at Beth's place. He'd cat-sat Monty on two occasions when Beth was away on holidays. When he'd first moved in nearby, it hadn't taken long to discover where the friendly cat called home.

He liked the story of Beth Langille's place. Local lore had it that the entire block had been farmland owned by a man named Jack who sold eggs all over the city. In the fifties, he'd sold it on the stipulation that one house be built to his personal specifications. There were various oddities in Beth's house like lever-style door handles throughout and a thick marine-glass picture window that had a faint hint of turquoise at the edges. Dennis let his gaze drift to the view which, at the moment, showed no more than low lying clouds in the evening gloom. The stars and the lights of Grouse Mountain were absent tonight.

By six thirty, the kitchen, dining area, and living room were filled with neighbours enjoying, amongst other dishes, Sofia's made-from-scratch lasagna—which meant she had made the pasta and used her own bottled tomato sauce. There was a chicken, mushroom, and rice casserole courtesy of co-captain Jenny Lee, and Nina had brought a savory pork stew. They had begun with appetizers of chicken wings, the usual cheddar and crackers, as well as Pearl's sausage rolls and ended with an assortment of desserts, including warm apple pie and ginger bread with lemon sauce, Beth's specialty.

Conversation roamed over countless topics, including local crime. Pearl popped in after all, and Constable Argento turned up as planned. It was nearing nine when Jenny got around to saying a few words about Block Watch and paying tribute to Edith for her long years of service to the neighbourhood. Then the constable formally thanked Edith and presented her with a certificate and a ten-year anniversary pin. Everyone raised their coffee mugs in a toast then clapped. Early birthday wishes were offered as well, with Edith beaming as she opened a few small gifts.

※

"Ready to go? I'll see you home, Edith. I've an early job in West Van tomorrow morning."

Dennis rose and gave Edith his hand so she could pull herself up from the deep armchair. She groaned a little and with a wry smile said, "I'll take you up on that offer."

After saying goodbyes all around, they walked in companionable silence over the lane toward her back gate, which he opened with a mock bow. Edith let out a small gasp as the back door light revealed the kitchen door was open at the top of the stairs.

"Oh no." Edith was about to rush ahead, but Dennis caught her arm, shook his head, and put his finger to his lips.

"Shhh," he whispered. "You know better than that. Someone could still be there," he scolded her gently. "We need to call nine-one-one. You go back to Beth's and call while I stay here. Too bad my cell is at home—I only use it for work."

"Stay out of sight, Dennis. You need to be careful too. Don't want to scare anyone off if they're still inside. Get over by the cedar."

Before long, Dennis saw headlights coming slowly up the lane from Nanaimo. Dennis stepped out, waved the police car on, and pointed toward the back of Edith's home. Two officers exited the cruiser, gesturing for him to stay put.

Soon after, one appeared at the door and called out, "They've been and gone. With neighbours at the side not in, they accessed the basement. The one window that doesn't open and has no bars has been smashed. You can go get Mrs. Todd please."

First thing Edith did was tell Dennis to go home and get to bed. "I'm fine; the officers want me to check everything with them. You go."

"No, the window downstairs was broken and needs to be boarded up when they're done dusting for prints. Ken's sure to have some plywood around. If not, I'll check with Gino or Alan. And I'm staying to keep you company after they finish, just for a little while," he insisted. It was obvious despite her bravado Edith was rattled. In the several weeks since Ken's hospitalization, Dennis noticed how she'd begun anxiously rubbing her hands.

Later, he followed Edith along the hall to the master bedroom where he saw various belongings dumped on the bed and floor. A jewellery box was overturned on the dresser with rings, earrings, broaches, and necklaces strewn here and there. Traces of fine dust remained from the forensics duo who had arrived quickly.

"I'll get you to put the drawers back in for me, Dennis." Edith shook her head at his offer of further help. "I can do the rest myself."

"Is anything missing?" It was then Dennis recalled his morning discovery. "Hey, what about the locket I found? It was in a bunch of roots that came out from under the garage."

"Oh, that. It's okay, I'm wearing it, but a small sapphire ring is gone as well as my short string of pearls. Usually, they're tucked away elsewhere, but I had a few things out earlier to see what I'd wear tonight. Otherwise, there wasn't anything much of value—just costume jewellery. The police said it was likely someone looking for things to pawn for drug money. A twenty, a ten, and some loonies are gone from the desk. That's all."

"Guess you were surprised to see the locket."

"You could say that." Edith searched for words. "It's been missing a long time and I'd forgotten it. Thanks."

She didn't seem as thrilled as Dennis had hoped she'd be, but of course, he chastised himself, she was upset and tired.

❧

Dennis dragged himself back to the sober present. He'd been planning to ask if there were any leads on the break-in when he picked up his cheque. Now he would never have that conversation with Edith—or any other.

FOUR

Sunday, November 7

A new day arrived cold and clear with the North Shore mountains sporting a light layer of snow. Beth watched puffy white clouds drift across a pale blue sky, the sun highlighting the frosted peaks. She stood motionless staring out her front room window, sensing the heaviness of heart that signaled the weight of combined losses. Monty rubbed against her ankles and flopped down, baring his tan-furred belly for a rub. "Not now, boy, I need to get out."

Passing through several residential blocks, Beth zigzagged her way to the park at Trout Lake. Despite unsettled thoughts, she felt some of her usual pleasure in seeing the deep red of Japanese maples, bright purple berry clusters on beautyberry shrubs, the faded hues of papery hydrangea flowers, and some rhododendrons whose stubborn second blooms decorated backyards with pink along the way. The smell of wood smoke floated in the air, reminding Beth she needed to clean out her fireplace. Once, a scruffy shih tzu, more mop than dog, barked at her through a slatted gate until she'd disappeared from view.

In John Hendry Park, the same willows that wept gold each year around the anniversary of her son Robbie's death wept now for Edith too. Beth swallowed hard as she strode past them. Two crows, their feathers gleaming ebony, strutted with confidence beneath the trees, stopping now and then to peck in the grass. Beth recalled an old children's rhyme: one for sorrow, two for joy... not much of that today. She wiped her eyes and blew her nose. The lake was a soothing, calm blue-grey with multi-shades of green and brown from bushes and trees reflected along the water's edge. It would be easy to let memories of her young son take over, but now was a time to savour memories of Edith, her friend and good neighbour.

The first time Beth had met Edith was seventeen years prior on an icy December morning three days after she had moved in. A loud knocking at the back door had sent her former cat, a calico named Jessica, galloping into the bedroom, where she promptly tunnelled under the comforter. Beth had always appreciated her as an early warning sign, but she had to admit it was far more pleasant having Monty the socialite around.

Through the door's sheer curtained window, Beth had seen a short, buxom, brown-haired woman waiting, cradling a plastic bag like a bulky baby. Beth had opened the door to a big smile and a barrage of information. The woman had declined to come in further than the porch.

"I'm Edith from just across the lane. Brought you some things I found last week in the garbage behind your garage. I don't know what happened to the rotisserie rod, sorry."

Beth recalled her initial confusion about what she was being told, until it became clear that Edith had retrieved items she recognized as parts of the McClary Easy Princess stove Beth had acquired with the house. Edith had hauled a broiler pan and grill out of the bag as she continued talking.

"These were all crusted with burned food. Nothing a little elbow grease couldn't fix. I don't know what my late neighbour's family was thinking, just wanted to get back to Comox, I guess. Anyway, that aside, I'm sure you're going to like it here—it's a good neighbourhood."

When Beth finally got to introduce herself, Edith flashed a smile again, saying, "I'm having my traditional neighbours' afternoon Christmas tea on the fifteenth. Two o'clock. No need to bring anything, several of us have already made enough goodies. Next year you can pitch in."

With the invitation proffered in the form of an edict and her delivery made, Edith had pointed out her home and marched out of the yard with a little wave, leaving Beth somewhat amused by the entire episode and very glad since then that Edith had given into her nosy nature and rescued the oven parts.

After four brisk turns round the park with the air crisp and the gentle warmth of the sun on her face, Beth could feel the result she'd aimed for. When she entered her back porch to the ever-comforting presence of Monty, she was ready to make some more calls.

❦

Truth is, Beth thought as she hesitated outside Ken's hospital door, *I never get any better at this, even though I know from experience how much support during these times is appreciated. During my own tragedy, I didn't dissect people's words; I was warmed and comforted by their caring.*

She took in a slow deep breath—*peace*—let it out gently—*love*—and entered the room to find Ken up, comfortable in an armchair, his balding head bent over an open bible on his lap.

"Ken, I'm so sorry. I know we were all praying for a miracle, but perhaps the miracle was that Edith lasted long enough for you to say goodbye."

Slack-faced, Ken raised his head. "I guess so. She did say my name a few times and squeezed my hand once. I wish I could have figured out what else she was trying to say. She was upset and was saying it over and over, something about 'way ten, way tin.'"

"I thought Edith was asking for you. Something like 'wha or wheh-ten'—I thought it was 'where's Ken?'"

"No, it wasn't that because when she finally did say my name, it was definite. The other was more the 'ay' sound. And then there was one like 'tin' or 'ten.' Way tin. Maybe it was one word."

"Whay ten, way tin, waytin," Beth repeated without pause. "Ah. Waiting. Sounds like waiting. What do you think?"

Ken's face brightened slightly, and his voice grew stronger as he strained to recall Edith's words.

"Suppose so, but waiting for what? I need to know what happened. Susan told me Edith had almost reached the other side of the street. Just a minute," said Ken, "one time, Edith repeated another word or words before the 'way ten' and they had an 'r' sound. It was likely that she'd waited to be sure there were no cars before she crossed like she always did. Susan reminded me it was dark and wet. Edith is always… *was* always careful. I think she was just trying to tell me she'd waited and had been careful."

"Or maybe Edith was trying to say that . . ." Beth let the sentence trail away. "Well, I don't really know." It dawned on her that Edith's agitation could be more than the result of the head injury. Maybe Edith was trying to tell them it was no accident. Had Edith been waiting or had the car been waiting? Beth wasn't about to say that out loud and upset Ken. "Hopefully the police will find the driver. Bill Yeung said he saw them pick up something from the road so that might be a clue to the car."

Monday, November 8

At the beginning of the day, Beth sighed as she wrote down some tasks she was planning to accomplish. It was difficult to concentrate, to keep her mind from revisiting what Edith had said in the last conversation they'd had, from sliding off into more speculation about the accident and from trying to make sense of Edith's mutterings.

The evening before, with the conversation she'd had with Ken fresh in her mind, Beth had devoted more time to thinking about the sounds she'd heard and spelled them out in several ways. She'd compared them with her previous effort. Perhaps Edith's distress was just that she wanted them to understand she'd been careful, had waited, and that it wasn't her fault. But could it be the other way around? Had the car been waiting for her? Knowing Edith had a pair of the sharpest eyes on the block, Beth was beginning to believe that was possible. Edith had been an ideal neighbourhood watchdog: observant, concerned, honest, reliable, and—well, yes—Beth had to admit, rather nosy in her pursuit of information. But while Edith may have gathered gossip, she only shared what she believed had bearing on the wellbeing of the neighbourhood. Finally, Beth decided to talk with Susan this morning and see what she thought.

Using the pretext of reporting on her visit with Ken, Beth began her to-do list by calling Susan, currently off work, to see how she was coping and told her what Ken had said about Edith's talking.

"Oh, I don't know really," said Susan. "Mom knew who we were, but she wasn't making much sense. I couldn't say for sure what she was trying to tell us. The word 'car' seemed pretty obvious to me, except she couldn't pronounce the 'c,' and I think she was saying 'raining' one time, so maybe she was just saying the rain made it hard for the car to see her or something."

"Yes, I suppose that could be it," Beth said, hesitated, then added, "But actually, what if the word was 'waiting?' You know, like 'car waiting,' if you put them together. I began thinking of the two threatening letters your mom received recently, as well as that horrible call from Harry Anders' nephew. Edith told me all about it. I gathered Harry Anders is quite well off. Your mom was very worried he was being taken advantage of and likely being tricked out of money."

Susan was quiet as she gradually digested what Beth said. "Yes, I know about him and about the letters. And of course, there was the break-in October thirtieth. I see what you're getting at," Susan said, "that Mom was the target of a vendetta of some sort, and she thought the car accident was part of it."

"I've been leaning that way," said Beth.

"Maybe she got too close to finding out something really damning. She did that once before. Harry's nephew sounds like a real weasel. I hear all about him. I mean heard—oh gosh, I just miss Mom so much." Susan's voice thickened then faded.

"I know you must. Your mom was so full of life and was totally into her family—and all of us who live around here too. I've envied your relationship with her."

Susan cleared her throat, recovering her composure. "Thanks, Beth. And I've appreciated yours with her. Perhaps it would be good to tell the police what we've talked about," Susan said. "Will you do that? Please."

"Yes," said Beth, motioning a thumbs up signal to the cat who gazed at her intently as though he understood. Like a toddler vying for attention, Monty almost always turned up when she was on the phone.

"And I have another favour to ask: Dad would like you to

collect the mail. He forgot to ask you. He says you have keys to the basement door. He doesn't want stuff piling up. Just put it on the kitchen table and I'll be over when I can."

Beth said, "Not a problem, and I can let you know if anything looks important. I'm sure Sofia and Gino are watching front and back."

"Yes, and Alan is too. I'll let them know you'll be going in. I've set timers on two different lights by the way. Dad and I appreciate this, thanks so much."

Beth replaced the receiver feeling pleased with the outcome of the call. She sat and had a cuddle with Monty and made up her mind to take a quick trip to the corner store to check in with Bill Yeung. She had lots of time before Cathy was due to pick her up for lunch and a shopping excursion at Metrotown. Her long-time friend, who hailed from school days in Nova Scotia, worked part time as an occupational therapist at Lions Gate Hospital in North Vancouver where she lived with her husband Bob, a successful real estate agent.

She was glad to see Bill alone behind the counter of his shop. He was perched on a stool with the *Vancouver Sun* spread out in front of him. He looked up and greeted her by her first name. He lived with his wife on the upper floor of the square, two-story, wood-framed building, which they had managed long before Beth moved into the area.

"First time I've seen you since . . ." his words trailed away. "Jenny Lee was in to pick up a paper this morning. She told me about Edith's death." He shook his head. "It's impossible to think of the neighbourhood without her."

"So true. With Ken in hospital, it's extra sad," Beth said. "Bill, I came to ask you if you have the number for the officer who was here. I remember the time I had some summer chairs stolen off my back deck, and I was given a business card before the policeman left, so I assume they gave you one."

"Oh sure, I'll write down the name and number for you," Bill said. "Do you know something?"

"No, I came along after the accident. Edith's daughter wants me to call the police, but she forgot to give me a contact number. I guess you've had a thorough questioning. Could you help them at all?"

"Not really. I happened to be near the front there restocking one of the shelves, but I was concentrating on what I was doing. By the time I looked up, the taillights of a dark sedan were all I saw. I couldn't even really tell what shape the lights were." Bill said.

About to tear the note from his pad, he hesitated and handed her the business card instead. "Why don't you just take this. There's another name written on the back. It's the sergeant in charge."

"Thanks," Beth said as she slipped the card in her pocket. She lingered in front of the counter, determined to learn as much as possible. "I can understand how you wouldn't see much at this angle from the counter. What about any witnesses on the street? Police say anything?"

Bill was clearly eager to share his story. "I think the first man to go to Edith came from the end of the lane. Then someone stopped their car and put their flashers on. There was another fellow across the street bringing his dog back from the park, I guess. You might know him to see him—he has that cute Welsh terrier he walks all the time."

"I've noticed them around. Don't know him."

"Well," said Bill, "the officer spoke to him, but it wasn't for long. Still, I'd guess he saw more of the car than me. The first person on the scene came in to get some smokes afterward. He said the police picked up two bits of orange plastic from the road. From a signal light, I guess. The fellow who stopped his car didn't see anything because the car that hit Edith was long gone. He started directing cars to the other lane. Dangerous really with the visibility so bad, but the police arrived five minutes later, thank God."

"I just find it hard to believe any driver could miss those red lights," Beth said. "There are two, in fact. I know Edith would have been looking both ways. Anyway, no one in their right mind would have crossed against the light."

Bill shrugged his shoulders. "There are lots of iffy drivers out there these days, and really, conditions were dreadful." He sighed. "Maybe the driver was speeding and was trying to stop but slid into Edith, then panicked."

Beth nodded. Looking at the scene of the crime—as she had begun to think of it—she felt a solidifying of her belief it was not a simple accident. Edith was ultra-careful. Her mind raced ahead to its chosen conclusion. It was a hit-and-run in the most calculated meaning of the words. Someone had meant to hurt Edith.

"You'll let me know when the service is?" Bill said.

"What? Yes, of course—it'll be at St. Jude's, I presume, but I'll make sure you know. When will depend on what Ken can manage, I imagine."

With Susan's request that she tell the police about the verbal and written attacks on her mother, Beth felt more justified and as ready as she'd ever be to phone Sergeant James. It was a letdown to be forwarded to voicemail. Beth fumbled her way through a short message identifying herself as Edith Todd's neighbour and saying she was calling on behalf of the family. She closed by saying Mr. Todd and his daughter had information that could be important to the accident investigation.

Time out with her friend Cathy had been pleasantly distracting and offered the comfort of someone who knew her well. Beth arrived home relaxed. She listened to the businesslike voice of Sergeant James informing her he'd be available to see her the following afternoon when he would be in his office. A constable would call in the morning to set an appointment. As her edginess returned, Beth decided to skip her photography class that evening. A leisurely bath and the light murder mystery *Evans Above* by Rhys Bowen, which had been languishing in her bookcase since last Christmas, was far more appealing. At last, she'd be able to tell Cathy she was reading it.

※

Tuesday, November 9

Beth was thankful when the phone rang just after nine the next morning. She tried to give the constable from the hit-and-run team some background on the purpose of the appointment but he drowned out her explanation with instructions of where she needed to be at two o'clock. She was to present herself to the reception desk in the lobby of the VPD building at Cambie and Sixth, after which she would be escorted to the meeting with Sergeant James. Beth felt like she was being summoned to the principal's office.

Sergeant James was sitting behind his desk when Beth was shown in. It was not just his manner that seemed intimidating: a sober giant rose to his feet to greet her, offering his large right hand over the desk. He jotted down a few notes while he listened to her halting report of what Edith seemed to be saying according to both Beth and Edith's family. She relaxed a bit as she clearly outlined the reasons for their concerns. As an afterthought, Beth added that the Todd home was broken into in late October. Sergeant James rose and asked to be excused, with an apology but no explanation, and left her waiting for fifteen minutes.

"I wanted to check if Mrs. Todd reported the threats," he said upon his return. "There was nothing on file and the Block Watch liaison officer Constable Argento knew nothing of them. I gather Mrs. Todd was a rather zealous captain and had gone beyond safe practice in the past. Constable Argento thinks the break-in at the Todd's was in keeping with the local crime happening in your area. And as for the blind parishioner with a scheming nephew, that sounds like the plot of a mystery book. It seems Mrs. Todd, while well-meaning, had an overactive imagination."

He continued just as Beth opened her mouth to object to the last part of his statement. "There's no need for you to worry, we're doing everything possible to locate the car and through that, the driver. It's just a matter of time. We'll contact the family to reassure them. There's no way to be sure of what Mrs. Todd was saying. Confusion and incoherence are common symptoms of a head injury. An interview was attempted during her short conscious period, but I'm afraid none of Mrs. Todd's responses made sense."

Sergeant James went on to reiterate that what Beth thought she'd heard could be anything and that perhaps the shock of losing her close neighbour made it difficult for her to accept the accident was just that.

"Constable Argento did say Mrs. Todd was a very effective Block Watch captain and I *am* sorry for your loss," he offered in a softer, conciliatory tone. "Unfortunately, it's the time of year we begin to see an increase in these kinds of tragic accidents related to darkness and the poor weather."

Beth nodded, understanding there was nothing more she could say that would change the sergeant's mind. Her cheeks felt dragged down by lead weights.

In what seemed to be a reaction to Beth's downcast expression,

Sergeant James said, "If it's any reassurance, we do have some evidence left at the scene of the accident. It takes time to unravel some of these cases, but I'm confident it can be solved."

He stood up and assured her the case was being pursued with due diligence, including an ongoing public appeal. With a final reminder that body shops were on the alert, he ushered Beth toward the door. His assistant accompanied her to the lobby.

Afterwards, Beth drove home on her usual route along Nanaimo, her mind stuck in a circle of unpleasant thoughts. She found herself reliving the accident scene she had glimpsed the previous Thursday, keenly aware now that it had been Edith she'd seen being lifted by the paramedics. She took vague notice of the almost-bare trees and stucco homes approaching then receding past her left and right. Her teeth were as clenched as her fingers on the steering wheel when she slowed, light blinking to indicate a left turn. While she waited for the oncoming traffic to abate, she made an effort to relax.

A shoulder roll, a deep breath, a long exhalation.

Beth recognized she was feeling more hopeful the car would be identified, heartened by the confirmation that there was some useful evidence. But it was another thing to prove the accident was intentional. *Edith deserves better.* Sadness pulled at her like the undertow of a rushing river. She wondered what the Welsh terrier owner had seen. *I can find out.*

Despite feeling spent, Beth felt anger starting to penetrate her gloom and goad her to action. She was unwilling to set aside her gut feeling there was an explanation for Edith's fatal accident, and it wasn't just being in the wrong place at the wrong time. The other possibilities needed to be explored. In the time it took to reach the back lane, she decided that if the police weren't going to open other areas of investigation, she would do it herself. And she would contact Constable Argento herself to feel him out. Perhaps he would be willing to help if he got to hear the explanation of her and Susan Todd's concerns straight from her.

Waiting for her garage door to open, Beth looked at the now lifeless windows of the Todd home. It was of 1950s vintage, similar to Beth's. As she had been reminded by Susan, Beth had keys to the basement door from five summers ago when Edith and Ken had their recreation room altered to enlarge Ken's workshop. After the job was finished, Edith told her to keep them "just in case." Now, Beth had a legitimate reason to go into the house to sort the Todd's mail and report to Susan. What if she just checked to see if Edith had written down anything relevant? She'd often referred to 'my notes' when speaking of Block Watch activities. That would be okay, wouldn't it? After all, Edith had wanted to talk with her about something important.

When she stepped into the back porch, a thump from the living room signaled Monty was on his way to greet her. Beth sighed and bent to lift him into her arms for a prolonged hug.

"Who's my favourite fellow then?" The cat purred with gusto, butting his head against her chin. Holding Monty's soft warmth against her neck, Beth's thoughts swung back to consider what could be helpful in her pursuit for answers. There were Edith's personal Block Watch files. *And there's a journal somewhere . . .*

FIVE

Wednesday, November 10

A good deal of the dreary grey morning was taken up with Beth dissecting her intent to search for clues in Edith's home. She had to do it if she was to learn anything of Edith's secret. But what would people think if she was found out? She'd busied herself with two loads of laundry while she went back and forth with the decision. Beth coaxed herself to take the time needed to prepare a grilled cheese and tomato sandwich. It always felt comforting, a reminder of her childhood years. She heated some soup and sat with a *Courier*, the local paper that was delivered twice a week, propped up in front of her. Afterwards, she could recall little of what she had read and had no recollection of eating her sandwich. *So much for comfort.* Her mind had roamed through a crowd of thoughts about Edith's death and the last few days, effectively erasing the present moment.

Beth pushed through the drain from yesterday's overall disappointment and her recent waffling throughout the morning. A single thought brought the final decision. She had no doubt Edith would approve of her intent. Edith clearly had something specific on her mind. *Find the journal.* Knowing that Beth journaled, Edith had once confided that she began a journal during a time of severe stress over her younger daughter's death, saying, "I keep it private in a very safe place." *It may take some rooting about to find but I know Edith; she'd want me to look.*

❦

Down the lane, Mike Mahoney Junior left home under his own grey cloud, his guts in a knot. There had been no way to avoid his mother's demand for him to accompany her and his father to busybody Edith's funeral. It would be a downer for sure. And it meant missing work. He used to like her, but for a while now, she'd been on his case with sharp asides about getting himself "on the straight and narrow." He resented her interference. As if his mom wasn't bad enough. She rattled on about how too much drink and hanging out with the 'wrong sort' could affect one's future prospects. It was dark and rainy, and his mom was pissing him off again.

"You need to get full-time work. This piecemeal job of yours won't pay for university fees. We can only help you so much. Have you checked in with the employment office at Safeway headquarters yet? You know your dad already put in a good word for you. Why hasn't the Manpower employment agency contacted you? Didn't you leave a resume with them? Don't they offer some retraining courses? You've got to get back to your studies. You're wasting your talents."

On and on. The probing only ended when he snapped that he was following up a lead in Burnaby—a lie. He'd need to eat some humble pie later but now he had to get away from the voice that was wailing behind the slammed door, "You haven't even finished your breakfast."

He pulled the hood of his Taiga jacket over the mop of dark blond hair he'd inherited from his father. He'd get a haircut—that would lighten the mood when he got back. *Catch the sky train out to Metrotown, that's what I'll do.* Then he could show her the stamped return ticket to prove where he'd been if she grilled him. He could easily spin a tale and get Norm to vouch for him.

From the first time they'd met, Mike felt a kinship with skinny Norm Jervis ("call me Legs," he'd said, but Mike never did) who was conveniently nearby across the lane. Norm and his girlfriend Tara had been living in a makeshift basement suite in her uncle's house for eight months now. Mike had overheard his mother say she was sure Tara's mother Mazie, a Kelowna divorcee, had designs on her former brother-in-law Alan Whitman since his wife, Mazie's sister, had died less than a year before. Barely four months after Evie's passing, she had called and asked if Tara and Norm could stay with him until they found a place of their own.

Tara had promptly got work at the downtown Hudson's Bay department store, but Norm, who had said he was unemployed like Mike, offered Mike the understanding of a fellow down-on-his-luck job seeker. On the April morning Alan drove his niece to work for her first day, he had introduced the couple to Mike. Tara, her thin face framed in black curls from a new permed style, had given him a quick grimace of a smile while her fingers fidgeted with her purse clasp. She had been visibly anxious about what was to be her "first day on the job in the big city," as her Uncle Alan explained.

After the car rolled off down the lane, Norm and Mike had stood for nearly half an hour talking about their respective work history, comparing notes on stupid bosses, lame coworkers, and the unrealistic demands of snotty Manpower agents. His mother's sharp call for him to take out the garbage had curtailed this meeting of minds.

"Wanna have a drink later?" Norm had said. "What about four at the All Hours Tavern up on Kingsway. Know it?"

"Yeah," Mike had said with a thumb up. "Meet you there."

Later at the tavern, Norm had drained his fourth pale ale and let out a loud burp. "Sorry, man." He'd leaned forward, smoothing back the shock of mousey brown hair that kept obscuring his dark eyes.

He'd paused as the lyrics of Shania Twain's "The Woman in Me" floated through the pub from an old jukebox.

"Hey, I know we don't know each other really, but I got a line on some work and maybe you could get in on it," Norm had said, slurring some words. "My cousin Rich says he's hiring. Needs a few guys, he says. I was hoping he'd come through. My gal is giving me the gears 'cause she's got a job and I don't."

Mike had set his empty glass down. "Know what that feels like. Mom is after me every day to get a job *and* get back to university. What's your cousin got going?"

"Rich owns and runs a car dealership and repair shop from a big outfit on Vulcan Way in Richmond. Pacific Coastal Auto Company. You must have seen ads in the paper and on TV. It's new and used cars and auto parts. He's a bit older, mid-forties. He's doing great. Hell, he even has a place in Palm Springs. Ever been there? Anyways, Rich is sending someone to pick me up at ten tomorrow. I mentioned you. You should come along. Whadya say?"

Mike recalled that conversation as the start of his renewed hope for the future. His few years at UBC had not enthused him, though he did complete three years towards a BSc. It was too much toil, not enough money, and little fun. Unable to fit in more than ten hours of work a week and maintain his grades, his social life suffered as did his bank account. He insisted he needed a break to work and make some money. His dad had been okay with it. However, his mom was livid. And the fact he'd moved in with his new girlfriend Charlene, who had also dropped out of university, did not please her. Charlene already had a small apartment thanks to a doting uncle who had offered him a job waiting tables at the restaurant he owned. Mike had been amazed at how much extra he could make in tips—plenty of big spenders ate at Le Crocodile. Even his parents had come and tipped him. But the work had been boring. Worse, Charlene had turned out to be a control freak. He'd escaped as soon as his savings allowed him to take off to Europe. His mom's objections had been softened by him agreeing that she had been right when she'd warned that Charlene wasn't right for him. What was meant to be a short trip to Europe had turned into two years, after which his folks had to send him money to fly back from London. His mother had welcomed him home with arms opened wide. And there he'd been—stuck in a rut for nearly four years working here and there and doing the odd night class to keep his mother at bay.

❧

The day of the interview, Mike had made an effort to dress neatly—he'd ditched his ball cap and wore a navy sports jacket with the new pair of Levi's jeans his mom bought him for his birthday. She'd quizzed him later about the silver Cadillac she'd watched him and Norm get into. Where did you go? Who was that exactly? What kind of a job interview? He'd been glad he had something positive to tell her even though he knew what her reaction would be.

"Cousin of Norm's, Mom, Richard Belmont. Owns a large Chevrolet dealership with a busy repair shop and parts supply section. You may have seen his picture in the paper sponsoring charity events? He's hired us each to drive delivery trucks casually. But that's just to start. He pays more than minimum wage. I'll be able to get some money put aside to pay you back and to get back to some studies."

"Never mind that. Is your driver's license still valid? What do you know about driving trucks?" she said, her forehead beginning to wrinkle. "You need a special license, don't you?"

"They're not big trucks, Mom, just delivery vans. Anyway, if I need to upgrade, I'll do it. Mr. Belmont told me this will work into more," said Mike. During the mini-interview he'd had with Rich, he'd handed over a one-page resume, which produced a positive reaction. Now it occurred to him he was glad he hadn't mentioned his university years to Norm, or he might never have been asked to go along.

"Well, be careful. I think I met this Richard Belmont at a Christmas event I attended hosted by the Lassiter family. He must be okay. Just keep looking for something better, something permanent. You haven't talked properly to your dad yet. He can help you. We don't want you wasting your talents on menial work. You still need to take one more course to finish your first degree then go on to the next so you can command a good wage in a job worthy of your talents."

Mothers. He needed to have some good money coming in. That's what he needed. He had to get out from under his mother's thumb as soon as he could.

The car dealership was a place to start, though Mike hadn't imagined it would lead to a criminal act, though minor, that had him spooked. It had happened two months after he'd been driving for Rich's outfit. Rich had called him into the office and spoke quietly of the delicate nature of some of his dealings. *Delicate?* Mike had wondered about that.

❧

"Too many meaningless rules out there to follow," Rich had said. "I admit, I dodge some of them. Doesn't hurt to take some shortcuts and get ahead." Rich smoothed back his wavy dark brown hair. His unusually pale eyes bore into Mike's. "I have a small, trusted group of employees. It's kind of casual. I think you should be part of it. Norm'll fill you in." Rich had followed up with a firm handshake.

Mike had felt nervous but figured there was no good reason to turn Rich down. He'd wanted to show he was serious and was sure this would lead to more work and more money. Rich was obviously making big bucks and was cool to be around. The guy had nerve as well as heart; after all, he made regular donations to the food bank and showed up in the local charity events pages Norm said. So what if the rules got bent now and then? Rich was just making a point about how two faced some systems were. Mike could see how he would need trust his employees not to make waves.

That evening, Norm had treated him to a Big Mac meal deal and told him about The Pizza Club.

"There's just a little test, an initiation of sorts," he'd said. "It will be your ticket into the inner circle. Rich needs to know you can stay cool under pressure. Everybody's done it. It's nothing really."

"What's this 'nothing?'" Mike had asked, thinking it might be like the beginning of his freshman year.

"All you gotta to do is lift a couple new-release video tapes, then we'll all get together on the weekend, order in pizza, have some beers, and watch a movie. I'm sure you'll be fine. Just don't get caught." Norm had laughed.

When the time came to "earn his place," as Norm had said, all Mike could think was, *don't get caught*. He had tried some slow breathing to ease the queasy feeling in his stomach and offset the light-headedness that accompanied his fear of failure. He'd felt guilty before he'd even done anything. He'd been told he could choose any store he wanted, so he'd decided on one in Richmond away from his neighbourhood. Norm had driven him there in a "club car," chattering away as if it was a fun outing.

"Gotta keep an eye on you and watch you carry out the mission. I can run interference if it's needed. Just pretend I'm not here."

Sure, Mike had thought.

They'd parked at a nearby mini mall, and Mike had walked to Blockbuster Video with Norm trailing him at a distance. Mike had chosen a Friday afternoon, reasoning that there would be lots of people renting videos for weekend viewing. His plan had been to tuck the videos under one arm inside his jacket, pretend he was leaving while casually picking up a movie guide by the door, then make a mad dash for it. He had cased the area the previous week, so he'd known exactly where he would go hide to wait out a possible chase. He'd worn a throw-away red ball cap and a black windbreaker that he would reverse to grey as soon as he was out of sight round a corner.

As he'd entered the store, he'd thought he might faint; his hands had been slick, underarms sticky. He'd almost collided with someone leaving. The young blonde at the front counter had called out, "Good afternoon."

"Yeah, hi," said Mike and had strode to the back wall where the latest releases were lined up. He'd spent about five minutes picking up several boxes and pretending to read the covers. All the while, his innards had churned as if he was in a small boat on heavy seas. Norm had entered the store and was methodically examining videos for sale then came to stand where he blocked another customer's view. Mike had taken a long deep breath and began walking to the front with two hidden video cassettes. A young mother with her whiny little boy provided an unexpected distraction as he'd picked up the movie rag and took the last few steps past the detector to the door, pushing it open, breaths shallow, feet moving fast. He had heard the alarm and a shout behind him but had made it around the corner headed for his hiding place before anyone got out on the sidewalk. He hadn't been a track champion in high school for nothing. Still, he wasn't in the same shape as then and the short sprint to take cover in a nearby lane had him gulping for air. His breathing had slowed as he'd forced himself to sit casually on the back step of a random business to have a pretend smoke. He'd bummed a cigarette from one of the mechanics, but it hadn't been worth smoking and risking his mother's keen nose. Mike had gradually relaxed into a sense of calm and success. *Norm can wait.*

In time, Mike would swear to his father that he didn't know what was going on at the dealership, that it wasn't his fault. Yes, he was there, he'd confess, and he did finally realize it was a very bad scene, but he was also very frightened, and at the time, he saw no way to escape serious personal harm.

SIX

Wednesday, November 10

Beth roused herself from a short sitting meditation at the sound of her pocket timer. It was a relief to get moving. She called Ken's hospital unit to leave a message that she would drop in to see him after dinner in the evening, and since she was considered family, the unit clerk offered the news that he was being discharged the next day.

Aware of the possibility that Susan could turn up for some of her father's belongings, Beth found herself hesitant about her plan. She shook her head in rebuke of her sliding resolve. If she was in the house and Susan arrived, it should be fine. She would break off from checking around to head for the mail.

She rooted around at the back of a desk drawer where, tucked in a small box, she found the Todd's keys. Should she take some rubber gloves? There were some thin ones in the bathroom cabinet from a long-ago attempt to colour her hair to cover some of the grey. What if there was another break-in? There was no guarantee it wouldn't happen again while the house was unattended. She may be an amateur, but she'd been watching *Exhibit A: Secrets of Forensic Science* regularly since it began airing in 1997. *Don't be silly, your prints aren't on file anywhere,* she thought.

Beth stuffed a small pad and pen in her pocket and decided to bring her SLR camera and macro lens. The camera happened to be loaded with black and white film because of a photo course assignment. If she found Edith's journal, she could take pictures of some of the journal pages but would rely on notes just in case the photos were poor. That was assuming she could find the journal.

Since Beth had no idea how long she would need for her task, she decided it would be better not to be seen coming or going by anyone. She used the pretense of pulling a few straggly weeds near the back of her garage while she scanned for any activity in the lane. *Nothing. Good.* Beth placed her hand on the latch of the Todd's picket gate and opened and closed the gate with exaggerated care. She passed the flower bed that Dennis recently finished. He had waived the cost of the bulbs in Edith's memory. If anyone happened by, Beth could honestly say she was checking the Todd's mail then try harder to avoid being spotted upon leaving.

At the basement door, which was shielded somewhat by a large camellia bush, the guilt about what she was going to do surfaced briefly as she handled the keys. Two were needed for this entrance—one key for the handle and another for the deadbolt lock. Ken and Edith had dispensed with their alarm system some years back after an upgrade to a newer version resulted in several false alarms, but they'd left the warning stickers in place as a deterrent. The recently broken window had been replaced and bars added. Beth had learned upon joining Block Watch that an alarm was not a substitute for sturdy hardware, so she had followed the Todd's example. Edith had confided in Beth that anything of great value was in a very safe place in the house. Beth had a good idea of what that safe location might be, though not exactly where. Many of the homes on either side of the lane at this end of the block had been constructed by the same builder. There was a safe place in her home behind a false wall, which Beth hadn't discovered until two years after she'd moved in. Whether it was another of Jack's quirks or was the builder's signature, she didn't know.

Beth slid the first key in and turned. It didn't budge. The other key worked at once, and Beth winced when the lock opened with a loud clunk. To her relief, when she retried the other key, the bolt lock retracted with only a low rasp. Pushing the heavy wood door inward, she stepped onto a cement floor in a dimly lit, unfinished area where two small horizontal windows were covered with faded orange burlap curtains. Ken's rake, a shovel, and other garden tools hung in a neat row on a nearby wall. There was a workbench with some wood pieces lying neatly at one end along with a toolbox. The oil furnace seemed like a brooding metal octopus with arms snaking away into the upstairs vents.

Despite the legitimacy of her presence in the house and her own voice reassuring her that all was well, Beth felt like a trespasser. She wound her way around some boxes to push a sliding door aside, entering an area where she found one bedroom and the stairs that led to the kitchen. Beth flicked on the stairway light and started up. *Creak.* The lifeless house was giving her the creeps. Her sadness over Edith's death and Ken's grief seemed a literal weight in her heart. She knew her own sense of loss was compounded by personal sorrows.

All at once, she was at the top of the stairs, doorknob in her hand, turning it slowly. She nudged the door open to the silence of the main floor. Here, she was in familiar territory, having been there on a variety of occasions from intimate chats over tea to more formalized Block Watch meetings.

Beth voiced a tentative, "Hellooo?" and waited. She prepared herself to hear Susan's voice. A second louder hello was not answered either.

From the kitchen, a T-shaped hallway offered central access to the bathroom, the main bedroom, the living room, and two smaller rooms, one with dining furniture, and one which Edith had converted into an office and sewing room. Beth would begin there. *Pick up the mail last,* she reminded herself.

Beth gave thanks that the window was covered with sheer curtains so she couldn't be seen but there was enough light to work by. Beginning with the datebook lying open on the desktop, Beth thumbed back through the past two months. Her eyes teared as she saw Edith's entry for a hair appointment that very day. Beth noticed an address circled in red jotted in the margin of one of the pages, so transcribed it to her notepad. The sharp ring of the desk phone brought her head and her heart rate up. Susan must have disconnected the answering machine. Beth stood by, willing the person to hang up. By the time the jarring sounds finally stopped, her resolve needed some boosting. *Deep breath.* There was still the Block Watch binder to check and Edith's journal to find.

The former was easy, marked in capital letters on a shelf nearby. In it were several dividers, one of which was labelled 'Current.' A ruled page had one entry. It simply read '*see if Alan can get me a sample of Norm's handwriting.*' A plastic sleeve at the back of this section held two envelopes: one had 'Block Watch Witch' scrawled on the front and a skull and crossbones where a stamp would go. This would have been the one left on her doorstep at Halloween. The other had come by post and was franked on the eighteenth of October. Beth placed the letters in her casual canvas shoulder bag. She admitted to herself she was feeling annoyed that Edith hadn't told Constable Argento.

Glancing at her watch, she was surprised that twenty minutes

SIX | 53

had passed when it felt like less. *Get a move on.* She needed to find the journal, take whatever pictures she could, and leave. She walked quickly to the primary bedroom. Using a chair to step up, she searched the upper panels of the closet for the same configuration as in her own closet. Her belief that she knew where to look was shattered when she failed to find a hidden compartment there or in the other bedroom. She was headed back to the office when the sound of the door chime nailed her to the spot. It chimed one more time. Seconds later, the clang of the side gate latch galvanized her into action. She took a slow breath and crept to the basement door, which she'd left ajar. Beth eased herself through and waited. She stood still as a lamp post while someone tramped up to the back door. After a loud round of knocking, the person clumped down the steps. *Did someone see me come in?* she wondered. It took Beth a moment to decide she shouldn't let herself give up just yet. She had to try her best to find Edith's journal so she could find out what Edith wanted her to know.

Another ten minutes of rising tension and looking through drawers, shelves, and the office closet found her holding it, disbelieving her luck and the answer to its hiding place. It had been in plain sight. Beth's good fortune, although it startled her at the time, was in knocking aside a thick sewing manual as she checked the bookshelves. When she'd righted it, it seemed far too light. Curious, she'd opened the cover to find a simple spiral-bound journal nested in a hollowed space.

"Gracious, you went to a lot of trouble, Edith," she murmured and let a small smile tug on her lips. With tears not far away, Beth made a quick decision—forget the note taking and photos, she would take the journal and letters home to photograph and return them promptly. She needed to leave; she'd been in the house long enough. She placed the mail on the kitchen table, retreated back through the basement, locked up, and slipped through the lane gate while holding her camera at the ready as a prop. But there was no one in sight. *As far as I know*, she thought.

Once home, Beth shoved what she had found out of sight in a desk drawer and promised herself to leave any exploration of them till the next morning. The combined forces of anxiety and grief had given rise to a sudden dread that she was out of her depth and that anger was causing her to act in poor faith. Perhaps she had it all wrong and had already made a fool of herself in engineering an approach to the police. The thought that followed was that she shouldn't have removed Edith's personal papers. *Pointless thinking that now; I'll focus on what I can learn from what I've taken and return Edith's belongings as soon as possible.*

❦

Thursday, November 11

On Remembrance Day, the dull grey skies and cold drizzle did little to boost Beth's tenuous calm. She switched on the TV and ate some hot oatmeal while watching the ceremonies in Ottawa, joining in for the two minutes of silent prayer. In particular, the laying of the wreath by the Silver Cross Mother never failed to move her. She thought of her dad and the picture album from his days in the Royal Air Force. He hadn't been a pilot, but as ground crew, he was an integral part of the war effort and proud of his service. She owed her Canadian citizenship to him. In 1941, he volunteered to be part of the Commonwealth Air Training Program. While serving in Debert, Nova Scotia, he met and fell for a local girl. They married before he was posted back to England. Her mother followed by ship to join him, and when the war was behind them, her dad decided to take early discharge and emigrate. In 1947, they left with Beth in tow, bound for Halifax. Later, there'd be another daughter, Jane, and eventually a son, Peter.

Beth stood before the bathroom mirror pushing a comb through her short, Twiggy-like cut. It would soon need a trim. Upon first awaking, she'd laid quietly reviewing the ethical dilemma she had created for herself. She had stepped over a line. However, if not entirely comfortable, it felt right. *I'm doing it for Edith. She had something very important she was going to share with me, so dammit, I'm going to do this.*

Beth resisted the strong urge to go look at the letters and Edith's journal until after she had shed her pajamas for some jeans and a long-sleeve turquoise turtleneck. She added a cardigan, as the house was taking some time to warm up after having cooled a lot during the night. She settled at her desk and flipped quickly to the most recent entries in the journal where she found Edith had briefly written of her suspicions about Norm as well as Harry's nephew. Edith had felt the threats and the break-in could be related to either of them. Edith's last entry on November 2 revealed the significance of the locket.

> I'm wearing Emma's locket. I need to keep it safe till I decide what to do. The locket should not have been where Dennis found it. I will never forget when she disappeared. I met her in the lane that day. Emma touched the locket and said it was the anniversary of her parents' fatal accident. I cannot bear to think dear Emma did not run away but it must be true. Must talk this over with someone.

This had to be it—the main reason Edith wanted to talk to her. *Why don't I know of this person,* Beth thought, *given how important Emma seems to have been to Edith?* Using the macro lens with her den well lit, Beth took pictures of several journal pages and the two threatening notes, any of which could have some bearing on the accident being not an accident at all. There were only four frames remaining on the film when she finished taking pictures. She decided to waste them and develop the film immediately.

In the unfinished part of her basement near the furnace was a small darkroom. Her brother Peter had created it for her one summer several years back. He'd been visiting in between carpentry contracts. Beth pulled on a warm fleece vest and headed downstairs. Once the film had been loaded onto a reel in a stainless-steel canister in the complete darkness, she turned on the light and took the container to a sink area. The rest of the process involved presoaking with tepid water, adding developer, then using an acetic acid stop bath followed by fixer. Beth placed the tank under the tap and let water flood it several times before inverting it to drain. She welcomed the peace that concentrating on the development process had brought her. Finally, she hung the film in the darkroom to dry after carefully wiping it down with a clean sponge dedicated to just that. Emerging into the kitchen at the top of the basement steps, Beth found it was near noon and the day had brightened with pale sun now slanting through the dining room window.

🍀

Beth fought off the urge to join Monty for an after-lunch nap on the couch. Her hunger had been blunted by eating too much and her momentum had faded. But napping might spoil her sleep and she had to get up early the next day for work. That kept her from giving in and also prompted the idea that soon she would consider retiring completely. She now had another job for as long as it took—to make sure Edith's death did not go unpunished if it was the deliberate act she thought it was. It seemed an enormous undertaking. What was the quote her counsellor had shared with her? *The secret of getting started is breaking your complex overwhelming tasks into small manageable tasks, and starting on the first one.* That was it. Mark Twain.

It dawned on her she could try using the steps in an infection outbreak investigation as a way to organize herself to probe Edith's death until she could get to the library to see what books there might be on how criminal investigations were handled by the police.

In the den, Beth found the study materials she had used in preparation for the last professional certification exam she took. *Worth a try,* she thought. She settled at her desk to adapt the steps as best she could.

Write a case definition:
> A planned hit-and-run accident

Assess need for consultation:
> Family and friends (like Ken, Sofia, Dennis)
> Block Watch— Constable Argento, co-captain
> Jenny Lee
> Bill Yeung
> Other?

Obtain appropriate laboratory specimens:
> Tangible evidence like the poison pen letters, documented witness information that implicates suspects

Seek additional cases, current and retrospective:
> Have any other Block Watch captains been targeted?

Characterize case(s) by person, place, and time:
> Edith Todd, seventy-nine years old, Block Watch captain, struck down on the crosswalk by the Good Luck Corner Grocery on Nanaimo Street at approx. 6 p.m. Friday, November 4, 1999

Formulate tentative hypothesis: (identify suspects)

> 1. Was targeted to interrupt her influence on Harry so nephew can profit
>
> 2. Was targeted to keep her from discovering the criminals who are stealing from our neighbourhood—maybe gang related?
>
> 3. Was killed to prevent her from reporting the locket that could ultimately result in someone's arrest for the kidnapping/murder of Emma—that would mean the kidnapper/killer must know it was found

Test hypothesis:
> Develop a plausible scenario for each possibility

Communicate findings (oral briefing / written report):
> Alert hit-and-run investigating officer and Constable Argento as appropriate

It was becoming clear that this undertaking she had committed to was too much for an amateur like her. She pushed away the defeated feeling and thought about how the protagonist in most of the mysteries she read often had a sidekick or mentor or some kind of support. Why didn't she choose someone who could help and who she could trust to keep quiet? It would be wise to invite someone into her confidence. *What if something happened to me and no one knew I'd been silenced? Ridiculous. Don't be melodramatic.*

Beth spent the rest of the day forcing herself to concentrate on other activities. There was a new Michael Connolly mystery to read, a call to make to her dad, some dress pants to be hemmed, and any number of household chores should she choose to do them.

By seven in the evening, Beth returned to the darkroom. Five hours had elapsed, and the emulsion seemed properly set. She cut the film into short strips and went into the dimly lit darkroom to produce a contact sheet from which she chose the crispest images to process. Like the proof sheet, she slipped each into developer, followed by the stop bath, then the fixer. Next, she agitated the prints in a tray under running water. Finally, they were pinned up to dry. The next step would be to get the journal and letters back to Edith's office, something she'd do on Saturday. Beth decided Friday's mail could be checked then too in case Susan Todd had come to the house. And on the off-chance she was there, the journal would need to be concealed and be returned another day. Getting it back safely to where it belonged was a priority now.

SEVEN

Friday, November 12

At the downtown Vancouver office of the United Organic Food Growers Consortium, in an unprecedented departure from habit, Michael Mahoney Senior, the chief financial officer, was having a coffee break before he started his workday. He wished family relationships could be as uncomplicated as numbers. Sure, he knew numbers seemed an enigma to lots of folk, but as long as the correct equations were used and calculations were verified, they told the truth. Numbers didn't lie unless someone was deliberately skewing the input data.

Since Mike Junior had returned home following his spending spree in Europe, life seemed more chaotic and was filled with tension between his son and wife. Home was not a comfortable place to be right now, which was why he had been coming into work early several times a week and staying late on occasion. Today, he knew that extra time was needed to compose himself in order to be ready for an important 9 a.m. meeting. Nina was annoyed that he had to be at work at all today given that he had yesterday and tomorrow off. Every year, they had the same discussion about why his company did not generally allow four-day weekends when the statutory holiday fell on a

Thursday or a Tuesday. A three-day work week wasn't good for productivity. Which reminded him of Mike, whose three or less days of work each week was not compatible with harmony, not to mention the state of his son's bank account. The sooner Mike got off his duff, had regular work, and moved out again, the better. Michael had resisted Nina's suggestion they think about turning the basement into a small, contained suite for Mike to rent. His son needed independence.

Michael sighed with the realization that he'd been much less available to his son over the past six months, but even before that, he'd let years slip by. A large company merger was the focus of his attention now. A lot of number crunching and negotiations were involved, all of which created overtime hours. He wondered if he could have averted Mike's current situation, which saw him under Norm's influence and working in a job that didn't use his talent for numbers. Mike had shown even more aptitude than Michael for figures but sadly, not the same drive.

Perhaps he and Nina had given him too much. Although, to be truthful like the numbers he loved, he couldn't shy away from pointing a finger at Nina, who had always been an overly doting mom. He stretched his back and stood up to head for the executive washroom. He barely looked at himself as he washed his hands and poured a few mouthfuls of cold coffee down the drain. Still in good shape at sixty-five, Michael stood a tall-enough—in his view—five foot eight. An easy man to approach by most people's reckoning, his hair was tinged with grey, his usually bright brown eyes tired. Back in his office, he cast a glance at the clock and turned to the sheaf of papers in the red folder. *Better try to get home early today.*

❦

It was shaping up to be a usual busy last day of the formal

work week in the modest infection control office at Highcrest Hospital situated in Champlain Heights. In the mid-1970s, based on the growing recognition of the importance of preventing health care-related infections, a small infection control team was created at Highcrest consisting of a medical microbiologist and an infection control nurse.

Beth arrived for her first shift of the month just before eight o'clock. She clipped on a pager and listened to the taped report left for her by Donna Boudreau, the infection control nurse who had been hired when Beth left. Beth willed herself to pay attention, to block the pull of other thoughts.

She grabbed a few papers sitting in the inbox, one of which was the daily operating room slate. Later, she would check it for scheduled incision and drainage procedures, or any other surgery that could point to possible wound infections. She then scanned the previous day's patient listings for alert codes indicating isolation of some sort was required.

A voicemail left by the evening charge nurse on the extended care unit requested a visit "first thing in the morning" to check out some diarrhea cases that were not clearing up. It seemed to be one of Murphy's laws for someone to panic at the end of the week and let the office know that a problem had been brewing. Beth logged on to the patient care information system to access the unit listings. With a few deft keystrokes, she produced a printout of the cases to check and ran a practiced eye over it for new admissions, highlighting those that looked suspicious for infection of any sort. The hospital had 236 beds serving a variety of community health needs. While changes to the provincial health care delivery system had created centres of excellence at other lower mainland hospitals, Highcrest continued to offer a range of general services outside of these specialties. The eight-bed emergency was quick to transfer any cases assessed in triage as requiring critical specialized care to facilities like Vancouver General Hospital.

A soft knocking sound brought Beth's head up. Petite and neat in a crisp white lab coat, her shiny, mid-length black hair tucked behind her ears, lab manager June Ishida stood framed by the doorway, holding more reports.

"You look worn out. Bad night?"

"Been out of sorts for days now," Beth said. "You'll remember Edith, one of my close neighbours. She died on the weekend."

"That's sad, Beth. I'm so sorry. Of course. I met her once and she's come up in lots of our conversations. What happened?"

"She was hit by a car and ended up at VGH. It was around six last Thursday evening, dark of course, and wet. Even though Edith was in a lighted crosswalk, someone plowed into her and kept on going. I've never understood how someone can do that."

"Listen, let's have lunch together," said June. "Even if you're busy, you have to eat. It's been a while since we've managed to see one another. You can tell me more then, if you feel like it."

Beth nodded, pressed a tissue to her glistening eyes, and shifted her attention to June's hand. "What have you got there?"

"Sorry, these are going to add to your work today—got an odd situation here. There are four cultures. Some have a small mix of organisms, but primarily, they've grown the same Aspergillus. I've not seen it in surgical wounds before. More often, it's associated with immunocompromised patients, but these are different. One of the patients is in the urology unit, two are in general surgery, and the other is having dressing changes as an outpatient. The four of them came up late yesterday."

Frowning, Beth scanned the reports. "Okay, I better pop up to the wards to look at the charts before Dr. Harris gets here."

Beth's workday progressed steadily with her planned ward visits, negotiating the transfer of two patients to single rooms for isolation, returning a few 'how do I . . .' calls, leading a half-hour education in-service on influenza, and in the midst of it all, taking time for lunch with June in the cafeteria. Dr. Harris had reviewed all the cases and results with Beth and spoken to the four attending physicians regarding the Aspergillus problem. The lab was on full alert.

Around three, Dr. Harris, in his casual Friday attire of jeans and a sports jacket, tapped on the door to get a final report on the latest issues since he was on call over the weekend.

"Do you think you might be ready to leave in about half an hour?" he asked, and fielding her puzzled look, he added, "There's a tech coming to install a new phone and internet hook up for me so I'd like to use this office for a while. Don't worry about repaying the time—after all, I wonder how many extra half hours you've clocked up over the years."

At home, Beth opened her back door and, in her rush to get to the ringing telephone, almost stumbled over Monty.

"Hello, is Beth at home?" a somewhat familiar male voice said. "It's Dan Argento."

🍂

Saturday, November 13

Interesting, **Beth reflected** over her second cup of coffee the next morning, the Friday *Courier* paper in front of her on the table, *how one day at work now produces a weariness that feels like I've worked the whole week.* She knew that was exaggerated, but she recognized that the gaps between what she called her "helping days" were taking an understandable toll on the continuity she enjoyed when working full time—continuity that aided in the efficient response to some of the ever-arising infection control-related situations at the hospital. In general, she had been able to leave minor issues resolved or updated for Donna's Monday morning return. One more nonhealing wound, this time from a plastic surgery case, had grown the puzzling Aspergillus. A full investigation into the outbreak was underway. She would have to wait two weeks to find out if the problem was solved or not.

Thoughts of the previous workday gave way to those about how to complete the task of getting Edith's journal back into its hiding place as quickly as possible. Although she had escaped detection once, Beth wasn't convinced she would have the same luck on a Saturday as she'd had on a weekday, so she needed to do it in the daytime to avoid using a flashlight. Any lamps set on automatic timers were not in Edith's office.

The items she had taken from Edith's home were burning a proverbial hole in Beth's desk drawer, especially after talking with Constable Argento yesterday. She had bought a little time so she could gather her thoughts by asking him to call back in ten minutes. He had been kind, empathizing with how significant a loss Edith's absence was to her family and neighbours. When Beth had touched on the same issues she'd aired with the sergeant, he'd responded calmly, saying he judged that Beth's concerns were brought about by her own grief and attempt to make sense of a senseless loss of life. In the beginning, she had thought he might be more receptive about the signs she felt pointed to foul play given he knew Edith's personality so well. Beth had briefly considered sharing the fact that Edith said she had something important and secret to discuss with her. Beth cast that thought aside. Maybe later. The constable had obviously been sincere in insisting she could call the Block Watch office any time to contact him if there was anything else. She'd decided she just might do that once she figured out how to handle the subject of the locket. He'd rang off saying he'd be at the funeral if his workload allowed.

Around ten, Nina Mahoney also nursed a second cup of coffee and had a fashion magazine open in front of her on the kitchen counter. Unlike Beth, she wasn't reading. It was merely a prop while she waited for her son to emerge from 'his' bathroom and come upstairs. She had heard him get up twenty minutes earlier. She intended to have a serious talk with him about how he was wasting his time and talents. She had some good suggestions to make. Mike's blindness to the way Norman—she refused to call him Norm, he was no friend of hers—had put ideas into his head was holding Mike back. It was creating a wedge between her and her son. She had thought that Michael would be here for the talk too, but when she'd raised the subject last evening after Mike left for the pub—another bad habit picked up from Norman—Michael had claimed he had to go into the office early to finish some more paperwork to do with the merger. She hadn't been able to help herself from raising her voice to say that he seemed to be spending more time at the office than ever, and what about his family? *Don't we come first?*

She'd been happy when Mike was forced to return home having used up his savings—it was just like old times. The three of them together. She remembered Michael bringing her and Mikey home from the hospital. It was the beginning of their perfect little family; all she'd ever wanted. There was no way her son should be driving trucks for a living.

Nina was troubled by his developing insolence. She hated that he was often coming home drunk. She needed to save her beautiful boy. It wasn't his fault he'd been let go from his previous job with H&R Block tax services. It was clear his last boss had had it in for him from day one. *Likely felt threatened by Mikey's brilliance,* she thought. She heard the bathroom door creak open. *Why hasn't Michael fixed that yet?* She went to the top of the steps and called softly.

"Morning sweetie, what would you like for breakfast?"

❧

Sunday, November 14

With the swishing sound of the dishwasher at work in the background, Beth looked out her living room window at the soggy day. Monty jumped to the narrow window ledge; his attention fixed on raindrops slipping down the glass. He pawed at the glass, amusing in his industrious effort to catch them.

"Silly boy," she said with a smile, ruffling his head.

The almost-bare trees lining the block looked forlorn. *Looks like it's stopping.* The temperature was a balmy 12 degrees Celsius thanks to a system dubbed a Pineapple Express sweeping up from Hawaii. Further up the street, she saw a Welsh terrier straining at the leash held by its master. This was the dog walker Bill Yeung had told her about. Dashing to the closet, she yanked her purple rain jacket from the hanger, which clattered onto the hardwood floor and sent Monty skittering away. Her umbrella was on the back porch, but her hood would do, and her keys were handy in her purse, which hung from the bedroom doorknob. In less than two minutes, Beth was out the front door. She could see the dog walker had been delayed, chatting with a woman she barely knew but was familiar with from brief contact during a jury selection several years before. Trying to recall the woman's name now would be no use. Beth slowed and stopped a respectful distance from the three. The terrier started pulling in her direction, distracting them from their conversation.

"Hi, I'm Beth." Two heads nodded. "I just wanted to check if either of you knew Edith Todd, a neighbour across my back lane. Perhaps you heard about the accident recently at the crosswalk near the corner store?"

The woman smiled. "I'm Trisha, we crossed paths once at the courthouse, remember?"

Beth nodded. "Joe here told me about the accident," Trisha said. "He and Digger were out for a walk and saw—"

"No, no. I didn't really see anything," Joe interrupted whatever was coming next. "There was a car speeding away. Told the police—total blur. That's all. How's your neighbour?"

"Edith passed away from a head injury." Beth gulped. "Her funeral is tomorrow. I thought I'd let you know in case you want to go. She'd lived in the neighbourhood a very long time and a lot of folks knew her through her Block Watch activity."

Trisha nodded. "I knew her casually over the eight years I've been here. Used to see her over at Safeway demonstrating new products, so we'd have a chat. I'd go if I wasn't working. What about you, Joe?"

"No, sorry, I never met her that I know of. I moved to my place near Slocan and Twentieth about a year ago."

"It's been nice to meet you—I'd better let you get on with Digger's walk. See you both around then," Beth said as she turned to walk back to her house. She filed away the thought that she needed a chat with Joe when he was on his own. She would have to watch out for him. She wanted to know exactly what he'd told the police.

After lunch, Beth decided it was as good a time as any to try to get Edith's journal and the two letters back in place. She tucked them in a Ziploc bag and used the large inner pocket of her rain jacket to conceal them. *This time,* she thought, *it will be fast.* She'd remembered another reason to trot out if she met someone. She could say truthfully that she was returning the Tupperware container of Edith's that had been left behind the night of the potluck. Still, she felt nervous with the bulked-up inner pocket reminding her of her dishonesty. She put her hood up to shield her face giving her a false sense of anonymity. Her charmed entry and return of the items ended when she re-latched the Todd's gate on her way back. She saw Nina exit in a hurry from her own yard. Beth willed her to not look up, but she did. *Rats.* Nina offered a perfunctory wave and began to run down the lane. Beth smiled, thinking that for all Nina's grumbling that Edith was too interested in her neighbours, Nina could be just as nosy. *I'd best be ready for a question sometime.*

EIGHT

Monday, November 15

Edith's 11 a.m. funeral found Beth unsettled and disappointed—an unhappy start to another week. The solemn Catholic ritual seemed dry and impersonal compared to other denominational services she'd attended. Still, the hot drinks—she found the aroma of the coffee soothing—and sweets served afterward in the church hall allowed for some pleasant personal reminiscences with neighbours and Edith's family and church friends.

Ken Todd, looking thin and pale and clad in a black suit, moved like a rusty robot. He kept repeating that he was at Susan's in Richmond. He spoke of having an open house when he returned home eventually. Ken was seated while Susan and her brother Glen stood behind. They wore blank expressions, broken now and then by the odd half-hearted smile when some happier recollection outweighed the pain of the occasion. Two young grandsons, looking solemn beyond their years, stood gravely on either side of their grandfather, completing the tableau.

The church had been full. In addition to Edith's family, friends, and congregation, there had been good representation from the homes on either side of the back lane. Alan Whitman, Ken's old friend, understandably empathetic, hovered near the family. Dennis offered bear hugs to a few of the ladies he knew would accept them in the spirit offered. Mike Mahoney, who had abandoned his parents, stood in a corner sipping a glass of apple juice, barely raising his eyes.

Sofia, her soft dark hair newly dyed and set, sniffled into a tissue nonstop, her eyes red-rimmed. She stood with Beth for a time.

"It's a nice turnout. Even some young people are here. Well, not that young—it's a shame Nina still treats Mike like a teenager. I think he's almost thirty. Edith would know," Sofia said quietly.

At one point, Beth heard someone murmur behind her. "Look what the cat dragged in."

Beth scanned the room to see Pearl Simmons ushering in her sister Maggie, who was clad in oversized black rubber boots and a double-breasted purple coat. Beth cast a surreptitious glance around and saw Nina whispering to her husband Michael, who had the grace to look embarrassed as his eyes met Beth's, knowing she had heard Nina's remark. It seemed Bill Yeung had also heard the aside; he nodded to Beth, and they went to greet the sisters.

"Good to see you both—Pearl, Maggie."

"Maggie didn't think she could manage the service, but thought this would suit her," said Pearl. "We've known Edith and Ken for forever it seems. Maggie and I will miss her very much."

Maggie nodded. "Very, very sad," she said in a small, dry voice, addressing the floor.

Pearl linked her arm in her sister's and steered her toward a chair. "Let's get you something to drink before we speak to Ken."

❦

Nina, wearing a pantsuit topped with a grey patterned wool shawl, watched the room from behind a raised teacup. It was hard to pretend she was deeply moved by Edith's departure to the so-called better world. For as long as she could recall, Nina had felt on edge not knowing when Edith might thrust Emma's name into the conversation. *Why do that? Emma lived on our block only a short time.* Nina also welcomed the relief that she would not have to deal with Edith's recent pointed remarks about Mike anymore. But poor Ken—for him, she was sad. In her view, widowers often seemed to manage poorly on their own.

❦

Eventually, Beth saw Ken and his family alone and went to fill what looked to be an uncomfortable void.

"This must seem so unreal to you. It's dreadful we've lost Edith this way. I have some idea of what you're going through," said Beth, clasping Susan's hand and turning to Ken next. After the number of years she'd lived in the neighbourhood, Beth knew her own background of having lost a young son, as well as her mother, had been shared around. Ken began to rise unsteadily from the chair where he sat.

"No need to get up," Beth said as she leaned to take his hand. She searched for what else to say as the hum of low voices swirled around a pocket of silence.

"I've something to ask of you, Beth," Susan said into the lull. She brought a small, clear plastic bag from her purse. "I'm wondering if you would return this to the ICU. Dad and I are sure it's not Mom's. We've never seen it before. We'd really appreciate it if you could do this for us; I just can't go back there again. I can call the unit manager to tell her about the mistake. I'll give her your name if you agree."

Dennis's approach interrupted Beth's reply. He gestured at Susan's hand. "Hey, I see you've got Edith's locket. I found that," he said.

"What do you mean?" said Susan. "This can't be Mom's. The middle initial is wrong."

"Oh," Dennis said. "I found it when I was pulling out the Hypericum roots. I had a chance to ask Edith if it was taken in the break-in and she said no because she was wearing it. Seemed like it was hers. She was weary and upset about the burglary, of course. She did say she hadn't seen it in ages. She didn't say anything else. Are there photos inside?"

"It's got two small black and white pictures," said Susan, gently prying it open to show Beth and Dennis. "It's in amazing condition. Nice looking couple. I have no idea who they are." Ken shook his head in silent agreement.

"Maybe they're old family relatives," Dennis said.

Throughout this exchange, Beth remained largely quiet, offering the odd 'oh' or 'interesting' to the remarks. She realized this was the locket spoken of in Edith's journal and it was an uncomfortable reminder of the intrusions she'd made.

Beth cleared her throat. "Maybe one of the neighbours lost it when in the yard? What about Evie?"

Susan replaced the locket inside the bag. "I'll check it out with Aunt Alma to see if she knows anything," she said, closing her purse and the subject with a snap.

In the evening Beth's thoughts revolved in an endless loop through a maze of questions. What was Edith trying to tell them when she repeated her garbled words so often? Who broke into the Todd's home? Was it just a coincidence? What was Norm up to and was it Mike whom Edith was trying to protect? Who sent the mean letters? Was Frank Nolan so desperate to get his uncle's money he may have run Edith down? The threatening notes could be linked to anyone. Was there any chance of identifying the sender of one of the envelopes? The old locket seemed to be the most alarming possibility for someone wanting Edith out of the way. It clearly belonged to the missing woman who used to live somewhere close by. Edith had known something was very wrong with the locket being found where it was. Beth suppressed the petty annoyance she had toward Dennis for blocking her chance to get it. Edith wanted it kept safe. Beth needed to find out a lot more. She hoped getting some sleep would bring some order to her thoughts.

Tuesday, November 16

It was an effort to get out of bed on the dreary morning following Edith's funeral. As Beth became more conscious, her mind roamed over the events and thoughts of the previous day, drawing her into the increasingly familiar tangled web of speculation.

Monty's insistent demands for his breakfast got her moving. In the living room, she pulled over an old 1970s TV table and sat to eat her breakfast while she watched some morning news. A report about a truck hitting a North Vancouver man on Lonsdale where the driver stayed at the scene brought her back to her ruminations. Beth decided what she needed was some down time. She would take herself to the Vancouver Art Gallery this morning, even though she and Cathy had already planned a visit there for later in the week on one of Cathy's days off.

Beth boarded a rapid transit train at the Nanaimo station thinking, not for the first time, what a convenient bee-line it was for her to get downtown. She had pleasant memories of her parents coming west for Expo '86. Using the Expo Line to access the exhibition site added to their awe of the whole experience.

Beth, unseeing, gazed out the windows as she recalled that her previous visit to the gallery had been somewhat chaotic because of a class of young teenagers on an educational outing. It was possible this visit wouldn't be the relaxing distraction she was aiming for. The teens had been chaperoned of course—by their teacher and one other adult—though that had not ensured complete peace. Having been a member of the art gallery for over five years, Beth had been amazed she hadn't run into this before, and she found it tested her patience. But she did notice the security staff were attentive and, in particular, had observed one man who showed skill and patience dealing with some rather unruly boys. *Aha—assess need for outside consultation.* She could almost see a lightbulb shining above her head. She perked up in anticipation she might see the same person or someone else in security who looked approachable. *What kind of training do they have?* she wondered.

Later, Beth congratulated herself on a successful encounter with the man she'd recalled from the time she saw him kindly but firmly disciplining several students. He'd looked relaxed despite his official alert posture, and there had been no students to watch today. She had been on the fourth floor admiring a selected display of Emily Carr's forest paintings, approaching *The Little Pine* (1931), one of her personal favourites, when she'd made eye contact with the man she was seeking. She judged was in his mid-fifties like her. With no one else in the room, Beth had felt comfortable striking up a conversation.

"This is one of my favourites," she'd said quietly.

"I have many favourites in this room," he'd said and nodded. The room had lapsed into silence again.

Beth had furiously thought of what to say next. She had seen the name tag which read 'C. Ross,' under which was 'Security Manager.'

"If you don't mind me asking, how is it, with the position you hold as a manager, that you would be patrolling a room?"

C. Ross had explained he considered it wise to regularly acquaint himself with the day-to-day activity in the art gallery.

After a moment, he'd added, "And I happen to like being around art."

"I have a nephew who wants to get into security work," Beth had fibbed, thinking it might be too personal to ask this man his background directly. "What kind of qualifications are needed?"

To her satisfaction, in the course of their short exchange, she'd learned that C. Ross was a retired police officer like one or two others on staff. Beth had noted his name and title in her pocket notebook once she'd left the room.

🌿

While she enjoyed a sandwich at the gallery café, Beth mulled over who else she wanted to talk with. Harry Anders. He would be easier to follow up on. Edith had spent regular time with Harry since his eyesight had succumbed to macular degeneration, which forced him into a care home. Beth understood that at one time, he and his late wife had been neighbours of Edith's and had attended St. Jude's. Sofia knew him as well and could provide an introduction. How should she play it? Beth wasn't ready to share her suspicions with any of the neighbours at this point. She had little doubt that Sofia or Jenny would be open to her ideas. However, if Edith had been hit on purpose and the driver lived in the neighbourhood, then she, as well as they, might be at risk. Perhaps she was being overly cautious, but keeping it all to herself was the best option for now.

What she really needed was someone, preferably an outsider like Mr. Ross, who could bring expertise and objectiveness to the concerns she had about Edith's accident. She'd do a little digging around this week to see what more she could learn. In particular, she needed to discover who Emma was and when she had disappeared. Edith had noted the locket meant Emma had not run away after all. It made Beth wonder if Emma was a teenager.

NINE

Wednesday, November 17

It was a quiet morning at the Vancouver Art Gallery. At the moment, the extreme windy, wet weather was keeping all but the diehards from venturing forth—at least so far—but Cameron Ross had hope it would pick up. Walking past the gallery's main doors, he glanced out to Robson Street where some of the remaining few autumn leaves, which had stubbornly clung on till now, swooped and soared like golden birds. Many trees would be reduced to stark silhouettes after this storm passed on. He checked in with the security office guard who was monitoring the wall of screens, which showed every inch of the gallery's exhibit rooms.

"I'm up on the second floor this morning, Terry. See you later. I can cover your coffee break." Terry nodded with a half-smile and kept his eyes on the screens.

Cameron headed right, up one half of the curved marble staircases, which hugged a circular rotunda. The art gallery was housed on four floors of an impressive heritage building built in 1907 that once served as a provincial courthouse. A contemporary installation of wood and shiny metal titled *Albatross Two* was on display there. As he moved, his athletic form, mirrored in the wavy structure, changed to a rippling figure with dark hair wearing black and white. To Cameron's mind, it wasn't exactly art, although he admired the imagination and enthusiasm of its creator. He'd worked at the gallery for over three years and rarely failed to be amazed at the range of works that were considered worthy of display. He was always impressed by the ingenuity of the curator and his staff who oversaw the choice and layout of the exhibits.

From the start of Cameron's employment at the gallery, the proximity to paintings, photographs, and other forms of art had offered a welcome escape from a police career that had left him drained. He'd been only too glad to leave the Vancouver Police Department and the serious crimes division behind. Here, he had found some peace and a new beginning, no matter the drop in salary. He looked forward to going to work from the moment he began the job. Over time, he became familiar with much of the permanent collection, counting himself fortunate to be in the presence of such inspiration daily. In particular, he had developed a special fondness for Emily Carr and made time to read about her life and art in the gallery library in his off-hours. He was as proud of her as if she was his very own eccentric ancestor.

A current temporary exhibit, *The Faithful Voice,* was drawing a lot of attention. The recent members opening night had been a crush of people eager to catch a glimpse of notorious artist Nikki Hartfield and her fourth celebrity husband. A handful of protesters had snuck in to proclaim that her art was heresy due to its heavy use of religious icons. The result of the disruption was an increase in surveillance with Cameron sharing some extra shifts until such time as the exhibit was dismantled.

He stood in a corner, quiet and alert as usual, despite the fact that in the room he was monitoring there was a lone elderly gentleman browsing. Cameron thought back on the previous day, which had offered up a stilted conversation with a woman who had nice blue eyes and said she was a member. He couldn't remember her name exactly. *Was it Bev?* She had engaged him in some small talk about art gallery security, complimenting staff in general on their professionalism and posing some questions. "I wondered what you watch out for apart from folks leaning on display cases? I suppose there are surveillance cameras everywhere." Then she'd asked about what type of training he and other staff had and something about a nephew being interested. Not the truth, he had concluded. She seemed a pleasant enough person; he didn't suppose she was up to no good. But the thought had crossed his policeman's mind.

❧

Thursday, November 18

In contrast to the day before, Beth threw back her covers eager to get up despite the crashing sound of rain on the roof. Monty went flying off the bottom of the bed. She'd been thinking about C. Ross. She made a face recalling how awkward she'd been in speaking with him, but she was buoyed up with the new-found knowledge that he was a retired policeman. He could be the perfect someone to help her. She wondered how soon would be appropriate to speak with him again. Since he seemed to be head of security, he should be easy to contact. She had no illusions about him reacting the same way as Sergeant James and Constable Argento. He'd need convincing that her suspicions were legitimate. She was an unknown entity to him. Somehow, she'd have to prove herself.

After she and Monty had had their respective breakfasts, Beth brushed her teeth and went straight to get her notebook. Sitting at her desk still wrapped in her warm fleece robe, she realized there were several theories to consider as she jotted down a few ideas, all of which she felt had substance. Finding the truth about Edith's death would be her priority until she could hand over some solid evidence to police. If she was right, in time justice would be served. *Uh-oh, that sounds like Edith.*

She reviewed her notes on what she'd found in Edith's office. She had begun to think of her Wednesday 'outing' as an investigative field trip. The letters would be difficult to trace if not impossible. The scrawl on one was messy, perhaps on purpose, and the other had words cut from newsprint. One was mailed, the other hand delivered. Could they be the work of someone living on the lane? Edith's intent to ask about Norm's handwriting showed she was leaning that way. While Emma's locket was the most intriguing, Beth came back to the one situation she could get started on almost immediately: Harry Anders.

"Sofia, how're you doing?" Beth said. She cradled the receiver against her ear as she opened her date book to be sure she had not overlooked a commitment.

Sofia offered a lengthy sigh. "Okay I guess."

"I wanted to talk to you about Harry Anders. It occurred to me he could be at a loss without Edith to help him with his Christmas cards like she always did. I'd like to offer to do it."

"That's really kind of you, Beth. I know he'd appreciate that; he doesn't have many close family members—well, except an elderly sister-in-law here and a niece who's in California and that nephew who's a leech from what Edith says… said. I'd offer myself but you know how horribly busy I am this time of year with what I do for family get-togethers, the church bazaar, and the bake sale."

"Do you have time to call him this morning to see if we can visit this afternoon? If not, maybe tomorrow?"

"Sure," said Sofia in a brighter tone, "I'm fine with that. I'll ring the church office and get his number."

Pushing her chair back from the desk, Beth heard a low rumble. She glanced out to the lane across the sad-looking remnants of her vegetable plot to see Dennis's red, rust-spotted pickup trundle past. She pressed her face up to the window to see if she could tell where he was headed and saw the top of the cab come to a halt somewhere near the Mahoney's, or perhaps it was Alan Whitman's. Didn't matter, it looked like he was here for a job and that would give her an opportunity to talk with him. She was especially interested in the locket; she wanted to know exactly how he found it.

Fifteen minutes later, after throwing on jeans, a tee, and her jacket, Beth was out in the lane, umbrella hoisted above her head, headed in the truck's direction. And there was Dennis—bar any face protection—looking like a cross between a moon walker and a Hazmat team member in his bulky rainproof gear. He was already up a ladder scooping out sodden, decaying leaves from the Mahoney's roof eaves. Michael would be at work, and Nina too, at her part-time receptionist job at a physiotherapy clinic. After a few minutes, Dennis backed down the ladder.

Beth spoke his name softly so as not to startle him.

"Hi," he said, "you waiting for me?"

"Yes. I saw you go by and wondered if you'd like to drop in for coffee or tea when you're done? It's time I scheduled you to clean my eaves too."

"Sure thing, that'd be great. I need to warm up. This is a rotten job in the rain, but I have to get it done today. I'd love some coffee. I'll be with you in a half hour or so."

Beth busied herself with measuring out the coffee and filling the cistern while she thought about how she would quiz Dennis without it seeming that way. She flipped the switch as soon as she heard the squeak and clang of her back gate closing.

"Come right in—no, no, take your boots off in the porch," she directed when she saw Dennis about to leave them in a sheltered corner of the deck. "They'll just get cold out there. You can lay your wet things on the dryer."

Monty lolled by the dining room heat vent. He answered Dennis's query as to his health with a short meow, unwilling to leave the blast of hot air.

"We can sit at the table or go into the living room. Your choice."

"Table's fine, can't see your great view of the North Shore today. Maybe it's snowing up there and ski season will start soon."

"That reminds me of Edith," Beth said. "She loved to see the first snows up on the mountains. She and Ken have the same view from the back of their place. I know everyone keeps saying this, but I can't believe she's gone. Everything is topsy-turvy. What about the garden work you were doing for Edith, have you finished?"

"Enough for now, I don't need to bother Ken about it. I wouldn't have been doing much more till late February or early March anyway."

"Must have been heavy work getting all that Hypericum out," Beth said, slipping in the key question next. "That's where you found a locket you said?"

"Yeah, it was just a fluke really. If the sun hadn't come out, I would have missed it. It was in the last bunch of roots I got out. Some went way under the garage so I just pulled out what I could and pushed a bunch of earth firmly back in place. Don't worry, I don't think the garage is going to shift," Dennis joked.

"So, I'm curious, what did Edith say?"

"I was curious too, but I only thought to ask just after the break-in. By then, she was bushed, she only said thanks and it'd been missing a long time. Didn't remember to ask her again when she called about my cheque, and that was the last time

I talked with her," Dennis said, bringing his coffee mug to his mouth to cover his distress and still his quavering voice.

"It's all right, Dennis," Beth said, giving him a pat on the arm. "You've spent more time with Edith in the last several months than would have been usual, so you'll be feeling her loss as much as the rest of us."

Frustrated to be no further ahead in her locket inquiry, Beth waved Dennis goodbye after arranging for his return to do her eaves. She tidied the coffee mugs away and returned to her den. Her mind revisited the many question marks. Who was this Emma who had run away? How did the locket end up in the Hypericum bed? Could Harry's nephew be a threat to him and thus had he been threat to Edith? And what about those letters? She so wished she'd pressed Edith about the 'serious matter' when she'd called that evening to invite her for dinner.

Hopefully, it wouldn't be too hard to get some information from other neighbours without revealing her intentions. Like going through Edith's office, it was underhanded. *But it's what I have to do*. Ken and perhaps Susan would the best sources of information. And there were others who'd been here a long time, like Alan Whitman, who should know about this Emma. By all accounts, he and Evie had moved into their place within months of Edith and Ken.

A talk with Alan could help on two fronts, she thought. Edith had voiced strong concerns about Norm being a bad influence on Mike Jr. She had even mentioned that in her journal. It was understandable that having known Mike since he was a child, she'd felt a special interest in his well-being. Beth would try to find out what Alan knew without, she hoped, letting on that she was deliberately prying. This was a whole new way of communicating for her—searching out information in a dishonest way. At work, the investigative process was entirely above board.

This was far different—the uncovering of facts that might have a bearing on Edith's death would be messy. *Okay, enough of this, where will I start?*

The question was answered almost immediately when Sofia called to say they could visit Harry in the afternoon and that she'd meet Beth at her back gate at one thirty.

❧

"Harry's a nice old fellow," said Sofia as they began walking down the lane. "He and his wife were parishioners at St. Jude's for as long as I can remember. Cora died at least ten years ago of a stroke around the time his eyesight started to go. It was sad when he had to move to Lakeview Manor. He can tell light from dark is all, I think. Edith would have told you about him."

"Yes. She'd been worried about him since his niece moved away. The nephew was not Edith's favourite person and I know the feeling was mutual."

At the front door of his ground floor unit, Harry Anders, smiling below a ruffled halo of white hair, greeted Sofia with familiarity and reached out his hand in the direction of her voice.

"You've brought the Beth I've heard Edith often speak of. Come right in."

"I'm pleased to meet you, Harry," Beth said. "Edith spoke of you as well. I know she enjoyed time spent with you."

He led them past several doorways to a surprisingly spacious living/dining area and pointed out a fiery red Burning Bush shrub still thriving outside his window. Harry settled himself in his Lazy Boy armchair while Beth and Sofia sat on the couch.

"I'd like to hear about Edith's service. I'm sorry I didn't make it. My nephew meant to drive me and accompany me, but he got the days mixed up." He paused. "Well, at least, that's his story. Frank isn't… wasn't all that keen on Edith. I suspect he didn't really want to go."

"I'm so sorry, you should have called me," Sofia said.

"By the time I knew Frank wasn't coming I thought you'd be gone since you usually help set out the prayer books. Oh well, I said a little prayer of my own. But please tell me about it. How are Ken and his family?"

They spoke about Edith's tragic accident and her family's loss. Sofia offered to take Harry to visit Ken sometime. Then talk turned to Harry and his life at the home. As expected, he warmly welcomed the idea of Beth helping him with his Christmas card correspondence.

To Beth's secret satisfaction, Harry invited her to come soon. "I always get an early start even though they're mostly local. It worked well for Edith and me." He brought out a white handkerchief from his pants pocket and dabbed at his eyes. Sofia patted his shoulder. Beth promised she would call to set up a time.

TEN

Friday, November 19

Beth's local library was a welcoming space. She'd escaped the noise of the demolition of a beige stucco home—a similar 1950s vintage to hers—opposite her tree-lined avenue. It was good to see that at least some of the shrubs on the property were being retained and the roadside maple, which still boasted some scattered neon red leaves, was protected. Renfrew Branch Library offered a quiet refuge from the loud drone of the bulldozer. It was a pleasant, easy walk away, often a favourite inclusion at the end of leisure walks along the Skytrain pedestrian pathway and explorations of residential streets and lanes.

Beth browsed through the mystery section and picked three books to check out, then returned to a reading area to open the most recent P.D. James novel. Looking toward the front entrance, Beth saw Nina Mahoney pull the door open. Immediately, two conflicting thoughts collided. One was that she would like to avoid her in order to continue a relaxing read and thus avoid fielding Nina's persistent suggestion that she join Nina's book club. The other was that she needed to speak with Nina and see what she could learn—without appearing to do so, of course. This was a perfect opening she mustn't pass up. They hadn't crossed paths since Edith's funeral.

Twenty minutes later, Beth was seated across from Nina at a bakery café nearby on Rupert Street. She allowed Nina to proffer the expected invitation to the book club and explained for the third time that she might join eventually but not right now.

"I don't understand, Beth, you have loads of time now—you're retired. I'm working three days a week and I have my family. My days are very busy, but I make time for this. I really enjoy the group discussions. I appreciate the books I read so much more. You will too," Nina said, trying to press home her point of view.

"You're right, but I'm not sure I'm a good fit with the group. How did you connect with them?" said Beth in hopes of figuring out how to steer the conversation. "I've noticed some of the ladies you've mentioned have their photos appear in the society pages."

"An old school friend invited me. Amy used to live in that two-storey white house on the corner of Penticton. She married into the Lassiter family from Ontario. Anyway, her husband is running his family's construction business here and they have a mansion on Angus Drive with—"

"That's right, I remember now," said Beth, forestalling any further descriptions of grandeur. "Edith mentioned once that you lived in the house on the other side of Alan's when you were growing up. You've been around a long time. I thought you might be bothered seeing your former home on a daily basis, with renters coming and going. There's been a fair turnover in the time I've been here."

"No, no, that's my past," said Nina with a tone of finality. "The moment Michael proposed to me, I knew his home was where I belonged."

"And your folks, where are they? I forget."

"Over on the North Shore where it's quieter. They're kind of out of the way. We don't get to see each other much," Nina said, breaking eye contact.

Beth felt herself floundering. Since she settled in her home, her relationship with Nina had been one of friendly acquaintance. It was not one that had ever included confidences. However, with the recent death of Edith, they had a loss in common and Beth hoped it would open the way to some less superficial conversation.

"Edith's accident makes me think about going somewhere quieter too," Beth lied. "Traffic seems crazier and crime in the city keeps rising. I guess the party was the last time you got to talk with Edith, was it?" *Damn*, she thought, *I've asked a question that can be answered with a yes.*

Beth didn't wait for a reply. "I've been thinking about what we can do to encourage Block Watch participation now that we've lost our best champion. Do you have any ideas? Edith was gung-ho on preventing any more area break-ins. You'll have read the recent newsletter. I was thinking Mike Junior might be another pair of eyes if he'd be interested in training for what to watch for. I understand he's only working part time at the moment. What's he doing exactly?"

Nina went on the defensive at once, ignoring the question. "Mike has no extra time at all. The part-time work is just a stopgap. He'll likely join Michael's place of business soon," she declared.

When the two women parted ways, the boost in motivation Beth had had from her achievements the day before now waned in the face of the minimal success she'd had with Nina. She corrected herself—it had not been a success at all. If anything, Nina had seemed more distant. Using the simple word 'only' about Mike's work had been a mistake.

A talk with Alan Whitman would go better. He was a kindly man who'd always provided advice and encouragement in the years Beth was starting her vegetable garden, though she'd been more acquainted with Evie, his late wife, through Block Watch and the fact she'd been Edith's best friend. With Edith gone and Ken out in Richmond, she was sure Alan would welcome a visit. She was itching to find out more about what Norm and Mike were doing if she could.

Beth's underhanded activities reminded her that Edith had felt Norm was sneaky. She had seen him nosing around two local properties and had heard the same from more than one neighbour—sources unrevealed. As well, in his short time on the block, Norm had been marked as a braggart because of his fondness for showing off any connection, however tenuous, to local celebrities, be they sports figures or TV personalities.

Rather than calling Alan, Beth decided she would go knock on the back door because if Alan was out and Norm answered, maybe she could advance her acquaintance with him past "Hi, nice day." She'd heard he was off work for a couple days because he'd fallen off a bar stool and sprained his ankle. He wouldn't be bragging about that, but maybe he would open up to a little sympathy. She marveled, not for the first time, at how one thought created another. Barstools led her to barmen and the reputation they had for listening to a person's troubles. Would Norm have blabbed anything at the pub he and Mike frequented according to Edith? But there was no way she was going to quiz a barman. *Ridiculous.* She shook her head. Her wild thinking underlined her need for help to sort out how to be most effective.

There were other people who sometimes became sounding boards. An image of herself sitting in the hairdresser's chair sharing some ups and downs of life niggled its way into her head. Knowing Andre for at least fourteen years, she had become more his friend than client and he would understand her cancelling. She knew Edith felt the same about Miriam. Beth didn't know her last name, but she knew where she worked. How many

Miriams could there be at Raymond's Hair Salon at Oakridge?

At half past three, she was sitting in a chair looking at two reflections. Miriam ran a comb through Beth's wet hair. Since her knock on Alan's door after lunch had not been answered, she supposed Miriam would be her last investigative task of the day unless Alan left a reply to her phone message. For now, her plan was to use Edith's Block Watch involvement to justify her queries. On a practical note, she realized she had better not distract Miriam too much from what she was doing or Beth might end up with more hair off than she wanted.

"I'm sure you knew Edith was captain of our neighbourhood Block Watch team. And that she was retiring from that the end of this month," said Beth.

"Yes, she often had interesting tales to tell," Miriam said. "I admired her energy and curiosity. I'm really sad to think she won't be sitting in this chair again." A single tear traced its way along the side of her nose.

Beth squirmed at the realization that she was sitting where Edith had sat countless times. She shook off the gloom that threatened to derail her intention of discovering if Miriam knew anything that could help. She quietly exhaled a deep breath.

"I'm assuming you and Edith likely talked about all sort of things over the years. Did Edith speak at all about the threatening letters she'd received recently? We're just trying to follow up on it."

"Sure," Miriam said, a small catch noticeable in her voice, "we talked about it. She's… she'd been my client for ages. I was amazed how she kept so much information in that head of hers. I recall she talked of a letter. It just happened the day before her last appointment. At first, she seemed to think it might have something to do with that blind man she helped out. Something about his hanger-on nephew who didn't like her and who she'd had words with. She also mentioned your area robberies and said she was keeping an eye on a couple of fellows. I told her that could be dangerous, and she needed to let the police do their work. Edith said they had too much to do, and she only wanted to help . . ." Miriam's voice quavered, and further words became unintelligible.

"Sorry, I didn't catch that."

"Last time, I told her… I said… you won't be any use if you help yourself into an early grave. It was just a little joke. Edith said 'what, little old me?' and we laughed."

That evening, Beth's phone remained silent apart from one call. There'd been no reply from Alan, but her mood lightened when her hoped-for visit to Ken was welcomed by his daughter.

Saturday, November 20

Beth sat in Susan's modest two-bedroom Richmond apartment sipping green tea, facing Ken across a pleasantly furnished living room.

"I'll give you some alone time," Susan said from the hallway. "Be back in about forty-five minutes, Dad, and then you, Beth, and I can take a little walk over to the park."

Beth didn't miss the frown on Ken's face in reaction to that statement.

"She's been badgering me," he complained after Susan was gone. "She's worse than the nurses."

"We all want you to keep getting better, Ken. The more physically fit you are, the easier it will be to cope with this very sad time. Edith would have been after you too."

Beth continued offering Ken various well wishes from a few of the more casually acquainted neighbours she had come across in the past few days. All the while, in the background, she was considering how to slip in the subject of the locket, hoping she could find a way to have Ken and Susan offer the locket to her again.

It didn't take long for the conversation to come to Dennis's work on the backyard and she had her opening.

"I gather there's a bit of a puzzle about the locket that Dennis pulled up by the garage," Beth said.

She was immediately frustrated when Ken began reminiscing about the building of their garage in 1960.

"It was perfect weather that summer. One of the best for our vegetable garden. I remember it well because I'd come into some money when a maiden aunt of mine left me a bequest. We jumped at the opportunity to have a garage. I had two chaps from Dicks Lumber come and do most of the work. Gino and Michael helped me get the cement poured."

"You put in the Hypericum then I guess," said Beth in an effort to bring Ken back to thinking about Dennis's current yard work.

"Yes. Edith liked how it looked in Jenny's yard against the side of the house. Someone else lived there back then, of course. The neighbourhood has seen a number of changes over the years. Son of a gun. How could I forget? That September everyone was worried about Emma. Very sad. Very upsetting."

"Who was Emma?" Beth said in breathless anticipation.

"Michael's first wife. Before your time. She walked off—never was found. The police took a hard look at Michael, but he'd been at work all day and there were two staff who'd alibied him. Emma'd had some problems, her pregnancy wasn't going well. She came over quite a bit to talk with Edith. Nice young woman. Edith became very fond of her. Edith said since Emma lost her mom and dad, she likely thought of her as a parent."

Just like me, in a way, thought Beth, then realized she'd missed the next part of Ken's story. "What was that again, Ken?"

"Oh, just that Emma was around eleven when they were killed in a car crash on the Patulla Bridge. She went to live with grandparents in Kelowna. What came out through the investigation of her disappearance was that she'd suffered with depression and had run away several times from her grandparents in her teenage years. Michael was devastated. I think he spent a year trying to find her with the help of a private firm. There was a long police inquiry because they still suspected Michael was involved but, in the end, the thought was she went away somewhere and killed herself. She became one of the city's many cold cases, I suppose."

A clicking sound from the front door lock signaled Susan's return. Realizing her chance was slipping away, Beth rushed to speak over Ken's voice.

"Goodness, there was an E on that locket Dennis found, wasn't there?"

"What's this?" Susan said from the doorway.

"Oh, Ken was just telling me about Emma, Michael's first wife. I suddenly thought about the locket's initials. I wonder if it could be hers?" said Beth, her throat feeling constricted.

"I suppose so," said Ken, "and there's Evie, Alan's wife, could be hers too. And the last initial could be her maiden name."

"I haven't had a chance to ask Aunt Alma yet," said Susan. "It may have belonged to a great grandmother or something. I guess it could be Mom's since after all, she was wearing it."

No, it's not your mom's. Is there any way to salvage this? Beth wondered. Unwittingly, Ken did just that.

"Why don't you try Alma right now while Beth's here," said Ken. "I never saw your mom wear it before and she never spoke of it. We could have Beth show it to both Alan and Michael if it isn't family jewellery."

When Susan returned from making a successful call to her aunt, she handed over the locket in a small black felt bag. "Maybe start with Alan since Evie was Mom's closest friend."

"Oh," Ken turned to Beth, "you'd better be careful about contacting Michael—Edith says… said… Nina never likes Emma's name being spoken, gets upset. Emma was like a sister to her." The reminder of Edith no longer being there closed in on Ken. His face crumbled; his eyes filled with tears, looking at Susan. "I can't believe your mom's gone. I don't know if I can ever face going home."

Susan moved over to her father and took his hand. "Things will work out, Dad. One day at a time."

❦

Finally, with Monty as warm as a heating pad on her lap and a soothing cup of chamomile tea nearby, Beth relaxed in the comfortable recliner she usually used while watching TV. She examined the gold locket with a magnifying glass and was amazed the photos inside were in good condition since it had been buried for well over thirty-five years. How did it end up in the garden bed if Emma ran away? *Exactly what Edith thought.*

Beth knew it would be easier to talk with Alan now. The locket could be her passport to quizzing any number of neighbours. Although it was wearisome to conceal her true motive, there was no denying she felt pleased with her efforts and the result so far. On the other hand, she felt nervous about continuing on alone.

ELEVEN

Sunday, November 21

A dark gloomy morning arrived with the North Shore mountains nowhere in sight, but Beth was undeterred now that she'd had her first success and a tangible clue in hand. She was also looking forward to talking to Alan Whitman that evening. But first she had some other work to do. She had reports to write just like in the police detective books. Even if little came of her amateur interviews, like the one with Miriam, it all ought to be recorded so she could remember what was said, and perhaps a review of her activities over time would lead to other ideas.

There were at least three areas of inquiry that clearly involved Edith: her activities in Block Watch (including her reservations about Norm), her suspicions about Harry Anders' nephew, and her fearful conclusion about Emma Mahoney. Within her files, Beth planned to detail any interviews and put down her interpretation and/or what she already knew that pointed to a particular deduction. She wanted to treat this like a job, devote concrete effort to it but keep time for personal activities and relaxation. She concluded, above all, that to accomplish these objectives, it was essential that she collaborate with someone like Mr. Ross. Having set down her ideas to her satisfaction in the knowledge that she would seek help, Beth devoted some time to a blend of chores and reading until it was time to head to Alan's.

♣

Alan Whitman dried the few dishes he had used at dinner. He wondered if Beth was going to try to get him involved in the neighbourhood Block Watch. He wasn't quite sure what the purpose of this evening visit was and had been trying to recall what she'd actually said. He had called Beth yesterday. There was something about a locket, something about Edith's break-in, and something about… he couldn't remember. Ever since Evie had died, he'd had trouble keeping things straight. His doctor said it was normal—no wonder, Evie had managed most of the social part of their lives along with household upkeep, correspondence, and telephone messages. As much as he felt some resentment toward Mazie for pushing his niece and her iffy boyfriend on him, he recognized that Tara and Norm had brought some stability to his days, especially now that Edith had died and Ken wasn't around, even if temporarily. These changes had triggered a return to higher anxiety as well as less oomph.

A knock at the back door signaled Beth's punctual arrival.

♣

It was her first time inside the house since Evie's passing. As Beth followed Alan through the kitchen to the living room, she remembered the layout was a mirror image of Edith and Ken's place.

Even though she was full from dinner, Beth agreed to some tea and shortbread when it was offered. It would be easier to broach the subjects she had in mind over a cordial cuppa. She began by offering sympathy for Alan's loss of Edith, his and Evie's long-time friend.

"Who would have thought?" said Alan. "Evie hasn't been gone that long, and now for Ken to lose Edith—this is just horrible." He ran a shaky hand over his thinning grey hair. "I talked with him yesterday. Susan is bringing him home to pick up some things tomorrow, so we'll have a visit."

"I got to see Ken and Susan yesterday," Beth said. "They asked me to check with a few of the neighbours about a locket Edith had." She pulled it from the small box she'd placed it in and put it on her palm to show Alan. "Dennis found it when he was digging out that garden bed at the side of Ken's garage. They're pretty sure it's not Edith's. Neither of them has seen it before. Susan thought the hospital staff had made a mistake. Could it be Evie's?"

"No, those aren't her initials. Her name was Matilda Evelyn Rider before we married. She hated Matilda because kids would tease her by singing 'Waltzing Matilda.' By the time she was in high school, she would only answer to Evie."

"No trouble." Beth tucked it back in her purse, reflexively swallowing her guilt about the fact that she already knew it wasn't Evie's locket. "This is a good opportunity to catch up a bit. I haven't seen a lot of you lately. I notice we have new neighbours next to you."

"Yes, nice to see those rowdy lads gone," said Alan. "You know that's the house where Nina grew up? Her parents Inga and Gus sold it and got a place over in Deep Cove quite awhile back."

"I know about the house. Deep Cove, that's nice, haven't been there in a few years. Nina mentioned they were on the North Shore when I asked but no more than that. Kind of closed up about it."

"Not surprising," Alan said. "Nina's folks didn't approve of her marriage to Michael. Gus said they didn't trust him. Talk around was that it had to do with his first wife's disappearance.

But he's okay, I've always liked Nina and Michael. Emma had problems. It was sad."

"I heard about her from Ken the other day." Beth veered away from saying more. "There's something else I wanted to ask. I know Edith and Evie were fast friends. Did Evie ever tell you anything about Edith's worries about Harry Anders?"

"No, can't remember anything." Alan shook his head and added quickly, "Is it to do with Block Watch? I don't want to get involved right now; I hope you understand."

"It's okay, I wasn't going to ask you to help with anything. I hear you've been volunteering at Trout Lake Community Centre. And I guess you're busier with Tara and Norm living with you. How's that going?"

"Not bad, I guess. It's nice having company. I realize how empty the place is with just me here when they're at work. Tara's a good girl. She's been suggesting I get a cat for company. She's worried about me when she's at work. Acting like a little mother." Alan offered a wan smile. "I think she's getting on well at her Bay job. She's a friendly sort and smart—a little gullible perhaps, at least when it comes to Norm. But maybe I'm being harsh."

"I've only met Norm a few times in the lane. I think Edith shared your concern about him; she wasn't too impressed," Beth said. "He's working though, isn't he?"

"Yeah, he's got a job with his cousin – seems to idolize him – but it's only part time at the moment. Nina must have told you young Mike is working there too. Driving vans or something for an automotive parts business at a car dealership. They work funny hours sometimes. At least Norm does."

"What do you mean?"

"Well, Norm might work the day and then say he has a leftover job to do and is gone for a few hours mid-evening. Tonight, he's out drinking with Mike. Tara went along. Not sure what she sees in Norm. I must say though, he loves his mom. He talks about her now and then and he calls her every week. Guess he's alright; he does do a few chores around the place if I ask. Tara is good; she'll often see something I don't and tidy it. And she likes to make meals. I've gained back some weight I had lost, but I'm not quite as dumpy as I was before." Alan made a half-smile.

After that, there was nothing appropriate Beth could find to say in order to set up a way to talk with Norm. *Time to go,* she thought, *Alan's getting tired.*

"Say hello to Tara and Norm for me, won't you? It would be nice to have a visit with them sometime," Beth said lamely as she left.

Crossing the lane back to her place, she was aware of her rising frustration with her lack of know-how. As soon as she was inside, she jotted down '*CALL C. ROSS*' in bold letters on a sticky note and put it by the coffee maker.

TWELVE

Monday, November 22

It was just after nine when Beth contacted the art gallery and found herself impatiently listening to Cameron Ross's voicemail message. *Darn*, she thought. At least she'd discovered his first name. She left her name and number, reminded him of their prior conversation and politely asked if she could meet with him briefly over coffee to get more information. There wasn't much time to feel crabby since her phone rang less than fifteen minutes later.

Cameron didn't wait for her to say more than hello. "I haven't any more information I can give you for your nephew," he said dryly.

"About that," Beth said hesitantly, "it was actually information I wanted for myself."

"You don't mean *you* want to train to do security work?" Cameron did nothing to disguise the skepticism in his voice.

"No, no, sorry, the truth is, I want some help in figuring out how to proceed in a situation I know of that I think is a deliberate crime, not an accident like it's been labeled."

"That's easy. Report it to the police."

"I've tried that; they're not interested in what I think. Listen,

I'm not an oddball. Would you be willing to meet me for coffee sometime so I can tell you about it, person to person? It involves a hit-and-run accident that happened in my neighbourhood."

"Are you part of Block Watch?" Cameron said. "You could run it past the liaison officer."

"Yes, we have Block Watch here, but I might encounter some bias. The person hit was our team captain, and she had a bit of a reputation for being overzealous. I really don't think it was an accident she was hit. She died from her injuries. Please, Mr. Ross. I just need someone with experience, who's neutral, to listen to me."

"All right, guess it can't hurt. Perhaps I can tell you what's important to include in a report for the police then you can go back to them. That's only if I actually agree it's worth reporting."

Beth smiled at the phone. "What do you suggest? In general, I'm free today and most of the week."

"Come today. I have an hour break at twelve thirty. Meet me near the coat check." He hung up.

Almost an hour disappeared as Beth mulled over how to present her "case" to Cameron Ross. He seemed brusque on the phone. Used to being obeyed, she guessed. The man was basically a stranger, and though he was no longer with the police, she still needed to be careful what she said. She was sure he would disapprove of her search in the Todd home. *No need to say anything about that.* She wanted to present herself as a grounded, intelligent, well-intentioned person—which she thought she was most of the time—with sufficient evidence pointing to the clear possibility of wrong-doing. It should help to tell him that in her job, detection was fundamental to the everyday work. Infection control was like fitting together the pieces of a jigsaw puzzle a lot of the time.

First, she would introduce the last words spoken by Edith's

own lips, their meaning more or less agreed upon by Ken and Susan. And there were the threats. She doubted a vulnerable old man who might be the target of a scheming nephew would interest him though. Having reviewed Edith's journal entry about Emma via the photos she'd taken, Beth knew the location where the locket was found clearly pointed to foul play. That would be the second point. Then she could go on with the rest. Beth jotted it down: what Edith said in ICU first, the locket next, and then the threats and break-in. This was like preparing for an exam. Tired from thinking things over, she stood and shook her head to clear the sluggishness that had descended like the heavy velvet curtain at the end of a Saturday night opera. She did a few stretches and went to wash her face.

"Well, Monty, what will be, will be. I'm going on a walk to return my library book." The tabby, who had been lounging beside a hot air vent, sat up and yawned.

❦

Beth arrived early on purpose so she could browse the art gallery gift shop. In the summer, she'd found some perfect gifts there to send east for Christmas—which reminded her she'd better get them wrapped and mailed soon. She hadn't taken a moment to think of much other than work and Edith lately. The bright coloured lights appearing around the city had barely dented her consciousness.

Coming back into the foyer, Beth saw Cameron Ross. She picked up her pace. He had just turned to watch the Hornby Street entrance.

"Mr. Ross, hello."

He turned back. "Good, you're on time. And it's Cameron, please." Beth shook his extended hand. "We'll go upstairs and grab a bite. I have forty-five minutes I can spare. Let's eat first and then you can tell me what's bothering you."

They were seated in a far corner at a table that had a reserved sign. *Reserved for staff maybe?* The moderate hum in the room from other voices offered some further privacy. Beth dipped into a steaming bowl of salmon chowder with feather-light biscuits on the side. Cameron had chosen a grilled turkey, apple, and brie panini with the house side salad.

"I'd definitely give the café full marks for having the soup at a proper temperature," she said. From there, between mouthfuls, she spaced out a few short remarks about the nature of her professional background, then fell silent to finish her meal.

In return, Cameron replied with comments that had her feeling she'd made a good impression. They made some small talk about the recent weather, then after her last bite of biscuit was washed down with some water, Cameron prompted her to tell him about her concerns. Beth took a silent breath, *here goes*. Her tummy was fluttering like the first time she'd presented the infection control orientation education to new employees.

"I believe the police could be overlooking some key evidence about the nature of the hit-and-run accident that caused the death of my neighbour Edith Todd," Beth said. She'd practiced that opening and was relieved it came off smoothly.

"All right. Go on." Beneath his short, businesslike haircut, Cameron's broad face and hazel eyes were attentive.

"There are a number of concerns I know Edith had. They could cast a different light on the accident." With her planned introduction safely aired, Beth felt her confidence increase. She outlined the words Edith had managed to say and the conclusion that she, Susan, and Ken had about them.

Cameron interrupted. "Even if that's right, it still doesn't mean she wasn't hit accidently. With the weather the way it was and who knows what other distractions, a driver pulling out may have seen her too late. A hit-and-run *is* a crime, after all, and the police will be working to find the person. There's no way it's not being investigated. I don't really see what the problem is."

"The problem is that there is other evidence I've told the police about that I believe could point to a deliberate act and they are not giving it consideration."

"Okay, let's have it. I've got fifteen minutes left."

"First, Edith received two threatening letters in the last three weeks. And she had seen some suspicious things involving one or two young men on the block. We figured it all could be to do with her Block Watch activities." Beth noticed that it sounded like hearsay though she'd changed to 'we,' hoping a collective might carry more weight.

"So, then it's best to go through your Block Watch liaison constable," said Cameron.

"Well, I think he's a bit tired of Edith often poking her nose into things. I gather Constable Argento said he'd heard nothing of the threats when Sergeant James asked him." Feeling rattled by the second interruption, she rushed to add that there had been a break-in at the Todd's near the end of October.

"All right, I suppose that could be something more than coincidence. But to me, it's still Block Watch. That it?" Cameron said. He didn't hide the glance at his watch.

"No, no, there's one other thing." Beth stumbled on realizing that with Cameron's questioning, she'd lost track of her pitch and overlooked the recently found locket. "An old locket was pulled out with some roots from under the Todd's garage by a hired gardener. Edith was very disturbed by its discovery. She said it should not have been found there. I was supposed to go over to her place the next evening, which was after the accident, for her to tell me more. Then on Friday, I learned from Ken Todd about a missing neighbour when he and his daughter asked me to—"

"A missing neighbour? Well, that will be under investigation," Cameron said firmly.

"No, it's a case from… like, thirty years ago or more. Ken told me it was a young woman named Emma Mahoney who disappeared in 1960." Beth hurried on, "We're guessing the locket could be Emma Mahoney's, but the family want me to ask other neighbours about it too." *If I was Pinocchio…*

"What was that name again?" Cameron was sitting straighter, at full attention.

"Emma. She was the first wife of a neighbour of mine, Michael Mahoney."

"Mmm. What else can you tell me?"

"Well, there is another situation that could be important. It concerns an older male friend of Edith's who's blind and very well off. She was positive the nephew is planning to separate him from his money."

"No. I mean about Emma Mahoney."

"Not much more. I gather she had a history of depression. It looked like she'd run away; some of her belongings were missing."

Cameron hesitated momentarily then leaned forward, an elbow on the table, hand cupping his chin. "Mmm. That sounds like it could be a case investigated by my uncle who was with the force at the time. Sergeant James must have been interested in that."

"He doesn't know. The Todds and I didn't make the connection till this past weekend," Beth said, recalling that she hadn't known about the locket until after she'd met with the sergeant.

"You should go back to Sergeant James," Cameron said. "I should think you'll be fine now. Just tell the sergeant what you've told me, and tell the daughter to keep the locket in a safe place. It will have to be turned in. Let me know how you get on."

"Sure. Thanks."

Later, at home, Beth took another look at the couple inside and hid the locket in her own 'safe place', wondering if the words guile and guilt were related.

❧

Throughout the afternoon, Cameron found himself distracted by Beth's lunchtime revelation. He was picturing how satisfying it would be to unravel this particular case especially if it was one of the ones his Uncle John regretted not solving. He must have been about sixteen or seventeen when his uncle spoke of a case that sounded like it could be this one. He felt a rising interest in finding out more and knew he would enjoy telling his uncle about this possible development after so many years.

❧

Beth wasn't looking forward to contacting Sergeant James again. He would no doubt feel she was being a pest, but she'd wanted advice and couldn't dispute Cameron Ross's opinion. She needed to review what she wanted to say before she called. She'd headed to Pacific Centre with the idea of doing some Christmas shopping and ended up at the back of the bustling food court where she nursed a hot chocolate while she jotted down what she remembered telling Cameron. She needed to be sure to stick to the same information. *Not telling the exact truth is unpleasantly exhausting,* she thought. What to do about the locket was now an issue—she bet, though, that Susan would tell her just to take it to the police. Beth pried herself away from unhelpful speculation, deciding to leave the calls till the morning when she was fresh. After that, she wandered around Hudson's Bay for an hour and came home empty handed.

Preparing her dinner that evening with Monty meowing

loudly as usual, Beth turned her thoughts to Michael Mahoney. It was not lost on her that the locket's appearance likely had Edith thinking that his first wife must be dead, not missing. He would become chief suspect—or at least that's what happened in the many books she read. If he heard via Alan about last evening's visit, she'd better have a story ready. *Sorry, it's in my safety deposit box*—that might do.

It was almost nine thirty when the phone rang, startling Beth from some TV viewing designed to drown out her inner voice, which was finding fault with her behaviour and plans. She rose quickly, tipping Monty onto the floor. He stalked away with an irritated flick of his tail.

"Beth, it's Cameron. I'm very sorry to disturb you so late," he began, sounding more friendly than at lunch, "but I've been thinking about your neighbour. I've talked with my uncle briefly about Emma Mahoney. It *was* a case he worked on. Give me some time. I need to see him. He lives out of town. Remember to tell Susan Todd to keep the locket in a safe place for now."

"All right, no problem, thanks." Beth squeezed in the words before he rang off. Her lips curved into a satisfied smile. *What a relief,* she thought. Tomorrow, she'd take the locket to her safety deposit box first thing. She hoped Michael Mahoney wouldn't hear of it ... *maybe I could say Edith told me to put it there if he does?*

❦

Norm Jervis was in Alan Whitman's small basement bathroom attempting to style the new shorter haircut he was trying at Rich's suggestion. His forehead felt naked. Tara wasn't home yet, and he was headed out to meet Rich for dinner before clocking an extra shift. It seemed he and Tara were missing each other more these days what with some of the hours Rich had him working. He chewed over the strange—he thought—message Tara's uncle had passed on to him about the Langille woman's hello to him and Tara. Talk of a visit sometime? Didn't sound like anything he'd want to do. Weird. They didn't know her at all. She was old. Well, not as old as Alan of course.

Norm went out the front door to avoid being seen by Mike. He was helping Rich with a special job later that Mike knew nothing about. Mike was never in on anything more than minor infractions because he seemed edgy a lot of the time. Norm was irked that his own idea to have Mike along for a small task Rich had entrusted him with had bombed. Except that it had brought about—what was that word?—*leverage, that's it. We have control.* That led him to think about how he got stuck with Mike in the first place. The guy had latched on to him as if they were long lost pals. When he invited Mike along to see about work, it was the fault of too many beers. He'd been flattered by the attention at first, not having any friends but his cousin and a couple of the guys at the shop. It wasn't long before he realized Mike was a momma's boy. He was always worrying what she'd say, what she'd find out, how she'd mess up his plans. It was clear Mike would never really fit in with The Pizza Club. Rich is right he thought. *Mike's a nuisance but we hafta keep an eye on him and watch what we say.*

THIRTEEN

Tuesday, November 23

Sugary frost dusted the rooftops as Beth stood at the sink hand-washing a few breakfast dishes. She looked across her backyard toward Sofia's and Edith's—it would remain Edith's for a long time in her mind—and contemplated the low feelings hovering around her. She knew they were a combination of her loss of Edith, the dark times after Robbie died, the end of her marriage and the slump following her mother's passing. *Focus on today.*

Beth felt impatient to get out, but the sun had only caught the chimney tops so far. She was going to devote time to search for 'Joe the dogwalker,' not the most noble of activities but necessary. It would be good to make some headway on her list. In the past week, through some random observation both from her living room window and while out on errands, she had already established that he seemed to have a couple usual routes. She had drawn the line at trailing him to his home. She'd made sure to exchange a small wave occasionally when possible and was pleased with this contact as preliminary to speaking with him.

Her plan was to walk parts of each of the routes several different times as necessary and make the opportunity happen.

And today would be a perfect day for walking. The recent low system had swept inland with a high settled over the south coast for a couple days. She could incorporate some errands west to Broadway and Commercial taking the Trout Lake circuit and later, if necessary, go east.

On her second venture out, Beth saw Norm, his spindly legs almost a blur, coming up the lane as if escaping from something. Obviously, his ankle had healed. She hurried to catch him just as he reached the gate of Alan's yard.

"Hi Norm," she said, then continued, since he looked at her blankly, "It's Beth. Remember? Tara introduced us a little while back. I'd met her at Edith's one evening not long after you moved in with Alan. I haven't seen either of you since. Guess you're busy working. It would be nice to have you both drop in sometime. Perhaps we can plan around your schedule?"

Norm shifted his stance. "Suppose so," he said, a sour look belying the words. He put his hand out to take the gate latch.

Beth scrabbled to keep the paltry conversation going. "I heard you hurt your ankle. Has it affected your job? Mrs. Todd, Edith, told me you and Mike are doing something for a cousin. What sort of business does he run?"

Norm ignored the questions. "Mrs. Todd. Oh yeah, her. Too bad about the accident and all. Didn't know her much. A bit harsh, wasn't she? She was like Mike's mom—after us about getting work. We *are* working," he said in a resentful tone. "Hey, I got to get going. Bye." Norm slammed the gate behind him and strode away.

Evening found Beth frustrated and weary. First contact with Norm was useless except perhaps as a set up for the next time. It was obvious he didn't want to talk. And how could she possibly have missed Joe? He must be away or maybe sick—after all, the flu season was well underway. The day had been a big fat zero with no sign of him anywhere. *Well, no,* she chided herself. *Not a big fat zero.* Groceries had been bought; the locket, now nestled in tissue in a small box, was safe in the bank; library books were returned and exercise had—well, she'd had more than she needed.

Beth's initial elation over Cameron's call had waned with her fatigue, and once again, her thoughts turned to the several possibilities about who had wished Edith ill. She realized it was natural that the only part of her story that was of interest to Mr. Ross—*Cameron, he'd said*—was the old Mahoney case. But she wanted his help with investigating Edith's death too. Perhaps it was time to choose a backup person to share her ideas and plans with.

Sofia would certainly have a vested interest in helping. She had lived next door to Edith and the two had been neighbourly friends attending the same church almost as long as the Whitmans. Sofia was a generous, capable person; however, by her own admission, her emotions were clouding her days and it might be too much for her right now.

There was Dennis, who was somewhat part of the neighbourhood still. He'd found the locket and maybe that mystery could entice him to help her out. In addition, his contact with various neighbours would be seen as natural so he could do some digging for her. Beth groaned aloud. *Horrible pun.*

What of Jenny Lee? She had already committed to assume the position of Block Watch captain. Her less lengthy relationship with Edith would bring a more objective view. Jenny was practical and level-headed, always willing to help. There was a 'but' though. Her only daughter—a single mom with two children—had come home to live a couple years ago and had never left. With both her husband and daughter working, and Jenny looking after the kids on her own, she had her hands full. Beth shook her head. It would be unfair to burden her with more.

Maybe it was best to choose someone outside of the neighbourhood. *June would be good.* Having known one another for fourteen years at work, she and June Ishida had gradually developed a friendship that included lunching in the hospital cafeteria when their workdays permitted and the occasional but nonetheless regular social activity away from work. She would definitely be objective. She would be at least as good a fit as Beth was for something like this given the investigative nature of laboratory work. Once she heard from Cameron Ross, she could decide.

There was just enough time to call Harry Anders before it turned nine. He gallantly brushed aside her apologies for not calling sooner and assured her he had more local than overseas cards to send. It reminded her she had her own cards to do and gifts to buy. *But it doesn't feel like Christmas should be happening at all.*

"Can you come tomorrow around one?" he asked. "Frank will be here to join me for eleven-thirty lunch in our dining room, maybe you'll get to meet him. I'll see if he can wait."

Beth thought it was too bad she was biased against Frank already. Edith had had little or no regard for the man. In the early days of Ken's hospitalization, she had shared both her indignation about a call she'd had from Frank as well as what she'd found out. It might be hard to find out more without Cameron Ross's help. He was fixed on the locket, but maybe in time—*oh well,* she thought, *I'll muddle on for now.*

Frank Nolan, according to Edith, was out to get control of Harry's money and had been pressuring his uncle to name him as power of attorney. This began as soon as his cousin, Harry's niece Pat, had moved to California to teach at the prestigious Stanford University. Harry's modest living arrangements belied the state of his financial situation—he'd confided in Edith that he'd made a bundle from the container business established by his father in the 1920s. Harry and his late older brother Edward carried on the flourishing business till the latter's passing and then Harry's own retirement. He'd sold at a fine price. Edith felt her fears were well-founded given she had overheard Frank twice trying to persuade his uncle to accompany him to see a lawyer friend who could 'take care of everything'. Both times, she'd been sitting next to Harry when he'd taken Frank's call. Because Frank raised his voice whenever he spoke on the phone to his uncle, his side of the conversation could be overheard by anyone in the room.

Beth recalled Edith quoting Frank's remarks with relish and anger when she'd talked about the offensive call he'd made to her.

"Said I was a nosy old goat. Told me to butt out of his uncle's business or else. He kept yelling at me. When I asked him what 'or else' meant, he said, 'it means you'll be very sorry. Stick to your reading and letter writing,' he said. What nerve," she had huffed. "I know his sort. He's a bully and sly. You mark my words, he's after Harry's money."

"Edith, are you telling me everything?" Beth had asked. "Frank seems to have had an extreme reaction if all you've been doing is helping Harry."

"Well… I did a little research on the iffy lawyer. I overheard the name. I asked one of our parishioners who's with a reputable law firm about him, and I encouraged Harry to let his niece Pat know."

"And?"

"Oh, I suppose he might have seen me outside his office building."

"The lawyer?" Beth had said.

"Frank."

"What? How did you know where to go?"

"Easy," Edith had said. "Harry had his business card lying around. Frank has an office in the Roberts Block building where my son worked for a few years during university. I'm going to see what I can find out about his business. A-1 Investments. Hah. That doesn't fill *me* with confidence."

It dawned on Beth that the Pender address written in the margin of Edith's date book was likely Frank Nolan's office location.

❧

Wednesday, November 24

As promised, it was another sunny day. Beth bent to give Monty, curled up by the heater, a farewell pat and stepped out into the four degree Celsius windchill after a lunch of hot beans and wieners on toast. It was an occasional indulgence reminiscent of her childhood years. She crossed Nanaimo on the green light at a smart pace, her tummy muscles tight, chest barely moving till she was on the other side. Her next breath was released in a great steamy cloud.

Harry's seniors' complex, which lay near the south end of John Hendry Park, came into view. Beth felt nervous about meeting Frank given his recent interaction with Edith. She tried vainly to put aside her preconceptions. *Act like you've never heard of him before,* she counselled herself, pulling her shoulders back.

Frank Nolan opened the door when Beth knocked on Harry's door. A short, middle-aged man stood before her. The impeccable pin stripe suit he wore was in keeping with Edith's description, though the welcoming smile was not.

"Well… you must be Beth. I'm Frank." He offered a limp handshake. "Uncle Harry is resting in his armchair. Do come in."

After ten minutes of vague pleasantries, Frank Nolan's smile faded and his pleasant exterior with it, though he professed himself "so very glad" to meet her. Beth hoped her own duplicity was not as transparent. She responded promptly though not gladly when he asked for her telephone number "in case I need to get in touch" and took his leave.

"That went well," said Harry, oblivious to any tension.

Shortly before three, Beth also took her leave after getting a good start to Harry's Christmas card list. Between the dictation and conversation, Beth learned that Frank, the son of Harry's late sister Rose, had grown up in Ontario the only child of a single mother. He'd had been in Vancouver barely two years.

"I think he's getting on fairly well, seems to like the big city life. Before she died, I told Rose I would look after him. My wife Cora was an only child. She and I never had kids so Frank and Pat are all there is of our family's younger generation."

"What's Frank's line of work?" Beth asked, curious what the answer would be given what she'd heard from Edith.

"Oh, he got a BA and took chartered accounting, and he's been managing investments successfully for years. Somewhere in the Maritimes, I think. Rose always said he had a head for predicting winners. Now Pat, she's the *real* brainy one." Harry went on to speak wistfully of his niece, daughter of his deceased brother Edward. "I feel closer to her," Harry said, "I've known her all her life, but she moved to California last year to take a job at Stanford. Quantum something—that's her field. She's home quite often though to see her mom and me."

❦

Thursday, November 25

Rain had returned in the early morning hours before Beth rose. She opened the bedroom curtains a crack and let out a small groan upon seeing a cascade of rain bouncing on her front steps.

It was meant to pour all day. Even so, she knew her impatience would thrust her out into the wet looking for Joe again.

By midmorning, Beth was walking along the side of her home out to the front where Joe often trailed by, his terrier leading the way to John Hendry Park. The light rain on her turquoise umbrella was a gift after the previous hour's torrent. She'd noticed that Joe went walking his dog in all kinds of weather, so it wasn't just luck that he was out on the blustery wet evening of Edith's so-called accident. Maybe he would remember something vital if she could only speak with him. She dawdled for a while in her front yard, appearing to check the garden bed along the top of her stone retaining wall, which was largely populated with small to medium evergreen shrubs, mainly azalea with a mix of Alberta fir and Mugo pine, before descending five cement steps to the sidewalk.

She turned and looked east, willing Joe and Digger to appear. *No such luck.* Aware of her reaction before at the recently infamous crosswalk, she focused on her mission when she carefully crossed at the light. Her wish took form. There, not two blocks distant down a lane that led to the park, was a lone hooded figure led by a Welsh terrier and heading her way.

Beth opened the exchange by greeting the rain-coated dog. "Hello, Digger, how are you today? Glad I ran into you, Joe. I wanted to ask you a few more questions about your memories of Edith's accident. I was quite close to her. I feel a need to help figure out what happened."

Joe's brow wrinkled. "I didn't really see the accident but sure, okay. We were just going to zig zag our way home but another turn around the park will be fine."

For a time, Beth and Joe followed Digger in silence along the curving dirt pathway nearest Trout Lake past the now mostly denuded willow trees. Bedraggled-looking bushes and reeds lined the water's edge where muted colours of tan, rust and grey offered their own beauty as a background to some scattered ochre leaves and maroon seed clusters. The rain had eased so Beth folded her umbrella.

"So, you're pretty sure you saw the car leaving the accident scene?"

"Yeah, sure. It was really speeding, and I looked up when I heard the loud engine. It whizzed by—we were on the west side of the road you understand," said Joe as he stopped to face Beth.

"What if we walked the same way back? That should help you recall it better."

"I suppose. We can cut across and go fifteenth to Nanaimo. That's what I did then. I didn't want to walk the entire park in *that* weather." This remark led to the inevitable rehashing of past soggy, windy autumn storms.

As they walked along the sidewalk, each casting their minds back to the evening of Edith's accident, Beth prompted Joe with a question. "The police spoke to you right then?"

"Yes, I'd crossed the street after the ambulance left, and we stood under the awning of the corner store. But I told him I couldn't identify the car apart from it being a dark colour. Likely black or even a navy blue."

"What size?"

"Well, I thought it seemed a full-size sedan, you know, not a compact."

"And you couldn't see a logo or anything like that?"

Joe answered with some annoyance in his voice. "Well no. I would have told the police that, wouldn't I? You must remember yourself it was wet and slick and there were streetlights and headlights bouncing off everything. Off the road, off the windshields."

"Yes, yes. I do. You're right," Beth hastened to pacify him.

"So, you couldn't see the person in the car? The driver would have been on your side. You said the noise made you look up before it passed by."

Joe said nothing at first, then his eyes widened slightly. "The face was indistinct, a profile, I've told the police. I've remembered something though. An odd sensation, I kinda saw double. I guess it was just reflected lights all over the car that seemed to blur my sight along with some rain on my glasses. The rain was in my face. No point using the umbrella in that gale. Had my hood secured. But I'm thinking now there might have been a passenger. Anyway, nothing else I can recall."

"I remember the poor visibility," Beth said. "It was a real challenge with headlights coming straight for me and reflections everywhere it seemed."

"Well, I guess that's what happened to that driver so he didn't see Mrs. Todd, but he should have stayed. I felt bad I couldn't be of any real help," said Joe.

"If there was another person, the police would add that into their public appeal. And maybe the person will call in. I think it will help the police to know what you've told me."

"Yeah, I guess I should call them," said Joe. "Okay. Got to get going now; see you 'round."

They parted ways, leaving Beth disappointed there was so little to go on. She started along her back lane then thought better of it, took a side lane to the street, and entered her front door to avoid passing the Todd's backyard. She wondered if she should just give up. Cameron Ross hadn't called again. She hoped he wouldn't bail on her. *I can't figure this all out with just June or one of the neighbours,* she thought.

In her current mood, the message in the fortune cookie she broke open later when she ate some ordered-in Chinese food was not amusing. *Be prepared to modify your plans. Your flexibility is appreciated.*

Even Monty was not his usual soothing self—he paced about the house, frequently meowing his displeasure that his wishes to be outside had been ignored all day.

♣

Cameron Ross had left just after nine to go see his uncle, John, in Squamish. The town, whose mainstay was the forest industry, lay about an hour's drive north of Vancouver. John Ross, retired from the VPD, was the younger brother of Cameron's late father Alister, who'd risen in the ranks of the RCMP before retiring. Cameron had been trying to visit his uncle more often since John had been forced to have his wife Lily placed in a nursing home due to advanced dementia a few years previous. Cameron pushed away some guilt about this visit being overdue. *The case of Emma Mahoney might make up for it,* he thought. He'd not told his uncle of the locket when he asked if he could come to catch up and treat him to lunch.

The usually scenic drive was unpleasant in the rain, but the cloud level was not so low that Stawamus Chief Mountain, just south of the community, was obscured. It appeared as a misty brooding giant on the right as he passed. Locally dubbed The Chief, it was a popular rock-climbing destination. While Cameron had faced danger in many forms during his career, the thought of scaling the monolith's granite heights held no appeal—he was keenly aware during his last year of policing that he had grown less comfortable taking personal risks. The moment he couldn't give his all to the job, he knew it was time to quit. It hadn't helped that his last years were tainted by a wrongful charge of conspiracy in harbouring a wanted criminal.

He let the passing blur of calming green quiet his angst. Yes, he appreciated nature, but he enjoyed the hustle and bustle of big city life despite having grown up on the outskirts of Prince George where his younger brother Ian, having followed in their father's footsteps, was with the RCMP detachment. Vancouver was an attractive city that allowed him to escape to water, mountains, or countryside in a few hours.

Aunt Lily and Uncle John, on his retirement, had chosen to get away and be close to the outdoor activities they had always enjoyed as an antidote to the demands of his work and schedules.

"Cameron, my boy, come in, come in," the older man said with a warm smile. His short iron-grey hair was slicked back, his trousers were pressed, and over a white shirt he wore a navy Perry Como cardigan. No flannel shirt or jeans today.

"Great to see you, Uncle; you're looking fit." They shared a short hug and John led the way to the kitchen where he poured them each a cup of coffee.

"Mary next door brought over some muffins. It's just past ten, let's have one."

"How's Aunt Lily?" said Cameron.

"About the same, you know—not talking, needs coaxing to eat. She's gradually failing. I'm glad we had almost ten years here and made a number of new friends before this happened. We'll drop in to the home later. The nurses tell me she's always calmer after I've been."

After exchanging some other family news, talk turned to work as it more often did since Lily's condition had advanced. Cameron described some of the minor altercations he'd dealt with at the gallery before he talked about how a woman, an art gallery member, had sought his advice about a neighbourhood car accident.

"Do you remember very much about that case involving the disappearance of an Emma Mahoney?" he asked his uncle, rather sure what the answer would be.

"You bet I do," said John, his head nodding vigorously. "It was one of a couple cases I kept my notes from when I left the force. I always thought when I had more time, I'd go over them again, but I never did. Lily and I moved, got involved with the hiking group, and at that time, Carl, Jill, and the grandchildren lived here and—"

"Did you keep your notes?"

"Yes. Somewhere. I know I didn't shred them. There's a mess of stuff in the basement. Lily and I always meant to get to it. What's this all about exactly?"

"Beth lives in the same block where the Mahoney's lived. Her neighbour died after a hit-and-run and she's got it in her head that it wasn't accidental. A locket that was part of the victim's valuables was found caught up in some roots that came from under this lady's garage. It apparently belonged to Emma Mahoney."

"Emma Mahoney," repeated John, a bright determined look in his eyes. "I'll turn out the basement tomorrow and find my notes."

FOURTEEN

Friday, November 26

As Beth approached the infection control office, she heard the chugging sound of a printer at work.

"I guess you don't need me today," she said to the back of the shapely figure who straightened up and turned to be greeted by an impish grin. All at once, Beth was feeling good about having a normal interaction and knowing she would have a day of familiar routine involving lab and ward staff she'd known for years.

"Oh, yes we do," Donna smiled, teasing back. "Not staying long. Just thought I'd do these unit lists for you. I have a meeting with Tom about the Aspergillus outbreak at eight thirty. You'll be interested in what we found."

"I'm all ears," said Beth as she locked away her purse after removing her reading glasses.

"More cases of the fungus were discovered in wounds early last week on two other units." Donna handed Beth a copy of the draft report. "I'll let you run your eye over that for typos and anything that isn't clear. There's a folder on my desk that has the raw data if you have any questions. Took over a week to get it sorted. Oh, I confess I didn't get to update the resistant organisms study data entries. Perhaps you'll have time to do some."

"Sure, no problem, as long as it doesn't turn into a crazy Friday," Beth said.

"Back to the Aspergillus," said Donna. "Altogether, there were three infections plus four cases where the fungus was present along with a more obvious pathogen—all wounds of one sort or another. The main thing they had in common was the use of a dressing tray."

Beth spoke up to show she wasn't out of practice. "With all the different wards involved, it must have come down to a single source away from the patient units."

"Yes. Once we determined that, Tom and I went to the central supply storage room. There's some major reconstruction going on and there were no physical barriers in place to prevent airborne spread of bacteria. No one thought of consulting us because it isn't a patient care area."

"Must have been a fair bit of dust."

"Yup. We did swabs of a variety of box tops and other surfaces. Aspergillus was growing on almost every plate. The area is all sealed off properly now, thank goodness."

"A logical chain of transmission," said Beth. "Supply services deliver the dusty boxes to the ward; staff opens them to shelve the contents and the outside of the dressing trays become contaminated. Then when the outer wrap is removed at the bedside to set up for dressing change, the contents become contaminated with some fungus. Transfer to the wound would be unavoidable."

"Exactly," said Donna. "It's a good feeling to have found the answer and it's been a good teaching experience for a lot of staff."

❦

Just after four as Beth locked up the office, June stopped by a moment, and they remarked to each other how fast the day had gone by. For Beth, it had been an effective distraction from the anxious feelings she was experiencing waiting for Cameron to call. It had been four days now, and she'd expected to hear sooner. She decided to hang on over the weekend before mentioning anything to June about help. Once she was home, impatience niggled at her again. She headed off to the park to walk it out of her system.

As Beth went in her usual direction around Trout Lake, a new opening presented itself. In the distance, she saw Tara looking zombie-like, carrying two Safeway bags. Beth picked up speed to narrow the gap between them. Perhaps she could get some information about what Norm and Mike were doing.

"Hi Tara. Been wondering how you're getting along these days. How's work going?"

❧

Tara Samson shivered even with many warm layers. A yellow wool tam was pulled over her ears. The perm had finally grown out and straight bangs escaped to form an uneven fringe tickling her forehead. She sniffled and hoped she hadn't caught her supervisor's cold. She was glad she had reached the point in her work schedule where she had a weekend off. She was looking forward to a quiet evening with her Uncle Alan. She would throw together a mild chili and serve it over rice with some store-bought coleslaw mixed with some grated apple and sunflower seeds. Last night Norm had said he was working another late shift. Privately, she was beginning to wonder what he was actually doing. Tonight though, he was having a meal with Mike at the pub.

Tara had begun to find excuses to not join Norm and Mike at the pub. She'd come to strongly dislike the drinking, the boasting, and the innuendos about their inside track with Norm's cousin Rich. Rich sounded like a trumped-up dictator, and she'd not changed her mind when she met him two weeks previous at his glitzy home in Tsawwassen. Then she thought further that she really didn't know what she was doing with Norm. Even though she'd only lived in Vancouver for eight months, she felt she had finally grown up. The retail experience and the encouragement at her workplace had increased her confidence—and in speaking with a few different young men from other departments, she realized she was having far more meaningful conversations with them than Norm. She was now sure she wanted to break up with him, which meant he'd have to find a new place to live. She didn't think his posh cousin would be inviting him to stay. Some buddies at work were in a house somewhere not far away, so they might take him in. She had a fair idea there'd be some whining and swearing. With these thoughts preoccupying her, she nearly bumped into Beth before realizing she was being addressed.

❦

"Beth," Tara said, mouth open, eyes wide, "I didn't see you. Sorry, what did you say?"

"That's okay. How are you doing? I can walk home with you. I was just having a quick turn around the lake to wind down from work. Let me carry one of your bags."

"Sure," said Tara, handing off the lighter bag. "I kind of went overboard buying some things for the weekend. I'm doing chili tonight and Uncle Alan has a sweet tooth so I'm doing some baking tomorrow."

"I know your uncle is really glad to have you here from what he said last Sunday when I dropped in on him. It hasn't been that long since your Aunt Evie died."

It would be hard to learn more about Norm in the short time the walk would take, Beth realized. Not only were her interview skills lacking, she needed lead-up time to get to her agenda and there would be no lingering at the back gate given the time and the icy breeze.

"Tara, why don't you come over for a visit tomorrow afternoon? Are you free? We can have some tea or whatever and a good chat. Alan said you like cats and my Monty loves visitors."

Tara beamed. "Sure, I'll check with you after lunch. By then I should know if the chill I'm feeling is just the weather. What's your number?"

※

Saturday, November 27

In the morning, which seemed to ooze toward noon, Beth's phone rang three times. First, it was Jenny checking if Beth could help deliver the Block Watch newsletters, then Sofia asking how she was, and later, Dennis changing the day he'd do her eaves. Finally, Cameron called just after one—about the time Beth was finishing up some lunch while thinking of how to politely withdraw her request for his assistance. He apologized in a way that immediately made her feel contrite about deciding he was unreliable.

"It's taken longer than I thought to get back to you. Sorry about that. I needed to coordinate a time with my uncle who's in Squamish. Better in person, I thought."

"That's okay," Beth said. Then she figured it wouldn't hurt to remind him of the other cases. "I've been busy talking to a few neighbours and forming some ideas about the other reasons Edith may have been targeted. I'm looking forward to your help. What did your uncle say?"

"That he's certain the locket should not have been wherever it was because he clearly recalls there was a solid witness who said Emma Mahoney was wearing it the day she disappeared. As did her husband. Lots to talk about. Can we meet tomorrow afternoon? I'm free. Are you?"

After they'd settled a time and place and she'd hung up, Beth thought about the fact that Cameron hadn't acknowledged her comments about the other possibilities for Edith's accident. Perhaps she shouldn't jump to conclusions, maybe his comment about 'lots to talk about' did include them. She'd make sure he listened to her tomorrow and see how he responded.

A short while later, Tara came across the deck holding a plate of cookies covered with plastic wrap. "Made some ginger sparklers from Aunt Evie's recipe box this morning," she said, "Uncle Alan's favourite."

"How kind of you. Those take me back to training days when I lived in residence. Mom sent me yummy care packages." Beth held the screen door open. "Come on in, and I'll put the kettle on. Go on into the living room. Pretty sure you'll find Monty there. Guess he's too lazy to come out to meet you."

To Tara's delight, the cat was in an armchair near the front window sitting up as if waiting for his visitor. "Hi Monty, you have a great view."

While Beth busied herself in the kitchen, she felt the familiar regret that her interactions with neighbours had hidden motives. *It's for Block Watch and Edith; it's important,* she reminded herself.

"This is soothing," said Tara after they'd settled at the dining room table where Beth had set a pot of vanilla rooibos tea with the cookies. "The last time I had tea like this was when Mr. and Mrs. Todd invited us one evening to meet a few neighbours. Of course, you were there. It seems a long time ago."

"Yes, I recall," said Beth. "Too bad Norm wasn't with you. Guess he was working?"

"Possible. Not sure. I think it was an excuse." Tara switched subjects before Beth could ask more. "Tell me about your home; it has a different feel with the kitchen, dining room, and living room flowing into one another. I like it a lot."

"I agree. I was lucky that the two offers before me fell through because I was really taken with the whole place. Well, maybe not the stucco exterior so much but an assessment of the place guaranteed it had 'good bones' as my realtor called it. Perhaps one day you and Norm will have a place of your own. Would you stay in the Vancouver area, do you think?"

"Uh," Tara said, pausing, "I'm not sure Norm and I are *that* serious, and anyway, our income is low. It's hard to save much."

Beth jumped in to see if she could find out what Norm had avoided telling her. "What exactly does Norm do? I know he and Mike work at the same place."

Tara paused again. "In some ways, I'm not really sure. He doesn't talk about it much except to keep promising it'll be full time soon. His cousin Rich owns a big garage and car dealership. Norm's working three, occasionally four times a week, and his shifts sometimes start midafternoon and go into late evening. He and Mike are driving vans and delivering car parts all over the place, I guess. Even out to Chilliwack. Norm is doing some extra stuff for Rich and that keeps him in a good mood. But he gripes about the pay still. I've heard Mike talking about training to be a mechanic to earn more."

"That's a switch," Beth said. "Mike was at UBC and planned to study higher mathematics last I heard. His dad is a successful accountant at a big company."

"Yeah, it's come up in talk at the pub when we're out… not that I go with them much anymore. Lately, I've stopped. I'm getting tired of that scene. They do nothing but talk about sports, the money they plan to make, and what they'll buy. Seems they've got enough to spend on lots of beer."

"You're sounding a little unhappy, Tara. Would you rather be back home?"

"Not really. I came first because Mom wanted me to keep Uncle Alan company. He's a dear and I like it here and I like my job. Norm was pushing to get out of Kelowna too. He'd had a little mix-up with the RCMP and that spooked him."

Beth leaned toward Tara slightly. "Goodness, what happened?"

"Norm wouldn't tell me. Didn't want to upset me, he said. But I heard rumours from my girlfriends. They said there was a robbery of some sort and there may have been drugs involved. Someone's boyfriend was talking about it. Anyway, it never made the papers, and Norm said the police had nothing on him when I asked. Swore to me that someone tried to frame him for something he never did."

"Maybe someone was trying to deflect interest from themselves." said Beth.

"The trouble is," Tara said, lowering her voice, "between you and me, I'm not so sure that's true."

The squeak of the screen door and a loud knock on the inner door made them both jump. From their seated positions, neither had heard or seen who'd come across the deck. Beth swiveled around, leaned to look out the dining room window, and saw what appeared to be a man's back. He wore a black hoody with the hood up and had a small backpack slung over his shoulder. Beth was irritated because the interruption prevented Tara from saying more.

She opened the door to a moody young face. "Come on in, Norm."

"No need, I'm here to get Tara," he said, standing still.

Behind Beth, Tara protested she hadn't finished her visit, that it was only two thirty, and shouldn't he be at work?

"You women can gab anytime," Norm said. "I've been able

to take off early so we can get out together."

The frown lines on Tara's face deepened. She stepped closer. "Why did you do that? You knew I was looking forward to time with Beth. I'm staying a while longer. I told Uncle I'd be back before four."

Beth had moved quietly aside, judging she'd best remain mum, but she didn't leave. With growing concern, she watched Norm's face, which was suffused with colour, first pink, now almost red. His expression had hardened to a plastic-like mask.

"Oh, come on, babe," Norm said, loud and firm. "Just get your coat and come home."

"No," said Tara. "And don't call me babe, you know I hate that. I'll be back before four just as I'd planned. My tea's getting cold." She turned toward the kitchen.

While Norm stood there glaring, Beth moved forward to shut the door. She tried to lighten the mood. "Don't worry, Norm; I'll kick her out before long and the two of you will have lots of time to talk and plan your evening."

"You stay out of this, you snoop," he spat at her.

Like a dust devil, Tara whirled back to face Norm, her eyes glowing. "What's gotten into you, Norm? Apologize right now. Go home. I'll be back by four."

Norm's face set into a sullen grimace. He mumbled something and turned to leave. As he did, Beth noticed the business end of a screwdriver poking through an unzipped section of his backpack. Of course, there might be some other explanation for the tool but added to his garb and the pack, it all fit with the working uniform of a property crime offender, something she'd learned about during Block Watch training. She paused to make sure he left her yard.

Beth found Tara in the living room stroking Monty and murmuring quiet endearments to the cat. She looked up. "I'm so very sorry, Beth."

"Not your fault. Maybe Norm isn't so happy at his work after all."

"Don't think it's that. It's more likely he knows I've been unhappy with him the past few weeks. I should really go and talk to him now, but I want to stick to what I said about four. Sorry to drag you into my personal troubles."

"It's okay, do you want to talk about it?" said Beth, feeling extra guilty but hoping perhaps she might still get some more information about Norm.

"There's not much to talk about. I want to split up with him, and I may as well get it over with tonight. Can we talk recipes? I need some ideas for dinner meals."

Perhaps I should call myself 'the two-steps-back investigator,' Beth thought as she fought to shove aside her frustration.

FIFTEEN

Sunday, November 28

Cameron Ross woke early, disturbed by the hoarse calls of crows creating a fuss in the maple tree outside his bedroom window. While he put on some coffee, he sensed an underlying discontent about the planned afternoon meeting with Beth Langille. He thought it may be wise to keep his involvement to a minimum. Perhaps once he'd given some clear advice, he would opt out. He could follow up on the Mahoney case through channels of his own. Beth appeared to be nice enough and smart—except for the fact that she was so caught up in her attachment to her friend Mrs. Todd who had died. As a result, she seemed out to prove there was a sinister cause for her friend's accident. Hit-and-runs were not uncommon, and accidental collisions occurred more frequently in dark, rainy conditions. Those were the sad facts.

The locket was a different matter. It wouldn't be the first time a chance find like that had opened up a fresh investigation into a case that had ended unsatisfactorily. It had nothing to do with the hit-and-run, but it had resulted in Beth coincidentally bringing his attention to the discovery. It was one of those happenstances he'd come across more than once in his career—an inadvertent discovery many months or years later, which led to arrests and convictions. Like in the movies. No, like real life. He knew from experience real life could be stranger than fiction as the saying went.

Just take the circumstances that ended his marriage. He pushed the last forkful of egg and sausage into his mouth and chewed slowly. That his wife of nine years turned out to be someone who had committed an ugly crime was a stunner.

Sometimes, it seemed only yesterday that he and Tina had dined out with his buddy Ron Poole and wife Barb at a favourite Italian restaurant on Commercial Drive. Cameron would never forget that evening. It was the last Saturday in March 1992. He supposed he recalled it so well because he, Ron, and Barb had gone over and over it trying to pinpoint if there was anything that might have signaled Tina was going to vanish—though in the end, she didn't get far. The next day, Cameron had begun a stint of day shifts. He came home to a note saying she was joining her friend Viv for a shopping excursion in West Vancouver then would stay over for a girl's night. That had been a lie.

And Cameron was not likely to forget his humiliation on the Monday—or through the long months that followed. A senior colleague he'd had little respect for had come sauntering over to his desk and waved a printout under his nose.

"Hey, Cam, bet you knew about this. You do know who *this* is," he'd said loudly. "I've been to the superintendent to give her the original."

Cameron's face had turned rosy as he'd come to life, reaching out to grab the wanted poster. "That's my wife, dammit." He'd recognized the silver dolphin earrings right away, but Tina's hair was different. The name below was different too. Rosalia Conte.

He'd faltered, saying, "You got Tina's photo from somewhere, and this is a sick joke." But everyone nearby had heard the question mark punctuating his protest.

"No, it's not," the officer had said. "My sister is in town for a family visit. Her hubby is a police detective in Miami. They went to Arriva Ristorante on the weekend and he recognized your wife as someone from Florida charged with manslaughter over ten years ago. He took a photo of your table with their new digital camera and sent it on to his boss who faxed this to my office."

From then on, Cameron's life had changed dramatically. It was like living someone else's life. Tina's—Rosalia's crime and capture as well as his alleged culpability had been plastered all over *The Sun* and *The Province* papers. Or it felt like that. When Tina had finally been extradited to Florida to stand trial for the death of a neighbour, the press coverage faded away.

Cameron had been removed from active service and placed on desk duty until he was cleared by internal affairs of knowingly harbouring a fugitive. He had not been allowed to communicate with Tina—she was still Tina to him—until almost a year later when he got back to active duty. It was a stilted phone call. She'd said she loved him, but he couldn't believe it. What a patchwork of lies she must have fed him over the years. To blot out the betrayal, Cameron had thrown himself back into work, transferring from vice to homicide. He shoved the past away and came back to his current thoughts.

Under normal circumstances, Cameron would have told Beth the locket must be handed over to the police without delay. The accidental find combined with the coincidence that his Uncle John had headed the investigation into the disappearance of Emma Mahoney was influencing his own actions. Cameron knew his uncle would be thrilled if Emma's case was solved. And for his uncle's sake, he wanted to be part of the process that uncovered the truth. *Really, there's no question, is there?* He would need to reach out to his friend Ron to get in on the missing person case. If he could somehow see it through to a positive result, that would be ideal.

❦

Around noon, Michael Mahoney eased his pearl-grey Audi close to the cedar fence at the back of his home. When he pushed it, the back gate swung open with a harsh creak. Nina had stopped him when he wanted to oil it. She stressed that she wanted to know if someone was entering the yard. He had been to the office for a few quiet hours of number crunching but promised he'd be quick so he could have a chance to talk with Mike about job prospects at the consortium satellite office that had opened in Surrey in late September. Despite Mike's part-time work, it seemed there was rarely a time for Michael to catch his son during the week, and even if Mike was home in the evening, Michael felt too weary to tackle what had become the overriding contentious issue in their home. Nina wasn't helping much with her continual nagging of both him and Mike.

Dark clouds began a slow drizzle, adding an extra layer of gloom to his mood. He took in the disarray of the backyard, including the old rambler rose and a rangy orange blossom bush against the back of the house. The former had three sad red roses hanging on; the other looked bedraggled. No matter their condition, they always reminded him of Emma. When they bought the house back in 1958, the realtor had told them the owner had planted them so his wife could have a bouquet each summer to mark their wedding anniversary, a date which just so happened to be within days of Emma and Michael's anniversary. But he had to keep such thoughts to himself. Nina had made him promise, first when they started dating and again when they got married, to never talk to her about Emma. He knew Nina, a teen at the time, had had a close attachment to Emma, viewing her as the sister she'd never had. Later, when he'd applied to have Emma declared dead so he and Nina could marry, Michael had failed to convince Nina to join him when he returned to see the counsellor who'd helped him cope with the loss of both a wife and unborn child. The small flutter in his chest was suggestive of troublesome symptoms he had experienced after Emma vanished. He quelled it deliberately by changing his focus to his plans to clean up the yard. He should have done so before but there was still time if the weather dried up a bit to get all the bushes and such, back and front, tidied up. Mike could help. It would do him good to contribute.

Tantalizing smells of chicken soup and Nina's smile met him as he opened the door. She gave him a side hug.

"Lunch will be ready in half an hour," she said, "and Mike says he's staying home today. He got up late and is showering now." Then she shook her head. "I wish he wouldn't stay out so late drinking with Norm. You've got to convince him to lose that dead-end job."

Michael's own smile faded. "Right," he said. "I'll be in the den."

♣

On her way to meet Cameron, Beth tried to keep her mind on driving and not get sidetracked by the key points she had looked over during the morning. The day had turned miserable by midday. Miserable was her description when it was steady rain with the cloud cover so low, she felt suffocated. She knew Cameron had latched onto the missing person case of Emma Mahoney. He had emphasized his uncle's dissatisfaction with the outcome of the investigation. However, despite what Edith had said in her journal about the locket and her not-so-veiled insinuation that Emma had been murdered, Beth was convinced evidence about the two other situations must not be ignored. Both could fit with someone having it in for Edith. They needed to investigate everything, not just choose the one that seemed the most likely and logical fit. Cameron would know that from his police experience—it was something she'd learned during her years in infection control when conducting outbreak investigations. Beth hoped she and Cameron could come to an agreement about how to proceed. Personal biases needed to be set aside.

Beth realized she had been thinking in plural ever since she'd had the first coffee meeting with Cameron. However, she had serious concerns about the wisdom of continuing an arrangement with him cast as a mentor rather than partner. Could she extricate herself? The bigger question was how could she? She'd been biting her lip all morning and now her tongue sought out the sore spot again.

Beth sighed. It didn't feel like Christmas at all. How could it with Edith gone? The annual second-Friday-in-December afternoon tea would not be happening in the Todd's cozy living room. There would be no teacups raised in toasts to the festive season with assorted neighbours who regularly attended to appreciate Edith's melting shortbread cookies and contribute their own specialties. Beth acknowledged the fact that it was a tough time of year for her ever since her darling Robbie had died. This year, she would allow herself extra kindnesses; she had learned over the years there was a way to give the sad feelings their due then move on to the joys of Christmas. It would be tougher to do this year with Edith's recent passing.

Beth turned into the Oakridge underground parkade, wondering if Cameron lived in the area. She found a spot close to one of the mall entrances and made her way toward the tea shop and café. It took her a moment to recognize Cameron who, at a glance, was an attractive fellow casually dressed in blue jeans and a leather jacket. She reminded herself not to forget how businesslike he'd been before and that she mustn't let her ideas get sidelined. He was outside the shop doorway waiting with briefcase in hand scanning the corridor. As he came toward her, Cameron's serious face relaxed with a welcoming smile, and Beth's shoulders relaxed too.

"Thanks for coming. I've been thinking we'll have more privacy in the food fair area. The noise there will cover our conversation better than here. You okay with that?" he said.

Beth nodded and walked along till they settled on a corner table that had just been vacated by a couple pushing a baby stroller. The surrounding tables were busy with chatter and laughter. It felt very much at odds with Beth's general mood considering the subject matter they were about to cover. She hoped she could tune it out.

"What'll you have?" said Cameron.

"It's okay, I'll look after myself," Beth said with a small smile to soften her refusal of his implied offer. "You go ahead while I get sorted here." She didn't wish to be obligated to him for anything other than his help. She stuffed a mauve knit scarf down an arm hole and draped her purple Gore-Tex jacket over the chair. Then she set a thin plastic folder of papers on the table.

"I've brought my files," she announced when he returned.

Finally, when they faced one another over their respective hot drinks—hot chocolate for Beth and a large coffee for Cameron—he launched into background on his uncle and what he'd said. Gradually, Beth lost her calm feeling and grew as taut as thinly stretched elastic. She wondered how she could effectively assert herself with this man whom she barely knew and whose career was rooted in authority and an expertise she could not match.

"My uncle called last evening to say he'd found his case notes,"

Cameron said. "I jotted down the key points and he's going to send some photocopies to me by expedited mail tomorrow."

"And I've photocopied some of my notes for you about the two other situations that could also have a bearing on the accident," said Beth quickly to counter any expectation that the cold case was all she was there to talk about. "But do go on," she added.

Cameron opened his mouth to say something then shut it and reached for his notebook.

"All right, there is one hard fact that proves the significance of the locket. Emma Mahoney was definitely seen wearing it the day she disappeared. It was your Mrs. Todd who gave a witness statement to that effect. On the day she disappeared, Emma had stopped and spoken to her about it being the anniversary of her parents' death."

"Well then," said Beth, "Edith was right to think Emma came to harm. What if someone knew Edith had the locket? In any case, I'm pretty sure she was trying to say she'd been run down on purpose. And so are her husband and daughter."

"You may be right," Cameron conceded. "Despite my thought that Mrs. Todd's accident is just that, there's a reasonable chance she may have met with foul play. Since the locket was found in the Todd's yard, it would seem a neighbour or someone who was a frequent visitor to the neighbourhood must have had something to do with Emma Mahoney's disappearance. I'll see what I can find out through a friend at the police station. I'm hoping I can be involved given that the cold case team is often overwhelmed. If not, I'll just have to let them do their job."

"Good," Beth said through clenched teeth. "I'm anxious to hear what *we* are going to do and when." She pulled some papers out of her folder. "Let me tell you what I know about the other two situations I believe need attention."

Cameron sat back and folded his arms. At least he hasn't covered his ears, Beth thought. Beth was sure Cameron had noted her sharp tone, but he almost seemed amused by her pushiness. He then offered a brief comment on not getting sidetracked by red herrings.

"Think of them as red flags, Mr. Ross. Will you give me the courtesy of listening to what I have to say?"

This was met with an unexpected grin. "It's okay, Beth. I'm listening. I'm on your side. Why don't you call me Cam?"

By the time Beth had finished her descriptions of the circumstances she believed needed scrutiny, Cameron had only nodded and said 'I see' throughout.

"So, what is it you see... Cameron?" *I can't call him Cam*, she thought. "What *I* see are two or more people who could easily have wanted Edith harmed. Who knows if the threatening letters are from the same person? Seems Harry Anders' nephew could be a nasty piece of work. He threatened Edith by phone—maybe he sent the letters. Or if Edith was close to naming the person involved in the break-ins and he knew it—"

"Well, they seem like long shots to me, but sure, you could be right," Cameron said.

He announced it was time to create a list of actions required to gather information in each area of concern. In the end, as Beth had expected, it was decided Cameron would focus on Emma Mahoney and leave the rest to her.

"It's best you be the one to interact within your neighbourhood on those other two situations, but," he hastened to add, "I guarantee I will be available to speak with you and go over whatever you learn and then we'll see . . ."

Yes indeed, Beth thought, *we'll see.*

❧

Nina's announcement that she would let the "boys" go off and do something together in the afternoon while she relaxed with the novel she was reading for her book club was met initially with silence. Each family member sat in their appointed places at the round glass table, which Nina had cajoled Michael into buying a few years ago to replace the old but perfectly good chrome and Arborite one. Michael missed the latter, which gave the kitchen a homier feel.

Michael broke the quiet. "Good idea, dear. What would you like to do, Mike?"

Nina answered. "I bet he'd like to go to Lee Valley Tools. Or maybe take in the flea market on Terminal?"

"Uh, dunno, Mom, I'm not feeling so great."

"Well," said Nina in her mother-knows-best voice, "it's a good idea not to drink so much and stay out so late. If—"

Michael interrupted what was likely to become a morality lesson. "Let's do Lee Valley, Mike, perhaps there's something there you'd like for a Christmas present."

Later, as they strolled through the aisles of the store, Michael felt the most comfortable he'd been in weeks around his son. Mike was relaxed, even if hungover, and was obviously enjoying their conversation about the various tools displayed, which led to some reminiscences about small projects they'd done in years past when Mike was younger. This opened the door for asking questions about his son's professed intent to become a mechanic at the Belmont autobody shop. Michael had already decided he would give his son a chance to explain what he wanted to do and not try to dissuade him at this point.

"The only thing is, Mike, you don't seem to be getting ahead with your plan. You're driving vans and making deliveries, or has that changed?"

Mike shook his head. "I'm still new, really. I don't want to rock the boat."

In the end, Michael convinced Mike to go talk with "the boss" because he'd been there well over six months. He had faint hope that Nina would support him in this encouragement. She stormed out of the living room and began making a lot of noise in the kitchen with dinner preparations. When she returned, she threw an ultimatum at them.

"I'm putting you both on my own six-month probation—no, four—after that, if you can't show me you are settled in a program and doing well, Mike, you and your dad will have to work out something else."

"Okay," the two men said in unison to her retreating back as they shared a look of solidarity.

Mike lowered his voice. "Dad, thanks, I'll let you know how I get on tomorrow evening."

❦

Norm Jervis was alone drinking at some pub on Main near Twenty-seventh—he couldn't remember its name—so he wouldn't run into anyone he knew. He was on his fourth beer, on his second helping of fries, and considering a switch to rum and coke for dessert. He grimaced at the thought because it quickly conjured up the scene last evening with Tara when they were sitting in a small café sharing a large slice of chocolate cake. That little bitch had told him it was over.

"It?" he'd said. "What, you quit work or you got fired?"

"No, I mean *we* are over. I'm sorry. Let me try to explain, Norm. We've been together almost three years but living here in Vancouver has shown me that you and I are not really compatible anymore. I feel I've been growing up, but you seem stuck.

Working with your cousin seems to be a dead-end, and you've changed since working with him. You seem more secretive for one thing. I'm not happy with how you talk or behave. It's best you move out as soon as you can. Maybe you can share with those guys you work with who live over near Victoria."

Kicking me out—effing hell. She's the one who changed, not me, Norm thought as he gulped the last mouthful of Molson and signaled to the bartender. *Stuck-up bitch. Better off without her. And best to get away from that nosy broad Langille.*

"Hey man, pour me a shot of whiskey." *Rum with coke is for sissies.*

SIXTEEN

Monday, November 29

While Mike Mahoney Jr. waited to speak with Richard Belmont in the small waiting area outside the office on the second floor of Belmont Motors, he studied the butter yellow walls surrounding him. They were covered with testaments to Rich's charitable activities. The food bank was just one of his pet causes. There were group pictures of him with notable people from fundraising events like a golf tournament for ALS and a cycling ride for cancer research. Rich looked like he fit right in with local celebrities. Handsome face, big smile with straight white teeth, and perfectly coifed hair. From behind the secretary's desk, a glossy poster that advertised a local Christmas gift donation event completed the feel-good ambiance of the room.

But Mike wasn't feeling so good. Norm had dragged him out drinking again last evening and his mom was mad. He cast his mind back to the trip into work, which began with a phone call just after seven, much to his mother's further annoyance. It was Norm saying they would be getting a ride with his pals who were renting a house west of Trout Lake. "Be out in the lane just after eight," he'd barked then hung up. This morning, Norm's face was pale, eyes as puffy as marshmallows. He'd grunted in response to Mike's "How're you doing?"

Mike had picked up on the fact that something was wrong on Saturday night when Norm insisted on going bar-hopping. Norm complained about anything and everything more than usual and didn't answer when Mike asked about Tara. *Must've had a fight,* Mike thought. Norm proceeded to get falling-down drunk, leaving Mike aggrieved that he had to shell out the full fare for a cab ride home. It wasn't fair. Norm made more money than he did, supposedly for previous experience. Mike knew it would be no use asking for Norm to pay his share. This irritation added to the discontent Mike felt about Norm's increasing bossiness.

As well as asking Rich to approve him entering a mechanics course with on-the-job experience there, Mike thought he may as well ask for a small raise. Surely six months into the job he deserved more. He was a good driver and never once missed a deadline. The guys who sometimes came along to help speed up the deliveries thought he was good. His thoughts were interrupted when one of these men and a couple unknown to him came roaring along Nanaimo in a souped-up green Oldsmobile Cutlass, and swerved to the curbside at the bus stop to pick him and Norm up. Jimmy, the driver, one of the mechanics, had gestured Norm into the front passenger seat. Mike had to squeeze in back with the two rough-looking fellows. With the CD player blaring The Band album *Rock of Ages* all the way to work, a few nods were all the communication there was. *Never did get those guys' names,* he thought. He hadn't noticed them before and was wondering what work they did when the office door opened.

With a side jerk of his head, Richard Belmont motioned Mike inside. Rich's face was passive, stern even. Mike wondered if he'd pressed too hard for a private meeting. Rich went to sit behind his maple wood desk pointing Mike to the chair in front. He was thinking Rich didn't look as approachable as in his photos. There was no sign of the broad smile plastered over the walls outside.

❦

"What were you doing in there?" Norm said, scowling, as Mike was leaving Rich's office reception area.

Without waiting for an answer, he stabbed his pointer finger at Mike's chest. "You and Jeff have deliveries on the North Shore."

"I know, but we're not leaving for another half hour. There wasn't a chance to talk with you on the way here. I promised my dad I would ask Rich about getting my mechanic's certificate and apprenticing in the shop. You said you were thinking about doing the same."

"Nah, I've changed my mind. Rich is going to promote me to assistant manager of a warehouse he has out near Steveston. Part time to start so it'll make full time hours for me. I'll fill you in later at lunchtime. You better get going. You can help them load up."

Mike nodded and walked away.

When Mike was out of sight, Norm went to the reception desk, murmured that he'd like to see his cousin, and was buzzed in.

Rich was at the table by his second-floor window, pouring a coffee. In the distance, the lower slopes of the North Shore mountains were beginning to emerge, the foggy clouds clearing.

"What's up, Legs? Want a java?"

"Just wanted to ask about Mike. He told me about taking mechanics training and apprenticing in the shop. You good with that? It's going to put him too close to the action."

"Yes," Rich said, smoothing his hair back, "you're right.

Didn't want to say no right away. We've got to keep him around for now. I'm not exactly sure what's going on in his head. I think he'll go for being a salesman. Best that way. That business is legit. Mostly. You know what I mean." Rich winked.

Norm laughed. "Yeah, except for the special options for select customers."

Rich grinned. "Anyway, I wanted it to look like I'd considered his request. I'll tell him we have enough apprentices right now and offer sales. He can earn more money there. He's likely to be good in sales—he comes across as a nice guy, and I know from his resume he's smart. Told him I'd let him know my decision before he goes home."

"Oh, he gave you a resume, did he? You never asked for mine," Norm joked.

"Legs, you already know. Trust in family is everything." Rich grasped Norm's right elbow and shook his hand firmly.

❦

A few hours later, Norm sat opposite Mike in an empty office in the main building eating lunch. Mike munched on some celery sticks smeared with peanut butter, part of the lunch his mother had made. It made him feel like he was still at school, and he envied Norm's juicy double patty hamburger he'd apparently taken time to pick up at a local A&W. Mike wondered how much work Norm did for his larger paycheque—amount unknown.

"So, how'd the delivery go?" Norm said.

"Like clockwork," Mike said, and decided to ask, "What have you been doing?"

"Had a meeting with Rich about the warehouse position he wants me to take on. He says I can move up to manager if I do well." Mike was chewing so he nodded and avoided offering insincere encouragement. Norm continued, "Pay is better, which is good because I've decided to split with Tara and find a place of my own. I know you don't want to live at home anymore. Let's get an apartment together."

Mike avoided this unappealing suggestion. His mother was already agitated about his work; he didn't want to aggravate her further now. He changed the topic.

"I thought something was wrong. What happened with Tara?"

"It's no big deal, she's mad but she'll get over it." Norm swerved back to the main thing on his mind. "So, what about it, it would be cool to get our own place or maybe we could share that house Jimmy and the guys rent. I'm going to ask them. I've been hanging out over there a fair bit."

"Can't afford to leave home 'til I have more income. Sorry."

"Don't give up so easy man, that'll change. What about car sales? There's good money in that. You could share an office like this. You could use some of that knack you say you have with numbers and even move up to management. That would bring in some dough. Anyway, you need to check in with Rich's secretary. He wants to see you again."

There's that finger again. "I already know that," Mike said quietly.

❦

Beth walked into her multiuse back room to continue planning the steps in her investigations. A grey morning had dawned with none of the previous day's rain in sight, and even now, there was a brightening that heralded some sunshine to come. She glanced across her backyard and saw Dennis's old truck parked alongside Sofia and Gino's black Taurus in their carport. Dennis was likely starting the basement shelving job Gino wanted done. When Beth had reviewed her Sunday conversation with Cameron the evening before, she had decided that Dennis Greene and June

Ishida would likely be comfortable helping her. She had mulled over calling June but was loathe to break into June's evening knowing how early she arose to be at the lab in the morning. Instead, Beth had sent an email asking when a good time to have a chat would be.

Thinking of Dennis again, Beth figured since Cameron seemed disinclined at the moment to involve himself much with anything other than the Emma Mahoney case, the handyman-gardener with his familiar neighbourhood presence would be an ideal 'on-site' person, as it were. He could keep watch for anyone out of place and pick up information in casual conversation. Yet to be decided was what and how much to tell Dennis if he agreed. As far as June went, she would be a good sounding board and her objectivity would be a bonus.

The phone's ring startled Beth as she reached for it to leave a message at Dennis's home.

"Guess what, Beth, I just had to tell you. I saw Harry at church yesterday," Sofia said. "He's delighted with your help. That nephew was with him for the first time. Mother Mary, never thought, from what Edith had said, I'd see the day."

"Maybe he was making it up to Harry because he didn't bring him to the funeral," Beth said.

"That's probably it. Harry said you guys met last week."

"Frank was there when I arrived—seemed okay, I guess. Can't say I liked him, but I'm influenced by Edith's opinion. I'll do my best to keep tabs on Harry like she did."

"Don't forget, Edith had a really nasty call from Frank. Just be careful," Sofia urged.

"Don't worry, I will. By the way, can you ask Dennis to call me tonight?"

"Sure. I have something else to tell you before I get busy with some baking. I'm going to have Edith's traditional Christmas tea party here at my place," said Sofia.

"That's so good of you, we should really try to carry on what she started," said Beth feeling her eyes prickle and her throat close up. She grabbed a tissue to blow her nose.

"I'm glad to do it," said Sofia. "Planning it is making me feel happier. I'm not as weepy. I think of Edith cheering me on. Maybe Saturday afternoon, December eleventh?"

After the call, Beth turned to her files to re-order her thoughts, opening her workbook to a fresh page. She dated it and titled it "Who might hurt Edith on purpose?" Then she wrote her list of suspects.

1. Whoever kidnapped/murdered Emma Mahoney

2. The criminals who are thieving in our area—local person(s)?

3. Frank Nolan, who is after his uncle's money

Beth sighed, thinking that although number one could be the best bet it meant she was feeling largely excluded from working to find answers without much help from Cameron. Stop grumbling she told herself. *You're the amateur, but you still have lots to offer.*

She squared her shoulders, pushed herself back into the office chair, took a lined loose sheet of paper and began to write.

Timeline

Oct 15/99	Ken Todd has heart bypass surgery; leg harvest site infection leads to prolonged stay prompting Edith's more regular visits to VGH
Oct 18	Postal date stamp on envelope of a mailed unsigned poison pen letter

Oct 21- Nov 2	Edith, having time to spare, journals and logs her 'findings' as she expands her activities (e.g. she spied on Frank and drove to see where Norm and Mike work)
Oct 24	Frank Nolan phones; threatens Edith over her contact with Harry
Oct 28	Dennis finds Emma Mahoney's locket
Oct 29	B&E at Edith's (neighbourhood BW potluck evening)

She was forced to stop abruptly when a furry body launched itself onto the desk, scattering some papers. "No, no, no. Monty, get down, right now." She plopped him unceremoniously on the floor, tidied up and continued.

Oct 31	Threatening letter left on doorstep (Edith penciled date on envelope)
Nov 3	Edith calls me to say she has something very important to discuss with me
Nov 4	Hit-and-run "accident" resulting in Edith's death on Nov 6

All at once, Beth was crying. She fumbled for a tissue in her pocket, found none and quickly brought the arm of her long sleeve tee to wipe her wet eyes. Having written the bald words that reduced Edith's absence to an entry on a page, she now felt hollow. She was struck with the same feelings as when she'd tried to convince the police about her theory that Edith was targeted. She fought off the combination of sorrow, anger, and helplessness. It took a few hours and a walk to turn her mood around.

Don't give in, she repeated like a mantra, *you have help*.

In the afternoon, Beth dialed Harry and they decided to get together the next day. In the meantime, she had some reading to do before she thought any more about *her* two investigations. There were two library books she hadn't opened yet on detective techniques and observation skills. By the time she had skimmed through both books and taken some notes, played with Monty, taken a short walk, talked to Jenny about the Christmas tea plus done some light housekeeping, the afternoon had slid into her evening mealtime.

The phone conveniently rang before she watched the five o'clock news.

"Sorry, I was busy all day. Sofia says you might need some work done?" said Dennis.

"No, no, I want your help with something else. It has to do with Edith, ah—and Block Watch—something you'll need to keep to yourself for now."

"Oh… I don't know… what do you mean?"

"It's a little tricky. Edith was checking on a couple of people she suspected of being up to no good. She talked about it recently. She had more time on her hands with Ken in hospital, so she even tailed someone."

"Gosh, I don't like the sound of that," said Dennis. "Who was she watching?"

"One of them was a neighbour here; I won't name names. But she saw the person in or near more than one backyard looking around. The other person is someone related to a former neighbour. I've been wondering if there's a connection between either of them and the threatening letters Edith received." Beth stopped herself from speaking of the accident or the locket.

"What I thought was you might get in the habit of scanning around now and again whenever you're working around our block. Maybe you'll pick up on something that makes you wonder and you could tell me."

"Sure. I can do that when I'm around. Now that you've told me this, I wonder if the break-in at Edith and Ken's was on purpose."

"That's crossed my mind," said Beth. "How about you drop in sometime for coffee and we can have a chat? Are you working around here again this week?"

"Yeah, got something to do at Alan's, maybe Thursday. I'll be in touch."

Beth felt a welcome ease after her exchange with Dennis. She'd been able to keep it simple and stick to facts without entering into too much detail. When she and Dennis spoke face to face, she would judge what more to tell him.

Then a short call from Cameron set her scheming as to how to fulfill his brief request. Where did Michael Mahoney eat lunch, he'd asked. He wanted to look him over.

❦

It was after six by the time Mike Mahoney trudged up the lane. Norm and the guys had dropped him off on Nanaimo and were headed to a pub somewhere. Mike was just interested in food and sleep despite feeling happy about how his day had turned out.

It seemed life was taking a better direction than when he'd started out in the morning. Instead of being a student apprentice who would have to continue to stay at home until his apprenticeship finished, he'd been offered an opportunity to get on a faster track to independence. *And that doesn't mean living with Norm*, he thought. On Friday, he would start his new position as a salesman by shadowing Andy Fletcher, the top performer in Rich's business. Mike was seized with anxiety about telling his mother about the change in plans—it seemed he could scarcely breathe. Then he saw the Audi parked by the back fence. He hesitated at the back door, squared his shoulders, and entered. Only his dad was in the kitchen, stirring something on the stove. *Smells good.*

"Where's Mom?"

"Just getting changed—splashed some spaghetti sauce on her sweater. So how did it go, Son?"

By the time Nina returned, Mike had told his tale. His father was supportive as he expected. His mother was not.

"I don't like this at all, Mike. You're playing around. You're not going to get ahead this way. Okay, try it out. But your dad will agree with me—you must keep looking for something else. Right?"

Mike and Michael simply nodded.

♣

In the den of his modest home in Marpole, Cameron surveyed the broad plan for his inquiry into Emma Mahoney's disappearance. With the tangible evidence of the locket she was wearing on the last day she was seen, he had no doubt she had been the victim of foul play. Swapping shifts with a senior staff member who wanted a three-day weekend allowed him a leisurely start to his work week and time to do some errands. One of those was to pick up a large art pad. He used it for a clustering technique he'd found helpful in the past for brainstorming means, motive, and opportunity.

A blue file card with Emma's name in bold black capitals was fixed with painters' tape more or less in the middle of a wall of his home office. Areas of interest—each a page heading—radiated out from the centre: Victim Background/Habits; Last Seen; Husband Background/Habits; Family/friends; Neighbours;

Evidence; Theories/Suspects.

In the late afternoon, a courier had delivered a thin brown paper envelope. When he'd called his uncle, Cameron hadn't let on that the sparse contents had disappointed him. He'd resisted the urge to talk over the case with John and simply conveyed his intention to reach out to his former colleague Ron about his desire to participate in the cold case inquiry when it was reopened. It was fortunate his friend had risen to the higher ranks of the Vancouver police force and was well positioned to advise Cameron about whether there was a chance to help with the case.

Ron Poole had been his partner during the eight-year period Cameron had worked in the violent crimes unit. While other working relationships had faltered with Cameron's exit and switch to public sector security, the strong connection with Ron had not been lost.

"Hi, what's up?" said Ron answering Cameron's phone call. "You're not cancelling our racquetball game on Friday, are you?"

"Nope, this is business," said Cameron, "a case I'm sort of looking into . . ."

"Oh, trouble at the gallery?"

"No, it's an old case my uncle worked on eons ago," Cameron said. Then realizing the conversation would go far better in person, he followed up with, "Can you meet me before or after your shift tomorrow?"

SEVENTEEN

Tuesday, November 30

Cameron waited for Ron in the Starbucks at Cambie and West Eighth. Tucked in his pocket was a small notebook with information from his uncle's files. He looked it over discreetly as his foot tapped in nervous impatience. He'd found a table in a quiet corner, but it felt odd being there. It took him back to the times he would drop in before or after a shift when he'd worked out of the Cambie location years past. He'd given up the habit when he was suspended and put on desk duty. It wasn't surprising that many of his fellow officers viewed him with suspicion at that time. Not Ron though. Ron had stuck by him, having seen with his own eyes the naked disbelief in Cameron's eyes when he'd finally realized the wanted poster was not a hoax. His thoughts wandered through flashes of old memories as he sipped his latte. It was like seeing a movie trailer for a film he never wanted to watch again. A hand on his shoulder drew him away from his brooding.

"Same again?" Ron asked. Cameron was surprised to see his mug was empty.

Ron returned with two steaming drinks then lowered himself into the chair where he'd hung his jacket. "Good to see you. So, what about this old case you spoke of?"

"It's a missing person from 1960 that Uncle John worked on. He always felt badly that nothing came of the investigation. Emma Mahoney, a young wife, disappeared into thin air. There were circumstances that made it seem likely she'd run away or somehow killed herself. By coincidence, I've learned a piece of evidence has turned up that proves she met with foul play. As it happens, I'm well placed to do a little digging."

"Interesting. Tell me more," said Ron.

❧

Working out how to get what she wanted without tipping her hand was a drain, Beth moaned to herself. Her mind was sluggish. A half-finished crossword lay in front of her. She'd slept past her usual wake-up time because the radio music alarm had not been set. However, Monty hadn't let her rest long with breakfast on his mind. She arose half-heartedly to the chilly morning to shut him up.

Cameron's request niggled at her as she had another coffee with a heaping spoon of hot chocolate mix stirred in this time. She munched on raisin bread toast topped with peanut butter. Some wedges of apple offset Beth's slight guilt that she'd also had two squares of dark chocolate. Back to her problem—since Michael wasn't someone she saw often, the only way to find out where he went for lunch was to ask Nina. But that would have to wait until after her visit with Harry, she realized after looking at the clock. She promptly got herself ready and headed for the door.

❧

Beth walked north from Harry's seniors' residence to Safeway for some bread and bananas before heading home through John

Hendry Park. The Christmas cards she'd done for Harry were in the mail and though there were no more left to do, Beth had promised to keep in regular touch when Harry asked her. Had he not asked, she would have suggested it. Off to her right, a black lab had escaped its owner and dashed into the cold water of Trout Lake. Beth was barely aware of the man's exasperated pleas for his dog to return to him. She reflected on her luck that she'd been there when Harry's niece called from California. He had put her on the phone to introduce them then arranged for Pat to call him later.

Harry was very chatty afterward, obviously proud of his clever niece, who, he'd confided, felt like a daughter to him.

"She's so good with figures and the technology around these days. The Royal Bank is leading the way in online banking and investment services, she says. Still, perhaps now that she's so far away, I'd better transfer things over to Frank. He's coming to show me some papers later."

Beth didn't like the sound of that, and she'd done what she usually avoided—gave unsolicited advice. "Your niece will be home for Christmas; you should wait to talk it over with her then. It's only a couple of weeks till she's here. Sounds like she has it all under control and wants to continue to help you. Face to face will be much better for discussion than on the phone. If you don't have to change, it's likely best not to given how satisfied you are with your arrangement with Pat."

Harry had nodded. "Yes, I think you're right. I owe it to Pat to wait till she's here."

Beth was nearly exiting the park when a short, hard bark from an angry voice sounded in her ear. "You. Miss Langille."

Beth's breath caught. Her hand flew to her throat. *Miss Langille*? She turned to find Frank Nolan, his face contorted like an ugly gargoyle.

"What is it?" she managed, recovering from the unexpected startle.

"Stop putting ideas in my uncle's head," Frank said, his voice getting louder with each word. "He's a weak old man. He doesn't need another interfering woman messing up his head."

"I don't know what you mean."

"Sure you do. You're just like that Mrs. Todd—a meddling do-gooder," he shouted. He grabbed her right upper arm and squeezed tighter as Beth, now frightened, tried to pull away.

"Ow. Let go. You're hurting me."

"I'll hurt you more if you interfere again. Just you stay away from my uncle." Suddenly, his hand lost its grip when an umbrella handle struck his shoulder with force.

"What the hell?" Frank turned to see who had hit him.

"Hello Beth," said Nina Mahoney coolly. "What's going on here?" She still held her umbrella like a club.

"This is Frank, Nina, Harry Anders' nephew, he was just leaving," Beth said and stepped to Nina's side. "I'll walk home with you."

Frank stared after them, fuming and rubbing his shoulder.

"What on earth made him so angry with you?" Nina asked as they made their way east headed for the fateful crosswalk.

"Frank isn't happy I've been helping Harry the way Edith did—thinks I'm interfering. Maybe you didn't know he threatened Edith on the phone," Beth said. She thanked Nina and guided their conversation to Christmas, which felt far better than dwelling on Frank. She'd forgotten all about Michael.

In the evening, Beth, freshly shaken each time her mind replayed the incident, thanked the heavens yet again that Nina, an unlikely saviour to her mind, had come along when she did. Beth realized she had a good reason to call and suggest meeting for tea somewhere nice. It could double as a thanks and a way to find out about Michael's lunch routine. Any hesitation that Nina voiced upon hearing the offer dissolved when Beth mentioned the book club.

❦

Thursday, December 2

Tuesday's scare had Beth's motivation at a low ebb. But it returned with a midmorning call from Dennis. He was close to finishing up at Alan Whitman's.

"Can I drop in now? Sorry it's short notice. Slipped my mind. Half an hour okay?"

Beth quickly changed from her lounging clothes, tidied up the kitchen, and set about making fresh coffee while thinking, once again, about how to expand on what she'd already told Dennis.

By the time he knocked at the backdoor, Beth was still unsure about how much more to tell him, recognizing that the more people she told, the more likely it was her intentions would get around. And if she was right about someone harbouring ill will in any of the scenarios she imagined, then she or anyone she took into her confidence could be at risk. *Still, Dennis can handle himself.*

"NO," Dennis exclaimed when Beth told him about being grabbed by Frank Nolan and explained his relationship to Harry Anders, who was formerly from the neighbourhood and a blind parishioner Edith had helped out.

"He threatened Edith on the phone too," said Beth.

"So, you think he could be the poison pen writer too? What about the break-in?"

"I can't see him doing that," Beth said, "but a call and a letter? Sure. Now he seems to have me in his sights."

"Okay, I can help when I'm here. Remember, I'm not regularly around. You must have asked your neighbours—there are lots of them involved in Block Watch from what I saw at the October potluck."

Beth said a quick, "You're right," and gave Dennis a description of Frank Nolan. "I have a feeling he should stick out like a sore thumb. I've only seen him in a suit, smartly dressed. Fancies himself a hotshot businessman, Edith said once."

"Have you heard anything more about the break-in?" Dennis asked. "What was taken? I know Edith said her main jewellery was safe—which reminds me, Alan was telling me you have that locket I found. It's not Edith's?"

"Ken and Susan are quite sure it isn't, so they asked me to see if any neighbours lost it. Haven't had a chance to ask anyone else."

Beth guided their chat away from the locket by introducing the neighbourhood problem with property theft. Once she had talked about what to look out for—describing what Norm had been wearing on Saturday—they sat companionably sharing their sadness over the loss of Edith. Beth decided not to speak of Emma Mahoney's disappearance.

Afterward, she was on edge having learned that Alan was talking about the locket. *Why wouldn't he?* she admonished herself, *I didn't tell him to keep it secret.* This was something she needed to share with Cameron. What should they do? The locket *was* police business after all. She also knew that technically speaking, it was the property of Michael Mahoney.

❦

For her date with Nina, Beth suggested the Secret Garden Tea Company in Kerrisdale, which she knew would be a sure draw. Nina liked to frequent the shopping area near there, and at a Block Watch get-together one time, she had boasted about having met at the teashop to have high tea with her well-off friend.

The day was pleasantly mild, another gift from the south Pacific. People smiled in passing and chickadees twittered in the bare branches overhead as she walked a couple blocks from the residential parking spot she'd found. Beth arrived early to pick out as private a corner as possible. To avoid driving together, Beth had invented a podiatry appointment—not an entire fabrication, just so happened it was a couple weeks away.

She didn't have to wait long. Nina arrived exactly on time and settled into the paisley upholstered chair opposite Beth after removing and arranging a light turquoise wool jacket with care. They each chose a tea from the menu and agreed to share a plate of small pastries, during which Nina dispensed with the pleasantries and got straight to her pet subject. With an expansive hand gesture, she remarked how gratified she was that Beth was going to seriously consider the benefits of joining "her group."

At the outset, Beth knew she'd have to be careful how she steered the conversation. *Nina is not dumb.* But once they had settled into sipping and nibbling and hashed over the benefits of a book club, the subject of dining out seemed to come up quite naturally. She offered comments on several places she had tried.

"What about you and Michael? Have you any favourite places you go?"

"Absolutely. Michael takes me to Le Crocodile two or three times a year and we have a night out every few weeks at places like Chianti and Banana Leaf—and actually, even White Spot. Dad often took Mom and me to the drive-in on Granville— that was so much fun."

Beth took this opportunity to ask about eating downtown and manufactured a couple social lunches that were in the planning stages.

"I suppose Michael must eat out downtown sometimes. I'd

like to get some recommendations," she said to Nina.

Somehow, in the end, Beth managed to remain uncommitted to the book club without miffing Nina. It had been a demanding hour and a half for just one piece of information. Still, it was satisfying to have thanked Nina in a way that was appreciated.

"Thanks for a lovely time. I'll give you a call about our first January meeting," Nina reminded Beth when they said their goodbyes.

Too bad, Beth thought, *it might be worthwhile trying out Nina's book club, but once the locket is common knowledge, I don't think she'll be calling me.*

Beth was feeling contented that evening after returning home. She spoke with Cameron to tell him she'd got the name of the place where Michael often took his lunch.

"Good, I'll pop in on my lunch break tomorrow to see if he's there. And thanks for the potluck party photo with him in it that you emailed to me."

"No problem. Listen, there's a neighbour, Alan, who I got to ask about the locket recently because Edith's family wanted me to try to find out who it belonged to—"

"What? You didn't mention that on Sunday. What are you playing at? You knew it was Emma Mahoney's," Cameron said in an accusatory tone.

Beth jumped into an icy sea of silence. "Well, I started to, but you interrupted me. Then I forgot." *Partly true.* "It was a way to talk to this neighbour, Alan. I was really just trying to get some information about his niece's boyfriend Norm, the one Edith was very suspicious of."

"Why didn't the Todd's know who it belonged to? What did they say?"

"Since Alan's late wife's name was Evie, they thought it could be hers, though Emma's name was mentioned. Evie and Edith were very close. Only I knew it had to be Emma's. You said yourself you're thinking it might be the reason someone wanted Edith silenced. I thought the same thing then and decided it would be better for me to have it so they'd be safe," Beth said, now sounding as testy as she felt. Her guilt over the hidden truth of how she knew the locket was Emma Mahoney's had morphed into righteous indignation.

"That doesn't make sense," Cameron said bluntly. "The word *is* getting out and *you're* the one who will be in danger. Anyway, its coincidence the locket was found at all. We have to check with the gardener to find out if anyone might have seen him find it. Let's leave that for a moment," he said to allow Beth to settle. He was not immune to the strain in her voice.

"Here's the latest from my police contact. Ron, a former partner of mine, steered me to the correct division, and yesterday, I was able to meet with the head. I was given a deadline of two weeks to do some investigating then pass over any findings to a Detective McNabb, who I also met. He'll be lead detective on the Mahoney case. He'll also liaise with the hit-and-run team. I'm to have permission to look at the old case files at the station Monday but he expects the locket to be turned in as soon as possible. You and I need to meet for me to get it from you."

Beth let out a long breath. "What do I do if Michael Mahoney learns the locket has been found? What do I say?"

"You'll have to come clean. You've misled the Todd family. Tell them right away. Call tonight. Keep it simple. Tell them your suspicions about Mrs. Todd's accident, what she said to you, and how it resulted in you keeping your knowledge about the locket quiet. You can say the police have it. Given that they'll remember Emma Mahoney's disappearance, they should understand. And Michael Mahoney? Leave it for now. I think you'd have heard from him if he knew about it already."

"I'm concerned about his reaction," Beth said.

"Whenever you speak with him, just tell him the same thing you tell the Todds—that you decided you should turn it over to the police investigating the accident when you realized it belonged to a missing person and that there could be a connection to Mrs. Todd's death. You need to keep me out of it. I'll tell Detective McNabb so he can be ready for a call from Michael Mahoney."

Beth sighed. "I was only doing what I thought was best—Sergeant James didn't take me seriously. And there's still the possibility there's a different motive for Edith's accident."

"Yes, I understand you believe that," Cameron said quietly. "Just let me have a little time to get hold of McNabb tomorrow morning. I'll confirm for you that he knows as soon as I can—before you contact Michael Mahoney. Now, are you free for us to meet tomorrow?"

Beth scribbled down the time she and Cameron would meet the next day and took a few deep breaths before picking up the phone to call Susan Todd's number. As she listened to the ringing of the phone on the other end, she hoped that Susan might be busy and Ken would pick up. She felt she'd get a kinder reception from him. But it was Susan who said hello.

EIGHTEEN

Friday, December 3

Mike Mahoney admired himself in front of the staff washroom mirror. The crisp greyish blue shirt paired with one of his dad's ties made him feel professional. They went well with the new dark grey pants his mom gave him. He was wearing the navy sports jacket he'd worn to first meet Rich, having refused his mom's urging to put on the new jacket that had appeared in his closet along with the pants. He ran a comb through his newly cut hair and stepped out to start his orientation.

By midday, Mike considered Andy Fletcher a pompous stuffed shirt. It was probably compensation for his wide waist and lack of height, Mike told Norm as they sat eating their respective lunches. There was a lot to catch up on. Three days previous, while Tara was at work, Norm had moved out. He complained that with his and Mike's different work times, it wouldn't be as easy to get together anymore. *Maybe not such a bad thing,* Mike thought and carried on talking about his morning experience.

"Maaann, Andy's know-it-all attitude's a drag but he's on the ball. I've no problem understanding the figuring and financing arrangements required. Over the weekend, I picked up an old paperback called *How to Sell Anything to Anyone.* This guy Joe Girard sold 13,001 cars in fifteen years and made it into the Guinness World Records book back in 1973 for selling 1,425 cars that year. Really inspiring. My salary is much better. And there's commission for actual sales."

"Good for you," said Norm, poker faced.

"How about you? Tell me about the house, and when do you start your new position?" said Mike.

"The guys have the three upper floor rooms, so I'm stuck in a room in the corner of the basement. Don't worry, I can ride it out till you and I get a place to share. Rich isn't moving me until the end of January and my pay won't increase till then. Bummer." Norm pouted.

For the next five minutes, he ranted about stupid broads, Tara and Beth being the focus of his anger. Mike, glad no one was in the room, grew more uncomfortable as the time passed though was pleased the topic of apartment sharing had been completely overtaken by Norm's bitterness toward the two women. Mike pulled back his sleeve to check the time and announced he was sorry but had to go.

"Yup, mustn't make a bad impression on your first day, Mikey." Norm scowled and scratched his nose.

❧

Beth didn't know how many times she'd replayed the conversation she'd had with Susan Todd the previous evening before she and Monty had gone to bed. It was a tense exchange during which Beth stumbled a number of times, searching for what seemed like the right balance between expressing regret and explaining the logic of her decision to withhold information based on her fear that Edith's accident was deliberate.

At last, Susan seemed to accept Beth's apology, saying she

would tell her father. Beth's sense of guilt remained for she knew full well her confession still included a falsehood. It was one that would always exist since she had no intention of ever telling anyone that she had been reading Edith's journal. She could live with it, completely convinced it was done with Edith's consent.

By noon Beth was still waiting impatiently for Cameron to give her the go-ahead to call Michael Mahoney. She had flitted from room to room at first before settling to change her bed and launder some sheets and towels. At least it felt like work was being done as washing machine noises filled the house.

It wasn't till early afternoon that Cameron called and assured her everything was now in place for when Michael Mahoney called the police. This would be a more difficult call for Beth. She had the number of the consortium ready on a pad by the phone. Over several years, Beth had noted Michael's car home at varying early times on Friday afternoons. She hoped she'd be lucky catching him while he was at work. She went out to her garbage can to toss in a bag of vacuum dust and stepped out a few paces to scan the lane. No Audi.

Beth identified herself to the secretary and waited on hold, nibbling at a hangnail.

"I'm putting you through now to Mr. Mahoney."

"Hello Beth—everything okay?" Michael said in a quizzical voice.

Beth pulled out the small note page where she'd jotted down what Cameron advised her to say. She'd practiced a little before calling Susan but it hadn't helped a lot. She now faltered about how to open the subject—at least Susan had already known there was a locket.

"Sort of. I need to tell you about some jewellery that Dennis found when he was digging out that garden bed for Edith. He had given it to her, and she was wearing it the day she was hit—"

"What's that got to do with me?" Michael interrupted, impatient. "Can't this wait till this evening? I'm in the middle of finishing up a few things so I can get away early."

"No, it can't wait Michael." Beth blurted out the rest. "It's your first wife's locket. Edith was wearing it when she had the accident and the police have it now."

❧

Nina Mahoney heard a car in the lane and saw Michael pulling in. She smiled at the prospect of time to talk about her gift ideas for Mike before her son got home. She unlocked the door, then, hugging her arms to her body, stepped out to wait in the dry cold. She was alarmed to see her husband's faltering steps and drooping shoulders. He looked at her blankly.

"What's wrong? Is it Mike, has something happened to my Mikey?"

"No, it hasn't. Get inside, then we'll talk about it."

But Nina found he wasn't ready to talk and no amount of coaxing could get him to speak about whatever 'it' was until he'd had some quiet time. Michael got a Granville Island Brewing lager from the fridge, and without taking his jacket off, went straight to the den and closed the door.

Nina sat stiff as a cardboard cut-out on a kitchen chair, seeing nothing and fearing what 'it' might be. *Did Michael lose his job? He was at the doctor last week for a checkup. Has he found out he has cancer?*

After about thirty minutes, Nina heard the den door open. She went to the sink to run the cold water.

"Feel like some tea?" she said. "We'd better talk before Mike gets home."

"No tea," said Michael, "but yes, I need to talk with you. It's about Emma. Come to the living room."

Nina paled, her thoughts freefalling into the past. She followed Michael mutely and resumed her rigid posture balanced on the edge of a velvet wingback chair.

"No, come over here," said Michael. He patted the spot beside him on the sofa. He took her hand and began to tell her what 'it' was.

"Beth called me. Dennis found Emma's locket in the Todd's yard at the end of October and gave it to Edith."

Nina's face slowly suffused with colour as anger replaced dread. "What? How does Beth even know it was Emma's? Beth wasn't living here then."

"I'm not sure, but Susan passed it on to Beth to give to the police. It's Emma's alright. Beth described it. It has Emma's maiden name initials and pictures of her parents inside."

"Sounds fishy to me," Nina burst out. "Beth is overstepping like Edith did. Edith was spying on us all in the name of Block Watch. She saw burglars and criminals on every corner. And Beth didn't say anything to me yesterday. She's a retiree now with too much time on her hands so she's after attention. She has one hell of a nerve not giving you the locket. If it's even Emma's at all."

"Calm down, honey. I said it is," Michael said, stressing the words. "The description is accurate. I'll call the police tomorrow. I want to see it, and anyway, they'll need positive identification. This is really difficult for me, Nina. Please, I'll need your support." Michael pressed her hand more tightly.

Nina leaned into him and put her head on his shoulder. "You have it, Michael; I'll always be here for you."

❦

Seated opposite Cameron in a Chinese noodle house near Main and Fifteenth, Beth was feeling somewhat uncomfortable meeting over dinner out. It had seemed rather unprofessional and more like a date at first when she'd entered and Cameron had hailed her to a booth at the back. However, his brusque manner when they each ordered a combination plate and he stated it would be separate bills erased any sense of familiarity. *Good.* She had barely relaxed when Cameron's reproach over her handling of the locket set her on edge again.

"I presume you remembered to bring it."

"Of course I have," she said stiffly.

"Let's have a look at it then."

Beth placed a small white box in Cameron's outstretched hand. The reverence with which he slowly unfolded the pale pink tissue paper softened her mood. He gently pried the locket open to look at the photos.

"I took black and white pictures with my Nikon," Beth said. "And I've developed them. I can give you some copies if you like."

"Ah," Cameron said, with a fleeting smile, "a woman of hidden talents. Black and white is good. I need to turn in the locket right away. It would be good to have photos for my DIY evidence wall. How did it go with Mr. Mahoney?"

Beth proceeded to describe the uncomfortable interaction she'd had with Michael, speculating that she may have lost any friendship with the Mahoney's forever. This triggered her memory of the scary encounter with Frank on Tuesday and Nina's rescue of her. Her revelation completely ruined the air of goodwill that had arisen. Beth's face clouded over as Cameron gave her a lecture about putting herself in harm's way, reminiscent of Constable Argento's words to Edith. Except the constable had stressed his concern respectfully and kindly, Edith said.

Beth defended her actions. "My sole intention is keeping

Harry out of harm's way as you say."

It was good luck the food arrived before she launched a further rebuttal. Beth avoided Cameron's eyes and concentrated on her chicken with broccoli and mushrooms that came with rice and a choice of soup. They ate in silence for a time.

"I hope you're liking your meal," Cameron said. "A buddy introduced me to this place years ago, and I drop in here at least once a month."

Beth agreed it was good and they continued with small talk in which weather featured heavily. Finally, they were left sipping on tea from a fresh pot delivered by the restaurant owner. He had greeted Cameron warmly while casting an inquisitive glance in Beth's direction. It was satisfying to be introduced as a colleague here to talk a little business. Mr. Wang gave a brief nod and left.

"So, you say the police are allowing us two weeks to explore Emma's case," Beth said. "What do you propose? I don't want to lose sight of the other two situations even though it seems clear Emma was abducted or murdered and that's a compelling reason for someone to target Edith. Maybe they noticed she was wearing the locket. She'd had it about a week."

"Could be. So, let's concentrate on Emma for the next few days. First, I have to do a thorough read of the cold case file. I'm hoping I might be able to do that as soon as I turn in the locket. There'll be some re-interviewing to do. I'm betting that most people will be only too glad to help when they know the circumstances. I'll find out tomorrow how Detective McNabb wants me to introduce myself."

"What about me?" Beth said, purposely putting him on the spot.

"Yes, generally I'll want you along. Even if you don't know some of the folks from back then, you're from the neighbourhood, you know enough, and your presence will make me seem less intimidating. I'm aware of how I might come across at times."

Beth let that go. "So, what about the other two queries?"

"Well, I guess, just carry on and see what you can find out but without getting yourself into trouble like you did with Frank Nolan. As far as your neighbourhood concerns go, you should consult with your liaison officer. Argento, right? Now, it's going to be a busy two weeks. You'll need to be available to accompany me. I hope you can keep your days flexible. I'll see how much time I can take off from the gallery. We'll just have to see how it goes."

Beth decided just to nod and say okay before suggesting they ask for their bills. Later at home, she found her notebook and wrote a small report on the dinner discussion. Then she phoned June to see how her week had gone.

"Busy as usual, disappeared in a flash," June said. "Sorry I never got back to you. We need to plan our Christmas dinner out, don't we?"

"That's right," said Beth, covering up that she'd forgotten. "Any chance of this weekend?"

"Definitely," said June.

※

In a swanky restaurant in Vancouver's west end, Frank Nolan was entertaining clients, a wealthy husband and his wife, regaling them with stories of the wealth to be gained by investing in diamond mines in the Northwest Territories. It was the third such expensive dinner this week.

The hundreds of phone calls he had made over the last few months had finally started to pay off. It was galling to share space with seven two-bit businesses, but he couldn't afford a decent apartment and pay for his own office and secretary as well. Luckily, Rita was a smart one. She managed to keep all the phone lines straight, answering with the correct business name each time. Prestige Mining Investments was beginning to feel real to Frank. He had appropriated several reports from legitimate copper, coal, and other working mines in northern BC to give his unwitting future clients a sense of success and business longevity. This was far more exciting than the stock market and bond investment scam he'd had going back in the Maritimes. He had exited that scene in a hurry once he secured his money. Since he had used a fake identity and employed some makeup and hair colour to change his appearance, his disappearing act was made easy. He'd soon realized clientele here in the big city were generally shrewder, so eventually, Frank made a business name switch from A-1. Coming to Vancouver had another downside—he was forced to be himself in order to capitalize on his relationship with his uncle Harry. And capitalize he would, in time. *I just need to get rid of the interfering women in my uncle's life.*

The Ekati Diamond Mine, which he was currently flogging, was legitimate. What wasn't was his involvement in it. However, Frank did have a trusted contact on the inside. He'd met Lenny Hunt in the first few weeks he'd been in the city. Lenny was single, friendly, talkative, and hooked on gambling. They spent a couple evenings at the Riverside Casino bonding before Lenny flew back to Yellowknife broke. Frank loaned him some cash to tide him over.

From that first encounter, Frank sensed the mining industry offered the perfect opportunity to work up a plan for pulling in lots of money. He set out to learn everything he could. The information was there for the taking, courtesy of the BC government—all about the mining lifecycle: exploration, development, operation, and closure. After Lenny provided him with some details not publicly available, Frank wasted no time applying for a "Notice of Work" permit. It was in a smart black frame and hung in his little work cubicle. For some of the more reserved of his clients, he made a show of his modest office, pointing out how he was keeping overhead low in order not to squander their money—*hah*. He felt he'd hit on an attractive product to tempt the unwary in order to finance his retirement plan. It was a little like being Robin Hood he decided. In his previous incarnation as a portfolio manager, he wasn't picky who he took money from. It was far more ethical to restrict himself to taking from the rich and giving to the poor—namely himself. He gave himself an A for his new-found humanity.

NINETEEN

Saturday, December 4

At the Cambie Street police station, Cameron stood before the glassed-in reception desk for the second time in a week. Entering the building now felt easier than it had the first time, but the sharp sound of a backfiring vehicle outside put him on edge. He glanced around to see if anyone had noticed him jump.

He'd called and updated his uncle the previous evening. John Ross was pleased that a case that had long haunted him might at last get solved. He had always thought the husband did it somehow, despite his alibi. John might have finally accepted he was wrong if not for the fact Michael Mahoney had succeeded, less than three years later, in having Emma declared dead so he could remarry. *Mahoney must have pulled some strings,* John thought.

His uncle had voiced concern about Cameron's emotional health which Cameron had brushed aside, claiming he was okay. He'd only be at the station brief amounts of time; it would be fine. He promised that if he experienced any relapse of the old panic attacks, which had sprung up as he navigated both the lingering distrust around him and his own crumbling confidence, he would be sure to consult his old counsellor.

Fit, smiling, and casually dressed, Detective McNabb appeared from a side door and came to greet Cameron and, after a quick firm hand shake, motioned Cameron into the security elevator. Cameron internally shook his head over the youthful appearance of the detective despite his receding hairline, wondering just how much experience he had. *Likely older than he looks,* Cameron thought, *with this level of responsibility.*

"We're very grateful to have you helping out," said Steve McNabb. "As usual, we're overwhelmed with a backlog of cases. Newer cases take priority all the time. We better get you an interim ID pass because you're bound to be back here several times and you'll need something official to show out there in the big bad world when you do interviews."

Cameron relaxed. "I wondered about that. You'll already know I had an exhaustive check that cleared me not so long ago. So, what do I call myself?"

"How does crime unit consultant sound? Leaves your scope of activity wide open. Come on, let's get the locket registered as evidence, then I'll introduce you to the team. And, I've got the Mahoney file for you. I hear you go by Cam sometimes—is that okay?"

Later, as Cameron approached his 'desk for today,' where all the relevant files lay waiting for him, he pushed away uncomfortable memories of feeling like an outsider when he was confined to office work after the Tina-story got around. *I've a job to do here* he told himself, *so get on with it.* The fact that he had only been granted two weeks to contribute to the reopened case would limit his field of inquiry. He would need to narrow down as best he could which interviews might yield the most promising results. Certainly, after all this time, some people may have passed away or relocated. Beth would no doubt be helpful for the neighbourhood follow-up.

He lifted the top of the brown box. *A kind of Pandora's box,* he thought. Once the cold case investigation got seriously underway, fear and unease would be generated in different forms among all those it touched.

The first folder held the official missing person report. Cameron scanned the information, picking out relevant bits. Emma Mahoney was a pregnant twenty-six-year-old Caucasian female living in the east Vancouver neighbourhood of Collingwood-Renfrew with her husband Michael Mahoney. She had last been seen when she left her obstetrician's office located on Richards near Smithe around 2 p.m. on Tuesday September 6, 1960. The only sightings in her neighbourhood happened as she made her way down the back lane to catch a bus to her 1:30 p.m. appointment. She was described by her neighbours as sweet, thoughtful, and well liked.

Cameron paused to hold up a colour photograph of Emma. So, this was the first Mrs. Mahoney. He studied the open-faced smile of a pretty young woman standing beside the lower part of a painted totem pole. *Looks like Stanley Park*. Emma's long blonde hair was swept back from one side of her face, cascading in a gentle curve over the opposite shoulder almost to her hip. Cameron sighed, thinking of the waste of two lives. It would have taken a particularly cold-hearted person to abduct a pregnant woman.

❦

The second Mrs. Mahoney was stepping out her front door just as her husband picked up the phone to call the police.

"I'm just going out to run a few errands," Nina called over her shoulder. "Be back before noon." She didn't wait for a reply.

Against Michael's advice, she had parked her red Mini on

the street the evening before when they'd returned from the restaurant reservation she'd insisted they honour. Nina had also insisted on driving since she judged Michael to be too upset.

"Oh, it'll be fine here," she had said, not letting on she wanted to avoid any chance of running into Beth in particular or any other chatty neighbours. Soon enough, their family would become subjects of conjecture once the police started asking questions. She'd had nightmares after all the probing and speculation back when Emma disappeared. She knew blotting it out had saved her.

It was a cold, overcast day with a feel of snow in the air. Nina pulled away from the curb with little idea of where she was headed. She didn't go far and ended up in the parking area north of Trout Lake, sitting there with the motor running. She'd wanted to escape from the feeling of walls closing in on her. Memories from the time of Emma's absence had left her sleepless with worry most of the night. It didn't take much thought to realize that Michael would again become the focus of a police investigation. She'd awoke after a few hours of rest to an uneasiness that penetrated every pore of her body. With it returned the anger she'd first felt upon hearing Michael describe Beth's call. Now she wondered if the day she'd seen Dennis tucking something in his pocket was when he found the locket. Edith should have given it to Michael. It sounded like Beth had woven a tale about the discovery to distract Michael from her meddling. *That locket is ruining everything. Damn her anyway.* She would have a few choice words with Beth when she got her alone. Finally, Nina decided to go to Meinhardt's and browse in some of the other Granville Street shops beforehand.

❦

When Michael Mahoney heard the front door being unlocked,

he quickly tucked the worn photograph back in place. After he'd left a message for Detective McNabb, he'd pulled the picture of Emma from where it lay hidden under several old business cards at the back of his wallet. He had carried it around from the days of their engagement. He wondered what his precious Emma would look like now but thrust aside the question, recognizing the pointlessness of the thought. She remained dear to his heart, cute and blonde—forever young.

Nina sailed by the den door. "Honey, I'm just going to heat up some soup for us to have with lunch."

※

About midmorning, Beth had a visit from the interim Block Watch captain, Jenny Lee, who was delivering the latest newsletter to the neighbours who didn't have email. It reported that recent stats showed property theft had steadily risen during October and November in an area from Commercial to Renfrew and bounded by Twelfth and Kingsway. Part of it was the often-seen rise of pre-Christmas break-ins, both commercial and residential, vehicles included.

"Beth, I've decided I'll commit to being captain," Jenny said. "I'm just wondering, would you be co-captain? All you have to do is have a background check and attend a training session that Constable Argento and the Block Watch office manager present. You know a lot of the material anyway from reading the manual, but I know you'll still learn some new things and better appreciate the effectiveness of the Block Watch program."

"I guess I could do that. I've been a participant for years now and I'd be glad to help you out."

"Good, thanks. I'll put your name forward and let you know when the next training session is. Likely within the next two months."

After Jenny left, Beth gave some thought to how to find more information about Frank Nolan without getting herself into trouble, as Cameron had baldly put it. *He could have said it some other way,* she thought. She supposed that his police career had jaded him. *Maybe that's where his lack of tact comes from.*

She resolved to check out A-1 Investments. The lawyer was likely not so important. Beth had found his name jotted down in a steno pad that Edith kept with her Block Watch files. Beth would make sure the niece Pat knew about him. *Back to Frank.* She wanted to check on the legitimacy of his business. *Maybe,* she thought, *June would be willing to make a one-time inquiry posing as a potential client.* Beth would ask when they met for dinner in the evening. *Since Frank knows me, there's no way I can do it.*

Cameron phoned Beth around five and caught her breathless, grabbing the receiver just in time to keep it from going to voicemail. She still hadn't figured out how to interrupt the caller once a message was being left and vowed, yet again, to rectify that.

"Caught you at a bad time?"

"I was almost out the door, that's all," Beth said.

"Oh. Saturday night date?"

"Sort of. I'm joining a friend for dinner." She decided not to elaborate. "What's up?"

"I've made up an interview list which I'll send to you by email. To start, I'd like you to call Dennis Greene. Perhaps you could do that if you get in early this evening or as soon as possible tomorrow morning. I don't want to waste any time, so I'm hoping for anytime tomorrow afternoon. I need to know exactly how he found the locket. Anyway, I won't keep you now. We'll talk tomorrow. Have a good date."

"Okay, I'll call you tomorrow," said Beth, squeezing it in before the click on the line.

She picked up her keys and hurried out the door, fending off

Monty's bid to get outside.

"Nope, boy, I'm out and you're in. See you later."

Beth and June arrived at the Shaughnessy Restaurant around six, greeting each other with a hug at the entrance. It had become a Christmas tradition in recent years since their friendship had strengthened. Though June had a busy life with her work, husband, and two grown sons with young families, she made time to get together with Beth outside of work a couple times a year. They 'oohed' and 'aahed' through the restaurant windows at what they could see of this year's brilliant multi-coloured light show in Van Dusen Gardens before settling to peruse the menu.

Throughout the meal, their conversation covered everything from personal Christmas plans to the global worry, dubbed Y2K, that computer systems would not be able to change to 2000 at midnight New Year's Eve. Finally, Beth filled June in on what was happening in her neighbourhood concerning Edith and the locket.

"Goodness, it must feel strange, even scary, to think Edith knew something that got her run down," said June. "But it's good the police are investigating. Lucky you were able to get Cameron Ross on your side. You can relax and let them all get on with it."

"Not really," Beth said. "I want to be involved. I'm going to be present at his interviews. Also, there's another reason, maybe two even, that may have led to the accident being intentional."

"Is it that nephew person who grabbed you? I hope you're staying well away from him."

"I'm not planning to abandon Harry Anders," said Beth firmly. "I want to meet his niece Pat. She sounds like someone who is good for Harry, unlike Frank Nolan. But I *will* stay away from Frank. If he turns up at Harry's when I'm there, I'll leave—which leads me to an idea I wanted to run by you. It involves your help—only if you are willing and able, mind."

"Well, we've known each other long enough you know I won't say yes unless I'm comfortable with it."

Beth hesitated a moment as she swallowed her last mouthful of apple crisp. "Since Frank knows me, I can't check out his place of business without the risk of being seen. I know from Edith where his office is. I think Frank's lawyer pal is there too."

June said, "Wait a minute, the lawyer sounds tangential."

"You're right, I should just concentrate on Frank. The lawyer drew up the papers for Harry to sign. I suppose Frank could be leading him on too."

"So, what do you want from me?' said June.

"I'm wondering if you could pose as a potential client—just happen to stop in—you could say you saw the sign for A-1 Investments and decided you might surprise your husband with an unexpected Christmas gift of an investment certificate tucked in a box with a nice silk tie. String him along a bit."

"Sounds like a bit of fun," said June. "I've never told you I took drama classes in high school for two years and toyed with the idea of entering the Langara College acting program."

"Really? Then it sounds like you're in?"

"You bet. I'll do it on Monday. I have two vacation days I'm tacking on to this weekend to get some Christmas chores done. I wanted to do some shopping downtown, so it fits in fine with my plans."

Beth was home shortly after eight, pleased with the outcome of her exchange with June. A half hour later when Beth was slipping into some cozy pajamas, she remembered Dennis. *Still a reasonable time to call,* she thought. It wasn't surprising there was no answer on a Saturday night. She left a message for him to call her as soon as possible.

Sunday, December 5

Dennis, true to Beth's request, called at seven-thirty in the morning and apologized when he recognized he had woken her. She breathed slowly to calm her heart rate, which had leapt in fear that it might be bad news.

"I'm sorry. It sounded important. We didn't get in till late last night," said Dennis. "You did say as soon as possible, and I know you get up early."

"That's right," she said. "I am usually up by now, but Sundays I lie in a bit if Monty lets me. I was calling to tell you that the locket you unearthed over at the Todd's belonged to Michael Mahoney's first wife. She disappeared years ago and was never found—"

Dennis broke in, "That's terrible. He's such a nice guy. I never heard about that."

"That's because it happened decades ago, Dennis. You weren't in the neighbourhood then. Neither was I."

"Right, so what did you want to tell me?"

"The missing person cold case is being reopened, and as part of the investigation, you'll be asked to make a statement. I happen to know the retired police consultant who is helping with inquiries. His name is Cameron Ross and he asked me to contact you. I turned the locket over to him on Friday. This is really short notice but is there any chance you could meet him today at your place? I'll be there too."

"Well, yeah. I suppose so," said Dennis. "Vicky and I aren't due at her parents in North Van till five for dinner so how's about two?"

"Okay. I'll call Cameron just after nine. I'll give him your number so he can confirm with you directly."

Beth arrived at Dennis's before Cameron. She found his East Fourteenth Avenue address was an easy walk away and discovered, using her map book, it was opposite to Clark Park. She'd only been vaguely aware that some sort of grassy wooded area was there since she rarely drove the section of Commercial it bordered. In fact, it stretched almost through to Knight Street. It was one of the many prized outdoor spaces, second oldest after Stanley Park, contributing to Vancouver's reputation as a green city.

"I might have guessed you'd search out a place near a park," she said when Dennis opened the door of a modest white-picket-fenced house. "Nice area. I had no idea."

"Yeah," said Dennis. "We really like it here. Our landlady is great." His eyes veered over her shoulder. Cameron's 4x4 jeep had pulled in at the curb and he was coming up the walk.

As Beth made a formal introduction, Dennis hustled them both into the small entryway. "Let's get out of the cold. Living room is on your right. I can put your jackets in the closet. Would you rather be in the kitchen around the table? Will you have a coffee, Mr. Ross? There's still some in the pot and it's hot. Or could I make some tea for you?"

"No. No fuss. Thanks, Dennis. This isn't going to take long. Please call me Cameron."

When they were seated, sans coffee and with jackets draped over their armchairs, Cameron took out his notebook and pen. It took a mere fifteen minutes for Dennis to give a clear account of how the locket was discovered, ending with a comment on its state when he retrieved it.

"It was snarled in the roots. First, I thought I ruined it; I could see some links were pulled apart. But I suppose that's how it was lost. Anyway, I cleaned it up a bit with a rag and left it in an old envelope for Edith."

Dennis waved goodbye from the stoop, having agreed to be available to make a formal statement at the police station.

"So where will we go to have our meeting?" Cameron asked Beth as he held the picket gate open for her. "Can we drive over to your place? It'll give me a chance to see your neighbourhood and get an idea of where some of the folks I need to talk with live or used to live."

Beth, who had been imagining a coffee shop talk somewhere, realized she would have to say yes and thanked the heavens she had tidied up the day before. There was refrigerated leftover coffee from her morning breakfast, but she figured that might not appeal to him. More than one of her friends had wrinkled their nose when they heard of her habit. *Tea will do.*

"Sure," she said. "Uh, you're not allergic to cats, are you? I have a cat."

"No. I like cats. Never had one of my own, but I grew up with one—he was ginger, very much part of the family."

Beth directed Cameron to use the back lane and park in the indented area by her cement block fence. If either Sofia or Gino were looking from their place, they would be wondering who the man was accompanying her up the back steps. Time enough and they would know.

The personable tabby greeted them at the door. Cameron bent to ruffle his head. "So, this is Monty. What a handsome fellow you are." Monty flopped down and rolled over to bare his tummy. "I guess I've been accepted," said Cameron, crouching to rub the cat gently.

Beth shooed Monty out the back door to avoid encouraging such familiarity. "Easier to concentrate on our business with him out of the way," she said. "We can sit here at the table."

Over some steaming cups of green tea, Cameron expressed his satisfaction with Dennis's description of the extraction of the locket, twisted among plant roots, from under the Todd's garage.

"It's good to have that detail from Dennis," Cameron said. "It had a new chain added by Mrs. Todd, obviously. Given she understood the significance of the locket having turned up, I'm sure she must have kept the old chain."

"Yes, I'm sure she would have," said Beth. "Perhaps Susan can find it for you. At least you have Dennis to testify if need be."

Cameron then outlined his plans for interviews in the coming two weeks while Beth listened with interest, replacing lingering resentment with a will to be helpful in any way she could.

"There are a number of people to talk with," he said. "Michael Mahoney, obviously, and his wife Nina, of course. Detective McNabb and I agree it's best to interview them in a way that prevents them from comparing notes and influencing their statements. She and her parents lived close by and both of them were at home that day, so they need to be interviewed too. Are the parents still around here?"

"No. They're over in Deep Cove now, moved about twenty-five years ago," Beth said.

"I want to speak with Mr. Todd next, if possible, I think," Cameron said. "I've arranged to be at work part time while I concentrate on this case. Friday December seventeenth is the day I'll hand over my—er, our—findings. How're you fixed for availability to accompany me in the next while?"

"I'll be at Highcrest eight to four this coming Friday, and on Saturday there's a neighbourhood Christmas tea from two till four. My photography class has ended so besides some other social plans, I'm largely available," said Beth. *Clearly*, she thought, *there's nothing on his mind but Emma Mahoney, and I'm certainly not going to tell him my plans for Frank Nolan.*

"Well then," Cameron said, "first let me see what is being arranged for interviewing the Mahoneys; I need to coordinate with McNabb. As soon as I can, I'll check in with you about setting up a time to talk with Ken Todd and his daughter. Now, I'd like to have a walk around the block with you to get a feel for the immediate area." He raised his cup and downed the last mouthful of tea.

They went out the front door, which was noticeably bare compared to the three doors across the street with their festive wreaths. Beth made a mental note to get some Christmas decorations out once Cameron had gone. They confined themselves to avenue sidewalks, speaking quietly as she pointed out which houses were relevant. A few more Christmas trees had appeared in front windows since Friday, but Beth wondered if she would put hers up at all. Finally, they turned down from the top of Beth's lane to stop at Cameron's parked Cherokee.

"All right, thanks for the tea, and I'll talk to you tomorrow afternoon likely," Cameron said before pulling his jeep door shut.

Beth walked slowly to where Monty sat waiting patiently at the top of the deck stairs. She pondered her inner disquiet about being relegated to helper. It was she, after all, who had initiated contact with Cameron and asked for *his* help. True, she was schooled in a helping profession—and wanting to help had been in her bones from an early age, even before she learned that an aunt and a great aunt had been nurses. She relaxed into the understanding that it was appropriate. Cameron was the true sleuth—at least in regard to the cold case query. It was hard to believe it had already been three weeks since they'd met for lunch at the art gallery. Progress was being made—even if the answer to the accident that claimed Edith's life seemed a long way from being explained.

TWENTY

Monday, December 6

Because his father had an early meeting in Richmond, Mike got a lift with him to Belmont Motors and avoided being picked up by Jimmy, Norm, and the two tough guys, who he'd finally learned were Gerry and Ben. He'd been told they worked in a specialty parts department in back of the auto repair garage. Norm warned him they were touchy about any ice cream jokes—Mike had already figured out they weren't the joking sort.

"Good to see where you're working, Son," said Michael Mahoney. "It looks like a solid establishment. I hope this works out for you if you really want it, but remember, I'm ready to help you find something else. You could discover this isn't entirely rewarding. You only have one unit to complete for your BSc, and if you ace it like the others, you can move on and specialize. I know that Sun Life has an actuarial student program . . ."

"Alright, Dad. I'll see how this goes; I promise."

Waving his dad goodbye, Mike used his key to enter a staff side door and walked straight into Norm.

"Well. Aren't you looking spiff," said Norm. "Looks like mommy got you another new outfit."

"No. I borrowed the tie from Dad, and this is the suit I wore to Mrs. Todd's funeral."

"Oh," said Norm, "well let's not talk about her. She's not poking around anymore, but that Beth Langille might be a problem. You're gonna hafta check on her for us."

"What do you mean?" said Mike, feeling a sweat break out under his snug shirt collar.

"Rich will explain. He wants me and you to see him this morning. I'll let you know when. Gotta go, see you later."

At ten, Norm breezed into the Belmont Motors showroom and headed up the open staircase to Rich's office. He called out over the railing to Mike who was with a prospective buyer.

"Hey, Mikey, better get Andy to take over. We've got a meeting NOW."

❦

June Ishida veered right to take the Seymour exit from the Granville Street bridge. She disliked driving downtown in general and followed her usual pattern, heading for the familiar entrance of The Bay parkade.

She'd called Beth before leaving home to get any last-minute advice.

"Nope, there's nothing," Beth had said, "just be careful. You've practiced your story, I guess?"

"Oh sure," June had replied. "I have a fake name, but I'm associating myself with a credible Japanese family business name that Frank will be able to verify. It's one of the oldest and most successful businesses in Japan. Oh, and I created a calling card for myself."

"Okay, good luck. Call me when you can."

June planned to get her little 'show on the road' first then come back to do her shopping. She was wearing a pearl necklace and earrings set and had dressed in her only cashmere pullover—a flattering fuchsia pink—paired with her recently bought dress jeans and a black tailored jacket. A single antique diamond ring sparkled on her left hand. She was trying for an air of casual wealth. Mindful of Frank Nolan's temper, she had added some fake black-framed glasses thinking that might prevent any chance of future recognition. As well, since she rarely wore her hair back, she had managed to pull it into a stubby knob.

With the address in hand, she walked east on Pender. She found the three-storey brick-faced Roberts Block building on the north side almost at Hamilton. The directory inside the glass-doored entrance didn't have A-1 Investments listed. She hesitated, then she noticed a different investment business—Prestige Mining Investments. June figured it was worth a try and if it wasn't right, she'd say she'd made a mistake.

On the second floor, she pushed open a door that was affixed with a large, plasticized sheet that listed each business alphabetically. Behind a desk in the midst of a modest-sized rectangular room sectioned off into small offices, a plump young woman was slowly entering something on a computer keyboard while her right shoulder pressed the phone receiver her ear. She beckoned June forward, gesturing to what was a small waiting area by a table that held a copier and a printer.

"I won't be long," the receptionist whispered. "Have a seat."

June chose one of the two sturdy oak chairs, and from a matching coffee table, she picked up a dogeared 1996 Readers Digest from a small pile of even older magazines. She took a candid look around the room. The pale blue walls were rather faded compared to the eight bright white office doors behind the receptionist's desk. One door had the single word 'Prestige' emblazoned in red with 'Franklin C. Nolan, BA, MBA' below it. *Good, this is the right place after all*, she thought.

❦

Frank Nolan was surprised when Rita rang to say there was a walk-in, a woman, to see him. He figured it must be a mistake, or—and he sure hoped not—it was the overly picky sister of the brother and sister duo who had pledged a one-hundred-thousand-dollar investment. He had yet to see any of it transferred into the account he'd set up for his clients—*ha, ha*. With some apprehension, he opened his door. He let out a soft breath of relief when he saw a well-dressed stranger holding out her hand to him.

"Hello, Mr. Nolan. I'm Kitty Kurokawa. I was just on my way to Pappas Furs next door and noticed your business listing. I wonder if I might have a moment of your time to discuss mining investments?"

The meeting had gone well, and like an old-time movie villain, Frank now sat rubbing his hands in glee after doing a computer search at the colosseum-like central Vancouver Public Library, which had opened four years previous. He had opted to go there since the computer service at Roberts Block was a slow dial-up process. He dreamed of the day he could move his business to a better location. Kitty Kurokawa was the embodiment of a very wealthy, money-is-no-object client who could guarantee his financial future. *Along with control of Uncle's fortune, I'll be all set.* Kitty Kurokawa mentioned her brother was Toichi Takenaka, who Frank discovered had been president of a huge, thriving, family-run business since 1980. *Incorporated in 1909!* It was a worldwide construction and engineering firm. Their list of structures seemed unending and included two domes and an international stadium completed in 1997. Mrs. Kurokawa—*she asked me to call her Kitty!*—didn't just want to buy some shares, she wanted to buy a diamond mine in the

Canadian North for her husband for Christmas. A search on the Kurokawa name revealed what he thought was a likely scenario. Kitty must have married into another wealthy family whose traditional Japanese sweets dated as far back as the 1600s. She'd be worth millions. Frank's mind was full of exclamation marks by the time he left the library.

🍂

Beth was occupied through the morning, glad to be finishing off her local Christmas cards and keeping herself busy. Her mind was engaged in finding new ways to wish her friends well, which managed to keep her from wondering how June was faring.

Sofia had called. Though she'd said nothing about what or whom she may have seen at Beth's on Sunday, Sofia had pressed to go for a walk together and Beth had happily agreed. She'd been planning a walk anyway, plus she wanted to tell Sofia what was going on. They settled on meeting in the lane around one thirty.

"I see Rusty is joining us," said Beth. The good-natured beagle wagged his tail then moved past Beth to stare beyond the wrought iron gate toward her back steps.

"He's checking to see if Monty is around," said Sofia. "The only thing I don't like about walking him is when he catches sight of a cat and wants to take off. He's forever testing me; he walks with Gino mostly. For some reason, he behaved well for Edith. Or so she said." Sofia's eyes glistened.

Beth felt her eyes well up too. "Remember how she enjoyed using him on her occasional patrols? I bet Rusty knew he was on duty," she joked as they each managed a smile. "So, where are we headed?"

"Let's start up by the SkyTrain," said Sofia. "You know, the walkway by the tracks. Perhaps we can zigzag around some residential streets. There are a number of front yards I like to check out. They're almost like formal gardens with plantings year-round. Then Trout Lake? How's that?"

Beth felt good about having filled in Sofia on the cold case development. It would become common knowledge as the week progressed. Eventually, near Victoria Drive, Beth parted from Sofia who said she needed to pick up a few things at Shoppers Drug Mart.

As she walked briskly home, Beth reviewed her answers to Sofia's questions. No, the man you saw me with is not a friend. His name is Cameron Ross. He is a consulting investigator who was asked by the VPD to contact her because she's the one who brought the locket to their attention on behalf of the Todds. Yes, he's single, but this is a business type relationship. She was helping him. He will be interviewing some of the neighbours who were around in 1960. Yes, you and Gino might be on his list. Yes, you can tell Gino, but otherwise please keep it quiet until I tell you otherwise. Beth said nothing about what she and the Todds thought Edith might have said before she died or how it could be related to 1960.

As Beth passed the Mahoney's backyard, she heard her name shouted. She swiveled around in alarm.

"Wait." It was an order. Nina came flying down her steps and along the walk to her gate, her face twisted and eyes fiery. "Who do you think you are? I'll tell you. You're a meddling crusader like Edith Todd and if you don't watch out, you'll be sorry. Stay away from me and my family."

Her venom spent, Nina turned and rushed back into the house, leaving Beth with her mouth agape.

❧

In the office of Detective Steve McNabb, he and Cameron

were discussing the relative importance of some interviews over others. A decision had been made to interview both Michael and Nina at the station. "I'll interview Mahoney Senior. A female detective will handle Mrs. Mahoney's interview at the same time."

"I assume you'll have a profiler observing Mr. Mahoney," said Cameron.

"Yes. Even though he had an alibi, I saw from the files there was some fresh conjecture, linked to his remarriage, that Mahoney might have arranged his wife's disappearance. I have a team member contacting the two coworkers who alibied him at the time."

Cameron nodded. "Yes, it's unusual. Normally, he shouldn't have been able to remarry that soon."

"How about you find out when Nina Mahoney's parents can talk to you, then I'll request the Mahoney's to be here around the same time. That will prevent them from comparing notes beforehand about what questions they were asked," said Steve.

❧

All afternoon, Mike Mahoney Jr. focused on his increased salary and the nice new shiny cars around him. He tried to keep his mind off the outcome of the so-called meeting he was summoned to at ten. Afterward, he'd realized it wasn't a meeting as much as an audience with Rich the ruler and his puppet Norm. Since he was impressed by Rich's success and community standing, the uneasiness Mike had when he'd begun working for Rich had never bothered him much, except when he had to "pass the test," and even then, he had talked himself into believing it wasn't so different from the antics of freshmen at university. He believed Rich only flouted outdated regulations that hampered business. You couldn't always do things by the book if they were contrary to common sense. That had sounded like reasonable practice to Mike.

Now he wasn't entirely sure what was going on. He popped a Tums and rubbed a throbbing forearm. When Mike responded negatively to the request—no, demand—to watch Beth Langille and report on her, Rich had sidled up and put a hand out to encircle Mike's wrist.

"I want you to do as I ask. You're part of our *team,* right? What do you say?" Rich had said as he clamped his fingers hard around Mike's wrist long enough for his hand to become bluish and tingly.

Norm, who had been quiet till then, sided with his cousin—of course. Somehow, he had managed to sound both pompous and considerate. "I would do it if I was still living across from you, but I'm not. You have to do it. I think she's acting like that old snoop Todd. That one was out here once; I saw her. Another time Ben said he saw some woman idling outside our back fence."

"I don't understand what you're concerned about," Mike had stammered, his flesh burning with the imprint of Rich's fingers. "Beth Langille is just helping out with our neighbourhood Block Watch. You know. *Watch.* They watch out for things in our area. The break-ins are on everybody's mind. I have no idea why Mrs. Todd came by here. And it could have been anyone Ben saw. How would he know her?"

"Oh, Mikey, wake up," Norm had said. "Todd was spying on us, and her friend Langille would be in on it. We've got to stick together. You're one of us. You share the guilt."

"Okay, that's enough," Rich had taken over, clearly annoyed. He'd sent a 'shut-up' look Norm's way. "Mike, it's simple. I want to know what the Langille woman is up to, if anything, and fast. You've got till Friday—we'll meet in the morning, same time."

❧

Near dinner time, Beth heard from Cameron. It had been decided Nina's parents should be interviewed at their home, he'd said, and please would she agree to come along?

Beth appreciated the 'please.' "When?" she said.

"Same as the Mahoneys. Thursday. In the morning. I hope you can come. Now, what about tomorrow? Will you call the Todd's and pave the way for us to see them? Evening would be best so his daughter is there, but I could arrange to be free midafternoon if I must. And I'd like to touch base with a few of your other neighbours whose names I saw in the files. The last names are Simmons, Martinelli, and Whitman. Perhaps an evening or Friday afternoon?"

"I'm okay anytime but Friday; I'm working, remember?" *No*, she thought, *he doesn't*.

After speaking with Cameron, Beth got a call from June, though their contact was brief.

June described the space Frank Nolan was renting. "Even though his so-called office is shabby, it's clean and neat. And by the way, that must have been an old card Edith saw because his business is Prestige Investments now. There's a single secretary for eight businesses. He has credentials on the wall and an operating certificate from the BC Ministry of Mines and Forests. I have to say, he's a smooth talker, but it all sounded valid. Could be he's legit, though my hubby reminded me permits and certificates can easily be faked. Ted has offered to help if you want."

"Frank doesn't strike me as genuine," said Beth. "From what Edith said and what I've picked up in just a few weeks, he's definitely got his eye on Harry's finances. I plan to keep him in my sights. Could Ted do some digging online to see if Frank is registered with any organizations?"

"Maybe. But more chat will have to wait till lunch at work on Friday. Sorry. I have a ton to do. You be careful. See you Friday," June said.

"Good night," Beth said reluctantly. She was itching to know more.

TWENTY-ONE

Wednesday, December 8

Once Cameron had tidied up the paperwork generated by a complaint against a gallery employee from the recent protest of the Nikki Hartfield exhibit, he took a stroll through each of the gallery floors, checking in with the various staff on duty. At lunch, he thought over the interview he had conducted the previous day with Ken Todd. It seemed to him that Emma Mahoney's disappearance had a direct link to someone in the neighbourhood or someone closely associated with it.

Emma's locket had been documented as being on her person when she was last seen by none other than the fastidious Edith Todd. Cameron had already entered that fact, along with when and where it was found, in red near the top of his home wall display. He had listened attentively to what Ken Todd had to say about September 1960 and the building of their garage. Gino Martinelli and Michael Mahoney had helped. Ken had provided lots of detail. He seemed to be enjoying recollections of his past—a happier place to be than his present. The garage floor was a definite object of interest, not that Cameron had mentioned that to him. The cement had apparently been poured the morning of September seventh, the day after Emma went missing.

From the tone of Steve McNabb's voice over the phone, Cameron could almost visualize his eyebrows raising and head nodding as he listened to this bit of information.

"Aha. Guess we'll be getting permission to probe the garage floor," he'd said. "Your interview with the gardener established the locket was hauled out in the roots from under that garage. I wonder what else we might find."

❧

Thursday, December 9

Cameron maneuvered his jeep into the right lane of the Second Narrows Bridge to take the Dollarton Highway exit.

"We're early. We'll take the scenic route," he said to Beth who replied in monotone.

"Fine."

Over the past few days, Cameron had seen that Beth was a definite asset in the interviews he'd conducted so far with her neighbours. He found himself feeling pleased with her involvement and wanted to tell her so, but she'd been prickly when he picked her up for the drive over to the North Shore. She was sitting silently, gazing out the passenger window at the choppy grey waters of Burrard Inlet. He'd let her be for now. He wandered through some disparate thoughts about last evening's brief interviews. The Martinellis, Alan Whitman, and Pearl Simmons had confirmed they recollected the day the Todd's garage floor was laid, simply because it was the day following Emma Mahoney's disappearance and Michael had still insisted on helping.

❧

As they drove along Dollarton, which had already transitioned to Deep Cove Road, Beth reflected that it almost seemed like another country, an unfamiliar land of looming dark green mountains shrouded in early morning mist. Or was it spitting rain? It was hard to tell. She had a niggling sense of disquiet seated again as a passenger in Cameron's four-wheel drive, silver-grey Cherokee. In a way, this time it was more like being a couple. She pushed the feeling aside. When he'd arrived at her back gate to pick her up, she'd sent a royal wave to Sofia watching from her kitchen window and had made sure to act business-like when she opened the door to get in. Cordial greeting. No smile. Maybe that would help fend off any further remarks about how nice it would be for Beth to have a boyfriend. Boyfriend? She hated people her age calling themselves boyfriends and girlfriends. *Only appropriate for young people,* she thought. That got her thinking about Nina, whose verbal attack she likened to a teenage meltdown.

Beth clenched her jaw remembering Nina's glowering look as they passed by her earlier. She'd been righting a trash can in the lane outside her yard. In spite of Cameron's request at the end of the interviews for conversations to be kept confidential, it was no surprise that tongues were wagging about the reopened investigation. Beth mused about the local gossip she'd heard once that Nina and her mother had never had an easy relationship. When Beth had checked it out with Sofia, Sofia told her that Inga and Gus Pavlik had been living somewhat estranged from their daughter for many years. It seemed one or both of them were unhappy with Nina's marriage perhaps due to the age difference—information that Beth had already passed on to Cameron. She wondered . . .

Cameron's voice intruded on Beth's thoughts. "Are you watching for our next turn off? It's along here somewhere."

Ross the Boss flitted through Beth's mind. "Yes. We've passed

Caledonia so Panorama Drive will be the next left." *See, I'm on top of things.* Then Beth's critic piped up, *who's the teenager now?*

The Pavlik's pale yellow bungalow with adjoining garage was fronted by a generous-sized driveway where Cameron parked behind an older tan Sentra. The yard that faced the street—and what might have been a view were it not for low cloud cover—was well kept. It was obvious someone was keeping up the garden beds in front, but from what could be seen of the back, the same care was not taken there. A quick glance as they exited the jeep revealed a rundown barn of some sort and a tangle of mostly denuded bushes and rambling wild blackberry. Behind that, a thick wood staked its claim.

By the time they reached the front door, it had opened. Standing there was a sturdy grey-haired man who they knew would be seventy-eight now. Before greeting them, he turned back and called out to the dark interior behind him.

"They're here. Mum, our visitors are here."

"Mr. Pavlik? I'm Cameron Ross from the Vancouver Police and this is Beth Langille from your old neighbourhood."

Gus Pavlik looked at Cameron's ID card, stepped back, and offered his hand to each of them. "Come on into the living room."

He turned to lead the way to where a woman, whose face was as wrinkled as her husband's and whose brown hair was an obvious home dye job, stood in the dining room doorway.

"Dad?"

"Mum, go sit in your chair," Gus said gently. To Cameron and Beth, he said, "Mum's got some memory problems that started this year, but she's doing okay. Her memory from the past seems just fine so I think she can help." He sent a reassuring look to his wife. "Mum, we're going to talk about the time Emma Mahoney went away."

Once they were all seated, Cameron commenced his usual, now memorized opening remarks to set the stage for the necessity of signed statements and possible reinterviews.

There was a slight change to both Inga's and Gus's statements.

"I was off work that day. Went on a fishing day up Agassi way. I didn't see Emma at all because I left early to pick up a buddy."

"No, Dad," Inga spoke firmly. "Matt came and picked *you* up. You had Nina take your truck to the garage for you. Don't you remember? She got her license that summer and started to pester you about driving it."

"Is your wife correct?" Cameron asked.

Gus Pavlik's gaze veered off as if peering into the distant past. "Maybe. I suppose we might be able to check if you think it's necessary. Still have the truck out back. It's been in the barn for at least fifteen years. Had it towed there after the engine block cracked one winter. The service logbook I kept should be in the glove compartment."

"What about your friend Matt, Mr. Pavlik?" Beth asked to show Cameron she was paying attention.

"Oh, Matt's been gone a couple years now. Cancer. Might be right what Mum says. I remember there was one time we went fishing and Matt called in sick—he was a teacher. He'd only transferred to Palmer Secondary in Richmond the previous year. He felt so guilty missing the first day of school, he never called in sick again unless he really was. Yup, I think Mum's right."

Accepting that Mrs. Pavlik's understanding seemed mainly intact, Cameron asked what she recalled of the day Emma went missing. "I understand you were at home and could see the Mahoney place from your yard. Did you see Emma at all the day she didn't come home?"

Her answer, which tallied with her previous statement, was that she had not seen Emma since the day before when Nina and Emma had picked zucchini from their vegetable garden.

"Nina and Emma were good friends, you know," she said. "Emma's husband married Nina."

Cameron nodded. "Yes, we know."

Mrs. Pavlik looked at her husband. "Maybe the police will get him this time, Dad. Nina will be safe at last."

Mr. Pavlik looked embarrassed and ignored her statement. "Anything else?" he directed his question to Cameron.

Beth interrupted, "Do *you* have concerns about Michael Mahoney?"

"Used to think he might have done something," Mr. Pavlik said. "Mum's always felt that way."

"All right, there's nothing more for now. We'll be in touch if there is," Cameron said.

"I guess that didn't help much," Beth said as they began the return to Vancouver.

"It's hard to tell at this point. I'm just going to pull off to the side here," Cameron said when he turned onto another road. "There's time to alert Detective McNabb about the truck before Nina Mahoney is interviewed. It was a good example of how, after all these years, a statement can change. We know memories can be unreliable, but at times, just the right trigger will prompt something forgotten that turns out to be important."

As Beth left the jeep after they reached her back lane, Cameron earned a genuine smile when he complimented her on her help. "I'm glad you asked that question."

"Have a good day at work tomorrow," he added. "Can I call you in the evening?"

Beth agreed, thinking it might be the first time Cameron had asked if it was okay rather than expected it would be. Together with his sincere praise, it gave her the sense that this liaison was beginning to work the way she'd imagined.

Before leaving the house again to take her favourite walk, which included a circuit around Trout Lake, Beth contacted Harry Anders. She invited herself for a short visit to drop off some goodies. She had baked several batches of festive cookies—shortbreads and ginger snaps—for Saturday's tea and other Christmas giving. Surely, she thought, Frank Nolan would be holed up in the shabby little office June had described. Her luck held out and there was a bonus. Harry announced with a grin that Pat would be home for Christmas early the week of December 20.

"I'm looking forward to meeting your niece," said Beth.

"Don't you worry, I'll make sure you do," Harry said beaming. "She's looking forward to meeting you too."

❦

After his lunch break, Mike headed to Rich Belmont's office, more nervous than before, having been summoned from the showroom

floor once again by Norm. The 'meeting' had been brought forward from Friday since Rich decided to take three days off. With effort, Mike asserted himself and stalled for time by saying he'd be up in a few minutes as he needed to visit the washroom first. This earned him a snide remark from Norm.

"Make sure you wash your hands, Mikey."

Mike dried his hands. He patted a cool, wet wad of paper towel against his brow and to dry off, he used the pristine white handkerchief his mom had insisted no proper man should be without. He chewed an extra strength antacid tablet, all the while trying to remember the few points he had written down on a sheet of paper at home. He'd planned to review it that evening. What did he have to report? *Not much.* He might not be in Rich's good graces after today. He'd just have to wing it.

He'd overheard his mom complaining about Beth to his dad. It seemed Beth had passed on some family jewellery to the police. It had something to do with Edith Todd. He couldn't even begin to figure that out. He'd noted that his mom had called Beth "another Edith." His mother had clearly had some sort of falling-out with Beth because before this, she was set on getting her to join the book club. Climbing the stairs slowly, Mike continued pondering his predicament and realized the best he could do was tell Rich that Beth Langille had been around the neighbourhood with someone from the police who apparently was talking with neighbours about a crime back in the sixties. That ought to deflect Rich and Norm's attention.

Mike sent Beryl, the secretary, a feeble smile and nod when she gestured him to go right in. Whatever Rich and Norm were talking about was halted in midstream with his entry. Mike judged the immediate hearty greeting from both to be suspect. Was Rich talking about canning him?

"Want a caffeine fix to get you through the afternoon?" Rich said.

"No thanks." Mike just wanted to get the conversation over with. He blurted out something before he could think too much. "I don't have much of interest to tell you about Beth Langille. I know she's more involved in Block Watch since Mrs. Todd died. I told you the local thefts have continued to upset everyone. The only other thing is she's been seen around with a policeman consultant of some sort who is looking into a suspected murder case from decades ago. I heard my parents talking about it." Mike took a breath, waiting for Rich's response.

"That's all then?" Rich asked.

"Nothing more of note," said Mike. "Beth's retired but works every second Friday at Highcrest. And she might be helping someone, I think, over near Trout Lake as well as being involved with our local Block Watch, which you know."

"Well thanks, Mike," Rich said, holding out his hand. "That wasn't so difficult, was it? I value your loyalty." He crushed Mike's hand in a long shake.

Later in the afternoon, Norm ambled into the showroom. A customer had just been sent off with quotes for a Corvette hardtop versus convertible. Mike thought the fellow would likely never be back; he had quickly picked up on the tell-tale signs Andy taught him to look for.

Without a word of greeting, Norm walked over and stood directly in front of Mike. "I want to hear more about this policeman," he said in a low voice.

In the seconds it had taken Norm to reach him, Mike felt his neck and shoulders tightening again. Since he was able to answer truthfully, he relaxed a little.

"I don't know much else. I couldn't hear everything they said. Both Mom and Dad clammed up when I asked about it. I did hear Mrs. Todd's name once. You remember her place was broken into late October? My folks said it was nothing for me to worry about. The police are still investigating."

Like a snake on alert, Norm bristled, "Well, try harder to find out more."

❧

To Nina, the silence in the car felt ominous and allowed her thoughts free rein. The interviews were over. Before Michael keyed the ignition, he'd said he wanted quiet; he didn't want to talk about anything till later. Nina was feeling the opposite; she was dying to talk. Michael proceeded to drive them home without a word, unless the loud expletive aimed at the dark red Mazda sportscar that cut in front of him somewhere along Twelfth Avenue counted. Meanwhile, Nina seethed with the indignity of having been called out over a measly lapse of memory about an ordinary garage checkup. What right had they to treat her like that? Trying to follow Michael's demand to stay quiet frustrated her impulse to shout curses of her own—but there were some were words she wouldn't stoop to utter aloud in any company. She didn't want to lose face in front of her beloved husband, especially now. She must keep him foremost in her thoughts and actions because she could feel Emma's ghost luring him away.

TWENTY-TWO

Friday, December 10

After being occupied with the cold case investigation and being in Cameron Ross's company much of the week, Beth was feeling a troubling disconnect from her infection control persona. She drove south along Boundary Road toward the hospital thinking about whether she should give up work altogether. The resistance Beth encountered to getting up in the morning had started her on this train of thought. A partly sunny day was forecast—the clouds had been blown away in the night by sharp wind gusts that rattled the screen on her front door and whistled down the chimney. It was a night of broken sleep. The house felt icy. She hadn't wanted to leave the warm comfort of her bed even after turning up the heat. She'd stood near one of the registers while her nightie ballooned out with toasty air and Monty meowed for his breakfast. One day of work every two weeks seemed to be turning into an imposition on her time. *Ridiculous*. She supposed she could casually mention her leanings toward full retirement to Dr. Harris. What was the term? She'd 'put it out there'—that was what she'd do.

In the meantime, she was looking forward to having lunch with June. They'd spoken barely ten minutes on Monday evening.

Apart from the inquiry interviews, Beth had been occupied with the neighbourhood either being Cameron's assistant, helping Sofia contact those invited to the Saturday tea and baking in preparation, or providing Jenny with help in alerting Block Watch participants about two local incidents. One of the latter was a break-and-enter to the basement of a rented home where Christmas gifts had been taken; the other was the scaring off of a yard trespasser.

Everyone was on high alert. The renters who had previously declined to join Block Watch had now signed up and were clamouring to have all the information they could get about home security. At their own expense, they had added a strike plate to the basement door. The homeowner had agreed to replace the narrow, grassed areas at the sides of the house with loose gravel, which would create a noisy deterrent to anyone intent on gaining entry through the lower-level windows. *It's much like closing the barn door after the horse has run away,* thought Beth. However, she was aware it was not uncommon for thieves to return a second time to steal any new purchases made to replace what had been stolen.

As soon as she got to the office, Beth boiled some water to make a pot of Darjeeling tea. She'd risen late and had rushed her breakfast. She took a sip and swore.

"What's this I hear?" said June from the doorway.

"Sorry, I don't often swear like that," said Beth, embarrassed by her outburst. "Burned my tongue. What have you got there?" She nodded toward the papers in June's hand.

"Just a positive urine. It's an antibiotic-resistant organism from a new admission. We called to alert the ward. And there are two positive results back from BCCDC for influenza A in patients on our geriatric unit."

"All right. Thanks, I'd better get on here then," Beth said, fingering the reports. "See you later."

After flagging charts as necessary, Beth listened to Donna's taped report in which she learned that Donna had isolated the flu patients in a double room at the far end of their nursing ward. Next, Beth checked over the day's printed unit census listings and the daily OR slate. The familiar routines always satisfied Beth's orderly nature. Detouring through the laboratory several hours after her ward rounds, Beth caught June's eye from a distance, raised her eyebrows in a silent query, and pointed to her watch.

Beth was dipping into the cafeteria's broccoli and cheese soup special of the day when June arrived with her lunch bag and a mug of tea.

"How goes it?" June asked. "You look weary."

Beth let out a small groan. "Not too bad, my week's activities have done me in, not the work here. I've got the ward rounds done and checked out all the patients from the reports you gave me and some more besides. The morning flew by. I can actually devote some time helping Donna with the entry of cases to the research databases, unless there are any more calls. Come on now, what else have you got to tell me about Monday and Frank Nolan. It seems you pulled off your impersonation in grand style."

June smiled. "It was rather fun once I saw he swallowed my story. With my best clothes and jewellery, I felt the part. There was time to take a look at his credentials on the wall when he went out to get some coffee for us. He has a certificate for a financial analysis and investment management course from the University of Toronto Continuing Studies and an MBA degree from the University of New Brunswick."

"Oh yeah, I recall his uncle saying something about a BA and other degrees from back east. What sort of investing is he doing then? With a set up like that, it must be penny ante," Beth said.

"Well, he showed me several leaflets—one was for the Ekati Diamond Mine up north. I've been able to confirm it opened last fall. I'd told him I was interested in buying Canadian diamond mine shares for my husband—at some point I said I was attracted to the idea of arranging ownership of a mine. I saw his eyes light up like my sons did when they saw the presents under the Christmas tree."

"I think Edith's gut feeling was right on," Beth sighed. "How can I thank you for going to all that trouble for me?"

"By staying safe and… giving me the recipe for those yummy peanut butter shortbreads you brought today for the lab to share. Deal? Now what about Harry Anders?"

"I saw him yesterday and he told me when his niece Pat will be home. I know it's meddling, but I want to feel her out and see if she realizes what's happening. I just can't let Harry get stuck in Frank's clutches. If I'm off base, I'll apologize later.

❦

After working at the gallery in the morning, Cameron had a quick lunch at the Bellagio Café across Hornby then headed to the Cambie police station. Showing his ID and taking the elevator to the third floor seemed quite natural now. Detective McNabb's office was located near his team's hub of activity; two heads looked up from a phone and a computer screen and sent him friendly nods as he passed.

Pleasantries dispensed with, Cameron and Steve exchanged interview reports and settled to discuss their respective takeaways using the whiteboard in the room.

"Michael Mahoney's statement was virtually the same," said Steve McNabb, "almost word for word. No doubt he went over the details of that day for years and it's embedded in his mind.

He looked upset and seemed genuine, though I know there are people who are good at acting. The team hasn't been able to make contact with the two coworkers who gave him the solid alibi yet. We should take another look at whether he had an accomplice or might have hired someone. Guess the latter is not so likely. If it's not Mahoney, it must be someone in the neighbourhood or someone who would have been a regular visitor in the neighbourhood. Where the locket was found speaks to that."

"Yes," said Cameron, "my thoughts exactly. Maybe a neighbour, maybe a regular delivery person or even a relative or friend of one of the neighbours. It's wide open."

"Seems so. By the way, I've applied for a warrant to excavate the garage floor. Just waiting for the go-ahead. The locket and original witness statement are enough to justify the search."

"It'll be interesting to see if there is any change in the two alibis," Cameron said. "Too bad Mr. Pavlik's fishing buddy died. There's no way to find out about the timing of their fishing trip. Just wondering now if Mr. Pavlik made a mistake or was trying to conceal something. You know how the brain starts to speculate."

"Uh huh. Mrs. Mahoney's statement was also almost exactly what she said last time. She repeated that she'd last seen Emma Mahoney the evening before and that despite the age gap, they'd been close friends." McNabb pulled the statement closer. "Oh yes, and that Emma was very upset about having developed diabetes because of the pregnancy and was troubled her obstetrician might tell her next day that she had to start taking insulin to keep her blood sugar down. By the way, you saw the 1965 entry your uncle made during a cold case review?"

Cameron nodded. "I already knew he thought Mahoney had staged the disappearance—and that if so, he would have had to have an accomplice."

"Right," said McNabb. "Thanks for calling with that tidbit about the truck before the interview with Nina Mahoney was finished. There was nothing about it in her original statement. I asked her if she was forgetting anything, and she said no. After that, I confronted her with what her parents said. You should have seen the fireworks. I think she's a person who has to be right, never wrong. When she calmed down, she said maybe in her grief she forgot. I suppose there's a chance she could be covering for her dad."

"And I suppose a young Nina Mahoney might not have thought anything about taking her dad's truck to the garage on that particular day and she dismissed it," said Cameron.

"Suppose so. If the mother is correct, then three of them overlooked the truck. I think it should have ended up in at least one of the statements. You're right, in this business, the mind *does* start to wonder. Pavlik could have gotten his buddy to cover for him. He let Nina take the truck to the garage then picked it up himself later. Perhaps they were fishing nearby, some place like Rice Lake over in North Vancouver, not as far away as he said, and then Pavlik got his buddy to drop him off at the garage. Pavlik may have had strong feelings for Emma, saw her, picked her up, then acted on his gut urges. We know only too well it happens. I'll add him to the board in our main room with a question mark. In the meantime, there're other avenues to explore."

Cameron had been leaning back as they spoke and now pushed himself forward as the conversation was winding up. "Yes. I'm going to speak to a few more people in the neighbourhood with Beth along. She's been a great help. Then there's the obstetrical clinic to get on to. It's still in existence. Someone who was around back then could still be employed there."

"Okay," said Steve, rising. "Appreciate what you're doing. It frees up one of our guys to follow up on other cases. I expect we'll get the search warrant later today and execute it as soon as possible. Could be as early as Monday. Best that you and Miss Langille alert the Todd's. I'll let you know when it'll happen. Oh, please make sure Miss Langille understands that unless she is told otherwise, all communication must be treated as completely confidential."

Cameron felt an unexpected need to rise to Beth's defense. "It's Ms. Langille—or Beth, if you want. We've spoken already about confidentiality, but I can touch on it again. I trust her. She's a seasoned health care professional. She's no stranger to the importance of privacy."

While he was thinking about Beth, Cameron made a mental note to ask her about her other concerns. *Definite long shots,* he thought. But as Beth was readily accommodating him, he'd begun to transition from dismissing her ideas to genuinely wishing to help her.

❧

Monty was not amused when the phone rang, interrupting the progress of his dinner service. He'd come bounding into the kitchen as soon as he heard the can opener in action. Over the sound of the cat's vocal displeasure, Beth heard Cameron say hello.

"You haven't started getting your dinner yet, have you?" he said. "We need to have a chat and I thought we could do it over dinner. I'm just about to leave the Cambie police station. What about meeting me at the White Spot on Cambie near Twelfth?"

"Suppose so," Beth said hesitantly. She'd been looking forward to an easy leftover meal and quiet evening. "Couldn't we talk things over on the phone later?"

"This'll be better," Cam said. "Face to face is far better for discussion and planning during an investigation. But we can do it tomorrow if that's more convenient for you."

"No, I'm busy tomorrow, so tonight will be okay," Beth conceded.

"Okay, I'll head up there now. Just take your time. I'll get a booth."

For the second Friday in a row, Beth found herself opposite Cameron in a quiet corner at a restaurant. They had each ordered a burger plate with 'endless' fries.

"Have a snack?" Cameron said when she arrived. He'd pushed a dish of onion rings toward her.

"Not a favourite, sorry," she said. "So, what have you learned that you can share with me?"

"Nothing much at this point. I know whatever we talk about you'll keep to yourself. I made sure Steve McNabb understands he has no need for concern on that point. He's waiting for permission to search under the garage, and he wants us to break it to the Todds."

"That'll cause quite a kafuffle in the neighbourhood," Beth said. "Can't they just use a detector of some sort that looks through the cement? I've read about that."

"That's the first step, but it will depend on how thick the concrete is. The success of scanning is dependent on whether something like reinforcing mesh has been used."

"Anything come out of the interviews?" Beth asked.

"Maybe. It could be just a matter of dotting an 'i', but Steve McNabb thinks Gus Pavlik's truck should be checked to see if we can confirm what Nina's parents say about when it was serviced. I'd like you to come along again for that. Not sure when yet. What's your week like?"

Beth made a show of consulting her pocket planner. "Not bad. Let me know as soon as you can, please."

"Now tell me, what's happening with your… inquiries?"

Beth was a little surprised by Cameron's expression of interest. She was only expecting discussion about the cold case. Could it be he was actually beginning to care? She went ahead and described the recent theft activity, reminding Cameron of Edith's suspicions concerning Norm Jervis.

"Yes, I recall," said Cameron. "This is the fellow who lives with his girlfriend and her uncle next door to the Todd's. And what makes you think he could have anything to do with Mrs. Todd's accident?"

"Well, it's just one of two possibilities that might have led to the threatening messages Edith received and then someone acting on their anger. I know she sometimes took things a little further than might be wise. She liked to ask a lot of questions. That was just Edith. She thought he was the one either doing the local thefts or sharing information about our premises. I wonder if he was the person behind the nasty letters. I learned some background information from his girlfriend Tara—a nice young woman. I had her in one afternoon about two weeks ago for a visit. Norm apparently had a run-in with authorities in Kelowna over drugs. Maybe you could check that out somehow."

"Beth, I still feel this is something best discussed with Constable Argento. Have you anything more to go on?"

"Well, the break-ins seemed to really increase after he moved here. Anyway," Beth forged on, "Norm came knocking on my back door while Tara and I were talking. He became angry, abusive really—I have a hunch he was trying to get her away from me before she told me anything. She'd already told me about the run-in with the law in Kelowna. He's a coarse sort of fellow. Chums around with Mike Mahoney Junior and they work at the same place."

"The break-ins are a Block Watch issue," Cameron repeated. "The culprits need to be caught by police. As for me, I need to fulfill my obligation to help with the cold case."

Beth nodded. *Best abandon that topic for now and not bother to mention that I've asked Dennis to help keep an extra eye out.*

The arrival of their meals silenced any more discussion just as Beth considered how to approach the subject of Frank Nolan. Cameron finished half his burger plate before he was interrupted by a low buzz from his cell phone.

"Sorry, I'd better take this—it's Detective McNabb." He rose to find some privacy near a back wall where there were a couple of empty booths.

When he returned, Cameron had news. The garage search warrant had been granted for Monday. "McNabb wants us to visit Ken Todd and tell him in person. Any chance you could arrange that for tomorrow or Sunday afternoon?"

"Has to be Sunday for me," said Beth. "I have our block Christmas tea tomorrow at two. I'll call Ken and Susan tonight as soon as I can."

Beth spoke with Susan Todd shortly after arriving home. She'd sped along Twelfth Avenue after realizing it was already well past eight thirty. *Cameron's fault,* she'd thought. He'd ordered two green teas for them when he was away from the table to answer his phone and she'd felt obliged to stay and drink one. Fortunately, Cameron had moved on from what her concerns might be and was focused on the cold case once again. They'd parted ways having paid their own bills at the front desk. Beth left feeling relieved that she would have some time to prepare for the topic of Frank Nolan.

"Dad is in bed," Susan announced when Beth asked for Ken.

"That's okay; I'm only calling on behalf of the VPD consultant Cameron Ross to ask if the two of you are home on Sunday. He wants to talk with you both about plans to do a search of the area where the locket came from."

Beth thought she'd done a good job making the search sound not too invasive. Susan responded favourably and set a time of two thirty "after Dad's nap". Beth rang Cameron straight away to let him know.

"Good," said Cameron, "and thanks. Maybe you could pick me up like before? Saves two of us looking for parking. By the way, sorry we didn't get to talk about the blind fellow you're worried about. We can go over it afterward."

Beth noted Cameron hadn't forgotten—he was becoming positively considerate. She hoped it would last. But would he agree to help when he heard what she'd done?

TWENTY-THREE

Saturday, December 11

Nina Mahoney decided she would attend Sofia's Christmas tea despite the fact that she didn't want to. It was important to be seen and to keep up appearances. She was waiting, as usual, to take care of her favourite son. He'd been in a funny mood this week, didn't react to their in-joke by quipping back, 'Mom, I'm your *only* son,' and he hadn't gone out with any friends, it seemed, even that poor-excuse-of-a-friend Norman. When Mike had been out, he'd said it was for a walk around the neighbourhood or down to Trout Lake—*not like him at all,* she thought. *I wonder if he's coming down with something.* She looked at her watch. It was almost eleven thirty.

Michael was holed up in his den. The interviews they each had at the police station had cast a pall over the household. It reminded her of the Peanuts character who sometimes had a raincloud ruining his day. She wished the sun was shining, but at least the day was mostly dry. Nina shrugged off the weight pulling her down and headed to the fridge. She'd throw together a frittata that would serve as breakfast or lunch—if anyone cared to join her. As she whisked the eggs, she considered what to wear to the tea. *Likely the red dress and definitely my diamond drop earrings.*

❦

Beth thought it almost felt like the Christmas teas Edith had hosted over the years for the women of the neighbourhood, even though there were a few men this year. Sofia's home was warm and cheery, offsetting the chill of the on and off damp day. She had used some small-sized variegated poinsettias to good effect in the dining room where the table and sideboard were laden with tempting sweets and savouries.

Usually, conversation would centre on the season they were gathered to celebrate: plans for Christmas presents, favourite Christmas traditions, past Christmases remembered. This afternoon had begun that way, but once Constable Argento arrived, Christmas was forgotten. Jenny Lee thought it would be good to have reassurance with the constable present since angst was high over the uptick in successful thefts and Edith's recent death. Apparently, he had thought so too. During the conversations that followed, Beth heard someone say it was too bad Edith wasn't here to get to the bottom of it. There was an awkward silence for a moment until Dan Argento spoke up, agreeing that Edith had been an exceptional Block Watch captain. He added he had confidence that Jenny and Beth would do a good job of carrying on in her stead. As tea was sipped and calorie-laden morsels munched, talk seemed to be stuck on crime. Rumours circulating about the cold case investigation had given rise to some morbid speculation that overshadowed the general sense of seasonal goodwill. Nina kept to the periphery of the crowded room and away from Beth and Alan in particular, engaging in superficial chatter as she saw fit.

Sunday, December 12

Upon hearing that a warrant had been granted to search under his garage and in the area next to it, Ken became upset about the probability that the newly planted garden bed, which Edith had planned with Dennis, would be a mess and his property damaged. Susan moved closer to her father on the settee. She put a hand on his arm murmuring some words of comfort.

"I understand your worry," Cameron said, "but the excavation will be done carefully to preserve any evidence that might be found. I can assure you that the forensic team are professional and cautious when doing this type of work. Sadly, they're not strangers to this kind of examination. The area of the search will be cleaned up and the cementing, if needed, redone by a reputable company."

Once Beth had chimed in to remind Ken that he knew Dennis was reliable and could be counted on to put the spring garden back the way Edith wanted it, Ken agreed it must be done.

"Guess I don't really have a choice, do I?" he said, looking at his slippered feet.

"Not really," Cameron agreed. "What about your car parked in there? If you have the keys, I could move it to the front of your house."

From Ken's tired, blank look, it was clear he'd had sufficient upheaval for the day, but he pulled himself together enough to suggest he would call his neighbour Alan, who had room in his garage since selling his wife's car. That decided, Susan handed the keys to Beth for delivery.

❦

"Tell me a little about the blind former neighbour," Cameron said to Beth. "He was your other concern. His nephew disliked Mrs. Todd, I recall."

They were seated in a small coffee shop on South Granville, several blocks from Cameron's home.

"Sure. Edith was regularly helping Harry Anders with correspondence and lifts to church," said Beth as she decided, on the spot, to side-step talking about June's visit to Frank Nolan's office if she could.

Beth went on. "I was thinking you could come with me to talk to Harry and see what he remembers from that September. That would be a way to have you assess the situation for yourself. Harry has been mostly blind the last ten years. I gather he moved where he could have help after his wife passed away in the early 1990s. The visit needn't take too long. It's possible he could provide a fresh outlook on the neighbourhood's past. He told me he often thinks back on his years there. At the same time, you can get a sense of the nephew because I can prompt Harry a little with some remarks about his family."

If Beth expected that her suggestion might bring the topic to a close and help her avoid a confession about June, she was mistaken.

"I thought you mentioned you have some more information about the nephew; what's his name again?" said Cameron.

". . . Frank Nolan," said Beth.

"So, go on. Review with me what you've discovered."

Beth took an unobtrusive calming breath and began first with what she knew from Edith.

"It sounds like a family dynamic that will have to play out," said Cameron. "Seems about the same as what goes on the world over when money is involved. You know this fellow is temper prone. Best stay away. What have you learned since we met on the third?"

There it was. The sort of question she had promised herself she would answer truthfully and had already decided how she could do it.

"Well, I took your advice to keep myself out of Frank's way. I asked a good friend from work who is in my confidence to do a little reconnaissance."

Cameron sat up straight. "Reconnaissance. What on earth?" His voice was a lot louder than normal. She cringed inside and glanced about but no one in the coffee shop was paying attention.

Beth's sharp voice broke in before Cameron said more. "Just hear me out."

Cameron gave a small groan and sat back, arms folded.

Beth chastised him, "You look just like Sergeant James when he seemed to be humouring me. Are you going to listen properly?"

Cameron held his hands up in mock surrender. He leaned forward and reached for his unfinished coffee. "All right, all right. I'm listening."

"I was keeping myself out of harm's way like you told me. June, my friend at work who's the lab supervisor, is the only one I've talked with about some of what I've been doing since Edith's accident. And don't worry, I've told her nothing confidential," Beth hurried to add.

"I wasn't going to say anything," Cameron said. "I trust you."

Beth couldn't pass this up. "So, I'm forgiven for not telling you right away about the locket?"

Cameron nodded with a half-smile. "Carry on."

"I felt June out about going to Frank's office to see what he's doing. I learned then that she'd taken some acting in college so she was okay with it. She made up a story about a family link to a big business in Japan—oh, I didn't tell you June's Japanese. She disguised her appearance, went to his office, and pretended to be interested in engaging his services. Later, she called Frank to say she had to leave Vancouver indefinitely for Tokyo due to family illness or something like that. It seemed to work well."

"That's lucky. So, what is Frank Nolan doing?"

"I think he's flogging a fake diamond mine—well, not fake exactly since he's using the name of a real one. Ever heard of the Ekati Diamond Mine?"

"Nope," said Cameron.

"I looked it up—it's in the Northwest Territories, northeast of Yellowknife. Frank claimed he's handling the shares for a second mine that Ekati is opening. I couldn't find anything about that."

"This is all very interesting, but I can't see what it has to do with Edith Todd's accident."

"I'm just trying to establish that Frank is really dishonest. That's what Edith thought. He has a temper and seems a combative person, so maybe he plowed into her, seeing her by chance that evening," Beth said.

"Anything else?"

"Yes. Remember I said Edith heard Frank's side of the conversation twice when she was at Harry's. She said he was badgering his uncle to pick a time when he could bring a lawyer around. The second time, when Harry mentioned Pat—that's the niece now in California—Frank put her down, said she's too far away and that Harry was risking his savings. He was really putting the pressure on."

"Sorry, Beth, but this fellow sounds like a long-shot compared to the person who murdered Emma Mahoney. Once that person is identified, we may have found the hit-and-run driver too."

"That would mean someone would have known that Edith had the locket. I'm sure she didn't say anything to anybody."

"She told you," Cameron said.

"Uh, yes," said Beth. *Liar, liar, pants on...* "I meant anyone but me. Edith only had it a short time. When you and I went to see Dennis, I don't remember you asking him if there was anyone around when he found it."

"That was caught when he went down to the station to make a formal statement. Detective McNabb said there were a few people Dennis was aware of around that time. I wasn't told who, and even if I knew, I couldn't share that information," Cameron said.

"Sure, I understand." Beth pulled out her small date book. "Now, what about coming to see Harry one afternoon in case he can add anything to the cold case investigation?"

"That's fine, but I'm only interested in keeping to that agenda so let's stick to 1960," Cameron stressed.

"Couldn't I just ask him some leading questions about his niece and nephew so you can hear what he says about Frank?"

"Listen," Cameron said firmly, "I'm going to repeat my view that you need to be very careful with this person. You told me the niece is in town next week. From what you say, she's very smart. She may have figured it out already."

After they paid their respective bills and left the shop, the uncomfortable silence between them lasted until Beth reached her Corolla. "I'll call you after I get some times from Harry then. Bye."

"Fine. Bye." Cameron stalked away.

TWENTY-FOUR

Monday, December 13

Beth looked up from the few breakfast dishes she'd just slipped into hot, soapy water to see a police cruiser roll quietly past her back gate. Her mind was sluggish, weighed down with questions, but this was something to which she knew the answer. The rectangular window above her kitchen sink was another interesting feature which set her house apart from similar homes in the block. Cut into the inner wall of the back entry area, it offered a view to the backyard and lane through spacious exterior windows. Facing south, the porch acted like a mini greenhouse, and Beth had a number of succulent plants happily growing on a shelving unit. Atop a portable dishwasher was a comfy old blanket where Monty had basked in some midday sun on Sunday. Not today so far, the bamboo blinds that filtered the sun in summer were raised high to reveal ominous clouds. The day was a breezy four degrees Celsius, and Monty was in the dining room by a heat register, his paws twitching as he dreamed of warmer days.

Rusty's sharp barks brought Gino Martinelli out his back door over the deck to the railing to look at whatever was going on at the Todd's. Beth stripped off her yellow rubber gloves and went to her den to have a better view. The police forensics team had arrived. She saw Sofia carry the dog back into the house. Beth wasn't too surprised to see Dennis with his Blue Jays cap among the various police personnel. Later, she learned he'd been asked to point out the exact area where he'd pulled out Emma's locket with the roots. *No need to stand here gawking.* Beth headed back to the sink to finish her chore and think.

First thing that came to mind was a chat at the Saturday Christmas tea that had filled in one blank for her.

❦

"Oh, that looks yummy," Sofia said, ushering Tara into the dining room where the sideboard was set up with beverages and an extended table was laden with Christmas goodies.

Sofia's voice became tremulous. "Evie always brought white fruitcake. Guess your uncle told you. We missed her last year, she was already ill. Beth made Edith's shortbreads. Feels like they're both here in spirit." Sofia took a tissue from her pocket to dab at the inner corner of one eye.

"I bet they are," said Tara, for want of something to say, and laid her plate where Sofia pointed.

"Sorry to rush off, I've got to get more coffee on. It seems to be more popular than tea today. But *you* like tea, Beth told me. There's a pot of Murchie's English Afternoon blend just made. If you want herbal, there's hot water and various teabags."

Tara turned around when she heard Beth's voice. "You're looking relaxed. I'm so glad you came. Where's your Uncle Alan?"

"He'll be along soon, couldn't decide what shirt to wear," said Tara smiling.

"Alan mentioned the other day that it's quieter with Norm gone. No more coming and going at odd hours. How's it working out for you?" asked Beth.

Tara lowered her voice and confided, "Really well. I feel free. I finally realized what a controlling, selfish person Norm is. He called me, obviously drunk, late one night last week. Went on about how he shouldn't have walked out on me."

"I thought it was you who sent him packing," Beth said.

"I did—so I reminded him, and he got all huffy. Said he was doing just fine. He has his own room and is living with three great guys from work in a house on Thirteenth near Victoria. Get this—two of them are Ben and Gerry."

"Oh, like Ben and Jerry ice cream?" said Beth.

"That's what I said too. Norm shouted at me, 'no it's spelled with a G, nothing to do with ice cream, stupid.' Then he slammed the receiver in my ear."

Beth jotted down the names and vague address information in her purse notebook. Perhaps she should take a little stroll around there sometime, preferably in the darkness of early evening. *Or maybe not, even Edith wouldn't be that rash.*

❦

Beth moved on to the locket ... who could have known Edith had it? Cameron reported that Dennis said he only saw a few neighbours around the time he found the locket, and none were very close. Did someone see him from their window? Or maybe Edith *did* tell someone else. Beth doubted that since Edith hadn't even told Ken or Susan. *And strictly speaking, Edith didn't tell me.* Sigh.

Finally, Beth considered the previous afternoon—she and Cameron had taken leave of each other formally. I hadn't felt good. Beth supposed he thought her bias against Frank Nolan clouded her judgement and her efforts in having June involved had proved it to him. Still, maybe she could work in some conversation about Frank if Harry spoke of him.

It would be just natural for her to answer or comment. The visit was all set for tomorrow, and it would be a waste of an opportunity to nudge Cameron out of his attitude about the point she was trying to make.

The sound of a noisy jackhammer brought Beth back to the present. From the position she had, it seemed that a number of onlookers were gathering. *They needn't bother,* she thought. Cameron told her there wouldn't be anything to see once a white tented area was set up. She understood, mostly from reading and from TV reports, that the procedure was similar to an archaeological dig. She looked down at the still unfinished dishes. The suds had almost disappeared, and the water was cold.

The remainder of the day was devoted to writing Christmas cards, some reading, and a few phone calls. With all the activity out in the lane, Monty was housebound. He followed Beth around meowing his displeasure and going to the back door often to implore her to let him out. When the wet day finally turned bright, Beth went out her front door and walked around Trout Lake to escape the commotion in the lane. She lingered for a time, breathing in crisp air and the late afternoon orange-red sunset.

Tuesday, December 14

Cameron felt his excitement surge as he raced up two flights of stairs to the obstetrical offices of the Doctors Sangster, Bing, and Singh. *Sounds like a musical trio.*

"Thanks for sparing some time for me this morning," Cameron said to Gwen Taylor, who looked at his ID and shook his hand.

Gwen turned momentarily to ask the receptionist to disturb her only if absolutely necessary. Cameron guessed she was getting on for sixty with grey-tinged, pale brown hair. Her matronly bearing and quiet manner radiated calm and confidence. She closed the door that bore her name as they entered what looked to be the largest office in the clinic. Gwen pointed him toward a corner where a circular table had several chairs gathered around.

"My office doubles as a lunchroom and education centre," she answered his unspoken thought and smiled. "So, I gather you think I may be of some help."

When Cameron had phoned the office the day previous to inquire if Dr. Wagner was still in practice, he'd been told the obstetrician had passed away from a heart attack several years past, though the clinic still bore his name. His disappointment was fleeting though since the receptionist, in passing him on to the nurse manager, landed him a promising new lead. Gwen Taylor had been a UBC nursing program student doing a practicum experience at the busy clinic during the summer of 1960. She was willing to see him as soon as he wanted.

"This is a preliminary interview, you understand," he reminded Gwen.

She nodded. "Yes. I recall you said there'd be a final interview and formal statement taken at the police station."

"With your permission, I'll take a few notes." Cameron had gotten back in the groove, as he thought of it, getting the little housekeeping questions tidily taken care of before launching into the questions that would yield the best outcome, be it helpful or unhelpful.

"Going back to what you told me on the phone—you said you were in the clinic on Tuesday September sixth, the day Emma Mahoney had her appointment. However, you were sent home sick a short time before she arrived. But you're sure you may be able to help us because you saw her being picked up? I assume you were missed from any police inquiry due to being reported as ill that afternoon. Why is it you didn't come forward as soon as you heard about the investigation?"

"Well, I had my nose in textbooks and was having practicum experience at Burnaby General. I didn't return after that till maybe two weeks before Christmas just to say hi and Merry Christmas to some of the staff. Someone did mention the police interviews and Mrs. Mahoney's disappearance, but at that time, I had no idea it happened on my last day. It wasn't till we spoke yesterday I realized it *was* that particular day."

"Explain how it is you remember it was that day—it was a very long time ago," said Cameron.

"I'd just finished my practicum before the Labour Day weekend," said Gwen. "Classes were starting up again for my final year. Tuesday the sixth I went in for one last day. I recall the day mainly because of the positive evaluation I received and the coffee break farewell I was treated to in the morning."

"But you'd gone home with a cold, so how—"

"That's just it, I didn't go home, though I should have. It's another reason I remember the day since I was feeling really guilty for staying downtown to do some shopping instead, and in the process, likely spreading some of my germs around. I would have been infectious, and I *should* have gone home."

"So, what do you remember seeing?" said Cameron.

"I was walking north on Seymour a few blocks before The Bay when I saw Mrs. Mahoney get picked up. I noticed her ahead waiting on the sidewalk. I'd have known her anywhere—she was very striking with her beautiful hair. Apart from that, she was wearing a dress I'd seen before. And of course, she'd been visiting the clinic every two weeks while I was there, so I recognized her easily."

"I asked you to take some time before meeting with me today and think back to what you saw. You told me you saw Mrs. Mahoney from the passenger side. Have you been able to recall anything about the car?" Cameron asked.

"I've been doing my best to visualize that day," said Gwen, "but it's ages ago and I wasn't feeling the best, you understand. I've no sense that I saw the driver, but I have this feeling I thought it was her husband only because I seem to recall it wasn't a car, it was a small truck I think."

"Can you remember the colour of the vehicle?"

"Goodness, I have no idea. Maybe if it had been blazing red I might have remembered," Gwen smiled. "Anyway, I think it could have been a small pickup. But I would never be able to swear on a bible that it was."

"Don't worry about it," said Cameron, "you've been a great help. I'll let you get back to your patients."

❦

Cameron and Detective McNabb met before noon to hash over Gwen Taylor's recollections.

"Here's a stab in the dark—perhaps the truck Mrs. Taylor thinks she saw is Gus Pavlik's," Cameron said. "It's an off-chance, but maybe she would remember more detail under hypnosis. Your decision of course."

"I was thinking the same thing," said Steve. "Worth a try. Along with some credible evidence from under the garage, we just might get somewhere with this case. This morning, the forensic team recovered a partially degraded leather wallet buried two feet below the cement near the side where the locket was found. A preliminary scan revealed it contains a watch and a set of keys. Once they carefully disassemble the wallet, we'll know more."

"Can fingerprints still be found on objects buried that long? I've never worked a case this old," Cameron said.

"Fingerprints have been known to last forty years or more in the right circumstances. A thorough job was done in 1960 collecting neighbours' prints; lucky we have them for comparison."

"With all the hands the locket passed through before we got it, there would be nothing useful there, I guess. I recall Dennis Greene said he wiped it," said Cameron.

"Forensics checked it inside and out, but no luck, as expected."

Chair casters squeaked as Steve rolled back from his desk and came around to clap Cameron on the shoulder as he rose to leave. "Feels like we're getting somewhere, Cam. I'll call Gwen Taylor now. If she can come in tomorrow to formalize a statement, maybe she'll also agree to stay and meet with one of our consulting hypnotherapists. Then we'll see if we have something more concrete to go on. I'll be in touch."

※

Beth saw Cameron had parked in the south lot of John Hendry Park near Trout Lake. He hopped out of the jeep and waved when he saw Beth approaching.

"Hi," said Beth. "We're just headed to Hull Street, it's not far. Harry's looking forward to meeting you."

While they walked, Cameron spoke in general terms of his discovery of a witness whose information could break open the cold case.

"After all these years, it doesn't seem likely it'll be that easy to solve," said Beth.

Cameron frowned. "I realize that. However, some interesting information turned up when I interviewed someone from the obstetrical clinic. Could be a lucky break or nothing, time will tell."

By two, they had signed in at the reception desk of Lakeview Manor and turned left to enter the south wing through a fire door. Harry was standing with his door open, as if he was watching them approach. He waved, a grin lighting his face.

"I thought you said he can't see?" Cameron said in a whispered aside.

"Come in," said Harry, holding his hand out to be shaken during introductions, then leading the way past his tiny kitchen. Beth glimpsed a plate of her gingerbread figures sitting on a tray flanked by three mugs.

"Let's have a cup of tea. The kettle just boiled, Beth. You can do the honours."

After an exchange of pleasantries, Cameron asked a few key questions about the disappearance of Emma Mahoney.

"I remember talk in the neighbourhood, yes. We heard about it at church, you know, from Edith or Sofia and from our nearer neighbours," Harry said. "But Cora and I lived on a corner lot at the top of the lane, so we came and went almost exclusively on Penticton. I liked to turn from there onto Twenty-second and get to Nanaimo that way."

"You would have known the Pavlik's, I suppose," said Beth.

"Oh yes," said Harry. "Gus and I did some fishing together once in a while and traded gardening tips over the years. But we didn't know them so well that we ever had meals together. And then they moved away and that was that."

A few further questions from Cameron didn't yield any revelations. When neighbourhood reminiscences faded out and Cameron looked ready to shut down the interview, Beth couldn't resist leading Harry onto the topic of his family.

"I know you're looking forward to Christmas and having

your niece Pat home. Will you do anything special with her and your nephew? Maybe all go out to dinner?"

"Don't think Frank will want that," Harry said with a shrug. "I think he's intimidated by his cousin. They don't really know each other. Pat grew up here. Frank grew up in Guelph. He only moved here a bit over two years ago."

"Will he go east for Christmas?" asked Beth, trying to figure out how to find further traction on the subject of Frank even as Cameron, across the small room, gave a negative shake of his head.

"No, there's no one there anymore he's attached to, so he's told me. He didn't really know his father who upped and left when he was only a toddler. My sister passed away four years ago now. Since she passed, Frank says he's not much into Christmas. I told him I'd treat him to a New Year's dinner at the Hotel Vancouver. I'm having Christmas dinner as usual with my niece and her mom. You must remember to call me about meeting Pat."

"What about . . ." Beth tried to squeeze in another question about Frank just as Cameron rose from his chair to signal the visit was over.

When he and Beth were out on the sidewalk again, Cameron broke the uncomfortable silence between them.

"Beth, you know what I said Sunday. I want to concentrate on Emma Mahoney this week. Remember, keep out of the nephew's way. It doesn't mean you can't visit Mr. Anders, but you must be careful."

"You're right," Beth said, barely holding in her frustration. "Sorry."

Cameron said he'd be in touch the next day, and like Sunday, they said a less-than-cordial goodbye.

TWENTY-FIVE

Wednesday, December 15

The chilly, overcast day found Cameron Ross at the Cambie police station watching Gwen Taylor get settled in a comfortable armchair to undergo hypnosis.

It was ten after ten. Cameron stood at the one-way window of the room adjoining an office where Gwen relaxed in a comfortable reclining chair. Steve McNabb, who sat removed from the proceedings, and Eileen Finch, one of the professional hypnotherapists who consulted with VPD at times, were the only staff in the room. The audio tapes, one a backup, had been turned on the moment the therapist entered the room.

The hypnotherapist began the preamble, introducing herself, her work, and her experience. Her voice was soft and soothing. She asked Gwen to call her by her first name. Eileen described how the hypnosis session would progress before they moved on to an informal conversation about Gwen's interests.

Gwen Taylor proved an easy subject to induce into a trance-like state. She concentrated on the small silver ball that was held about a foot from her eyes. Soon, her eyes grew heavy and closed.

After a few simple questions to determine Gwen's readiness, Eileen said, "I'm going to take you back to the time you finished your practicum at the Wagner Obstetrical Clinic. Tell me when that was."

"It was September 1960, on the Tuesday after the Labour Day weekend," Gwen replied without hesitation.

꽃

As Gwen Taylor was leaving, escorted by Detective McNabb, Cameron thanked her for allowing him to view the session. The results had been encouraging, even exciting, he thought. He was seated in Steve's office when the detective returned. They exchanged a smile and fell into speculation that the truck Gwen had described under hypnosis as a grey car-like truck might be Gus Pavlik's.

"I'll go see the Pavlik's again and get a look at that truck and the logbook," said Cameron, "though of course, it still could be someone else with a truck."

"Yes," said Steve. "Maybe Beth Langille can find out if anyone remembers who else in the neighbourhood back then had a pickup truck. Like Michael Mahoney. And the other neighbour—Martinelli—who also helped build the garage."

꽃

By late morning, the Belmont Motors showroom was abuzz with several prospective buyers, one of whom Mike Mahoney was confident would be a sale since the man had owned two Camaros before. He requested time to look through the list of options and read more about the updated electrical system. Mike left him to it while he situated himself to be available to the other two browsers. From where he stood, he had a view of the used car lot. Andy had failed to impress a middle-aged woman with any of the new cars and had taken her outside to show her some choices there. But she had apparently left. Mike looked out and saw Andy alone speaking with Rich at the far end of the lot. Andy was waving his arms in every direction. All at once, Mike saw Rich strike out. He landed two swift punches to Andy's belly and face before Andy collapsed and disappeared from view. Mike gasped and stepped back from the window. Rich took a quick look around before he strode away. Mike felt sick; he hoped he hadn't been seen. He jumped a little when one of the browsers spoke.

"Something's happened to one of your salesmen," the man said. "I saw him having fisty-cuffs with a fellow out there. He was knocked down and still hasn't gotten up. You better go out and see if he's okay."

Mike called to Jeff, another salesman, that he was going out to see Andy. When Mike got to the scene of the altercation, he found Andy, lying prone, seemingly unconscious with blood oozing from above his left eye. Mike fought off panic. Oblivious to the cold, he pulled his sports jacket off, folded it inside out, bent down, and placed it under Andy's head. As he did, Andy's eyes opened.

"Oooh," he groaned. "Back of my head hurts like hell."

Mike wasn't about to let on he saw what happened. "Are you okay?" he asked. "What happened? One of the customers saw you get punched."

"Crazy car buyer, that's all. Angry that I stood firm on the price I quoted. I'd already lowered it."

Andy's scared of Rich too, thought Mike.

❦

Thursday, December 16

Mike was relieved he'd managed to avoid both Rich and Norm when he arrived at work early Thursday, though he knew there was no way he could dodge them all the time. He would have liked to have called in sick but for the fact Andy Fletcher would likely be absent. Jeff confirmed his expectation.

"Don't know when he'll be back. He has a concussion," said Jeff.

"No wonder, his head hit the pavement," said Mike, his mind flying to an image of Andy lying flat out like he was dead.

Memories of the two meetings in Rich's office added to Mike's edginess. He planned to busy himself with a client or disappear to the staff washroom to keep out of the way and hopefully avoid interacting with Rich at all. Mike recognized he was in a situation that had little chance of getting better, but his worries were shoved aside by the part of him that lusted after a bright red Camaro with a V8 engine like the one that sat in the showroom. *Just remember*, he told himself, *Belmont Motors gives its salesmen good deals*.

At noon, just to keep up appearances, when Mike saw Norm in the lunchroom, he walked over to join him. Norm was already halfway through a peanut butter sandwich. He was in good spirits, crowing about how he met a fab girl at a bar last evening. Mike relaxed and kept him on the subject, asking a question now and then. Soon Norm went off, leaving some balled-up wax paper, a crumpled paper napkin, and an empty Styrofoam cup behind. Mike refrained from pointing out the garbage can was just a step away.

❦

It was only quarter to nine that morning when Cameron called Beth from his cell phone.

"Don't worry. I know. I'm ahead of time," he said. "I'm parked across from your place. Couldn't concentrate at home with road work out front. I'll just look over some of my notes. Take your time. We don't have to be at the Pavlik's till ten."

"Okay, be there soon." She put down the receiver, thinking Cameron's tone had seemed unexpectedly friendly given the two tense exchanges between them and a terse phone call last evening. She'd take him at his word and not rush. It had been a restless night broken by bouts of wakeful worrying that she was getting nowhere and that she may as well abandon this liaison. She should stop stepping beyond the bounds of her ability. Just let the police do their job. They would find out who killed Emma and they would find out who killed Edith, if someone had. They were already considering the fact that Edith's accident could be deliberate now—*only in relation to the cold case,* she reminded herself.

She sat a moment to finish her second cup of coffee, her elbows on the table. Monty jumped up and butted his head on her shoulder.

"You shouldn't be up here," she said, without conviction, and bent her head to kiss his forehead.

Not long after, as she buckled up her seatbelt, Cameron asked, "Shall we take the same route?"

"Sure," said Beth, surprised he'd asked her opinion about something like that.

Traffic seemed heavier this time. They were late and apologizing at the Pavlik's front door near quarter past ten.

"Doesn't matter," said Gus. "Nothing special planned today."

While Beth went into the living room to greet Inga Pavlik, Cameron waited outside for Gus to get the key to the old building that housed the truck.

❦

"Here she is, my Datsun Coupe Utility," said Gus after fussing with the rusted door lock. "Pretty special back then. Got it in '59, a year after it came out—nothing much to look at now."

Cameron casually swiped a finger through the thick layer of dust on the hood. "It's grey."

"Yes, I thought that was more business-like for work. It's been here a long time. Always meant to sell it, just never got to it."

"Useful vehicle," said Cameron as Gus opened the passenger-side door, popped open the glove compartment, then handed Cameron the logbook.

Cameron found the September 6, 1999 entry that confirmed the truck had indeed been serviced that day. He showed it to Gus and said, "This writing here, would it be from the garage?"

"No, that's Nina's, the others are mine. I kept my own record since I was using it for work and for pleasure. You said some forensic fellows are coming today?"

"Yes, Mr. Pavlik. They'll be here in about fifteen minutes. The examination of your truck won't take too long. Just a routine check with some photos taken of your logbook. Backs up the change to your statement."

"Just like in the movies, eh?" said Gus.

"Yes, something like that."

Later, as they drove away, Cameron asked Beth, "Did you learn anything new from Mrs. Pavlik?"

"No. It was a little hard keeping the conversation going, but she seemed to want to go over what she said last time. She wasn't reeling it off as if it was memorized, which I took as a good sign. And how did you get on?"

"Fine. But I disliked having to mislead Mr. Pavlik about why the truck is of interest. I couldn't tell him we think Emma got into a truck of the same sort after her clinic appointment. Which brings me to ask if you'll do a little digging. Steve McNabb suggested it."

❦

Cameron used the underground parking at City Square since he planned to get some groceries after the impromptu meeting Steve McNabb had requested. He wolfed down a sandwich at the Food Fair before heading down Cambie.

"Just wanted to talk over our ideas before you come on Saturday to give the team your wrap-up report," said Steve.

"If we're looking to fit Gus Pavlik into a scenario, it would mean he came home early from fishing or he and his friend went somewhere close by," said Cameron.

"What about the writing in the logbook?"

"Mr. Pavlik could have dictated the information to his daughter, I suppose," said Cameron.

Steve thought a moment. "Right. We could ask Mrs. Mahoney but she's basically a hostile witness. Maybe Mrs. Pavlik is covering up about when he got home. With his fishing buddy deceased we're stuck."

Cameron shrugged. "This isn't getting us very far."

"Well, what we do have is this," said Steve. "Mrs. Taylor thought the vehicle she saw Emma Mahoney get into seemed to be a cross between a truck and a car and she said it was grey under hypnosis. Could be wrong, I know. How many families in that neighbourhood might have had a similar truck no matter the colour? I wonder how many pickup trucks there were with a rear seating area back then?"

"Don't know for sure," said Cameron, "but I think Chevrolet and Toyota both had coupe utility vehicles. Anyway, Beth will try and find out what neighbours had trucks back then."

"I'll get a comparison on the writing with Mrs. Mahoney's signatures from old and new statements. The digital photos we use now should be adequate. We're waiting on the lab about the items found under the Todd's garage. That's going to take a little longer with some current cases taking priority. There was a homicide and a suspicious death two days ago and another homicide this morning. Not a good way to end the year."

Cameron nodded, "Nothing more for now then?"

"I think that's all," said Steve, "except—I'd appreciate it if you can stay connected with us after Saturday. I'd like to confirm your consultant status if you're able to offer help with cold cases again. It will be on and off, depending on budget restrictions. You alright with that?"

"Certainly, but I'm back to work on Monday. Any time I can spare will be limited to the couple days I'm generally off in a week."

"Understood."

Standing alone in an empty down elevator, Cameron felt a rush of satisfaction about how the cold case was progressing and with the unexpected 'thrill of the chase', something he thought he'd lost. As he exited, two familiar-faced officers waiting to go up gave him a friendly greeting by name. It was very satisfying to feel welcome again in his old workplace.

TWENTY-SIX

Friday, December 17

In the Mahoney household, three unhappy people were stirring. Michael arose first, as was expected of him, to turn up the thermostat so the house warmed up before his family got up. Lying in bed, Nina could hear Mike having a shower and wondered why, like yesterday, he was up so early. He didn't need to be at work till eight thirty. Nina, who had talked to her father the previous day, had scarcely slept four hours, seething with anger that her whole family was under attack. The mauve half circles under her eyes seemed darker every morning. How could Michael sleep so soundly? And why did the police have to bug her dad about one measly oversight?

❧

Mike, who knew he was literally at risk of attack, finished his shower and called up the stairs. "I'm out, Dad."

Mike was both dreading going to work and glad he was off the coming weekend. He needed a break from his jitters so he could begin the following week in good form.

He already had an idea for leaving Belmont Motors behind. It would sound logical that his dad had found him an entry level position in accounting downtown. But he was getting ahead of himself. First get the Camaro. Then wait several weeks past a payday and just call in to say he'd got a new job. There was nothing in his work contract that said either the garage or the employee had to give notice. *I bet Mom will give me a loan then I can bail sooner.* He felt calmer now. The current situation would blow over. *Maybe Andy won't come back at all.* As he pulled on a fresh shirt, Mike was reminded that his wrist remained tender. He could almost feel the pressure of Rich's fingers again. That encounter and the attack on Andy would remain foremost in his mind during the day.

❦

The sounds of Monty bringing up a hairball catapulted Beth out of bed. It was barely five thirty. She rushed to the kitchen, grabbed a knife and paper towel, and headed for the living room.

"Monty," she wailed, "why do you always do it on my carpets?" Monty wailed back asking for breakfast.

Once she completed more cleanup while the cat watched, crouched nearby, she felt both awake and tired. After she failed to get back to sleep, she got up. Even after eating, showering, and dressing, it was still too early to call Sofia, the person she planned to mine for information. She'd invite her over for a cup of tea in the afternoon.

Subduing her impatience, Beth reclined in her armchair to read awhile, checking her wristwatch more often than necessary till she could make the planned calls. She got Sofia just after nine thirty and was disappointed but not entirely surprised to learn she was unavailable.

"But we can catch up a little now," Sofia said. "Do you have time now? I haven't heard how you and your fellow have got along with the interviews. And what about the garage, can you tell me anything? Gino is very interested. With all his years handling construction projects, he's never done anything quite like that."

"I have time," said Beth. *I'm the one supposed to be asking questions.* "Sofia, I've told you, Mr. Ross is not my fellow. He's a VPD consultant."

"Well," said Sofia, "you told me he's single. You look like a nice couple to me."

Beth got her off the subject by returning to Sofia's interest in the interviews. "The interviews are confidential so I can't tell you much, Sofia, but Mr. Ross has almost finished, I think. We went over to see Inga and Gus Pavlik again as a follow up. Mr. Pavlik was showing off his old truck before we left."

"I remember it. I've been wondering how they are. Haven't talked to Inga in a long while. We used to swap vegetables from our gardens. Mostly her zucchini for my tomatoes."

Beth felt uneasy given the conversation was taking place in the context of interviews. But she realized she could introduce the subject further now since Sofia remembered the truck.

"Sofia, I can tell you my impression of how they're doing, but please, do not share our discussion with anyone. I can't stress that enough. Nina is already annoyed with me and not very neighbourly right now with many of us. You saw how she was at the Christmas tea. She and Michael are having a hard time with Emma's case reopened."

"Right. I understand. Just between you and me."

In the end, Beth thought she'd done well learning that Gino had had a red Ford pickup before he changed to an SUV, and that Michael Mahoney had not had a truck, nor had Alan Whitman. That was all she found out. She left Cameron a short message. Beth wondered not long after, as she relaxed in a steamy bubble bath, if the phone would ring. And it did. *Too bad,* she thought; she never interrupted a nice, long soak, especially in winter. When she checked, there was a friendly thankyou reply from Cameron.

❧

At eleven in the evening, Frank Nolan was kneeling by his toilet, head over the bowl, barfing out his guts for the third time that night. It was hard to be angry and sick at the same time. He sank to the floor, grabbed the bathmat and lay his head down. He had thought he'd treat himself since it was likely the last time for a while. An expensive meal at the Four Seasons with a pre-dinner martini, an appetizer of bacon-wrapped scallops, and a bottle of Merlot to pair with the Filet Mignon entrée, followed by Tiramisu with a vintage port on the side hadn't been the way to drown his sorrow or boost his spirits. *Why was I so stupid,* he thought.

Everything had gone wrong. Frank's personal bank account had now shrunk to an alarming level. Vancouver was expensive compared to his previous locations. *At least I kept Uncle's ten thousand aside.* His prize idea—the diamond mine—was doomed not only because there were no investors anymore but because reason had begun to nag him. Here he was working his wiles without a disguise to shield himself. He was beginning to admit that it was just crazy luck that Revenue Canada had never caught up with him.

First, the Wilson siblings had backed out of their signed 'legal' agreement and stopped the transfer of one hundred thousand dollars to the investment account he'd created. Daisy Wilson, a large woman with a large voice, obviously wore the pants in the family. She had stalked in unannounced and delivered the news with glee. Her smug satisfaction was evident as her shiny coral lips curled into a smile. Frank knew better than to challenge her, so he swallowed hard and choked on his ire. He had a coughing fit while the horrible woman left.

The appearance of Kitty Kurokawa had briefly overshadowed his awakening common sense. Elation turned to exasperation in less than a week when Kitty finally called him to apologize, saying she was out at YVR waiting to fly home to a serious family emergency. Not wanting to burn any proverbial bridges, Frank again swallowed hard, but this time he offered sympathies and his services when next she returned.

For the first time Frank was truly afraid that 'practicing' under his legal name put him in danger of losing his liberty. He could see he had lost sight of what was in his best interest. As his reserve of "earnings" dwindled, he had let panic sway him. He gave himself a talking-to. His old ways must be abandoned, and he would set his sights more firmly on attaining the inheritance he so richly deserved. It would be a relief to have legitimate access to capital. Uncle Harry had no offspring. That upstart of a cousin, Pat, was raking in the dough with her brainy research; *she* didn't need the old man's money. That left *him*. This thought gave Frank enough energy to drag himself along the floor to the bedroom. He clutched a corner of a plush comforter and pulled it off the bed. With some of it bunched up under his head, he fell into a half sleep on the thin carpet. Sometime in the night, Frank dreamed he was grasping for thousand-dollar bills that floated just out of reach.

❦

Saturday, December 18

It was just after 3 a.m., and Norm Jervis, who had dropped the ladder and abandoned Gerry and Ben to their fate, was crediting his luck in escaping the police dog to a very useful item he'd learned of from a pro. His tools of the trade always included a spray bottle of bleach. Now, back at the house, he did a hurried packing job, throwing his limited belongings into a large tote and a black plastic garbage bag. He stuffed his backpack with any remaining items, then stripped his bed and pushed the linen into the washing machine. He wouldn't be sorry to leave the dark cubby hole. He made a thorough check through the drawers and left the room looking bare. Jimmy was away for a week so would not be implicated, at least in tonight's disaster.

It was too early to call Rich, and Norm knew better than to ask for a place to stay. He did not want to jeopardize his standing in his cousin's eyes by having him think he expected that kind of favour. Twenty minutes later, he called a Yellow Cab using the landline, gave a Richmond street corner as his destination, and wiped the phone. Since he had been entrusted with keys to the body shop, he would walk there and wait out the time in a small room used for breaks. It wasn't like he hadn't slept in a chair before.

At eight, after a few rough hours bent over the table with his head cushioned on some rolled-up T-shirts, Norm's neck was stiff and his back ached. He boiled some water and rooted around for the instant coffee. There was no milk in the countertop fridge, but behind some boxed cookies and the glass jar of white sugar, he found an outdated tin of Carnation milk. Yanking open two drawers, he saw plenty of mismatched cutlery but not a can opener in sight. He slammed his fist on the counter then spent several minutes massaging his hand, swearing.

Sweet black water—ugh. But it was hot and warmed his hands. He forced down two stale McVities digestives. Norm knew that soon Rich would leave to get to his office for nine. He always dropped in on Saturday mornings to check the ledgers he kept locked away. Norm also knew Rich wasn't fond of surprises like the news he was about to share. It would be easier to tell him before he arrived.

Rich answered the phone with a cautious hello.

"Morning, cousin," Norm began, "I wanted to let you know right away that I think something bad has happened to Gerry and Ben. They went out late and didn't come home."

"You called me about that?" said Rich in a terse voice. "Don't worry, they're likely sleeping it off at some friend's place."

"No, I don't think so," said Norm. "I heard them go out early this morning, maybe two o'clock. I found out they're doing some break-and-enter gigs on the side—and that's where I think they went last night. They've got a lot of stuff stashed in the garage."

"Stuff like what?" Rich growled. His voice rose an octave. Norm held the receiver away from his ear. "They're not stealing from our supply, are they? If they've been doing that then—"

"No, no, it's not like that," said Norm, rushing to offset an all-out temper tantrum. "There are cameras, DVD players, cell phones, bikes—that kind of stuff," said Norm.

He hadn't expected such a rant over small change compared to the hundreds of thousands Rich was raking in. He was definitely not about to tell his cousin he was involved. If Tara's old uncle hadn't suggested they pay rent, and if Rich was paying him a decent wage with all the risks he was taking, he wouldn't have had to create this source of added income.

"You'd better be right," said Rich, not quite so loud. "If they've been nabbed, this is serious."

"The guys are solid; I know they won't talk willingly but they might get tricked into giving something away. You're right. This could be trouble," said Norm.

"We have to get in contact with them; I'll call my lawyer to do that," Rich said, adding as an afterthought, "Where are you anyway?"

"At the shop—I cleared out of the house, don't want to be mixed up with whatever mess they're in. What if the police showed up? I already have a past arrest for dealing. Not that it was proven but—"

"I'll contact someone I know who has a rooming house and you can go there for now," said Rich. "What about Mike Mahoney, did he know about this?"

He was about to say Mike knew nothing, when in a flash, Norm recognized how to create the third person working with Gerry and Ben. He had no fears they would rat on him given his relationship to Rich. As well, being part of the "inner circle," they were well aware of Rich's strict rules about loyalty.

"Yeah, pretty sure he does; I think he's been helping them out."

🍁

Gerry Newman sat in the backseat of the police cruiser glaring at the floor. He had seen Ben being pushed into the cruiser ahead. When he had realized there was no chance of escape, he'd hissed a warning at Ben: "Let me do the talking; if you say anything, just give them Mike's name." *Yeah*, he thought, *divide and conquer—not effing likely.* They both knew to keep their mouths shut. Nonetheless, he was pissed off that Norm had escaped. He was the ringleader after all—it was his bright idea to form a team and make some extra cash. It had been going well for months. They'd gotten some sweet loot, Gerry thought, but they hadn't moved half of it yet. They'd started out heisting bikes, which generally didn't require them to go into residences. Many were left outside with locks that were easy to breech, and garages were generally easy picking.

Gerry's mind swung sharply from bikes to Mike Mahoney. A few weeks back, Gerry had offered to sell 'my twelve speed' to Mike. He had fallen for the 'thought I'd ask you first before I advertise' line. Now he could take the fall for Norm. Norm was always complaining about the guy, so he'd be good with it. They needed a third person and Mike would be perfect.

❧

Steve McNabb ushered Cameron into a conference room where four officers were present, either seated at the large extended oval table or helping themselves to coffee. Cameron knew three, and the fourth, one of the two women, was introduced as Robin Shay from the forensics unit.

At nine, McNabb casually called the small group to order, "Morning, team. Our deliberations will begin with Cameron and I giving an overview of how this investigation has progressed. Jump in any time with observations or questions. Then we'll tease out what we still want or need to know in order to, hopefully, lay Emma Mahoney and her case to rest. Over to you, Cam."

"On September 6, 1960, twenty-six-year-old Mrs. Emma Mahoney went missing sometime in the afternoon following her obstetrical clinic appointment. At the time of her disappearance, she was described as extremely nervous about her six-month pregnancy since she had developed medical complications. In the end, compelling evidence about her troubled youth due to losing her parents in an accident here on the lower mainland came to light. She was around twelve years old at that time. She went to live in the Okanogan with her maternal grandparents, suffered from episodes of depression and kept running away trying to get back to Vancouver. It was postulated that Emma Mahoney had either run away or taken her own life. The former seemed most likely given some of her personal items, including clothes and a suitcase, were missing from her home. The husband who was thoroughly investigated had a solid alibi, and since there were no other red flags, the case was eventually sidelined. Emma was never found and the case has been reviewed periodically with no leads until now."

"Interesting tale," said McNabb. "An acquaintance of Cam's brought this all to light in the course of asking for advice on what she thinks is a suspicious car accident."

Cameron continued. "The case was reopened because the locket Emma was wearing the day of her disappearance thirty-nine years ago turned up in tangled roots from under the garage of a neighbour who recently died after being run down. Now we've determined through my discovery of a witness, missed back then due to unusual circumstances, that Emma was likely picked up by someone driving a small truck. She apparently did not hesitate to get in. At the time, the witness remembers speculating it was Emma's husband, although she couldn't see the driver. It was the truck that prompted that assumption. Her statement concerning the vehicle has been confirmed through hypnosis."

❦

Mike Junior was pleasantly occupied dreaming of warm breezes, a turquoise pool, palm trees, and a Mai Tai in his hand when an unpleasant knocking sound dragged him away from the beautiful brunette who was bending to ask him his name. Then a voice was hissing in his ear.

"Mikey, get up right now."

Mike squinted at his bedside clock. It was only nine thirty. He turned away, burrowed into his pillow, and squeezed his eyes together. The irritated—and irritating—hiss continued.

"Get up. Get your clothes on right now. There are two policemen in the living room waiting to talk to you."

Nina Mahoney pulled open the closet door and grabbed a pair of black jeans, throwing them on the bed. She yanked open some tallboy drawers and dropped some briefs, socks, and a dark grey T-shirt on top of the jeans.

"Aww, Mom. It's Saturday. I'm sleeping in. What the—" Mike stopped short of swearing. He was awake. "Police?"

"You heard me. What have you been doing? Why would police want to talk to you? Wash your face. Brush your teeth. Comb your hair. Put those things on now and get yourself up there."

A little over ten minutes later, his stomach in knots, Mike stepped into the living room.

"Good morning, Mr. Mahoney," Constable Roy said after showing his ID. "I believe you know Constable Argento."

Mike nodded, relaxing a little.

"Hi, Mike," said Constable Argento. "We're following up on a report that you're in possession of stolen property. Will you consent to showing us where your bicycle is, please?"

*

Out on her front steps, Beth was, at last, acting on the impetus to do some Christmas decorating. She'd seen the VPD cruiser parked out front of the Mahoney's when she'd stepped out her door and wondered about it, but then got on with the job she'd set herself. December 25th was exactly a week away. Today, she planned to do some shopping along Robson after meeting with Cameron in his office at the art gallery. He was returning to his VAG post for a half-day to catch up and had suggested a short chat in his office later to tell her what he could about the progress of Emma's case.

Even with gloves, Beth's fingers felt cold as she wove the coloured lights back and forth up the black iron railing, avoiding, as best she could, the winter remnants of the honeysuckle vine. On one side, the filigree work extended up to the top of the outside ceiling in a narrow, somewhat more ornate section, which allowed her to plug the lights into an outlet normally used for a lightbulb. Beth finished her task and was folding up her sturdy step stool when she saw Mike headed for the police car accompanied by Constable Argento and another officer. *Oh dear*, she thought, *have Edith's worries come true?*

TWENTY-SEVEN

Saturday, December 18

Michael Mahoney watched his son's profile in the police car until he could see it no longer. He'd had a quick exchange with Mike as soon as Constable Roy told his son he would be questioned at the station.

"Don't say anything till I get there," Michael had said. "This is all a big mistake. We'll have it sorted out in no time." Mike had nodded, his face looking pale and strained.

When the charter rights had been read, Nina had been the first to lash out, accusing the officers of harassment. Looking directly at Argento, she expressed her displeasure in his lack of judgement. "That wasn't necessary. Mike is a fine boy; you should know that."

Mike had lowered his eyes in what his father assumed was embarrassment. At thirty, he was a grown man in most people's eyes—except his mother's. If only she could appreciate how effective he had been in taking on the car sales position. His sales numbers were climbing and many clients had expressed their appreciation.

In the brief conversations he had had with his son, Michael had determined that in just two weeks, Mike was feeling more confident in himself. He wished his wife could see what he saw in their son. She gave half-hearted attention to his success and quickly turned to her belief that he must move on from his dead-end job.

Nina fell silent, her gaze unfocussed. As Michael put on his jacket and grabbed his car keys, she shook herself out of the trance and announced she'd accompany him.

"Nina, two of us won't be able to be with Mike in the interview. Keep yourself busy here, and I'll call as soon as we're on our way home. Plan a nice lunch. I'm sure everything will work out." He gave her cheek a quick kiss.

In a police station interview room, Michael sat, relatively comfortable due to his past week's experience, while Mike fidgeted. Mike was hoping Constable Argento would do the questioning; however, Constable Roy sat down opposite the young man. After Roy engaged them in a preliminary casual exchange, he asked permission to record the interview, starting with the time and description of who was present.

Not much over thirty minutes later, Mike and his father were on their way home, both feeling a degree of relief.

Several floors above, the discussion amongst Cameron, Steve, and the others was coming to an end.

"Let's sum up where we are," said Steve, turning to the movable whiteboard in the room. "Jump in if something new occurs to you. We have two possible suspects: Gus Pavlik and Michael Mahoney. If it's not one of them, it's an unknown person—but not a complete unknown because with Gwen Taylor's recollection of seeing Emma Mahoney getting into a vehicle without hesitation, I think we can be quite sure it was someone she knew and someone who knew the neighbourhood.

That could still leave the field wide open, but we'll work with what we've got for now."

Steve motioned to Cameron, who continued. "Gus Pavlik may have returned early from fishing and picked up the truck at the garage even if his daughter drove it there. We have no way of rechecking his alibi since the person is deceased. I suppose Pavlik would know about Emma's appointment through Nina talking about it at home."

"The handwriting examination was completed this morning and came out as a ninety percent match for his daughter so he could have dictated the log entry," said Robin Shay. "Fingerprints from the excavation specimens are pending."

"We don't have enough yet," said Steve. "Let's move on to Michael Mahoney. Any thoughts on him?" McNabb answered his own question. "The idea has persisted that he could have paid someone to do away with Emma while he was at work. Then before he called police, he could have gathered some of her things together and got rid of them to make it look like she ran away. We'd have a hard time proving that unless someone out there knows something and answers our new appeal for information. We've just had the usual dead-end tips so far."

"We know that the next day, Michael Mahoney helped pour the cement for the Todd's garage floor," said Constable Chu. "As reported earlier, what was found under the concrete is in generally good condition since it was protected. The watch face is a good bet. And it's a bonus that there was a clinic appointment card covered by an intact area of the wallet."

Shay added, "Paper is far more likely to yield results after so long. We'll do our best to get the forensic results to you by Monday."

"Well," said Steve, "somebody who knew about the cement job put those things there. Waiting a few extra days is nothing compared to thirty-nine years."

"Since the Pavlik truck can't be proven as the vehicle that picked up Emma," said Cameron, "the forensic evidence is critical. Our witness's memory from so long ago can be questioned. There's nothing beyond the locket and wallet and their resting place as hard evidence of foul play."

"Not just foul play," said Steve, "murder. And it might not just be one murder—there's the hit-and-run accident of the neighbour Mrs. Todd."

※

Later that morning, Cameron met with Beth around eleven in his office at the art gallery. Their discussion didn't take long, as there was little Cameron could share except for the general fact that lab results were pending and that he'd been gratified to know his help—amended immediately to *our help*—was appreciated. He told Beth he'd be willing to turn some attention to the concerns she had voiced about Frank Nolan.

"It'll have to wait a few days, though," Cameron said. "I want to clear up some things here."

"Fine. I'll hear from you then?" said Beth, rising from a comfortable upholstered chair.

"Yes, and before you go, I've got a question for you." Cameron rose too. "Are you doing anything on Boxing Day?"

"Nope, I'm looking forward to a quiet day recovering from Christmas at my friends' place. They'll have their daughter, son-in-law, and seven-year-old twin boys visiting from New Brunswick."

"Oh. I was hoping you might join me for the open house my former colleague Ron and his wife Barb are having in the afternoon. I'd enjoy it much more having someone along and Ron would like to meet you."

♣

Midafternoon found Beth, glad to be taking a break from Christmas gift decisions, sitting alone in a corner of a busy Starbucks at Robson and Thurlow. She was nursing the last two inches of her grande hot chocolate. The usual lineup at the order counter and the clump of people waiting for their midafternoon drinks generated a buzz of voices. Her ears picked out small snippets as she let her mind wander in a bid to avoid her current quandary. "Oh well, when she said that I just walked off. . ." "And then guess what he did . . ." "No, the ball's in his court now . . ." Seemed like everyone was focused on issues of the heart.

Beth pondered her own feelings that her relationship with Cameron might be about to change. She wasn't certain if she wanted that, though she was aware she found it pleasant to be in his company when he wasn't acting like a big brother. Was it wise to alter the relatively businesslike arrangement she had with him? Beth remained uncertain that the someone who killed Emma was necessarily Edith's attacker. She still felt at odds with Cameron since it seemed he didn't think Harry's situation or the neighbourhood crime spree were relevant. His mind was, she thought, already pulling away from Edith despite his expression of interest in doing a background check on Frank. Given they were clashing over the complexity of the hit-and-run accident, Cameron's request for her to accompany him on Boxing Day surprised her.

In her mind, Beth replayed the conversation that followed his invitation, as best she could remember.

♣

"You realize," Cameron said, "I couldn't have managed all I did without you." Then he laughed. "Hell, I wouldn't have known anything about the locket or case at all if not for your determination to play detective."

"That's not fair," Beth berated him. "I'm not playing. You know full well an important part of my job is like detective work and there are some similar principles."

"Sorry, sorry," said Cameron. "I didn't mean it that way—well, maybe I did—I apologize and promise to work on my delivery. Really. I think this collaboration worked well."

"In what way?" Beth asked, not willing to let him off so easily.

With a sheepish look, Cameron went on to say he thought that even with some disagreements, they'd made valuable contributions to the cold case together. "You've shown me some of my biases, I think, and I'm better for it."

"Anything to help," said Beth with a small smile.

"So, what about it? Will you consider coming to the open house? Please."

❦

Beth's thoughts continued to spin like the voices around her as she let herself consider what it might be like to date again after so long. She reined herself in. *This is not a date. It's only a few hours. It's confirmation that Cameron sees you as a credible working partner.* She'd promised to think it over and would let him know tomorrow.

❦

About the time Beth was having the heart-to-heart with herself, Frank Nolan was rudely wakened from a nap by the jarring ring of his telephone.

It was Uncle Harry calling to let him know that Frank's cousin Pat would be flying from San Francisco Sunday evening and maybe he'd like to pick her up at the airport since she was arriving so late.

"Your Aunt Agnes is worried about Pat taking a taxi from there at one in the morning. I've got her arrival information right here and my next-door neighbour—you remember Bert—can read it out to you," Harry said, his voice hopeful.

"Sorry, but I'll be over on Bowen Island at a friend's place."

Frank was so used to lying, the words were out of his mouth before he thought of the consequences.

"But I could take you to church in the morning," he said, grasping the fact that he should offer something to counter the disappointed silence at the other end of the line and show he was a caring nephew.

❦

Sunday, December 19

Frank fidgeted as he sat beside Harry, attending the late morning mass at St. Jude's. He wondered how his uncle could stand it. His unlined raincoat provided no relief from the hard wooden pew. He squirmed. Frank tuned out Father Benson's voice to mull over what more he could do to build up good will and hurry Harry into signing the new Power of Attorney document before Pat visited him. He'd left it with his uncle weeks ago. It was time for positive action. He'd suggest lunch out on Monday. Over dessert, he'd slip in some remarks about how good it would be if Pat remained in charge of the Representation Agreement, and since he, Frank, was planning to stay settled in Vancouver, the accounts would be managed much more easily here than from afar. After lunch, he would drive them directly to get it done. Frank was picturing himself a dutiful nephew escorting a grateful uncle to his lawyer friend's office where a fresh document awaited the required signatures. In the meantime, he had missed all but the last of the scripture reading from Matthew 6. He tuned in just when Father Benson ended the chosen passage with verse 24.

"No one can serve two masters; for a slave will either hate the one and love the other, or be devoted to the one and despise the other. You cannot serve God and wealth."

Frank heard these words and was struck with an odd sensation he could not name.

❧

Beth appreciated her leisurely Sunday morning after a draining week. She phoned her father, which was good timing for him on the east coast. He had eventually given up the house her late mom and he purchased in their younger years and he had moved in with Beth's sister Janice and her family in Dartmouth. He was happy there in a self-contained suite with their garden to look after.

One thirty seemed a reasonable time to call Cameron. She was feeling a little nervous about accepting his invitation but reminded herself she was doing him a favour. She jumped when her phone rang exactly as she was about to pick up the receiver.

"Hello there, Beth," said Sofia's familiar voice. "I didn't see you in church this morning." She hastened to add, "Just teasing, but guess who I did see."

"I bet I know. Any chance it was Frank with Harry?"

"Right. It was obvious he didn't want to be there. He was off in the clouds somewhere. But it was nice to see Harry. He didn't even have to persuade Frank stay for the coffee hour. Now, that was extra surprising."

"Maybe not so much—Harry's niece is due in town. I bet Frank is out to score points," said Beth. "I'm looking forward to meeting her Tuesday afternoon. I'm hoping Pat will put Frank in his place."

The two neighbours spent a little time talking about their Christmas activities. As soon as she replaced the receiver, Beth dialed Cameron to accept his invitation.

❦

There was no question that Mike would be hounded out of bed like he was on Saturday. His parents were up early, and in whispered tones, he could hear them having heated words over breakfast.

"I told you nothing good would come from Mikey chumming around with that Norman, let alone working with him and his friends. You should have found him a job at your company."

"We went over all that yesterday," his dad threw back. "I told you; I believe Mike when he says he didn't do anything. Sure, he bought a stolen bike—that's just bad luck. The two who were caught red-handed are trying to divert some of the blame. They're setting Mike up. And by the way, it's time you started calling our son Mike. He's been an adult for years."

"He acts like a kid. I don't know where his good sense has gone. We need to guide him. YOU need to talk with him again and take some responsibility. You've got to get him away from that place." There was a pause before his mother continued. "Remind me what that constable said before you and *Mike* left."

"He told Mike he was free to go for now, not to leave the city, and that he would be in touch soon," his dad said wearily.

"I don't understand why they would want to see Mike again. Mike didn't do anything except make a poor decision."

"I told you yesterday. We're not a solid alibi for him. Since we were sleeping upstairs, they say Mike could have gone out the basement door after he got home."

Mike tried to sleep some more, but the distant grumbling

of his parent's exchange made him get up. They'd been sniping at each other since he'd moved back in and even more so since he went to work at Belmont Motors. He needed to move out. But his focus now was the false claim that he was taking part in the break-ins happening on the east side. Constable Roy had gone so far as to suggest he was the ringleader. Mike explained that all he'd done was buy the bike and tire pump from Gerry. He was in bed before one that night. He learned then that Gerry and Ben were in custody, nabbed after a break-and-enter. They'd said he was the one who got away. Obviously, they gave the police his name to try to shift some of the blame. *Yeah, they're the type to do that,* Mike thought as he showered. *Bet it's Norm who escaped. He's been tight with them since he moved in and even before that. The police will figure it out.*

Mike remained determined to survive at work till he could afford a red Camaro. *I won't ask Mom. Got to do it on my own.*

TWENTY-EIGHT

Monday, December 20

Mike Mahoney held the strain of the weekend in his neck and shoulders. He awoke feeling achy and sick to his stomach. In truth, he had noticed some heartburn most days for weeks. He wasn't at ease at home or at work. There seemed to be no escaping his tension with the added police burglary investigation poised over his head like Darth Vader's lightsaber. The unpleasant lethargy he experienced as he dressed and mechanically ate a bowl of cereal followed him to work though he roused enough to appreciate his dad's offer to drive him there. To each of them, the silent drive offered respite. Unlike him though, Mike realized his dad was looking forward to going to his workplace so he could immerse himself in numbers and blot out his own anxieties. His mom had stayed in bed.

When Mike pushed the 'Employees Only' door open and ran straight into Norm, he felt acid spurt into his throat. *What's he doing here so early?* Mike's eyes teared up; he began to cough.

"Mikey, Mikey, what's the matter, man?"

"Just a minute, need some water," Mike croaked.

Norm surprised him. "I'll get you some right away."

This was not the Norm he had come to know. Mike followed

him toward the showroom water cooler where Norm filled a small paper cup with water. Mike saw Rich standing at the top of the stairs watching them. *Ah, showing off for the boss.*

Rich called down. "Why don't we all have a little chat in the office? Come on up, there's water here too and there's coffee ready."

Mike's acid reflux kicked into high gear. He didn't trust himself to speak without having another coughing fit, so he gestured with his dad's old, brown vinyl briefcase toward the office he shared with Jeff and nodded. The case was little more than a prop but came in handy to carry his lunch most days. He chewed two Tums and sipped more water. Soon after, he lifted his leaden feet to climb the stairway. By the time he reached Rich's office, Mike thought he had a decent plan to smooth things over and eke out enough time to get the car he so wanted.

The reception desk was vacant; Beryl didn't start till nine. The door to the plush office was open, and as he entered, Rich ordered him to close it. To be sociable, Mike accepted the offer of the coffee already being poured for him. He went to a side table to add a little half and half then stirred slowly, shielding his shaky hand from view. Norm, who was unusually silent, slouched at one end of a leather settee.

"Well now," began Rich, "I understand you had some trouble on the weekend. Tell me about it."

"Yes," said Mike, "I take it you heard from Gerry or Ben. The police came calling on Saturday morning. They think I was out stealing things on Friday night with the guys."

"And were you?"

"No, not with *them*." The emphasis on 'them' got a rise out of Norm.

"Huh," Rich said, clearly interested in what kind of tale he was about to hear. "What do you mean?"

"I mean that I lift a few items from the yards of people stupid enough to leave things out to tempt me. If there are no Block Watch signs around, I check out houses that have no visible alarms and lots of cover—you know, taller thick hedges, that sort of thing. I stay well away from apartment buildings. Anyway, I was out canvassing a new area, so I don't know why they told the police I was with them. I wasn't."

"Oh really?" said Norm. It seemed he was about to ask more, but he got cut off by Rich.

"Risky behaviour. Didn't expect that of you. Better forget it," said Rich. "Aren't I paying you enough money? You live at home after all. And you've got perks."

Mike sensed a change from cold to tepid in Rich's manner. Norm remained watchful.

"Yes, I know," said Mike, "and I appreciate that."

He was rewarded by a smile from Rich and an "all right, have a good sales day—you seem to be a natural," as he was shown the door. Norm, now standing with his back to the room, looked out the window while Mike left. As the door closed, he heard Norm's muffled voice say, "He's just trying to get out of it. He's lying."

Still quaking inside, Mike took slow breaths and descended carefully to the sales floor.

❧

Detective McNabb stared at the fingerprint analysis that had just been delivered to his door by the division secretary. A name jumped out at him, magnified by his surprise. There were several partial prints of Emma Mahoney's from different surfaces, which was predictable. However, three unexpected fingerprints were found. All were Nina Mahoney's. A partial was lifted from the watch face and the plastic key ring tag and a complete one from the obstetrical clinic appointment card.

It bore a single date—Emma Mahoney's appointment for one week after the day she disappeared. Nina had handled Emma's wallet contents. She had been eighteen, and, McNabb thought, no doubt infatuated with and used by Michael Mahoney. But she would have known what she was doing burying Emma's belongings. He alerted two officers who were part of his unit.

"Michael Mahoney needs to be escorted here from his place of work, please. I've confirmed he's in his office back from an early lunch. He'll be waiting. We're going to detain him for questioning. Read him his charter rights. Put him in room three with the door closed and someone outside. Bonnie Chu and I are arresting his wife who is at home. There's clear evidence to interrogate and hold her. I'll put Mrs. Mahoney in room one with Bonnie at the door. They can each stew a little while before the interrogations. This isn't the best situation with evidence against Mrs. Mahoney and nothing on her husband. Of course, it's their right to remain silent. Still, perhaps we can shake loose the truth about Emma Mahoney's disappearance. We must keep them apart for now."

Half an hour later, Detective McNabb with Constable Chu at his side, waited at the Mahoney's front door. The doorbell tone echoed twice inside.

Nina greeted them warily and agreed to McNabb's request to come in. Inside, McNabb introduced Chu before stating the purpose of their presence. Nina controlled her shock, her eyes first widening then narrowing to slits. Her mouth compressed to a thin line as the detective spoke.

"Mrs. Mahoney, based on recovered evidence, I am arresting you for complicity in the disappearance and presumed death of Emma Mahoney on September 6, 1960."

After reading Nina her charter rights, Constable Chu said, "You can call a lawyer now or when we get to the station."

"I'm going to call my husband," Nina said.

"I'm afraid that won't be possible," said McNabb. "Your husband is at the station now, being detained as co-conspirator. If you don't have a personal lawyer, I can provide you with the telephone number to contact a legal aid duty lawyer. It's a free service."

Nina shook her head, lapsing into silence.

"Think it over on the way to the station," said Chu. "You might change your mind and want to have objective professional advice during the questioning. You're facing a very serious charge."

❧

Even though his uncle had declined the lunch invitation offered on Sunday, Frank decided to call and ask again. After he'd inquired considerately about Harry's night, he got right to it.

"What about it, Uncle Harry? It can just be soup and a sandwich. Or I could come over and join you in the dining room there."

"Sorry, my boy, the kitchen needs twenty-four-hour notice."

"Oh, come on, surely they can make an exception for me, your only nephew."

"Frank, they won't do that, no point asking."

"Tomorrow then?" said Frank.

"No. Pat is coming over right after lunch and then Beth is dropping by at two. It will have to be later in the week."

Frank barely managed to quell a surly reply and choked out that he'd get back to Harry about it. His face was an ugly puce when he hung up.

❧

Beth heard the back gate clang shut, put her latest Ngaio Marsh mystery book down, and got up to see who was in her yard. By the time her neighbour Jenny Lee reached the back door, Beth was opening it.

"Beth, I thought I'd deliver the good news in person," Jenny said. "Our local thieves have been caught. At least that's what Constable Argento seems to believe."

"Definitely good news!" said Beth. "Got time for a cup of tea? How did the police get them? When did it happen?"

"Overnight Friday, I gather. It seems they're the fellows who were 'working the East side' as the constable called it. Anyway, hopefully that's an end to it. Why are you frowning?"

"Before I tell you, let me ask—did you see anything going on at the Mahoney's on Saturday morning?"

"No, but I saw something today. What happened Saturday?"

"Mike was driven away in a police car with Constable Argento and another policeman."

"Ooh. Well, we know Edith had strong suspicions," said Jenny, "but I've never been convinced about Mike. That Norman was another story—I'm glad he's gone."

"Yes, but Mike works at the same place Norm does, and they've been pally. I'm sure Nina and Michael must be very worried, whatever is happening. They're keeping to themselves given the other investigation, but someone else is bound to have seen what I did and start talking." Beth concluded.

"Yes," said Jenny. "The Mahoneys have a heap of trouble right now. Not long after lunch I saw Nina escorted to a police car with two officers on either side of her. It was unsettling. They locked her in the partitioned back seat. Best we be noncommittal if either topic comes up." Beth nodded.

❦

Constable Bonnie Chu stood quietly by the door of

interrogation room one. Nina sat calm, aloof and unbending, facing the mirrored wall as she waited for Detective McNabb. She wondered if anyone was behind the one-way glass. She noticed a camera mounted in one ceiling corner of the drab, beige room and rearranged her Gucci silk scarf around her neck.

There was a tap-tap. McNabb entered; he paused near Nina's chair. "Mrs. Mahoney, are you comfortable?"

"Yes."

"Do you want a drink?" He put down a bottle of water in front of her. "Do you need to use the washroom? Constable Chu can escort you anytime."

"I'm fine."

The detective put his notebook and a file folder on the table as he sat opposite Nina.

"Mrs. Mahoney, I am going to begin video recording this session in compliance with federal laws. Have you reconsidered your decision to decline a phone call to a lawyer?"

"No, I need to speak with my husband."

"I've said it's not possible right now. Are you sure you don't want a lawyer present? We can wait till you call and arrange it. Remember, it's a free service."

"No," said Nina, sitting ramrod straight. She stamped her foot. "I have to speak with Michael first."

"I'll proceed then. You are being held because of the irrefutable nature of the evidence discovered on the Todd property. Some personal items were found under the garage floor that belonged to Emma Mahoney, and they had your fingerprints on them. How did that happen?"

McNabb paused. Nina stared at him, silent.

"I believe Michael Mahoney gave them to you to get rid of. He took advantage of your—"

"You've got it all wrong," said Nina, raising her voice to drown out the detective's voice.

"Mrs. Mahoney, the fingerprints *are yours*. Tell me how they got on Emma's keys and on the clinic appointment card we found. It was made out for the next weeks appointment after September sixth. How could you possibly have handled that?"

"Listen to me," Nina said with mounting agitation. She flung her hands about causing Bonnie Chu to rise in her seat. "I can tell you it's nothing to do with my husband."

"Who then?" said Detective McNabb. "*Who* has it to do with? Who have you been covering for?"

TWENTY-NINE

Monday, December 20

Michael Mahoney's mind was whirling. It was nearly four o'clock by the time he'd been delivered back to his workplace, having been released from custody with a warning from Detective McNabb. He had to get his head on straight before he called Mike. How was he going to tell him about his mother? It was unbelievable that two days after his son had been interviewed by police, Michael found himself in the same position only worse. He remembered very well being grilled in 1960. He knew that he had more scrutiny to face. Detective McNabb had made that clear. Michael was sure there must be a logical reason for Nina's fingerprints being found. She and Emma had been close. He was dumbfounded by the news that Nina had confessed. Did she believe all these years that he'd killed Emma and she had to save him? What was going on in her head?

Michael had penned a short, encouraging note and asked it be given to Nina.

Nina, honey, I know you'll agree Mike has to be our priority right now. I'll speak with him tonight. There's a highly recommended criminal lawyer who I know to call and we'll be there tomorrow midmorning. This mess will be sorted out.

Hang in there. Love, Michael

He was drinking the cup of chamomile tea offered by the office manager. It was okay, sort of soothing. Lori was aware he'd been on edge for days and whatever had transpired at the police station had pushed him over that edge. When he stumbled by her desk, she told him he needed a hot drink—and it wasn't the strong caffeinated coffee he brewed in his office.

He stabbed at the buttons on his phone, got the number wrong, and began again.

"Mike, it's Dad, quick call. I'm going to pick up some takeout from White Spot for us. Your mom is busy. You want your usual?"

"Sure," said Mike. "What's Mom doing?"

"I'll tell you when I see you at home. Have to go," Michael managed to say. He hung up, hand shaking. His whole body seemed close to collapsing. The room spun like his thoughts while he struggled to think how to break the news to his son.

❦

On the way to the police station after his workday, Cameron did his best to control his impatience with the late afternoon traffic and to subdue his anticipation about what he was going to learn about the apparent solving of the cold case. The brief telephone exchange he'd had with McNabb had offered no clues.

Cameron strode down Cambie and into the station, having parked at City Square like before. He made a sharp rap on the door frame, which brought Steve's head up and a smile to his face.

"Come on in and shut the door."

"So, whose fingerprints are they?"

Steve McNabb said, "Want to take a guess?"

"From your reaction, seems it was a surprise," said Cameron. He grinned. "Okay, I'll play your game. Gino Martinelli."

"No… Nina Mahoney."

"What?" Cameron stared at Steve. "Then Michael Mahoney must have had her under a spell. She was about eighteen."

"Yes, that's what I'm thinking. Nina Mahoney was arrested for complicity in Emma Mahoney's disappearance and presumed murder this morning."

"What about Michael Mahoney?" said Cameron.

"We brought him in. I interrogated him after I saw his wife. He repeated his denials, and at the moment, we have no evidence against him. I must say, he came across as believably shocked about Nina's fingerprints but perhaps that's because he realizes the truth is out. We released him for now with the standard warning, but not Nina. He's called to say he's retained a lawyer who will be present for her follow-up interview tomorrow. You know how some interrogations don't turn out the way you expect?"

Cameron nodded, waiting.

"I'd pegged her as a tough customer from last week's interview. The way she acted when Chu and I picked her up this morning was in keeping with my first impression. She asked to change and put on a red dress and some black patent high heel boots. She announced cuffs wouldn't be necessary – though I saw no reason to do that – then she walked between us like we were all headed to a gala."

"Sounds like she was ready for a fight," said Cameron.

"Get this though—in less than ten minutes, she caved in. We'd already told her that her husband was in custody when she wanted to call him instead of a lawyer. She refused representation. When confronted about the fingerprints and accused of helping her husband, she had a melt down and started talking. She adamantly denied Mahoney's involvement. Said *she* did it and raved about how it was the best thing she'd ever done.

Clammed up after that. Couldn't get another word out of her."

"Congratulations, Steve."

"Well, it's a little premature to think it's all sewn up, but we're close. Oh, I mustn't forget. While Nina Mahoney confessed, she denied she was driving the car that hit Edith Todd. She gave us an alibi for the time. We've been able to check that it's bona fide so we've handed that case back to Sergeant James."

🌿

Mike's office mate offered him a ride partway home, dropping him near Fraser and Broadway to bus the rest of the way. Mike had lost track of how many antacid tablets he'd had through the day. To add to the general upheaval he was feeling, he'd had a run-in with Norm who had sought him out at lunchtime while he ate his lunch alone in the office. He couldn't help thinking about the exchange as he stood on the crowded bus.

"Think you're a smarty, don't you?" Norm had said. "Rich seems willing to believe you. I certainly don't."

"Well, no, Norm, you don't believe me, because I'm sure you're the one who was with the Ice Cream Kids."

"Don't call them that."

Mike faked a smile. "Come on, you know everyone calls them that behind their backs. I don't care if you were with them, I just want my name cleared. I'm sure you don't want Rich to know what you've been up to."

"There's no need for him to know. Gerry and Ben won't give me up—they know what's good for them."

"So," said Mike, "I'm betting you're the ones causing all the fuss around our area. I guess you guys went into the Todd place in October and took Mrs. Todd's stuff."

The admission was out of Norm's mouth before he thought better of it. "That was me all the way," he said, puffed up with satisfaction. "Payback for her snooping."

"Well then," said Mike. "I'll keep quiet about that and more, just like your pals."

"See that you do," said Norm, showing Mike a threatening fist.

Mike backed up a few steps but spoke firmly. "I will—if you get me out of this."

❦

With a welcome seamless connection at Nanaimo, Mike got off near Copley and was soon trudging up the lane, feeling relief after the mental exertions of his day. He was looking forward to having dinner with his dad. He'd be able to tell him how he sold two cars today and enjoy a positive response. He felt lighter with each step that took him closer to home. He kicked his shoes off inside the back door, but when he saw his father's drawn face, his mood dropped. Something was wrong.

"Hi, Son. Why don't you freshen up? Our food is warming in the oven. It'll be fine for another few minutes." Michael managed a wan smile. "We've got two pieces of their pumpkin pie for dessert too. Go down and wash up."

"Ready, Dad," Mike called as he reached the top of the stairs after changing. "So, where's Mom? She didn't say she was going to be out."

"I can tell you about that over dessert," said Michael while he set out some plates. "What I need to tell you now is that when I got in, there was a call from Constable Argento about another interview they want to do with you tomorrow morning."

Ooh, thought Mike as his tummy did a flip, *that's why Dad looks worried.* "I don't have anything different to say to them. They can't really arrest me, can they?"

"No. Sorry, Son, I should have said right away. Argento said

I could tell you that a second anonymous tip came in about you. Two tips on top of the confessions that the guys in custody made are too many for their liking. They think you're being set up and they want your help."

They ate in silence, Mike's thoughts busily stirring up fresh anxiety.

THIRTY

Tuesday, December 21

Mike Mahoney woke to the same hollowed-out sensation he'd had before he finally got to sleep. His body felt limp, pinned to the mattress. He thought of clichés to describe what had happened last evening when his dad told him about his mom's arrest. He'd had the rug pulled out from under him, a punch in the gut, been struck by lightning… *punch in the gut, that's what it was*. He was sorry to know his dad had lost his first wife, but that was eons ago. There had to be a good reason his mom had confessed—his dad thought she was having a nervous breakdown. The police must have pressured her or something. Their lawyer would get her out. *At least,* Mike thought, *I don't have to call work and explain anything.* He wasn't due at the car dealership till one. That was one good thing. And the other good thing was a reminder to himself that his sales were up. There'd be a hefty bonus.

Breakfast was another quiet meal. Mike figured his dad was exhausted from a poor night's sleep like he was. On the way to the police station, idling for a red light, Mike stared out the window.

"I'm sure you're going to be alright, Mike," his dad said.

"Dan Argento always struck me as a thoughtful man whenever he dropped into any Block Watch meetings."

"Yeah, he's nice. I just want to get this over with." Mike returned to guessing what questions he would be asked and thinking of what he would say. He wondered when he might get to see his mom. His dad would have time with her this morning and maybe things would be okay after all.

❦

They were back in the same interview room as last time with Constables Roy and Argento. Argento began with a short preamble.

"Just a recap—this past Friday night, police were called to an apartment complex on Eleventh near Victoria, reported by a Block Watch member as it happens, to attend the scene of a break-and-enter in progress. Subsequently, two individuals were arrested, each of whom you know. They have now made a full statement identifying you, Mike, as their buddy who escaped arrest."

Mike nodded. Under the table, his fingers, gripped tightly together, were turning white.

Constable Roy took up citing the facts. "Later, we came to your residence and found you in possession of stolen property. We have your statement denying involvement. Is there anything you would like to add?"

Mike shook his head. "No, I was home all night, and I didn't steal anything, let alone the bike. I don't know anything about what Gerry and Ben get up to. I've never hung out with them."

"All right. What do you have to say to the fact that while we were at your home, there was a call from a man, received on our tip line, who also pointed the finger at you? And, last evening, another anonymous call was made to the tip line," said Roy.

"All lies," said Mike.

"Seems that could be so. We think *you* know who the third person is. You, Gerry and Ben are employed at Belmont Motors. We are speculating it's someone else you know at work. Is there something you want to tell us?" said Constable Argento.

"Uh… maybe. I need a little time to think," said Mike, proverbial wheels spinning in his head. "Can I talk to my dad alone please?"

"Interview suspended at nine forty-four. Constables Roy and Argento are leaving the room." Roy clicked off the recorder. "Just open the door and tell the officer outside when you want us back."

Mike's resolve to keep quiet had begun to crumble as his anger grew with news of the second call—*that rat Norm*—and with the shock of his mother's arrest. He turned his chair a little to speak to his father.

"Dad, I've got to tell you something before I tell the police. Please don't be mad at me."

"I don't think I have any energy to waste on being mad, Mike." Michael cast a worried look at his son. "What is it?"

"I know who called to tell the police it was me. It was Norm. I think he's trying to get me arrested and out of the way."

"Why would he—"

"Norm's stupid. It's going to backfire on him because I'm going to tell the police everything."

"Everything? What does that mean?" Michael's voice cracked. "What have you been doing?"

"Nothing. Really. I've done nothing."

Mike said the rest in a hurry, his words blending together at times, while he inclined his head and concentrated on the silver tie clip his father was wearing.

"I've been keeping quiet about Mrs. Todd's accident. I was a passenger in the car that clipped her. Norm was driving. After, Norm said Rich just wanted her to have a good scare. The car had some damage, but of course, that was all taken care of at the shop."

"What on earth were you thinking, not reporting something like that?" Michael blurted.

"Rich and Norm said I'd better button my lip if I wanted to avoid big trouble. I knew what they meant. Norm said I was guilty too."

"In the eyes of the law, yes, I think that's true," said his father.

"But I was only a passenger. It wasn't my fault," said Mike. "Rich hurt me twice on purpose—once while pretending to shake my hand. I've been so scared. I saw him punch one of the salesmen and *he* ended up concussed." Mike dropped his gaze further in an unconscious bid to invite pity.

Michael shook his head and sighed. "Mike, I really don't understand why you didn't talk to me before. We'll sort it out later. You've got to tell the officers everything. It might mean they want to keep you longer to speak with whoever is investigating Mrs. Todd's accident. You won't be getting to work today. In fact, I'm sure you understand from what you've told me about the threats and criminal leanings you describe that it's not safe for you to return there."

Mike saw his red Camaro clearly for one second before it went *poof*.

❦

As mandated under the BC Police Act, the Richmond RCMP detachment was notified by Constable Argento that he and a colleague would be attending Belmont Motors to pick up a serial break-and-enter suspect. That would be a starting point. Mike Mahoney's confession about the Todd hit-and-run accident was about to turn the tables on Norm, a self-engineered twist of luck he would never appreciate.

The constables followed the directions Mike had given. Argento remained outside the building while Roy went inside to meet Richard Belmont. He confirmed that Norman Jervis was an employee and asked to have him called to the office. He stood by, alert for any sign of tip-off, while Rich used an intercom to contact the body shop. Rich projected a friendly law-abiding citizen demeanor, overly so, it seemed to Roy. When Norm saw police, his face lost its pleasantly curious look. He'd arrived wondering if his promotion was being fast-tracked.

"Howdy, officer," Norm said, walking forward with nonchalant conceit. "Guess you want to talk to me?"

"Yes, Mr. Jervis. I need you to accompany me and my colleague to the Vancouver police station."

Norm threw Rich a breezy, "See you tomorrow then," after Rich told him to take the rest of the day off.

❦

The short, older lady was wearing a familiar blue raincoat and stood on the opposite side of Nanaimo. Beth took a slow deep breath as she waited near the Good Luck Corner Grocery for the crosswalk light to change. When they were closer, it was clear there was little resemblance to Edith except for the coat and the woman's general shape.

Beth spoke in passing, "Nice afternoon for walking, isn't it?"

She had to grin when the lady broke into a large smile, nodding her head vigorously like a bobble-head doll. It was enough to ease the tension from Beth's neck and remove the image of the ambulance scene from her mind.

She took a direct route to Harry's along the south side of East Nineteenth. In the far distance, she thought she saw Joe with his dog Digger. However, her attention was drawn away to a black sedan travelling east on the road, much faster, she judged, than the posted speed limit. Any safety Beth felt from being on the sidewalk was swiftly doused when the car veered with a screech. It came to an abrupt stop, on the grass verge, within two feet of her.

Frank Nolan jumped out of his car and rushed at Beth, who shrank back and began to turn away. His face wild with fury, Frank delivered a tirade of curses. He shoved Beth with a force that sent her to the sidewalk. She fell to the left, partly on grass, a hand reaching out to break the fall, and felt a stabbing pain in her wrist at the same time her breath was taken away by her impact on the ground.

Frank towered over Beth, shouting, "Get up. Get up and face me, you damn snoop." He waved his arms around and kicked out, making contact with her right lower leg. Beth howled with pain and tried to pull herself back and away, of two minds about whether it was safer to stay down or get up. Then, beyond Frank, she saw the cavalry riding to the rescue, as she told Sofia later. She went limp, a warm relief flooding in along with tears. Joe and Digger were seconds away.

Frank hurled another insult and shook his finger. "Go ahead, cry, you brought this on yourself you bit—"

"Hey, buddy, back off," said Joe, puffing up his chest and moving toward Frank with fists raised in a boxing stance. Digger stood by Beth barking at both the men. A homeowner who had stepped out her front door retreated with Joe's arrival.

"Who do *you* think *you* are, b-u-u-u-d?" said Frank in a surly tone, face no less menacing.

"Lightweight boxing champion when I was in the Navy. That's who. And I still work out. You better get out of here right now," said Joe, moving closer and making a tentative jab.

Glaring at Joe, Frank retreated and walked swiftly to his vehicle. He shook his fist and snarled a parting insult. Beth had dried her eyes; she turned on her knees and took the hand Joe offered.

"Jeez, who is that guy—do you know him? I've got his plate number. You've got to report him… oh, you're holding your left arm." Joe delivered all this with urgency, buzzing around Beth like a worker bee.

"Yes, I know him, he's harassed me before and did the same to Edith. I *will* report it," said Beth, wincing. "I'm on my way to visit his uncle who lives in that seniors' residence on Hull. Would you mind walking with me?"

"But what about your leg? I saw him kick you. Don't you think you should go home? You've had a shock. You're hurt. I'll walk you home. You can call with your regrets as soon as you get there."

"I want to go tell my friend and his niece what happened in person. I can call a taxi from there to get to emergency. I need my arm checked out."

"Before I forget, here's the license—and my telephone number," said Joe, scribbling another number on the back of an old grocery list.

"Joe, did you recognize that car by any chance?"

"Uh… no," he said, "should I have? Oh. I know what you're thinking—was it the car that hit Mrs. Todd? No idea. I didn't see the other car long enough or well enough to identify it properly. Sorry."

Joe left Beth tapping in the code to get in the front door of the seniors' home. She thanked him and said yes to his reminder to call the police and to call him later. *And I'll call Cameron*, she thought. Harry's apartment door was slightly ajar. Beth heard a woman's pleasant laughter combined with his low chuckles.

She knocked as she pushed the door open.

"Hello, it's Beth," she called out. "Sorry to dampen what sounds like a good joke," she said when she reached the living room. "I'm afraid I have to sit down. I've had a fall on the way."

As Beth described what happened, Harry's face wrinkled with alarm.

"I don't know what to say," said Harry. "I'm so, so sorry. I feel terrible. Are you okay?"

"I don't think Beth is okay," said Pat. "You likely can't see that Beth has hurt her arm, I think, from the way she's holding it. And I noticed a limp."

"Yes, I've been hurt, but I'm alright," said Beth. "What a way to meet you, Pat. And Harry, this is in no way your fault, not in the least. I regret to tell you this is the second time Frank has physically threatened me. First time was minor compared with today. I expect you can understand that I want and need to report him after this incident."

To which Pat, her mouth set in a line, nodded her ash brown curls in Beth's direction.

"I do understand," said Harry, somber and concerned. "You must call me tomorrow to let me know how you are."

❦

Beth was at VGH emergency patiently waiting to be formally discharged when Cameron turned up. Her wrist was badly sprained with no breaks evident, but an influx of patients from a multivehicle accident had tied up a lot of staff and meant a longer wait. Her leg, which sported a large nasty bruise, ached.

"What are you doing here? I said I'd call you when I'm done. Don't you trust me?" Beth said. She was immediately sorry for her irritability. The analgesic she'd been given seemed to be wearing off.

THIRTY | 289

"It's okay," Cameron said. "Yes, I trust you, but I was able to get away. I waved my VPD card under someone's nose out front. Did you tell them someone pushed you?"

"For sure. I didn't want them to think I'd fainted or was dizzy or that I'm an old croc for that matter. I'm okay, but I won't be safe driving until my wrist has a chance to settle. I do appreciate you coming."

"Glad to," said Cameron. "You can call the police non-emergency line to report Frank Nolan this evening if you want. The criminal harassment unit will then get in touch. Frank being accused and charged with assault may safeguard Harry's savings. There won't be much trust there anymore. By the way, ask for a copy of your emergency report if it's ready. It'll save time."

Beth offered a half-hearted smile. "Okay, thanks. There's something else," she said. "Frank's car is black."

Cameron shrugged. "Do you know how many black cars there are out there?" he said.

Beth glared at him. He apologized, instantly recalling that his assumption Emma's murderer had driven into Edith Todd had been wrong. "I'm sorry, yes. I see why you're thinking that, given his rash behaviour. His car should be checked out."

THIRTY-ONE

Wednesday, December 22

In the remand center at Powell and Gore, Nina Mahoney squirmed in the loose regulation clothing she was instructed to change into on arrival. It was humiliating. The small room smelled musty and on one wall, there appeared to be old blood spatter. She should have been treated with more respect, making it so easy for that detective. This was the thanks she got.

Nina was awaiting the arrival of a psychologist recommended by the lawyer who saw her yesterday. Michael had agreed to this over her protests and she was feeling totally misjudged. She stared, yet again, at the note Michael had written her. Certainly, Mike was a concern, but as Michael's wife, she should be his first priority now. She was sacrificing herself for him, just as she had from the very beginning. Surely, he understood? And she'd given him a wonderful son. He would get to see Mike marry and have their grandchildren. A surge of jealousy overwhelmed her. It was an emotion that thrust her back to the past, an emotion she knew well from an early age. Through the years, Nina had used various means to satisfy her powerful need to have what she knew she deserved. She had wanted and deserved Michael. Finding and marrying her soulmate was the best thing she had ever done for both of them, she told herself. *The Universe, in fact, presented Michael to me for the taking.* Her thoughts swooped back to relive *The Beginning*.

❦

Nina took the stairs two at a time. She ignored her mother's summons which faded away when she closed and locked her bedroom door. Her mum had learned that if she heard that familiar clunk, she was not to disturb her daughter. Nina lay stretched on the bed hugging her pillow. She'd just met the man of her dreams—and of her future. It didn't matter that he was married. She wouldn't let a minor detail like that stifle her profound joy in the discovery that her soulmate lived a stone's throw away. She had been on her way home from high school in early June walking up the back lane when she saw him digging over some ground by his fence. She stopped. Michael looked up and gave her a large smile. His sun-kissed, dark blond hair and lightly tanned face held her spellbound. His warm brown eyes had reached into her soul.

"Hi, I'm your new neighbour, Michael. I've noticed you live over there," he'd said, gesturing to a grey stucco house across the lane. "You must be Nina; I've seen you before."

Of course, he'd noticed her! She'd kept the inner tremor from her voice, softening her tone so he'd had to move closer to hear. "Yes, I'm Nina. Dad said he'd met you and your wife."

"Emma is at Safeway getting some groceries. You'll get to meet her sometime."

Nina couldn't care less about Emma; she was of no account. Still, she had smiled and said some appropriate polite words, offered a little superficial information about other neighbours, and received another bright smile before Michael had said he must get back to his yard work.

"Mum was talking about having you both over for dinner some time," she'd lied as she'd walked away. What a difference ten minutes could make to a life. Her whole body tingled with the absolute deliciousness of what the years ahead held in store. There was not a doubt in her mind that Michael Mahoney was meant for her.

Nina had been certain that time and good planning would bring them together. And it had. Nina closed her eyes and imagined she was safe in her old bedroom with the tantalizing images of the future she would create.

❧

The aching crept up on Beth, waking her gradually to the memory of why she was in pain. The acetaminophen, taken during the night, had worn off. She thought of how lucky she was to have fallen to the left. It would be awkward to manage various everyday activities for a while, but had it been her right arm, it would have been very inconvenient. Monty was quietly patient and careful around her, displaying the comforting sensitivity a cat is said to possess for its human in times of need. Gingerly stretching, while Monty observed from the bedroom doorway, Beth eased off the bed. Everything hurt, it seemed.

Sofia had seen her get dropped off at the back gate early last evening with a sling on her arm and rushed out to see if she'd eaten yet. Beth had phoned Sofia to ask her to feed Monty if she wasn't home by six. At the time, she'd simply told Sofia she'd had a fall and hurt her wrist.

"It's good you gave me your house that key Edith had," Sofia said after she'd arrived straight from her kitchen with a foil pie plate filled with homemade lasagna. "How come your policeman friend brought you home?" she asked with unconcealed interest.

"I only called Cameron because I'm going to lay charges

against Frank Nolan and I wanted some advice," Beth had replied.

Sofia had wrung her hands. "What happened? What did Frank do to you? Go. Sit. Tell me while I get this ready. Hand me that plate. I'll reheat the food a little in your microwave." Once Sofia's curiosity had been satisfied, it had taken only a little coaxing to have her leave Beth in peace to eat.

Beth admitted it was comforting to be fussed over. Cameron had seen her into her home and made her promise to call him before noon then left after extracting another promise. Beth mused a moment about how personal it felt. He had stressed she was to take good care and make sure she was feeling well for Boxing Day.

Not long after a slowly prepared breakfast, there were two calls from neighbours and one from Dennis Greene to offer help around her place. *All Sofia's doing,* Beth thought and smiled. But the smile faded as she remembered why she needed the support.

❦

Michael Mahoney sat in his office staring blankly at the desktop calendar. It came into focus. Three days until Christmas. The good weather forecast for the weekend was of little interest to him except for the fact it would not impact driving as had snows of other years. When he'd called to tell the Pavlik's about Nina, their acceptance of the news surprised him. Gus confided Nina had had some worrying behaviours in her youth and they could talk about it sometime. Inga insisted he and Mike come for Christmas dinner though they would have been going there on New Year's Day anyway. It was one of the few times a year they visited Deep Cove after the rift. Michael agreed for his son's and the Pavlik's sake. *It's time to mend fences* he thought.

If Michael believed Monday—when he first learned that Nina was being charged with murder then had to tell their son—was the worst day in his life since Emma went missing, it was nothing compared to yesterday's visit to his wife.

Michael's recollection of his and Nina's tense exchanges came in waves. From his first words— "Nina, darling, what can I say; there must be a mix-up!"—it was like a strange, disturbed woman sat before him.

She'd leaned toward him, her eyes boring into his, commanding attention. "There's no mix-up. I've taken care of things for you," she said coolly.

After Nina had delivered those words in an unashamedly satisfied tone, she'd described with relish how clever she'd been in her execution of the plan to free him. Michael had sat like stone on the hard chair opposite. His mouth had slipped open as he'd listened to his wild-eyed wife.

"Emma was a wimp, not fit to be your partner, let alone a mother. I looked after everything. You needed and wanted me just as I did you," Nina had said. "We were meant for each other; I knew that from the moment we met. It was easy to plan. Everything fell into place. Emma'd been an emotional mess for days, so I took her for a drive over to Seymour Mountain after her appointment. We talked awhile and that calmed her. Then we explored a forest path I'd found early in summer. I wasn't unkind. One really good conk on the head and she was gone. Out like a light."

"Where is Emma?" Michael had said, his voice strangled with the horror of what he had heard.

"How the hell should I know after all these years? I pushed her over a steep bank somewhere," Nina had said her voice ringing with emotion. "I don't remember. And *you* don't need to know; she's history. I'm the one who was meant to be the mother of your child. How can you not understand? You should thank me."

Michael had stumbled to his feet at the same time the attending female officer had come to subdue Nina.

"How can I possibly understand it?" Michael had said. "This is crazy. Are you trying to put the police off charging me? It's not necessary. My alibi is solid. Why are you acting this way? I know we've all been under great stress. You're having a meltdown. It's nothing to be ashamed of. We'll get some counselling."

"I don't need counselling," Nina had said with finality. "I just need you to understand that what I did was necessary so you and I could fulfill our destiny."

❧

In an interview room, Norm Jervis, having spent the night at the remand center, contemplated the bind he was in, his trademark scowl furrowing his face.

Despite his denials, he found himself held as a probable accessory in the Friday-night robbery. Gerry and Ben's bid to cover up for him had helped suspicions. And a full set of Norm's right-hand fingerprints, matched to his file on the provincial database, were retrieved from an empty pop tin thrown in the garbage under the kitchen sink. Norm recalled he'd downed a coke to quench his raging thirst before dashing out to the waiting taxi that night. He quashed an urge to pound the tabletop. He'd taken time to wipe down everything imaginable and then look what he did. *Stupid, stupid, stupid.*

Then there was the bombshell about a second pending charge that could only have come from Mike spilling his sorry guts. Norm finally got to make his one call just after nine.

"It's Norm, Rich."

"Where the hell are you, Legs? You're supposed to be here filling in for Gerry."

"The police are holding me on trumped up robbery charges.

I'm going to need a good lawyer if you're wanting life to return to normal."

There was silence for a moment. "What do you mean by that?" Rich said abruptly.

"Oh, just looking at things realistically. Send me that lawyer of yours to get me out of here. And can you call my mom, *your aunt*, please, and say you've sent me on a little job. Make something up. I don't want her worrying that I missed my Wednesday call to her. Tell her I'll be home in time to call at Christmas."

A growled "Okay" cut short by the crash of Rich's receiver was Norm's answer.

❦

In the afternoon, Pat Anders, at Harry's request, called her cousin Frank to make him aware that their uncle had decided he would not be transferring the management of his accounts to Frank.

"Is he there with you?" said Frank with undisguised irritation. "He's making a big mistake. Put Uncle on the phone. I want to talk to him."

"You can't. His home help is here attending to his weekly bath."

"Then tell him I'm coming over later to talk to him."

"Frank, don't bother doing that," Pat said firmly. "Uncle Harry is not going to change his mind and I'm not either. We both know what you did yesterday. Your behaviour is inexcusable. You hurt Beth; she had to go to emergency. She mentioned you've threatened her before as well."

In the background, Pat heard Frank's front door intercom buzz once, then longer a second time.

"Gotta go," he said, infuriated by the interruption. "Tell Uncle Harry I can explain." He set the receiver down carefully but barely kept his cool when he discovered who was buzzing for a third time.

Strange, I feel my whole life is on pause Mike thought. He couldn't see his future anymore—it was just a black wall. He was lying on the couch in the small downstairs rec room mindlessly staring at a muted television screen—his mother having decreed years ago there would be no television in the living room. Sounds of footsteps on the back stairs signaled it must be near dinner time. His father called his name.

"Yup, down here, Dad."

Michael Mahoney stood in the doorway, briefcase still in hand. "What have you been doing?"

"Not much. Slept in, walked to Safeway, picked up a sandwich for lunch, and got a newspaper to look at want ads, but haven't yet. What sort of day did you have?"

"It was slow—it's hard to concentrate with the situation your mom is in. I went to see her again today after work, but your mom seems to have withdrawn into herself and barely spoke to me. She turned her back on the psychologist this morning. Repeated to me that she was doing what is best for you and I."

"What does the lawyer say?" said Mike.

"Only that your mom will be detained until she has a thorough psychological assessment and that he will review what evidence there is before sitting down to talk with us both. It's led me to realize you and I should each begin some counselling sessions."

"I need to get some work," said Mike. "That will be my therapy."

"That will help, but I know from experience that it's useful to talk to someone who's objective. Someone who doesn't know us can be a big support—it would mean you and I don't have to lean on each other as much or on family or friends. There are going to be many hard days ahead, Mike, and we're going to need all the help we can get."

THIRTY-TWO

Friday, December 24

At Highcrest Hospital, Beth was working her last shift of the year. With Christmas Day peering directly over her shoulder, she was glad it was a half-day. Her arm had been gradually feeling more comfortable over the last two days. On Thursday, she'd done the remainder of her gift-wrapping by abandoning ribbons to use colourful bags and tissue. Finally, she was beginning to feel in the Christmas spirit, with nearby homes and shrubs draped with bright lights, wreaths on doors, cards covering her mantle and her own small tree sparkling in the front room. This afternoon, she would prepare cranberry sauce and a homemade dressing for the mixed salad she'd be taking to the next day's festive early evening dinner at Cathy and Bob's.

Donna Boudreau, also working the half-day, greeted her.

"Good to see you, but are you sure you should be here? I can easily manage today."

Beth nodded. "If it was my right arm, I might not be. But I'll be okay. Got it well strapped." She held out her left arm for Donna to inspect.

"All right then. I've got the ward census reports printed for us. Can you check if there are other lab reports of interest once you've settled in?"

Beth exchanged her winter jacket for a lab coat, locked her purse away then poked her nose into June's office saying a bright hello to get her attention. After June handed over a single new positive TB of a patient already in isolation pending results, they agreed to meet for a short lunch.

Sitting at a smaller desk at the back of the office, Beth ran her trained eye over the ward patient lists, highlighted ones of interest, and soon gathered her clipboard and folder, ready to set out.

"Looks like the morning is about to fly by," she remarked to Donna.

"Yes, I see our emergency beds are full. But no infections as far as I can tell from the admitting complaints. I'll drop by there later."

"Anything outstanding from yesterday?" said Beth before leaving.

"Just 2B. You'll have noticed there are two patients on respiratory isolation for influenza A. They're not long into their infectious period; both came from the same nursing home and have pneumonia. Hilde, the new assistant head, is on today and over the weekend. She may have questions. Yesterday, I stopped someone entering the room with an ordinary protective mask on. I found that someone on nights had stocked the cart outside the room with the wrong ones."

Out on the wards, Beth's sense of the season was reinforced with the variety of Christmas decorations on each floor. There was only one unit she had to remind to remove a bowl of nuts and chocolates from the nursing station to the staff room, but she complimented them on having put spoons out for serving.

The lab coffee break in the seminar room was a joint affair with June, the lab techs, the infection control nurses and Dr.

Harris, who, following his yearly tradition, set down a large box of Purdy's assorted chocolates. In the centre of the table, June had placed a large red poinsettia on a doily and ringed it with twigs of holly from her yard. Dr. Harris pulled up a chair, eyeing the assortment of baked goods contributed.

"Dig in. I suppose everyone has washed their hands?" he teased, knowing the particular care that was always taken in the handling of specimens, the setup of tests, and the analyzing of results. "And of course," he smiled, "I see Donna has put out some tongs."

Beth relaxed as she joined in the chatter about personal plans for the holiday weekend. She glossed over her Boxing Day plans and sent a warning look June's way seeing her about to ask more.

Later, heads together over a cafeteria lunch, Beth and June hashed over the attack by Frank and the nabbing of the property thieves.

"You didn't say what you're doing Boxing Day," said June between bites of a ginger cookie. "Thanks for this, by the way. You can always come for leftovers at my place. We'd love to have you."

"Thanks, but actually, I do have plans. Cameron has asked me to come to a Boxing Day open house at the home of one of his former colleagues. Said it would be nicer for him if he had company. He feels obligated to go, I think."

"Mmm," said June, "something brewing between you two?"

"No, no. I don't mind doing him a favour, so I said yes," said Beth.

"Oh, come on, I got the impression you were getting to like him."

Beth's eyes dropped to study her empty soup bowl. "Yes, I guess I am. Cameron's become far more considerate the last little while—there's a good man in there."

"He seems attentive from what you say about his insisting you call him the day following your emergency visit. Sounds promising to me," said June with a mischievous smile.

❦

Sergeant James from the hit-and-run team stepped into a full elevator and nodded to Detective McNabb, who stood near the back.

"Steve, can we talk a moment in my office before the day's gone?"

"How about now?" said McNabb and received a nod. He squeezed past a couple uniformed bodies to follow the sergeant when he exited on the third floor.

Coffee cup in hand and leaning casually forward on a small settee along a side wall of Sergeant James's office, McNabb learned about a suspect who had been brought in by the Robbery Unit for probable involvement in a break-and-enter from the weekend. The fellow had eluded the dog squad then likely called in a tip to shift the blame from himself.

"What he didn't know," James explained, "was that the two who were caught in the act had readily offered the same name. When the phone tip came in it raised a few eyebrows. Then a fourth call. Complete overkill."

"And this has got to do with me how?" said McNabb.

"The name Mahoney ring a bell?" Sergeant James was rewarded with a sudden shift in Steve McNabb's posture. "Got your attention now." He smiled.

Back in his office, McNabb checked his watch and dialed Cameron's direct line. "Cam, glad I got you. Can we set a meeting time next week for an update on some very satisfying developments in the Mahoney cold case? There's news on the Todd hit-and-run too. Why don't you bring Beth Langille along? She deserves to be here. With statements to be issued soon, there's no reason not to include her. I trust your faith in her. Can we aim for Wednesday, morning preferred?"

"Likely," said Cameron. "I'll check with Beth. There's a small favour I want to ask in the meantime."

"Ask away. If I can help you, I will."

"On Tuesday, Beth was hurt in an unprovoked assault by one Frank Nolan. There was at least one witness. She called in a report that evening and has pressed charges. I'm interested to know at what stage the investigation is, particularly whether Mr. Nolan has been approached. I have some concern he's a bit of a loose cannon right now."

"No problem. Can do," said McNabb.

❦

Beth answered her home phone automatically. "Infection Control, Beth Langille here."

"Was work that bad today?" Cameron teased. "Sounds as if you haven't left it behind."

"It was fine. I'm fine. Really," Beth said. "I'm just busy. How can I help you?"

"That still sounds like you're at work. But, hey, just needed to tell you about a call I had from Steve McNabb who wants to plan a meeting with us. He has some news to share about the cold case and the car accident. We can bring up Frank Nolan's car then if need be."

"Okay. When does Detective McNabb want to meet?"

"Wednesday?" Cameron asked.

"Okay, but not too early," Beth said. "Any time after ten thirty."

"Good, I'll give him a ring. Now, about Boxing Day—I thought we should aim to arrive at the start of the open house. There'll be more time for us to have a visit with Ron and Barb." Cameron hesitated. "Is it okay if I pick you up?"

We. Us. Beth recognized some resistance to hearing those words. They were supposedly attending as colleagues of a sort, yet her heart was sending out signals to the contrary.

"Sure, you could pick me up," said Beth after a moment. "I'll take a taxi home."

"Fine. Barring the unforeseen, I'll be home late morning Sunday from Squamish. I'll pick you up around twenty to two. I'll call you if anything changes. Oh… front or back?"

"Back is fine," said Beth. "Have a Merry Christmas… Cam."

"You have a good one too, Beth. See you on Boxing Day."

THIRTY-THREE

Sunday, December 26

It was ten past two when Ron Poole, wearing a friendly grin under his trim, greying moustache, opened the front door of an older, Oakridge-area home near Tisdall Park. Cameron and Beth had seen him and his wife through the window in the living room chatting with two couples as they approached the house.

Cameron supported Beth's affected arm by its elbow as they came up the steps. "I'm not an invalid," Beth said. "I'm *okay*."

"Just making sure," Cameron replied continuing to leave his hand in warm contact with her arm.

Barb Poole came up behind her husband to join the introductions. Tall, like her husband, her pleasant face was framed by layered silvery hair.

"Great to see you, Cam." She turned her grey-blue eyes to Beth. "So glad to finally meet you, Beth. Cam knows where the coats go. Come, let's get acquainted and I'll introduce you to some friends."

The warm welcome put Beth at ease. She stifled the remark she was about to make to stop Cameron from grasping the collar of her charcoal wool coat to help her out of it. This seemed like a date after all. She thrust that thought aside and accepted his compliment on her dress. The long-sleeved, mauve, fine corduroy shirtwaist she'd chosen was one of her favourites. The elastic bandage stabilizing her wrist was barely noticeable.

As she turned to follow Barb, Cameron said, "I'll get a drink for you, Beth. What would you like?"

There was an amused glint in his eyes. She wondered if he was daring her to say she'd help herself. "White wine would be fine… Cam," she said politely, "not too dry, if possible."

❧

"I enjoyed that; I hope you did too," said Cameron as he opened the jeep door for Beth shortly after four.

"Yes, I did. Your friends Barb and Ron are interesting people and very easy to be with. Thanks for inviting me along."

When they pulled in by Beth's back gate, Cameron's hand hovered near the ignition key.

He turned slightly toward her. "Mind if I come in for a few minutes?"

As soon as Monty heard footsteps on the deck, he raced from the living room and sat like a welcoming dignitary just near the kitchen entry. Inside, Cameron draped his leather jacket over a dining room chair, making himself at home. He bent down to stroke the cat, who rubbed against his legs. The homey scene wasn't lost on Beth. And after having Cameron at her side a good deal of the afternoon—there was no getting around it, she felt like his date—she experienced a surge of longing for the easy relationship she and Alex once shared.

"Couldn't cadge a cup of coffee, could I?" Cameron asked.

"Sure," said Beth. "Caf or decaf?"

Smiling, Cameron straightened up. "Decaf's fine, I don't need it as a pick-me-up; I stuck to the juice punch after my first two glasses of wine. Didn't want you to have any reason to turn down my offer of a drive home."

"Oh, you were plotting, were you?" said Beth, measuring out the ground coffee and wondering what on earth she was saying, sounding like a flirt.

"Sort of," said Cameron. "I wanted to check how you're doing because I've been concerned. Didn't want to bring it up while we were at the open house. You had a rough experience last week. I hope you're really taking care of yourself."

Beth turned her face away. She stood waiting for the water to run cold, conscious of a slight edginess and aware of her continued affinity for consolation. The shock of what had happened would linger for a while, she knew.

"I am. And I appreciate your concern—sincerely. Now, why don't you look in that drawer you're standing by and get some spoons out. And then get two mugs out of the cupboard above. The brew won't take long because I'm only doing a half pot."

When they were settled at the dining room table, Cameron told Beth what he'd learned from McNabb about Frank Nolan.

"He was visited by two officers last Wednesday afternoon and taken to the station to explain himself."

"But what's Detective McNabb got to do with it?" Beth asked.

"He was only checking for me. Once he'd offered to have you present on Wednesday, I thought it was okay to ask him. I didn't say anything else except that Frank doesn't want you being friends with his uncle," Cameron said.

"Well, it's nice to know Frank's been officially warned and will be charged. I hope he's one of those bullies who loses steam when he's caught out. He didn't stay long after Joe confronted him." Beth heard herself offer a second cup of decaf. It seemed the generous gesture and she found she wasn't in a rush to have Cameron leave.

"Shall I pick you up this Wednesday?" he said when they had finished. He stood close to Beth on the porch as she opened the back door. "Not saying you need me to, just asking," he added with a half-smile.

"No, I'll likely take the bus."

"Okay then, see you soon. It's been a very pleasant afternoon, thanks." And then he was gone, taking the subtle scent of sandalwood with him.

🍂

Wednesday, December 28

Detective Steve McNabb came from behind his desk to welcome Cameron and Beth.

"Come in, come in. I'm Steve. Good to meet you, Miss Langille. May I call you Beth?"

"Likewise, Steve," said Beth, nodding as she shook his offered hand. "And yes, Beth is fine. Thanks for having me here. I know it's not usual. I gather you have good news to share."

"Sit down." He gestured to a small circular pine table with a couple seats, closed the door and pulled around his office chair. "I *do* have good news; I think you'll be satisfied."

"Well, come on," said Cameron, "don't keep Beth in suspense."

"Okay, okay. Well, the Emma Mahoney cold case has been put to rest by a confession after the suspect was told we identified their fingerprints on Emma's watch and on an appointment card. Those were some of the items found during the garage floor excavation. They were Emma Mahoney's and obviously buried there at the same time as the locket you turned over to Cameron. Since the arrest report is being released as we speak, I can tell you right now. It was Nina Mahoney. She admitted it in short order which doesn't happen all that often." The office fell silent.

"I can hardly believe it," Beth said after taking a few moments to digest this unexpected news. She grimaced. "She would have been so young. I don't know what to say. It's horrifying. Of course, I know you've both seen all kinds of unthinkable behaviour."

"Yes indeed," said McNabb. "Crown counsel will decide what exact charges to lay but Mrs. Mahoney will be detained and tried in due course."

"Are you satisfied she wasn't coerced by Michael Mahoney?" said Cameron.

"Doesn't seem likely. And his alibi remains unbreakable. There's no way to prove he did, and it seems very probable Nina Mahoney won't implicate him even if he did. She boasted that she planned it all herself. We were already feeling he was believable when he was interrogated. He seems devastated by his wife's confession; I'm told he looked as if he'd aged ten years after his visits with her."

"I guess that wraps up the hit-and-run accident that killed my neighbour Edith Todd too," said Beth. "Perhaps you know I always thought she was targeted."

"Yes, Cameron mentioned it. And you were right. However, the hit-and-run accident wasn't Nina Mahoney's doing. Sergeant James filled me in last week about an unexpected development that happened during an interview about the city's east side thefts. You're with Block Watch, so you'll know about those."

"This is sounding like another lucky break," said Cameron.

"Fortunate for us, but not the yahoo whose plans backfired on him. I'll tell you what happened, but not who. The news release will be next week. The Mahoney's son was interviewed a second time when it became clear he was being set up by the real instigator of those robberies. It was hoped he could and would identify the real ringleader. At the beginning, he didn't seem inclined to do more than repeat his claim of innocence, but when he heard about the second tip called in, he had a change of heart. He told the interviewer he'd confronted the tipster who had then more or less boasted he was involved. Then out of the blue, young Mahoney said he had something else to report. He admitted to being a passenger in the car that hit Mrs. Todd. Said the driver claimed he was 'just' trying to scare her. It was the same person who called in the tip naming Mike as part of the break-and-enter team."

Beth's hand flew to her mouth to stifle a shocked exclamation. "Oh no, poor Michael! He has both his wife and son facing serious charges."

"Yes," said McNabb. "And for your information, Sergeant James called the Todd family to tell them someone has been charged for the accident. They'll be given some details before the news release."

❧

"We ought to have a debriefing of our own, Beth," Cameron said when the elevator doors closed on the two of them. "You've got time?"

"I've got nothing but time at the moment," said Beth. "Christmas is over. My leisure time has increased with the end of the cold case and our hit-and-run investigations. I'm not due back at work till January seventh."

"Well, let me drive you home, and on the way, we could stop around Commercial and Twelfth. How does Café Algarve sound for a hot drink? I'd like to pick up some of those good Portuguese buns they have."

They were settled sipping coffee for several minutes before moving from chat about their respective Christmas days and the clear cold spell to a recap of the cold case and the other revelations of the morning's meeting with McNabb. Although they hadn't been told who admitted to being the driver of the car that hit Edith Todd, they speculated it could be Norm.

"You must be feeling just as much relief as the Todd family that the hit-and-run is solved. I realize you had a special bond with Mrs. Todd," said Cameron. "I don't think I ever said I'm sorry for your loss."

Beth wondered how much she wanted to say. To speak of anything much other than the cases was moving into uncharted territory. They had shared minimal personal information. She only knew that Cameron had a mother and brother in Nanaimo and his retired policeman uncle in Squamish, that he'd alluded once to being divorced and had left his career at VPD to take on the less stressful position he had now. As for her background, Cameron knew of her profession, her ties to Nova Scotia, and how long she'd lived in her East Vancouver neighbourhood.

"Thank you. I was very fond of Edith. She became something of a mother substitute over time. I'd lost connection with my own mother and then Mom passed away without us having cleared the air. Edith meant a lot to me. I'm really glad I was trusted to be included today. I feel I deserved to be there."

"Those were the very words Steve McNabb used when he called me last Friday to set up today's meeting, and I completely agree. You earned the right to be there. I'm glad you approached me last month. I think I tried to put you off at first, didn't I? But I got caught by the name Emma Mahoney just like you got hooked by what you thought your neighbour was trying to get across before she died."

Beth nodded and smiled. "I'm content now. I'll never know for sure what Edith said, but I'm glad her effort to try and tell me whatever it was, spurred me on."

Later, when Cameron left Beth at her back gate, she began to wish it was not the last time. She turned before slipping out of the jeep to say, "The coming weeks are going to feel quiet and tame compared to all the recent activity and upheaval, but I'm looking forward to a relaxing change. It will be good to get to the art gallery and see what's new there. Hope you have a very happy new year, Cam."

"I will, thanks. You too. Promise to look me up when you come to the art gallery?"

"Sure," said Beth, "you can count on it."

THIRTY-FOUR

Saturday, January 1, 2000

Beth anticipated her quiet evening and was reminded of her childhood years as she covered the few handwashed dishes with a fresh tea towel. It had been one of her mother's habits if the dishes weren't being dried right away. From about age eleven, it had been her job to wash and her brother's to dry. When cousin Leah came to stay for a week each summer, she took over the drying and they had giggled their way through the process. At times, her mother would call out to them from elsewhere in the house, 'You're having too much fun out there; don't break anything,' but it never sounded disapproving. The memory resurrected the particular sorrow she'd controlled until recently. Edith's death was like losing her mother a third time. The first time was when Beth went home to tell her parents that she and Alex were divorcing.

Her mother's face went still then hardened as she said, "Divorce? Never. No one in this family has ever divorced. You will stay by Alex's side and help him heal. I won't hear any talk of divorce."

"Mom, I've supported Alex through his depression while dealing with my own grief. I'm bushed. We've seen counsellors separately and together, but he's grown away from me. He's obsessed with what he thinks he must do to atone for missing Robbie's early symptoms of leukemia. Alex feels responsible for the delay in treatment that might have saved our son. There is nothing more I can say to convince him otherwise. He's decided to dedicate himself to Doctors Without Borders."

"Then you must go with him. You have your nursing expertise."

"Mom, listen to me. Alex is the one who asked for the divorce. It's going to happen."

Her mother had marched away with a parting remark, "You're both a shame to this family."

From that moment on, Beth felt motherless. Only her father, steadfast in his loyalty, saved future visits home from being ordeals. The second loss was her mom's death, after a brief illness, three years previous. Beth had felt a guilty relief that she no longer had to cope with their divided relationship but was left with deep regret that she had not made it home in time to tell her mom she loved her. Beth resumed counselling and journaled to a point where she believed she'd resolved her "mother issue" – until Edith's accident. After all, she'd had the more pervasive task of navigating the limitless sorrow of losing a child, a despair deepened by Alex's desertion. Now it seemed to her she was more ready to absorb her losses, put them away in the depths of her heart for safekeeping and embrace the future.

Beth turned off the kitchen light and stood still staring at the white expanse of her yard. She pondered how the resolution of Edith's cause of death had brought her to a place of relative calm and peace.

She'd had a good day on her own having had a pleasant New Year's Eve dinner with Sofia and her family. A call to Harry Anders found him in more than his usual good cheer.

"Guess what happened," he had said and, like a child, rushed on to the answer. "Frank came and joined us for Christmas dinner. Pat called and persuaded him. He knows I'm not going to change my banking arrangements and that we're very upset with his behaviour. He tried defending himself of course. We let him know he's family but we expect better of him. So, we'll see how it goes."

With a few more calls to and from family and friends, and a magical walk around Trout Lake in gently falling snow, this first day of a new year and new century felt like an optimistic beginning. By all accounts, 2000 had rolled in without any serious computer failures, which was a relief. *Not to forget,* she thought, *there's Cameron… Cam.* He'd called to say 'happy new year' and to recommend the current exhibition at the art gallery. "Let me know when you're coming," he'd said, "we'll meet for lunch," and she'd agreed.

Beth chose two lavender scented candles to place in the brass holders on one side of the fireplace and shooed the cat aside as she lit each. She sat quietly for a while on the couch opposite, gazing at the flickering flames. Monty hopped up on her lap. There was a deep content beneath her lingering sadness. *I'm certain Edith would be overjoyed if she knew her mumbles got through to me. And I know Mom loved me and wanted the best for me.* Beth stroked Monty's soft fur for a time before the fiery heat enticed him away.

EPILOGUE

February 17, 2000

Nina Mahoney, after a full psychological evaluation, was found mentally fit to stand trial. However, due to doubts about her stability, she was remanded into custody to await said trial. The jury deliberated for three days. On November 30, 2000, she was found guilty of first-degree murder and sentenced to life imprisonment.

March 22, 2000

Frank Nolan was found guilty of assault causing bodily harm and ordered to do nine months of community service beginning Monday, March 27.

May 25, 2000

Michael Mahoney Junior appeared before a judge to face charges of failing to report a serious criminal act. He was remanded into the custody of his father until a court date could be set. He was relieved to learn that due to the fact Norman Jervis had confessed to the hit-and-run accident, his testimony would not be needed when that case was heard.

November 6, 2000

Norman Jervis was convicted of manslaughter, defined as a homicide committed without the intention to cause death, for the accident that resulted in the demise of Mrs. Edith Todd. He was sentenced to six years in prison. As he was led from the courtroom, he tried to assault his lawyer and shouted that his cousin Rich would be sorry.

January 10, 2001

Michael Mahoney Senior and his son left for a four winter getaway to tour selected locations in New Zealand.

May 19, 2001: Victoria Day Weekend

Beth Langille and Cameron Ross were wed during a simple ceremony in the backyard of an East Vancouver home. The afternoon was a pleasant eighteen degrees Celsius and sunny with scattered clouds. A modest number of family, friends, and neighbours were in attendance. A private wedding dinner party was enjoyed at The Pear Tree Restaurant in Burnaby. A week later, the couple flew to Nova Scotia and to England to travel and celebrate with other family and friends.

October 3, 2002

After an extensive investigation over two years, Richmond RCMP, in one of the largest drug busts in the community's history, arrested **Richard Belmont** and nine of his employees. The sophisticated drug lab hidden in the basement of Belmont Motors auto repair shop took three days to dismantle. Because he was found guilty of a far more serious crime, Norman Jervis's willingness to provide inside information on his cousin's activities profited him very little—a single year was dropped from his sentence.

January 15, 2004

Tara Sampson-Kerr returned from maternity leave to her position as women's wear manager at the Hudson's Bay store in Metrotown Mall, Burnaby. She, husband Brian, a pharmacist, and baby Evelyn moved from her uncle's home to join the Oaklands Housing Cooperative in June.

Acknowledgements

The Death of Edith Todd fulfills my desire to write a mystery book, at the same time as paying tribute to the Vancouver neighbourhood where I lived, contented, for two decades. Most locations are factual for the time in which the story is set, with a notable exception – the hospital where Beth works.

I am forever indebted to my writer friends for their unfailing support and candid feedback. Karyn, Kiran, Lei-Lani, Torill, James and Stephan: I couldn't have done it without you. I am so grateful to have met you all at a writing course seventeen years ago.

A huge thank you to family, friends, and colleagues – many of whom have provided significant useful advice. With patient guidance from Friesenpress, I am happy I can now answer a resounding 'yes!' to the recurrent question 'is your book finished yet?'.

In closing I wish to acknowledge VPD's effective Block Watch program which provided some of the inspiration for my fictional 'whodunit'.

Anne L. Walsh, Vancouver, B.C.

CPSIA information can be obtained
at www.ICGtesting.com
Printed in the USA
LVHW030043120423
744005LV00001B/2

9 781039 159204